PENGUIN BOOKS

Shorelines

A well-known Canadian journalist, Roy MacGregor has
received two National Magazine Awards and an ACTRA
Award. After writing for *Maclean's* for several years, he
became a *Toronto Star* columnist. He is now the Ottawa
Bureau Chief for *Maclean's*.

Born in Whitney, Ontario, in 1948, the author was raised
in Huntsville, Ontario, and spent many summers in
Algonquin Park, where his grandfather was Chief Ranger.

Shorelines was his first novel, followed by *The Last Season*
published in 1983 and now also in Penguin.

SHORELINES

A Novel by

Roy MacGregor

Penguin Books

Penguin Books Canada Ltd., 2801 John Street, Markham,
Ontario, Canada L3R 1B4
Penguin Books Ltd., Harmondsworth, Middlesex, England
Penguin Books, 40 West 23rd Street, New York,
New York 10010 U.S.A.
Penguin Books Australia Ltd., Ringwood, Victoria, Australia
Penguin Books (N.Z.) Ltd., Private Bag, Takapuna,
Auckland 9, New Zealand

First published by McClelland and Stewart Limited

Published in Penguin Books, 1985

Manufactured in Canada by Gagne Printing Limited

Canadian Cataloguing in Publication Data

MacGregor, Roy, 1948-
 Shorelines

ISBN 0-14-007493-7

I. Title.

PS8575.G74S56 1985   C813'.54   C85-098638-9
PR9199.3.M2555S56 1985

For Ellen

SHORELINES

1

The day before had been a Tuesday, Hallowe'en of 1961, with a cold rain ignoring the mayor's eight-thirty curfew and lasting the night. By Wednesday noon, when the mill whistle signalled lunch – just as it had blown the night before to call off trick or treating – the rain was still falling hard, with the sky hanging over the town in a thick army blanket, one tuck behind the reservoir hill to the west, the other back of Rock Hill to the east. To the north and south, where the land flattened slightly along the river, sky and ground ghosted together in a grey mist. And out on Vernon's Main Street you could hear the rain twice, once when it hit and again as it washed in thin, quick waves down past The Bay, past the bowling alley and the hardware store, and down inadequate culverts into the Vernon River, which was already booked solid with the transport of dead leaves.

On the low side of Main, the rain flooded Odon Fuller's yard and threatened his eighteen-month timetable. So he worked anyway, in high rubber boots and a clear forty-nine-cent slicker, his milky hands shivering as they worked the waxed paper off the reconditioned, four-cycle Harley Davidson motorcycle engine. Just what they shook from wasn't clear. It could have been the expense of the engine, the $153 Fuller had taken fourteen months to shave off his pension, or it could have been the cold, or even old age. Fuller was, after all, going on seventy-four and would be three-quarters

9

of a century old in mid-April, 1962 – *blast-off day* – and he couldn't be sure there was even time to fill, choke, and fire the engine, let alone book his trip to Stockholm for the presentation of the Nobel Prize for Physics. For that, at the very least, was going to be due the man who would invent the world's very first flying saucer.

Odon Fuller was the sole resident of Vernon concerned with the abstract on that day. For the other 2,910 citizens, Wednesday, November 1 was a time of inescapable fact. It was neither a day for heart attacks nor tow trucks. The town's only ambulance was blocked in by both wreckers having bogged down as they tried to winch out an abandoned '51 Mercury Hallowe'en pranksters had dumped on the ambulance owner's lawn. Not that everyone in town was as upset as the ambulance owner. The afterglow of two new Ontario lacrosse championships still lingered from September. Only the past Saturday night the Legion had staged the awards banquet, a remarkable success despite one of the third-string peewee players having farted loudly during the mayor's speech, upsetting several members of the women's auxiliary.

But it was a time of reassessment; the town was still trying to shake free of the hangover of 1960, when the Muskoka Leather Company had closed on September 1. The tannery – a huge, stinking mass of yellow concrete in the hollow by the river and the CNR railway yard – had *been* the town for sixty-seven years. People rose and ate to its whistles, and they took pride in the joke that, since the tannery had been the largest sole leather producer in the British Empire, people all over the world were walking on a piece of Vernon.

Soon after the closing the local Chamber of Commerce had even taken it upon itself to compile a seductive chart of Vernon goodnesses to present to various industries in the hope of attracting them into north-central Ontario. For those who lived in the town, however, it was hard to recognize themselves clearly on paper: 2,910 people, two banks, the Royal and Toronto Dominion; two schools with 700 students; twice daily CNR express train service; skilled labour at $1.25 to $1.75 an hour; unskilled at eighty-five cents to $1.25 an hour; and women at fifty to eighty-five cents an hour.

How this could say anything about what Vernon *really* was all about, no one could understand. Where were the nods around the morning mail pickup? Where were the church bells, the overtime hockey victories, the parades, the view from Rock Hill? Where was the time Farmer Simpson shot out the town hall clock with a .303 Lee Enfield simply because he liked his weekend right where it was and wanted it to stay there? And where was the living room Tom Thomson painted in the spring of 1917, when he was courting a Vernon girl, the paint barely dry before they found him bloated and floating face down in Canoe Lake?

Such Chamber of Commerce arithmetic added up to a town as faceless and forgetful as a gravestone: numbers without life. A short walk out from the town, out along the Fourth Concession, there was the Anglican cemetery, St. John's, and the quick facts on the last stone on the low side told as little about the people buried there as the business statistics did about the town.

HARVEY TURNER
August 5, 1856 – February 9, 1932

His Wife
MELISSA BURTON TURNER
March 22, 1858 – October 3, 1935

There was nothing added about their daughter, Janet, who would have married Tom Thomson back in 1917, but for his peculiar death. And there was certainly nothing about her story or what she might have known about the drowning. All the gravestone offered were dates, something to serve as mere parentheses around what really happened in a person's life.

2

On that same day, Wednesday, November 1, 1961, a five-year-old Chevrolet Biscayne moved north toward Vernon. Blue, with rust bubbling about the headlights, the Chevrolet had come up Highway 11, leading away from Toronto, up through the forty-fourth parallel to the forty-fifth and past a ragged billboard which announced: YOU ARE NOW HALF-WAY TO THE NORTH POLE.

Eleanor Philpott saw the sign as she approached it, looked twice to make sure and wondered out loud whether the message was intended as a warning or a greeting.

She worked her cigarettes out of her purse, tossing the pack onto the passenger seat, put one to her mouth, and turned it when she saw the filter bobbing out past her nose. She suddenly realized how tired she was. With a long blink she took her sight out of its locked-in focus and looked over toward the west, out of which direction the storm had been coming since morning. It looked worse now; a heavily-bruised front was building for a larger attack still, with nothing beyond it but further threats.

She brought her thoughts back into the car. Her accelerator foot tingled with sharp pins, stung harder when she dared move it. With the radio little more than whining static now, the loudest sound in the cab was the scratch-wheeze-scratch of the left windshield wiper. Outside was a quieter, almost soothing engine knock, and through the opening in the no-draught she could hear the indistinct sizzle of the worn tires as they pushed ahead through the rain.

With luck, she'd find a decent hotel in this wilderness, though where she could only pray. The dash lighter popped. Eleanor reached for it, suddenly aware that her hand was trembling. She lit the cigarette.

All those lonely 150 miles from Toronto still hadn't prepared her for what lay ahead. She put the lighter back and drew on the cigarette as if she'd just risen from being a full minute under water. It calmed her somewhat, as did the brief change in the weather as the Chevrolet's tires fried noisily along the residential part of Main Street and she could look to the west out over the bay and the distant narrows. The storm cloud, though menacing a moment before, was suddenly breaking slightly, and though rain continued to dimple the windshield, enough to require wiping, the lowering sun was hanging in several long sleeves over the bay, the thin, silky light stabbing into the whitecaps and then bending like straws as the clouds moved along.

Eleanor had never actually been in Vernon before, though she had seen it. Back when she and Rudy were still together they had gone with the Maynards to their cottage on Lake Nipissing for a week, and Barney Maynard had insisted on flying his heavy old single-engine Stinson—even though Eleanor had pleaded with Joyce Maynard to talk him out of it. But Barney had won; they all flew up together and it had been every bit as bad as expected, Barney smart-alecking the old four-seater into phoney stalls and steep banks. Joyce had finally screamed at him when she saw the murder in Eleanor's eyes, and Rudy and Eleanor had spent the rest of the ride huddled in the back seat with an Ontario road map between them, trying to keep track of where they were as Barney, subdued, followed the boring lead of Highway 11.

She remembered Vernon vaguely from that trip. Quaint, she'd said. Rudy, who came from a small town not unlike Vernon's size in the Ottawa Valley, said it was the kind of place people retired to, and she'd looked down through the wing struts and wondered why. The town looked pretty enough, lots of green and blue from that height, with fair-sized lakes on both sides and a river that split the town as irregular as the crack in a morning eggshell. But what did people *do* there? And *why*?

Today, she wondered this again. She looked around and all she could see, apart from the houses and empty street – well, it was close to supper time – was a numbing amount of bush and water. Cottaging she could understand, but she couldn't quite fathom people living in such areas year round, let alone right now, with the autumn clinging to the town like a damp newspaper: cold, grey, persistent. Eleanor wondered if she wanted even to touch the town, let alone sift through as much of it as she could in the coming days.

But her decision had already been made. She'd find out the true story. And no matter how much it hurt her or the person who waited unwittingly at the end of this long drive.

Main Street surprised Eleanor by falling away to the right as the road passed over a rise and dropped quickly down toward the river. It caught her off guard and her shift into second came loudly, grinding, causing the car to lurch excitedly as it came to the turn-off into the Muskoka Hotel parking lot. A good omen awaited her – a spot that didn't require her backing into – and Eleanor's mouth curled between a smile and a search for another cigarette, finding neither.

For a long time after she turned the ignition off, Eleanor sat watching the Muskoka from her side mirror, the water misting over the reflection so the walls of the building rippled and ran. It looked, if nothing else, functional: red brick, square, sturdy, boring. She felt no commitment; there was no reservation made, certainly no one expecting her. If she wished, she could simply turn the key and be gone again as if this had never happened. She checked her watch: three and a half hours and she could be back in Toronto.

She checked her face in the mirror, aware she was stalling. The mirror was wide but too squat to fit all of her face in at

14

once. It made the cheekbones seem even wider, too high when she looked at her mouth and too low when she stared into her own eyes. When she centred the image the split and sweep of her newly-cut bangs forced a diamond of her face that was most unflattering. And, she knew, entirely wrong. Eleanor agreed with the doctor when he suggested that she knew very little about herself – hell, she agreed with *everything* he said, though this time she had genuinely meant it – but she was most certain about one thing regarding Eleanor Philpott: the inside did not go with the outside. She had a face gifted with assurance, a captivating look of strength that was as deceptive as mascara. "In darkness there is mystery, love," her hairdresser had said on Saturday when he talked her into letting him style her black hair so it formed a curtain across her forehead. "People will just *have* to get to know you."

She smiled at the thought. *Then I am not alone*. Her face quivered, as if shaking off the notion, and again she reached automatically for her cigarettes, finding them under the open map on the seat. She put one into her mouth but made no move to light it. She closed her eyes: a small time for the Eleanor inside.

But brush your damn hair back from the mystery and what are you left with? *What?* A librarian (very mysterious, that) who can't find a job, who can't keep a husband – who has perhaps even lost her mind. A forty-three-year-old basket case who worries more about the past than the future... yes indeed, people will have to get to know the notorious, mysterious Eleanor Philpott, who has remained these last many months cleverly disguised as a notions clerk in the Eaton's store at College and Yonge. Eleanor, who can't keep the till cash flow in balance and can't keep her floor manager's hands off her breasts. Eleanor, who snubs everyone – herself included – who just *has* to get to know her.

She opened her eyes, looked once more at her watch, as if the day might have taken the opportunity to sneak away on her, then did a quick calculation. She could probably be home before ten.

But then I'd never know.

She lit her cigarette, reached over into the back seat, and struggled with the overnight bag and umbrella. She got out, slammed the door locked, and then walked completely around the car, making sure all four doors were locked, steeled herself, and ran quickly around to the front, dodging the light rain.

Inside the hotel's main lobby there were a few people with packed shopping bags waiting for the bus and an oddly-dressed old man with a cane, who'd fallen asleep in a high-backed leather chair near the door. Eleanor moved, unnoticed, through the lobby, coolly fielded the deskman's small talk, and checked in with a sureness of manner that amazed and delighted her. Almost as if she did it weekly. It was, however, the first time she'd ever checked into anything herself.

She signed her name and pushed the register back to the deskman, noticing as he looked down at it that his head seemed to sit on his nose rather than the other way around. The nose came up, seeming to shrink as it now rested on the background of his face.

"Mrs. – uh – Philpott," the deskman said, his mouth rising above randomly-arranged teeth. "Welcome to the Muskoka. If there's anything we can do for you, just let us know, okay?"

"Well," she said, voice firm, convincing. "Maybe you could help me out." She pushed the paper with the name "Miss Janet Turner" toward him. "Any ideas where I might find this woman?"

The deskman examined the paper.

"Where did you park?" he asked.

"In the side parking lot," Eleanor said, the sureness missing from her voice.

The deskman pushed the paper back to her, spinning the words so they faced her.

16

"Well, then," he said. "It's kitty-cornered to where you parked. Brown frame house. She has the top floor. Rents out the bottom."

Eleanor swallowed. Instinctively she turned in that direction and looked back toward the lobby doors. It was dark out now, and still drizzling. The old man in the chair was watching her. She could hear his cane tapping on the chrome arm of the chair.

"You family?" the deskman asked.

Eleanor didn't answer. She turned and moved back across the lobby, out past the old man who seemed to be asleep again and out the door into the growing dark and the rain. When the umbrella went up the sound changed, the rain hollow on the cloth, and she was suddenly very aware of what she had done: *acted*. Acted impulsively. And now she was walking purposely across the street and up toward the blurred two-storey frame house. And that meant that the motion begun in the lobby was having a follow through. Again good.

There was a new sound now. A hum, high-pitched and steady, from above. Eleanor looked up toward it and saw a large green hydro transformer on the pole just outside the upper window of the house, out of which glowed a dim light. The transformer hum seemed to penetrate everything, beyond the rain in intensity and obviously more lasting. It was difficult to make out but there was a small animal, dead, caught on the wire as it touched the plastic connector leading to the pole. A squirrel, Eleanor decided, and shuddered.

She looked toward the light leaking out under a pulled shade, first window on the second floor. Eleanor watched for several minutes, wondering whether she'd rather have a cigarette or enough courage to actually knock. Lighting up a cigarette might draw attention to her, though, standing out in the rain, a stranger. Knocking would be even harder to deal with.

The choice obviated itself when the light in the window

fluttered and a shadow – bulky, Eleanor thought – moved slowly past the window and then the blind came down tight.

Eleanor shivered. She shrank back into the safety of her collar, instantly aware that she could not knock now. Perhaps later.

3

Russell Pemberton had been snoozing in the lobby of the Muskoka Hotel when Eleanor arrived. He probably wouldn't have even noticed her if it hadn't been for the sharp crack of her heels on the marble floor – a city walk, he instantly knew – and when he looked up he'd noticed she was smoking while she walked. Bad enough that women smoked when they sat, Russell thought. Like his mother had always said, "A whistling woman and a crowing hen is neither good for God nor man," and they could throw smoking in there as well, he figured, though he reminded himself smoking had come along after the Bible, not before.

Too bad about her, too, because this was one fine-looking girl that walked up to the reception desk and started talking to Archie about a piece of paper they handed back and forth. Russell figured the woman for her early forties, to his mind the best age possible for women. Unfortunately, for the ones who'd married somebody about their own age, it was also the worst age possible for men. Russell knew; he'd seen enough friends go through it.

But she was a looker, all right, standing there with her elbows on the counter and one leg lifting and falling behind her like a hand pump. Russell knew what that meant; he didn't go to every movie up at the local and fail to pick up something about life and women. When a leg moved like that it meant passion, clear and simple. When he looked at

19

the rest of the girl he had to nod: jet black hair, thick and shiny in the strong lights at the desk, nice high cheek bones – strength there, Russell thought – a mouth with a city-splash of lipstick, but possibly good-humoured under all that, and the rumour of a fine figure under that heavy coat that fell past her knees. Lordy, take away the cigarette and you've got something.

Russell Pemberton had been sitting, as usual, watching the passengers gather for the evening bus to Toronto. He liked to see people moved emotionally, even though his eyes weren't much good anymore. But you didn't need perfect vision to appreciate a long handshake or a sneaked kiss that often as not missed. Russell liked to sit by the door in the high-backed leather chair with the chrome handles and imagine they were all saying goodbye to him. Sometimes his eyes would water, and he'd be sitting there dabbing at them with a handkerchief, but he never missed a day. He knew he struck an odd figure: at seventy-six he still held onto a boyish face, large, fleshy, spirited, behind a proud nose, his true age hinted at by yellowing cataracts in once sky-blue eyes, and grey-white hair that had turned as soft and weightless as a floating milkweed seed. He'd sit this time of year with an insulated red hunter's vest on, red scarf with little yellow seahorses, cane set against one leg and his blue toque with the yellow tassel smoothed across the other.

Russell had watched Eleanor leave. He thought he detected fear when she passed by him, but it was difficult to say for sure, considering his poor eyes. For a moment after she'd gone he wondered who she was – not many strangers in town this time of year – and what it was that was bothering her.

Grabbing his cane, he pushed up on both armrests – bad knee cracking like a finger snap – and moved slowly over toward the desk, the lobby fading in and out of sight as slow blood rose to keep up with him. By the time Russell reached the reception desk the popping lights were gone; he rapped his cane on the marble counter and Archie looked up from the paper he was staring at.

"Russell! *You'll* know."

"Know what?" Russell growled.

Archie spun the register around and shoved it at the old man.

"Her. You know her?"

"I can't read that."

"Philpott – Eleanor Philpott, from Toronto."

"That woman?" Russell asked pointing toward the door.

"Yah. You know her?"

"Why should I know her?"

"She asked about Janet Turner."

Russell felt lightheaded again. He could feel his jaw tremble with instant anger.

"Asked what?"

"Just where she lived's all."

Russell turned in the direction of the frame house. *What was she doing there?*

"She family, Russell?" Archie asked. "I asked her but she didn't say."

Russell was already going in the direction of the lobby doors. He answered quickly over his shoulder.

"She *ain't* family."

Just then the Toronto woman came back in from the street; she moved briskly past him in her city isolation and on toward the elevator. *Not even a glance*, Russell thought. He couldn't tell from that whether she knew who he was and was deliberately avoiding him or whether she was just ignorant. Probably ignorant.

From just inside the lobby doors he could see the old Turner house, lights on, blinds drawn. He wondered if the city woman had been stupid enough to knock. If she had, and he presumed she had, then he hoped Jenny had not heard it. Or at least had the sense not to answer.

He went back to his seat, settled, and fussed about the city woman. If he weren't so tired he'd go on up to her room and find out for himself. What did she want with Jenny? *Who was she?* . . . God, he was tired. . .

21

. . . Spring of 1900 . . . Russell and Jenny – as he had always called her – were both fifteen that spring. Both were graduates of fifth class, as far as the local schooling went, and Russell, anyway, was finished with education for good. Jenny still talked about school, perhaps going elsewhere to study. But the fact remained that Jenny, though bright, had never got the hang of such things as grammar or drawing; Russell, not nearly as bright, was a complete failure at mathematics, Jenny's best subject. In one way, failing math was a blessing in disguise; Jenny kept passing notes back to Russell which he kept as much for their scent as the answers they contained.

They had remained close friends after graduation. Russell lived at home, while picking up odd jobs around town and Jenny lived with her parents, helping out her mother while her father was away working the bush camps. Russell also helped out his mother, though in this case she became his employer.

Abigail Pemberton, widow, had an herb garden that nearly overflowed the half-acre she owned on upper East Street, and her medicines were only slightly less in demand than the services of the two local medical doctors by the 1,400 people of the town.

It was a boom time for Vernon. Most of the town had accidentally burned to the ground six years earlier, and the old wooden buildings had been replaced by new, far more prosperous brick ones. The main wood in evidence formed the sidewalk up and down Main Street, as well as the bridge over the Vernon River. There was much talk of a steel bridge across the river, as if the shift from wood to brick to steel was a natural progression the new century brought with it.

Russell would never forget that spring. Some of the snow banks had piled up over eight feet high that winter, and when the runoff came it looked for a while as if the town would merely give in to its funnel shape between the two hills and slide down into the river and away. The town was brought to a stall. Wagons couldn't move up through the

22

muck of Main Street; horses couldn't keep their footing long enough to pull; people bogged down walking. Despite this, Russell ran for his mother, all right, but at considerable expense. He wore high rubber boots and learned to press his toes high to make sure the actual boots followed each step he took. After a while he could tell just by the sucking sound how far his boot had slipped down into the muck.

It was a busy time. Grippe had hit the town and the doctors seemed out of their element. Half the town was down with it, and a number of the original pioneers were already dead, their old bodies unable to stand up to the violent spasms and heaves of the disease. No one seemed able to keep down food, and certainly not any medicine, and some of the older folks were saying the grippe was spreading through footprints. They argued that the men were picking it up by walking around where animals had been, and for a while there were no shoes or boots to be seen in a single house in town. Russell discovered while making deliveries that he was expected to pull off those big boots, regardless of how dirty his hands got, and leave them standing like a couple of clay statues while he popped in a minute and collected for his mother's remedy.

Abigail Pemberton was in a panic. During the first part of the grippe scare she'd been busier than ever before. She'd rise at four and grind up her dried raspberry plants for Russell to run to the pregnant women around to stop them from miscarrying. She had her penny royal for making them sweat, her boneset to bring down the fever and even the odd sprig of feverfew to stop them from feeling nauseated. Feverfew, Russell's mother always told him, was the only thing to use when the ague struck: headaches, chills, fevers, shivering, long sweats – it didn't matter as long as you had some finely-ground feverfew from Abigail Pemberton.

Each day, for two hours until breakfast, Russell would work with the mortar and pestle until the grains were fine enough to dissolve in hot water. Then his mother would go to the slotted cedar box just outside the door, open it, and pull out the orders that had arrived during the night. There were often thirty or more orders to fill each day, which meant Russell would be going full out on his deliveries until well after supper.

Toward the end of the grippe epidemic, though, Abigail Pemberton's business almost collapsed. Her remedies were giving relief but no full cure. When the talk about the disease travelling on people's shoes peaked, the prevailing wisdom was that a layer of sulphur in the shoe was the answer; that way, any illness that figured to get at you through your feet would be subject to an instant, successful ambush. So while the general stores ran out of sulphur in less than two days, Abigail's orders trickled off to nothing.

So she figured two could play that game, and invented a cure so odd and confusing that no one would dare question it. Working with Russell, she chopped up a pile of strong onions as fine as the knife could manage, dumped them into a large spider cooker over the fire, added an equivalent amount of rye meal and vinegar, and created a large, thick paste. Into this brown sludge she sprinkled spearmint leaves and crushed woodruff, just to give the concoction a pleasant odour above the onions. They then packaged it all into small cotton bags, and Russell went about selling the mixture to people who promised to heat it all up again in a pot of boiling water and spread the bag over their chest at a temperature as high as they could bear, higher if possible. At twenty-five cents a bag, Abigail Pemberton made a killing, and, coincidentally, by mid-May the grippe had left town.

Russell knew that Janet Turner's house had been hit. Both her mother and father had come down with it, and Jenny hadn't had any time to talk when Russell stopped to make his delivery. She was caring for her parents and would meet him at the door. She gave him the money, a quick smile, and turned back inside. She looked haggard, worn, her hair dirty and clinging, and there were deep lines under her eyes. Russell felt sorry for her.

He saw her again over by Rock Hill closer to the end of

May. He had been rabbit hunting and was coming back from the hunt with two small kills, one with just a smidgeon of white left from winter along its flank, and he was swinging the rabbits on the cord and looking down at the barrel of his father's old .22 when he heard her calling.

"Russell! Hey! Russell Pemberton!"

Russell looked up, practically dropping the rabbits. Jenny's voice came as clear as the air. She stood with her mother on the edge of the opening, a handful of wildflowers alive against the white of her dress.

Russell waved and went over.

"Jenny," he said, genuinely pleased. "What're you doing?"

"Hello, Russell," Mrs. Turner said, her voice slightly edged with the effect of his forgetting to acknowledge her. She was also carrying some flowers and a small basket filled with new ferns, still tightly coiled, fiddleheads, some of the townspeople called them, though Russell had never tasted them. Mrs. Turner was in black, and her face was a grim contrast to the spring sun.

"Mrs. Turner," Russell said, tipping his hunter's cap the way his mother had always insisted.

"You wouldn't believe the flowers, Russell," Jenny said, and she pushed her handful toward him. "We've seen violets, Dutchman's breeches and more adder's tongues than you could count."

"No trilliums, though," added Mrs. Turner. "It must be too early yet with all the water that had to run off."

Russell set down his gun and his rabbits. He saw Jenny look at them, then glance quickly away and move toward the lily-of-the-valley they'd originally been headed for. Mrs. Turner turned to more picking as well, and Russell watched Jenny move as she picked the tiny white flowers and arranged them in small bells around her bouquet. She'd changed considerably since he last saw her. Fresh again, he had to say. Gone were the deep purple eyes and the tightness around the lips. Her eyes now were clear and alive – full of mischief, as Russell's mother would say. Her

25

hair, obviously washed that day, bounced high and black as she jumped from one flower clump to the next one. The greyness of her cheeks that Russell had seen only weeks before was now a pink that rode high on her cheekbones, and the mouth, now relaxed, had the same effect on Russell's knees as did the outline of her developing body. Little wonder, he thought, the older fellows he knew were asking him more and more about her.

Russell moved off into the shaded part of the bush, where the budding maples towered with young leaves and the forest floor was grey and brown with the decay of dead leaves. He only had to walk about fifty yards until he came to the side of the hill and, as he expected, found a dozen or more trilliums. He picked five, and circled them around a purple one which looked slightly devilish among the white. He came back and handed them to her.

"Why, Russell," Jenny said, "where did you find them? They're beautiful."

Mrs. Turner came over, her heavy black boots slipping on the new moss. She looked, sniffed, and scowled.

"What's that stinkin' Johnny doing in there? You'll spoil it."

"No it won't, Mother," Jenny said, her voice still light and happy. "I like it there."

Russell smiled and felt as if he'd just taken a very important step.

"It's very nice of you, Russell," Mrs. Turner said. "Come now, Janet. It's time we were getting back to get your father's supper. Do say hello to your good mother for me, Russell."

"I will, ma'am."

"Thank you for the flowers, Russell," Jenny said, and gave him a look of frustration with her mother.

"You're more than welcome, Jenny."

"I'll be seeing you around, I hope."

"Yah," Russell said. "Sure thing."

Russell didn't see Jenny again in the flesh—though he'd spent considerable time with her image in his daydreams—

until the last day of that month. He was coming back from an early-morning delivery to Mrs. Bullwark of a small bottle of rose petal vinegar for her migraines, and was killing time, whistling and kicking a round stone down the road toward Main Street when Jenny called from her porch.

"Russell!"

Russell grinned and turned, his hands still in his pockets. He knew her mother must be out for Jenny to call as unlady-like as that.

"Morning, Jenny. Lovely day, isn't it?"

"*Lovely!* You don't know the half of it, Russell Pember-ton. Don't you get any news?"

"News about what?"

"About the world, idiot. Pretoria has been captured! Sur-rendered yesterday. They're saying the war's almost over! It came over the wire first thing this morning. Are you going to the parade?"

"Parade? Me?"

"Parade *everybody*, silly. There's already been a petition presented to Reeve Wright and he's proclaimed this after-noon a holiday."

There was a loud explosion from Main Street. Russell jumped, pulled his hands from his pockets and braced him-self as if a dog were about to attack him. Jenny laughed.

"It's just a firecracker, for land's sake."

Russell looked and saw several of the young men he knew running from a can on the roadway. Several were holding their hats; all were laughing. There was another roar, muffled this time, and the can flew higher than the upper balcony of the Olympia Hotel. Older men, lined along the sidewalks, rocked back and forth on their feet, their faces red with enthusiasm.

"Come on," Jenny said. "Let's get in on the goings on!"

It had been as easy as all that. A chance meeting. A rare coincidence. And suddenly they were seen together having fun. Russell never forgot walking that short block down to Main Street, Jenny holding onto his forearm with both

27

hands and smiling as if she'd won the war herself, Russell puffing out his chest, as if he himself had stood between Queen Victoria and Kruger, and walking lightly on the balls of his feet, praying the lift of his new felt hat brought him up to and beyond the elegant Miss Janet Turner.

And what a day it had been! They walked up and down the boardwalk streets, watched the boys and their fire-crackers, raised their hands in victory salutes to friends across the street and even joined in an impromptu singing of "God Save The Queen" at the corner of Maple and Main. Russell sang with all he had – his mother said he had a good voice, the only thing of value his father had left him when he walked out on them – and Russell prayed that this, if nothing else, would impress Jenny Turner. For he'd just realized he was in love with her...

...Jenny Turner. Lordy, Russell reminded himself as he moved out of his doze and back into the reality of the Muskoka lobby, she was one hell of a girl. Why he'd decided that day sixty-one years ago, he didn't know. He just did, that's all. Despite all that had happened.

Fool that he was, he kept thinking it would all be just a matter of time. He'd get a real job away from his mother. Jenny would get the training her mother kept talking about, secretarial probably. That was fine. He could wait for all that, too.

"Mr. Pemberton? Russell?"

What was that? Russell couldn't place the voice at first and jumped when the hand started rocking his shoulder.

"*Russell!* Wake up."

Russell blinked his eyes. They'd been running again; one eyelid wouldn't open and the other would but the eye wouldn't focus. He reached for his handkerchief, letting the toque drop, wiped carefully, and looked again. He recognized Archie by his nose, big as a galvanized eavestrough elbow, Russell always said. Archie was leaning over, hands

28

on both knees, and looking at Russell as if he were a badly-tuned television set.

"You nodded off, Russell," Archie said, his voice full of the type of patronizing concern Russell despised. "Okay?"

"Okay what, Archie? Of course I'm okay."

Russell looked around to see if anyone was eavesdropping on this conversation. There was no one there. The bus had gone long ago.

"It's nearly eight, Russell," Archie continued. "You'd better get going on up if you're going to catch the game, eh?"

The game? Oh, the *game* – Russell remembered. Toronto and the Canadiens. Lord, yes, he must hear the game, though it was hardly the same now that the great Richard had retired.

"Here," Archie said. "Let me help you up."

He reached and took Russell's arm. The old man shook him off impatiently, rose himself with a loud crack from his knee. Russell fumbled for his cane, tapped it sharply on the floor and stood up straight.

"She come back down?" he asked Archie.

The deskman blinked, not understanding.

"Who?"

"That city woman. She come back down?"

"Oh, Mrs. Philpott. No, Russell, she didn't. You want me to tell her you were asking for her, though?"

"No."

Russell walked slowly off toward the elevator, found it waiting, and pushed the familiar fifth-floor button without looking.

Who was she? he wondered as he moved down the scarlet carpet to his room on the southwest corner, the best view of all the hotel for overlooking Jenny Turner's house. A Tom Thomson buff, more than likely. Always pestering poor Jenny. Murder. Suicide. Ghosts... more crap than Russell could properly keep track of. Why couldn't they just let it alone?

Russell turned the key to his room. *She'll have me to answer to if she doesn't mind herself, I promise her that.*

He didn't bother with the light. After twenty-seven years in the same room he didn't need one. He turned on the radio to the CBC affiliate. Three years ago he'd given up watching on the lobby television: his eyes were getting so bad the only time Russell knew anybody had scored was when the players all hugged each other. With the radio he could make up his own pictures, and quite frankly he found them more satisfying.

Russell went to the window, raised the blind, and looked down on Jenny's house, the streetlight on Hunter's Street spreading a cone of yellow down toward her lawn and showing a renewed intensity of the rain. There was a light on in her bedroom, he thought, but couldn't be sure, with his eyes. He hoped she was going to sleep well. Perhaps in the morning he'd call on her.

He looked up over her house toward the reservoir hill where they'd often walked in the spring and fall. In the distance lightning flashed, a quick flick like a lighter in a dark bar, and in a few moments the sky growled as if it were vaguely hungry.

He removed his clothes, with the light still off, placed them neatly over the small desk and chair. He put on his flannelette pajamas, made sure the top button was done up in case it did storm badly, and climbed into bed.

The voice came on the radio. Good old Foster Hewitt, Russell thought. He wouldn't find a better friend tonight.

"Hello Canada and hockey fans in the United States..."

4

Eleanor's room was on the far side of the Muskoka on the fourth floor. Her window overlooked the lower part of the town and the river, and it seemed to her the storm had anchored itself now over the big hill to the east. She could see lightning firing out over the lake, the clarity of the islands in each flash making the town seem pale and distant. She stood shoeless and smoking a cigarette, absently watching the storm as if it were a news report she had little interest in, but had even less inclination to get up and turn off.

There was a light rap at the door. She stubbed her cigarette, carefully put her shoes on and moved to answer the knock.

It was the deskman.

"Sorry about the delay, Mrs. Philpott, but we've been having room service problems of late. I had trouble coming up with even a sandwich."

"You did, though?" Eleanor asked.

"Roast beef on white, if that's okay. And no trouble with the drink."

"No, that's fine. Thank you for that, anyway. Can you just put it on my bill, please?"

"Certainly. No problem."

Archie moved into the room and set the tray down on the veneer writing desk. He looked quickly around—suitcase unpacked, still sitting open on the bed, the local paper spread out on the desk, an open carton of cigarettes – and then began unwrapping the sandwich plate from the large napkin he'd carried it in.

"No. No thanks. Just leave it please, I'll do it later," Eleanor said.

Archie stepped back, flustered.

"Of course. Later."

Eleanor pulled a dollar bill from her open purse on the desk and gave it to him, both of them acting as if the tipping existed apart from them. Archie pocketed it quickly and backed toward the door.

"Oh, by the way, Mrs. Philpott," he said as he grabbed the door, "find everything you were looking for – earlier, I mean."

Eleanor stiffened. Wouldn't do to have him ask too many questions, as this was to be her little secret until she knew for sure.

"Yes, fine, thank you."

"Was she in?" he asked.

"No," Eleanor said. "It wasn't important anyway."

Archie nodded with satisfaction and closed the door.

She had lied, and felt badly for it. But to have said anything different would only have encouraged more talk, and there wasn't anything Eleanor wanted to say about it – at least not yet. *Not important*, she'd said. Only important enough that she'd thought about little else since last March, when her mother died.

She looked at the bedside telephone and remembered when the threatening ring had come through: Aunt Rita calling long distance. Could she please come back to Philadelphia immediately. Her mother had taken a turn for the worse. The second stroke in a week.

Next morning she was on an economy flight out of Malton Airport. She'd considered calling Rudy to tell him, but hadn't. As far as Eleanor was concerned, Rudy no longer considered her part of his family – so how could he be expected to feel for an old woman from another city in another country. They'd only met infrequently, anyway, and Rudy hadn't seemed to care much for them. Nor they, really, for him. Sometimes Eleanor felt her mother had taken Rudy as a personal affront, his clumsiness threatening her fine china, his long silences ridiculing her idle chatter. He had no need to know. It didn't matter, anymore. It was a beautiful late winter day, with the snow below too bright to watch pass for long. She'd seen ice huts out on a small lake the plane circled over following takeoff, many of them painted a flat green so they looked as square and basic as a cluster of houses in a Monopoly game. During the approach into the Philadelphia airport she saw a school let out for recess, the bright coats of the children contrasting with the starkness of the snow-covered schoolyard. She had never seen this much snow in Pennsylvania. She leaned her forehead against the glass and looked out over the wing at the recess – the fifteen minutes that used to hang suspended for her – and she wished it could all be so simple for her again.

But it wasn't. Her father had long since died and her mother had had yet another stroke. Pretty soon she'd have no more connection with Philadelphia than the marking on her birth certificate.

Her Aunt Rita met her at the airport. Eleanor saw her first on the other side of the glass as she went through customs. Rita was standing with her back to a pillar, her best hat and coat worn for the occasion, and tissues hanging from the top of her black purse. She had her hands together, as if giving a recital, and her face looked drawn and worn, the usual heavy make-up around the eyes smudged and tracing to show where the tears had travelled. Eleanor thought Rita looked like she should have been at a funeral, not an airport, and then wondered if perhaps something further had happened since they had talked.

When she got through with her luggage, Rita was waiting at the automatic doors. She sighed and looked at Eleanor as if Eleanor was still six years old.

They hugged. Rita tried to kiss Eleanor on the cheek but

Eleanor, seeing the lipstick coming at her like a rubber-stamp mouth, managed to avoid it. Using her much longer arms, she held Rita at a distance and acted as if she were seeing her aunt for the first time in years.

"How is she?" Eleanor asked.

Rita sniffled. "Worse, dear. Much worse. I was in last night and she didn't even recognize me."

"Can she talk?"

"Yes, poor dear—but..."

"But what, Rita?"

"Myrna's in the past, poor thing. She thinks you're still a child."

Then she's as healthy as you, Eleanor said to herself.

The room was functional, if stark. Rita had arranged for fresh roses and gardenias on the table and there were already cards from people Eleanor remembered in a slightly out-of-focus way. Most of the cards were scriptures, which Eleanor always thought covered both ends of the matter: a little biblical support for those going up or those going down in health. It didn't matter much: the sender's tracks were covered.

Her mother lay in the bed as if she'd been fitted, the sheets designed about her. As long as the old woman was sleeping, Eleanor could handle it all, for then her mother didn't fully exist. For the moment, she felt nothing. There was only a frail, white-haired mass with drawn cheeks and sunken eyes. Eleanor thought she would have to put her mouth to her mother's nose just to make sure she was still breathing.

This was not her mother as she remembered her. The old woman lay there with her hands moving in front of her as if working some invisible loom, then plucked absent-mindedly at the blankets covering her. Rita told Eleanor her mother was making sure she was dressed to meet the maker, and said it with such conviction that Eleanor hadn't dared laugh. She'd laughed once, when Rudy told her about his grandfather's death up in the upper Ottawa Valley and how the family had handed the coffin out the window so the door wouldn't be cursed, and Rudy had become very upset with her, saying that was the way things were done there and Eleanor had no right to judge.

She wondered what would become of her mother. For herself, she rather fancied that people died the way plants died. They ended up in the ground and they rotted and that was that. It wouldn't hurt because it wouldn't matter: you were dead and dead meant the end, *finis*.

Naturally, Rita wouldn't have bought that even if Eleanor had bothered to tell her. Rita came and sat on the metal chair by the side of the bed and wept. And the tissue pile grew about her feet, though it would have required little effort for her to find the waste-basket. Eleanor thought that Rita let them drop where they may because she didn't want to offend her dying sister by demonstrating that tears were something to be cleaned up. Rita was obviously sitting there promising God the world – which He, presumably, already had – if only He'd intervene.

Eleanor also hoped He would, only not in quite the same direction, and that it would be over quickly. She felt that way at least until the third day in the hospital room, when Eleanor was sitting alone with her mother – Rita had said she'd take the "evening shift" – and the old woman's eyes fluttered open with the clarity of a child's and she started talking to someone who must have come from the same dimension as the complicated loom. She spoke in a voice that reminded Eleanor of nearly forgotten days, when her father smelled of scraped pipes and her mother knew the answers to questions Eleanor couldn't imagine having the foresight to ask.

"You're sure it'll be all right, Willie?" the old woman asked. Willie had been her pet name for Eleanor's father. "How old is the baby again?"

Eleanor passed that one off without too much trouble, but the wandering continued for a good two hours while Eleanor sat there dumbfounded and a giggly nurse came in and acted as if it were all right that the old lady played with her

35

marbles, that she'd seen them come and go, and far worse than that, and that Eleanor had no need to feel embarrassed just because her mother had fallen out of her tree.

"It's a sad thing, Willie, isn't it?" she said later that afternoon. "I know, I know. She's better off with us, poor, wee thing. But I do feel sorry for the mother. I can't help it... I know, Willie, the roast is a bit overdone... I had to let the meter man into the basement, dear..."

Wasn't that just like her mother, Eleanor thought: apologizing by rote. You'd think if she were going to get a few words in with her dear Willie at this time she might have asked him why he was so tight with his money.

...But what was this "poor, wee thing"? Eleanor had been an only child.

Eleanor looked closely at her mother. The skin of the old woman's face was now close to the colour and texture of an abandoned hornet's nest, the hair limp and thin and pale as tracing paper. Once she'd been blonde as goldenrod, Eleanor remembered.

And then remembered again. Her father had been pink-faced, and red-haired. Not exactly what you'd expect to produce a black-haired and dark-skinned daughter. Not that this was the first time Eleanor had wondered about that, but it was certainly the first time in more than thirty years. She'd asked her mother once at a time when she was dearly hoping she'd been adopted – preferably something as exotic and noble as an Indian princess – but her mother had simply laughed and hugged her and said she was the black sheep of the family, and probably took after Uncle Harold on her father's side, a dark and brooding man with a heavy scar that looked like a red caterpillar walking up his tea-coloured cheek.

Now she was asking again. Her mother's breathing faded into a deep sleep that sounded like a boat rubbing against dock tires. The door swung open and Rita came in.

"How is the poor dear?" Rita asked, as if Eleanor's mother was in another hospital.

Rita had a new bouquet, this time daffodils – expecting a second rising, Eleanor thought – and she hurried about from the bathroom for water to the bureau, where she arranged them as the centre attraction. Rita was wearing a very sober dress, compared to her usual pinks or yellows. She's enjoying this, Eleanor said to herself, getting a bigger kick out of death than she ever got out of life.

"Has she talked much?" Rita asked, still not receiving an answer to her first question.

"Some," Eleanor said.

Rita stepped back from the flowers and pulled a pink tissue from her sleeve.

"Was she... wandering?" Rita asked.

"Some, yes."

Rita looked pityingly at her ill sister. "Senility, I suppose."

"I suppose," said Eleanor. Her voice sounded as if it came from someone else, someone very tired.

"You go back to the apartment now, dear," Rita said. "I'll sit with her now. You get a good rest, huh?"

Doctor Stroud, a busy man with curling hair billowing up over the top of his shirt and a shiny bald head, came in then. He was carrying a clipboard and checked out Eleanor's mother as if she were an incubating egg, not a deathly-ill person, and when he'd finished he moved the curtain back to the wall and signalled the two women outside. Rita exited with a great handful of tissues and an expression that said she was about to catch hell from the teacher. Eleanor lit a cigarette.

Stroud wasted no time with small talk.

"Your mother's dying, Mrs. Philpott. Quite frankly, I'm surprised she's hung on this long."

Eleanor wasn't bothered by the bluntness. She could see for herself.

"How much longer, Doctor?"

"It's difficult to say. Another hour. A week, maybe."

Rita inhaled as if she'd had no air since she'd arrived at the hospital.

"Will she come round at all?" Rita asked. "Will we be able to say a proper goodbye to her?"

Jesus, Eleanor thought. *She's thinking about herself again.*

"Perhaps," the doctor said. "There might be a few minutes of clarity. You know, all that talk about 'the calm before the storm' and all that..."

"Oh, I do hope so," Rita said.

"Well," said Doctor Stroud, "I must get going. Your mother's resting comfortably, Mrs. Philpott, and you needn't worry about her. She's in no pain."

"Thank you," Eleanor said.

"Bless you, Doctor," Rita added.

Two more days passed without much change in the old woman. Eleanor and Rita swapped shifts, Eleanor sitting and dozing in the chair all night long with a spare blanket draped over her legs. A nurse came in every hour and Eleanor drifted between the methodical and difficult breathing of her mother and the efficient shush of nurses' nylons as they scurried in and out at regular intervals.

Just before breakfast on the fourth day, Eleanor was awakened from one of these fitful sleeps by a new sound.

"Eleanor, is that you?"

Eleanor sat up, blinked. Her mother's head had turned and the old woman was looking at her.

"You've come, Eleanor," the old lady said, her voice now as Eleanor had last recalled it. "I'm glad to see you, dear."

The calm before the storm, Eleanor thought.

"Hello, Mother," she said. "You're in the hospital."

"*I* know that. I've been in enough of them, you know."

Eleanor smiled.

"How is Rita?"

"Fine, Mother, fine."

"Well, make sure she doesn't get soppy about this, will you? You tell her listening to her is a whole lot worse than actually dying. No don't. But sometimes I think I'll be glad to get away from her."

She knows she's dying!

"How long have I been here?"

"Six days, Mother."

Eleanor drew closer and smoothed the old woman's hair back from her forehead. The hair felt like cobweb to Eleanor: visibly there, but without substance. Her mother's eyes were there, though, glistening and clear, and looking at her with what Eleanor could only take for a certain calmness.

"Mother? . . ." Eleanor began.

"Yes . . ."

"You were talking a lot in your . . . sleep," Eleanor continued.

"Oh dear . . . was I interesting?" her mother asked, and the dry corners of her mouth cracked into a smile.

"As a matter of fact, *very* . . . . You talked about me when I was a baby, Mother."

"You were a good baby, Eleanor."

Eleanor swallowed very hard, toughened to the task. She found herself whispering.

"But was I . . . was I *yours*? . . ."

"What? Speak up, Eleanor."

Eleanor closed her eyes.

"Was I adopted? Tell me, *please*, Mother."

The old woman turned away and stared at the window. Eleanor could hear her breathing, the pace unchanged. Eleanor hung her head and stayed on the edge of the seat, looking down at the stitching in the blanket covering her lap. After a few moments, she steeled herself again.

"Mother? . . ."

The old woman turned back, slowly and with great effort. And Eleanor noticed that her glistening eyes were now running. She looked at Eleanor with a hollow, disturbed expression.

"Mother . . . was I adopted? I have to know."

"What do you have to know, dear? You're my daughter."

"Mother . . ." Eleanor said, very deliberately, as if to prepare the old woman for the toughness of the next question. "Did you and father *have* me?"

The old woman stared at her for a long time. Eleanor watched her mother's eyes perceptibly tighten and loosen about the edges, as if she were concentrating on a very complicated problem.

Eventually her mother's mouth opened, no sound, but opened slowly as a thin film spread over one side of the dry mouth and then broke with the gentleness of a fish breaking water in the evening.

"... You don't want to know that, do you, Eleanor?"

"Please... you're still my mother, I just want to know who it was gave birth—"

"I don't know," the old lady said and turned again to face the window. She fell silent.

There was a commotion in the hallway. Rita's voice; early for her "shift" yet again. Eleanor turned as if she might hold up a hand the way a librarian would and gain some more time, alone and in silence. But Rita stormed through not even looking in her direction. She had an armful of Hollywood magazines, a fresh box of tissues, and a box of chocolates. Eleanor thought she looked more like she was going to the movies than to sit by a deathbed, and for a moment she wondered if Rita's mind could differentiate between the two: had it really gotten to the point where a good cry was her main pleasure in life?

"And how is she this morning, my dear?" Rita asked. "Any change?"

Eleanor chewed the anger off her bottom lip and turned with a smile borrowed from whatever reserve had let her put up with Rita for so long.

"Mother's much improved, Rita," Eleanor said with intentional coolness. "We've been talking."

Rita stopped organizing her death watch and looked at Eleanor as if she'd just said the old woman was checking out and going home.

"Talking?" she asked.

"Talking," Eleanor said, forcing another smile. "Come say hello to her."

Rita literally scrambled over and pushed in past Eleanor's arm. Eleanor had the distinct impression Rita was angry, as if she wondered how the old woman dared come round in her daughter's presence and leave her own sister to pick up the scraps. Rita's face came close to her sister's, the eyes wide and the powder and perfume overwhelming.

"It's me, Myrna – *Rita*!" she said.

Always thinking of yourself first, Eleanor thought.

"Rita. Your *sister*!" Rita was calling as if the old lady were deaf. "Do you know me?"

Eleanor wondered why there was no response, and she looked over Rita's shoulder into the face of the woman who had been lying there for all these days. She was no longer the person Eleanor had just been talking to. The calm had come; the calm had gone. Quietly, as it should. It would soon be over.

Thunder kicked through Eleanor's room at the Muskoka Hotel. She ate her sandwich, the roast beef tasting like binder twine, she decided, and sipped slowly at the Scotch and water. She rolled it around in her mouth and swallowed it in a manner that ensured each taste bud was given an equal opportunity. Then, with her one arm folded tightly against her waist and the drink held out in the other hand, she walked to the window and watched some more of the storm.

Her plan of attack would begin in the morning. She might try and get a look at Miss Janet Turner, might even try and "accidentally" speak to her, but the real test with Janet Turner, if it ever came, would have to come later. First she'd try the local paper.

Eleanor gave herself until the weekend. Monday she was due back at work, and she wanted to leave Vernon with an answer, one way or the other. She'd sleep now, begin in the morning. The drive had drained what little energy her curiosity had spared.

41

5

She tried to anticipate the alarm pins falling in her Baby Ben travelling clock. Eleanor knew roughly the time – seven-thirty – and that she was in a hotel in some town called Vernon. Her eyes hadn't opened yet. She was just awake enough to know she was still asleep. She liked that feeling, fearless and full of wonder, and usually tried to hang onto it for a few extra minutes before she got up. If the alarm did go before she could catch it, she counted the day ruined before she even opened her eyes.

Eleanor lay for a few minutes, blinking her eyes and thinking of Marilyn Monroe. She sometimes wished she knew Marilyn. Hers was really the only Hollywood star career Eleanor ever followed. Usually, she paid more attention to directors than to the plasticine people who worked as moving props. But Marilyn... well, Marilyn Monroe was different: she seemed to have no control over the events surrounding her life, which was something Eleanor could well – particularly now – sympathize with. Marilyn had been created by circumstance, which was precisely the way Eleanor was beginning to see herself.

She'd first come across a story on the actress in one of those silly magazines Eleanor felt were pardonable only in doctors' offices or hair salons. This time it was in a Bloor Street beauty parlour. Marilyn was talking about the famous pose that had brought her to fame. "When I posed for the calendar," the actress was quoted as saying, "all I had on was the radio." Eleanor had thought that was funny, and she'd started laughing, and because of the dryer being on she hadn't realized how loudly she'd laughed until she looked up and saw the salon's staff and the other patrons scowling over in her direction.

She considered that an important touchstone. It had been, Eleanor contended, one of the very few times the *real* Eleanor Philpott had appeared in public. Eleanor rather liked the idea that she'd made a fool of herself.

And all thanks to Marilyn Monroe. She'd prowled after magazines for more mention of her and she'd usually been rewarded. Mostly it was just gossip or something funny that Marilyn had said – like the time she claimed Chanel No. 5 was all she ever wore to bed – and that was all Eleanor had ever expected. What she didn't expect was that within a year she had decided that she and Marilyn Monroe were kindred spirits. She dated their relationship from the day she read an interview with the actress in which Marilyn said the following: "I am trying to find myself as a person. Sometimes that's not easy to do. Millions of people live their entire lives without finding themselves. Maybe they feel it isn't necessary."

Eleanor came to believe that in some small way she and Marilyn Monroe were like complementary colours: opposites that could work together, like red and green, and Eleanor had a pretty good idea who was the green in this relationship. But she felt that she, like Marilyn, existed as someone else's idea. She acted out a *concept* of Eleanor Philpott; it was not the role she wanted. Eleanor thought her personality was of the sponge variety – she soaked up what others sent her way, stored it, and delivered it right back to them whenever they touched her – and what she'd really like to do was take that sponge and shred it down until an Eleanor Philpott that was acceptable to her emerged.

She had had some tiny wooden dolls given to her when she was a small child. They came from Russia and were egg-shaped and came apart in the middle, and if you opened the largest one there was a slightly smaller one inside, and inside that another, and so on. The doll seemed to come apart in layers until, five dolls down, there was a tiny one that was of solid wood and would not peel off to reveal anything new. Eleanor thought she would one day like to get down to that in herself: the final definition.

She sat up in bed, convinced it was coming.

The feeling began to descend in the manner of pigeons landing in a park, a deep flutter that seemed less a sound than a spasm of the ear drums; but then, thank God it lifted. She'd started having spells like this shortly after Rudy left.

The first time had terrified her. One moment she had been talking to Joyce Maynard over the phone, laughing about something Joyce had said, and the next moment she was crying and not knowing why she was crying. She just sat there helpless, with the tears pouring out of her and her body shaking in short, violent snaps. She seemed to drift away from herself: she could see the tears and the red face and the terror in her own eyes, and she could see the little receiver lying on the arborite table facing her and Joyce's voice squeaking out of it, far away and distant and full of fright and concern. The whole thing seemed so futile to Eleanor from her new viewpoint, so absolutely vacuous and worthless and wasted and so undeniably sad. But why it would be sad, she didn't know.

Joyce had come over by taxi, and when she got there Eleanor was still sitting on the kitchen chair with the phone off the hook and sobbing, though now there were no tears. Completely detached from the scene, Eleanor watched Joyce run to the body Eleanor had jumped out of and hug it and start crying herself, and Eleanor's only reaction was that life is a waste of effort. If we all have to die some day, she thought, we might as well get it over with so we can stop worrying about it.

And then she'd come back. It was as if the moment between the first cry and the end of it was no more than whatever it took for Joyce's voice to travel between their

44

places by telephone, but in actual fact Joyce's body was here. Eleanor stopped crying, pulled out a cigarette.

Joyce had seemed unsure what to do. She kept on hugging Eleanor to comfort her, but all of a sudden Eleanor seemed to require less comfort than she did. She looked at Eleanor, as though she were surprised to see her. She sat back, took a cigarette, though Joyce was usually a non-smoker, and asked Eleanor if she'd like to talk about it. Eleanor lit her own cigarette and passed the match over. Later, Joyce had made coffee and grilled cheese sandwiches. And in a graceful manner during their lunch she suggested Eleanor should go and see a doctor.

But Eleanor hadn't. She regarded the problem as a cold, something that had come and had bothered her but was now gone and forgotten. She put it down to the fact that she hadn't let herself go when the marriage broke down. She'd read somewhere that when people can't absorb their own emotions, they tend to store them up or stifle them for the time being, only to have them all come out later like forgotten preserves, usually a whole lot mustier than when they went in. She'd been crying for Rudy, it was as simple as that.

But of course it wasn't. At work a few weeks later Eleanor heard that distant flutter. She'd immediately become distressed with everything around her and within her. Nothing seemed right. She felt less distant this time from herself, but eternally sad – and again she could find no reason.

She had walked up toward the coffee shop hoping to clear her head, and the employees who passed her all said hello or good morning as usual, but although Eleanor answered them back exactly as she always did, this time she couldn't shake a conviction that their lives added up to nothing. And she'd suddenly felt lonely and very scared.

She'd gone into a cubicle in the washroom and locked the door. For a while she just sat there looking at the snub-nosed hanger on the door, wondering if she couldn't find some solution in its manufacture: clean, efficient, discreet. And then she'd started to cry. Afraid that someone might come in

45

and recognize her by her shoes she pulled her feet up and sat on the toilet with the lid down and tried to harness her sobbing. Eventually, it stopped.

After that second time Eleanor phoned Joyce at her office and Joyce phoned a cousin of Barney's who knew someone and Eleanor eventually found herself sitting by the kitchen phone with the number of a doctor written on a torn piece of a cash receipt from work. She made the appointment and went to see him – the first thing she'd said was she didn't really know why she was there (and she was still going). It didn't hurt. After a while she'd even warmed to Doctor Klotz. He somehow reminded her of the best days with her father, days when she'd lean down over the back of the big chair in the living room and he'd smoke his pipe and read the comics out loud to her and they'd both laugh long and loud. That was as close as the two of them ever got to sharing jokes, even if they were always someone else's jokes, and she'd treasured those memories ever since.

Doctor Klotz, a man with granite features and wavy hair, which he combed straight back and let dribble over his collar, had talked about things like menopause – God! it made her sound so old – and depression, and he'd told her not to worry, that hers didn't seem severe, and she could take a tranquillizer when necessary. But he'd asked her about her parents a lot, as she'd expected, and though at first she had a lot of trouble talking about anything apart from where they lived and where they spent their holidays, and how she always got less allowance than any of her friends, she eventually loosened up and began telling Klotz things she didn't even think she knew herself.

She even told him about how she used to make herself huge bubble baths, when she was a teenager, every Friday night, when the local symphony gave its weekly radio concerts. She'd sit her green radio on the tub ledge and turn it up as high as the volume lever would go and cry while she listened to Handel and Mozart. Sometimes she thought about reaching up and pulling the radio in with her and letting all her schoolmates who were out that night try and figure it out. Klotz listened to it all and then asked her if she'd ever masturbated during these times. The way he asked seemed as natural as a salesman asking if he could help her, and she answered "Yes," as easily as she'd told the story. This, she decided, was getting pretty damned close to the final doll inside.

Eleanor got up, wrapped the light sweater around her shoulders, and walked over to the hotel-room window. She raised the venetian blinds and blinked out into the day. She felt she was seeing Vernon for the first time, as if it had changed magically overnight.

Eleanor rubbed her eyes and shivered tight to the sweater as she squinted out into a fall light that looked as if someone had taken the time to wash it on the way down. Eleanor had never seen colours so clean. The morning light was spreading in from the lake, like spilled paint, running up against the current of Vernon's river, and up into the better part of town. It was just now working its way down the side of the Muskoka Hotel and Eleanor was momentarily blinded by the light dancing along the lake, as if the water had been glazed over by broken glass. It was a sight she had never before seen. In the city, morning was something you heard about over the radio or smelled in the coffee pot.

She lit a cigarette and stood a long time by the window, watching the sun work up river toward the bridge and the small shops by the river. She thought of Doctor Klotz and how he was really the reason why she was here. If it hadn't been for all his questions about her parents she might have let sleeping dogs lie and never come to pester some old lady about something that might or might not be true.

That March day in the Philadelphia hospital was still with her. Just before noon her mother had died in her sleep. Eleanor felt relieved, but it was not an emotion to be shared with Rita, who was burbling hysterically. Instead, she pretended to also be overwhelmed with grief; at least that saved her from comforting Rita.

Eleanor handled the funeral arrangements with the usual crisp efficiency she reserved for ordering out of the catalogue or having her superintendent raise the heat in her apartment. Most of it was done by telephone, where her voice didn't necessarily belong to her. What had to be done in person was done by rote: the result of an idea Eleanor had about responsible people dealing with such things. As far as she was concerned, she was never personally present.

But at the actual funeral she could neither escape the situation nor herself. They buried her mother from the funeral home. There were but five other mourners—only one of them, Rita, actually mourning—and Eleanor sat in the tiny chapel as quietly, respectfully, and as totally under control as did the lawyer who was serving as executor, and the frail, white-haired doctor who said he'd been a bridge partner of her father's when they'd both belonged to the Philadelphia Professional Club. The minister spoke quietly and with merciful swiftness above Rita's sobbing.

Throughout the ceremony Eleanor played with her wedding ring, all these months later still working up to removing it. She turned it around and around on her finger until the fat below the first joint turned red with irritation. The skin there felt thicker, calloused, and when she compared it to the base of her ring finger on her right hand she realized for the first time that this had become a consistent nervous habit. The sensible thing would have been to simply take the ring off and admit that whatever she and Rudy had once had was over. But she kept it on. Not to keep people like Rita from opening sores they had no right to gloat over, but because the ring meant Eleanor still had some identity.

"Amen."

Eleanor looked up as the minister closed his prayer book. He smiled knowingly and with great sympathy at her. She admired his timing. He came down from the makeshift pulpit and took her hand warmly in both of his. She smiled her thanks and he moved on to Rita, who took both of his hands in both of hers. She would have lunged into the comfort of his robed chest had Eleanor not quickly taken her elbow and steered her away to thank the others for coming.

Rita cried all the way back to her apartment, and didn't stop once she arrived home. While she busied herself in the kitchen, Eleanor sat in the afghan-covered chair by the television, leafing backwards through the latest *McCall's* and tracking her aunt's kitchen movements by the sniffling. The kettle went on; the cookie tin shook slightly, then gasped open as the tight lid popped; cutlery rang; the refrigerator door opened, closed, opened and closed again. There was a prolonged blow of Rita's nose and then she edged backwards through the saloon doors carrying her special-occasion tray, a plastic coated watercolour print of England's Tower Bridge, which had, twice in the past, been referred to as London Bridge in Eleanor's presence without her having corrected Rita. The tea had already been poured and Rita set the tray down on the coffee table and took a seat on the edge of the chartreuse sofa opposite.

"Dear Eleanor..." Rita began, and paused, as if dictating a letter. "If I only had your strength..."

Eleanor reached for her cup and said nothing. Four decades of Rita's cloying sarcasm had inured her to virtually anything her aunt could say. Why Rita didn't come right out and ask Eleanor if she was too cold-hearted to cry was perfectly understood by Eleanor, just as it was understood that Eleanor would not answer. Would Rita comprehend Eleanor saying she was too private a person to cry anywhere but alone? Not likely. For Rita such tears would be wasted effort, a bit like dressing up to make a phone call.

"Rita?..." Eleanor began.

"Yes, dear," Rita said. She pulled a tissue from her sleeve and dabbed at closed eyes.

"Can I ask you something very important?"

Rita's eyes snapped to attention. "Of course you can," she said with enthusiasm.

My God, Eleanor realized, she's acting as if I'm a child again. Does she expect to tell me what a period is?

"Did *you* know I was adopted?"

Rita's mouth opened, a signal to Eleanor that her aunt was about to lie.

"Why, whatever gave you that ridiculous notion, dear?"

"Mother did."

"When?"

"When we talked. Just before she died."

"Oh, poosh," Rita said, a smile gaining in confidence. "Your mother wasn't herself, Eleanor. You know that."

"She was this time," Eleanor said with certainty.

Rita's smile lost its footing. "What did she tell you?"

"Just that, that I was adopted."

"That's all? Just like that?"

"Well, in so many words she did. It's true, isn't it?"

Rita paused for effect, looked down. "Yes. It's true."

Eleanor expected the answer, but not the rising anger within. "Why wasn't I told?"

Rita looked surprised at the question. "But what good would telling you have done?"

"I had a right to know, Rita."

"There was no law, dear. Your parents had to make a decision and they decided what was best for you."

Eleanor controlled her anger and angled off a bit. "You lived with us when I was little, Rita," she said. "You would have been there when–"

"When they brought you home. I was, yes. Heavens, you were only two weeks old and your mother and I didn't know a thing about babies." Rita laughed, as if the subject had been successfully changed.

"Where did I come from then?" Eleanor asked.

"A home," Rita answered, eyes closed to indicate this was

50

indeed a great sacrifice. "One of those homes for girls who, you know –"

"Where?"

"Here. Right here in Philadelphia. Now that's all, everything. That's all I know about you before you came."

Rita got up quickly and grabbed Eleanor's cooled tea. She set the cup beside her own on the souvenir of London serving tray and, ducking under Eleanor's stare, moved quickly toward the kitchen. The saloon doors swung shut behind her like final quotation marks for their conversation.

For a moment Eleanor continued to stare after her aunt. *Something is wrong here*. She followed Rita into the kitchen, where Rita stood with her back to Eleanor, rinsing the tea dishes in the sink.

"I have a *right* to know, Rita," Eleanor said, the threat in her voice surprising to her. "And you are *not going to keep it from me!*"

And in half an hour it had all come out, nicely mixed with sighs and lowered voices over the kitchen eating nook, as if someone might be listening in.

Eleanor's parents had wanted a child but one of them – Rita said her mother – had been unable to have any. Eleanor's father had had little trouble getting his wife to agree to adopt. He had less success, however, with the proper agencies. A large, ill-tempered and impatient man, he probably would have preferred to order a son out of the Sears-Roebuck catalogue. The agencies wanted interviews, some even approaching his associates for references. Invariably, they found out about his bad temper and asked him about it. Naturally, he denied there was any such thing, practically throttling one interviewer to prove it.

In the end his impatience won out. A few well-placed phone calls and bribes and he was soon sitting down with a woman who ran a financially troubled home down along the south shore. A generous "bequeath" would of course be forthcoming, he assured them, and fortunately there was a

51

Canadian girl in her ninth month, who would be heading for home immediately after the baby was placed. No Pennsylvania connection; not even an American one. Whatever paperwork that had to be done could be done later, making the adoption virtually as legal and proper as if they'd gone through the proper channels. Only this way, the baby would arrive much faster.

When it turned out to be a girl he almost cancelled the deal. Myrna, however, prevailed upon him to at least agree to go down with her and have a look at the child. Rita had gone with them and once the prospective father tickled Eleanor a few times to get the feel of her, he was sold on the idea. Large, dark, and furious, Eleanor seemed to put to shame the two tiny boy babies there.

She had been only four days old at the time and her crying had brought the real mother hurrying in from the hallway, thinking the baby needed an early feeding. When she saw the prospective parents cuddling her baby she realized what was up and turned to leave, only to have Myrna and Rita call her back. They talked for five minutes or more, but Rita could remember very little of the chance encounter. It had, after all, been forty-three years ago.

"Oh, we didn't have much to say, really," Rita said. "I mean I felt odd talking to her anyway. You know why. I asked her where she was from and she said some name in Ontario. If I only remembered the name, you might recognize it—but of course I don't. I asked her why she'd come here—a darn silly question I now realize—and she didn't even bother to answer me, which I now think was probably the right thing to do. Foolish of me, that."

Suddenly Rita flushed, as if suddenly remembering something else. She giggled nervously. "Though that was hardly so foolish as when your father turned around—he never was much for tact, that man—and he asked her in his big booming voice if there was any Indian blood in you, you being so dark and all."

"And?" Eleanor invited.

"My Lord, that was embarrassing to Myrna and me. But she just stood there and took it and kind of even smiled. Myrna shut him up fast, though. Sent him packing down the hall with you wailing away. And was she ever apologetic to that poor girl.

"But, as I say, she didn't seem to mind much. She just smiled this cute little smile of hers – my she was pretty – and said some people often said the father was an Indian, but he wasn't. He was an artist, she said, just as proud as punch too, like it was "engineer" or "doctor" – something really important, you know. And she said just as matter-of-factly as you can imagine that he'd been killed."

"What happened to him?" Eleanor asked. "Did you ask?"

"Your mother asked if it had happened overseas. The war was still on, of course. But she said No, he'd died in Canada."

"How?"

"Eleanor. For heaven's sake – even your Aunt Rita knows when to stop. Gracious."

Late the next evening Eleanor had flown back to Toronto. She sat with her back to the man beside her and did not acknowledge the stewardess's call for the meal. She simply watched the turbo-prop sparking in the night air. She was thinking, trying to decide what to do about all that Rita had told her.

She tried to imagine what the mother who had given birth to her looked like, what her father had been like, how he had been killed. It was all so vastly romantic, like those dreamy poems back in high school. She'd loved those poets – Keats, Wordsworth, Shelley – loved their poetry, until the English teacher broke them down like a Meccano set, anyway. Perhaps her father's death was better left alone as well.

But that would have been like the Eleanor Philpott of old: it's not worth getting stung to find the honey. She was now Eleanor Philpott, Thursday-at-three-thirty patient of Dr. Richard Klotz, psychiatrist, and she was "under doctor's orders" to examine the past. Eleanor smiled out into the night. Dr. Klotz will be fascinated. She would savour this Thursday's session. For a change she would have something to tell him, and he would listen with interest. He would say, as he always said, just the two words: "Go on."

She would, too. Not that there was much to go on with, but she would try. Anything to break the boredom of Eaton's. Anything to help her forget about Rudy. Anything to help Dr. Klotz find the real Eleanor Philpott. No, that's not right— anything to help her find herself.

She would find out about this mysterious woman with the pretty face and the dead lover. It would please Dr. Klotz. And, who knows, if her past was not as she remembered it, then surely her future couldn't be as she dreaded it would become.

6

As she had anticipated, Dr. Klotz was full of encouragement. If he doubted she would be able to come up with anything, he hid it well. "What have you got to lose?" he asked at the end of the session. He said it would be a healthy diversion, a harmless exercise at worst and a solid grip on her past at best. Either way she would be able to turn her thoughts outward rather than inward, and, as he put it: "Your mind could do with a good airing."

That same evening she took a large piece of foolscap and very carefully wrote down each of the leads Rita had given her. She printed each word with care, slowly going back over each letter and deepening them as if she feared their fading, escaping. But the real problem was that there wasn't a great deal to write down:

> mother
> pretty
> Ontario
> small town or village
> father
> dark (Indian?)
> artist
> engaged (?)
> killed (?)

There was also the matter of her own birth certificate. After returning from Philadelphia she'd gone to her file desk and examined it carefully. It gave a date, February 26, 1918, and a place, Philadelphia. But the name on it was Eleanor Marianne Daniels, the family name of the adoptive parents. Nothing in brackets; nothing, apparently, in code. She looked at the registration date – March 5, 1918 – and realized it had probably been done within days of her arriving home. She remembered Rita's talk about the paperwork having later been taken care of and she realized the birth certificate was a virtually useless lead, its only value being that she could assume her real father had died somewhere in the nine-month span between late May, early June 1917, and her birthday in 1918.

She thought about an ad in the paper, perhaps in the *Telegram*'s personal section, but had to laugh when she considered what it was she could say at five cents a word:

> *Lost:* parents, somewhere in Ontario, 1917-18. Markings: mother pretty, nice smile; father very dark and dead. Write Eleanor, Box 35A.

No, the only sure things – if anything from Rita was ever sure – were that the father had been an artist and the mother had come from Ontario. And he had probably been killed before her birth. That wasn't much for Eleanor to go on. Ontario was quite foreign to her. She had lived in Toronto a full five years with Rudy but barely felt comfortable with the Yonge-Bloor corridor in the downtown core.

Five years – it hardly seemed so long since she'd been living in Philadelphia and she'd let Pauline, at the library, talk her into a blind date. She had gone, she thought then, only because the man was from Toronto, and she knew nothing of Canada. She went also because the date was to a minor-league hockey game – Rudy Philpott was apparently in public relations with a major league club in Toronto – and she'd never seen one. It was not an emotional decision to go out with Rudy – she was long past waiting for Mr. Right – but it was a meticulous librarian's decision: take it, examine it, and file it away. At the age of thirty-eight, life for Eleanor had become a detached accumulation of experiences, small proofs she did indeed exist.

But Rudy was different then. In the next four months he'd come back to Philadelphia five times. When he returned to Toronto that fifth time, Eleanor had gone with him, still wearing the same clothes she'd worn that afternoon at the civil marriage ceremony, which she'd hastily arranged and carried out much to the disappointment of her mother. How things had changed since, memories of Rudy now including week-long silences, heavy drinking, his lost job with the hockey club, the terrifying night he hit her and she'd slept on towels piled in the bath tub, the bathroom door locked, waking in the morning to find he'd packed and gone. She lived alone now. And she had a job in the notions department at Eaton's College Street store, openings for librarians having become a rarity. She even found herself nodding while the other women – or "girls," as Beek referred to them – snubbed the downtown store workers, as if marble pillars and a puny art gallery up the stairs could stretch their eighty-five cents an hour farther than the girls a few blocks south could get out of their pay. For Eleanor, it was a matter of putting in time. Straighten the buttons when the manager patrolled... dust off the purse rack... do pre-inventory on the school supplies... hold breath until morning coffee... lunch... afternoon coffee... *closing*!

It hurt. But none of it so bad as the stockroom stalks of Wilson Beek. Beek, Eleanor decided, had to have been adopted himself, by parents with a humour so twisted they'd searched until they found an appropriate face for their peculiar name. Wilson Beek's nose seemed to have come from parrot genes, and the way this nose curved back to a small, knobby, bald head gave the skinny man a profile not unlike a comfortable cane. It was his hands, however, not his nose that so disturbed Eleanor. As floor manager, it was Beek's task to assign staff to unpack new shipments in the rear stock room, and it was Eleanor who usually was selected. From the other women he must have known about Eleanor and Rudy – she wished she'd kept it to herself, but it seemed like idle enough talk over coffee one morning – but he certainly showed very little sympathy. What he did offer was a series of quick finger flutters up and down the side of her dress. And though she was quick to angrily brush his hand away, he always came back. He knew she needed the work. But that wasn't the way he phrased it.

"I know just what you need, Eleanor," he would say out of the side of his mouth. He didn't elaborate on what it was he had on his mind. He didn't need to. Eleanor was intent on keeping it just in his mind, whatever the cost; she only hoped to avoid the coming scene that would surely cost her the job – or at least avoid it until the job was expendable.

If only she could get back into library work. Each day she read through the wanted section of the *Globe* and each day she saw nothing, at least nothing for her. What few opportunities there were went to graduates in library science, masters degrees usually, and Eleanor had only a general arts college education. All she had to offer were three things that didn't count for much: experience in the United States, desire, and a true love of books. The interest in books she had picked up from her father – not through inheritance but through good fortune. In his panelled den he kept beautifully-bound and gold-embossed editions of Faulkner and Conrad. He had purchased them through a mail-order house and had never read them. They cracked when Eleanor opened them. But what was adventure for her was simply furniture to him: they finished off the oak bookcase.

It had been a long battle against that upbringing. When Eleanor first moved out on her own, at the age of twenty-six, she forced herself to learn something of a suitably obscure and esoteric subject, the school of geometric abstraction. It fit in nicely with the dull talk at the few parties she attended, parties stocked with bored librarians, the odd drunken literary editor and even, once or twice, a lecherous poet, who seemed to think he could translate Victor Hugo into a quick feel. Eleanor honestly liked Chagall and she did adore the works and thoughts of Marcel Duchamp. She could list the titles of the latest works by Jackson Pollock and she could scowl appropriately at the earnestness of an opportunistic imitator. It was a trick but it worked. She knew nothing but a few catchwords of art, just enough to fake it. And she rationalized it by believing the others were faking as well.

It was inconceivable that her real father had come from the school of geometric abstraction. Perhaps her father hadn't even been an artist. Rita's memory had failed before. And even if he was, who was to say he was well-known? And yet, Rita's recollection was all there was to go on, and Eleanor knew she must go on and on. If she had to begin this search, she might as well begin by assuming that this Canadian artist who died – Rita had said was killed – would at least merit having his death recorded.

The next morning she called in sick – something she'd never done before – and at ten o'clock Eleanor found herself walking in the front doors of the city's central library. It felt like coming home. The first thing that struck her was the smells – she remembered reading somewhere that this, surprisingly, was the strongest memory, far more definite and lasting than sight or sound. First the smells, and then the quiet settled her. It was the librarian rising in Eleanor: silence meant well. After all those dreary years in the Philadelphia library system she was once again in her own element. There was still the Library of Congress Cataloguing, the cross-indexing of files, the periodical index, the newspaper files – it was all essentially the same, if Canadian.

In ten minutes she was sitting at a highly-polished oak desk with a 1917 edition of J. Castell Hopkins' *The Canadian Annual Review of Public Affairs*. A thick, red book that opened onto a stern photograph of Prime Minister Borden, the review claimed to contain all that happened of any significance during that year in Canada, and while much of it was spent on the war effort, there was also – much to Eleanor's delight – a Canadian obituary for the year 1917, beginning on page 835.

She quickly discovered, however, that the list included no artists at all. In London, on October 6, Drake, M.D., Fred'k Phineas, died. Editor Hopkins considered Drake an "Eminent Medical Man." De Martigny, M.D., Adelstan, who died in Montreal on November 14, however, was deemed to be only a "Prominent Medical Man" by Hopkins, and Eleanor wondered if this was merely an innocent oversight or an example of J. Castell Hopkins' condescending attitude toward the French.

She tried a few other reference books without luck. Her first fear – that her possible father hadn't been prominent enough to warrant mention – was joined by a second – that no artist was considered of any importance during the year 1917. She began to hope that whatever had "killed" him had been sufficiently grisly to force the newspapers to report his death as a crime of interest, if not involving an artist of public concern. She could check the murders.

Eleanor looked at her watch. Twelve-thirty. If she skipped lunch and stayed till near supper time, she might make it through one of the Toronto newspapers from the time. She went back to the reference librarian, a red-haired woman, who looked like she was kept on a shelf at night – *Christ*, Eleanor thought, *did I once look like that?* – and asked which paper was considered the best for reference purposes for that year. You'd have thought Eleanor had asked where she'd bought that lovely dress, for the woman brightened considerably over Eleanor's interest and in two minutes had Eleanor's oak desk covered with the bulky bundles that made up the Toronto *Globe* for the year 1917.

When Eleanor saw the mass of print she felt like abandoning the search. Fortunately, however, much of 1917 she could eliminate. Going by her own birth date – February 26, 1918 (presuming it was at least *fairly* accurate) – she had simply to count back nine months and begin no earlier than May. Rita hadn't said much about Eleanor as a baby, apart from the fact that she'd been healthy, so Eleanor presumed the conception took place some time between early May and late June of 1917. But that still left over half a year for the artist to get killed. And she already knew the chances of it being reported were slim.

The *Globe* was overflowing with war casualties and Eleanor wondered if Rita had been wrong, if the artist in question had indeed been killed at war with all the rest. Beginning in May, the German counter-attacks on the heights of the Aisne and in Fresnoy were inflicting heavy allied casualties. There was also the North Sea engagement, heavy fighting near Lens, Bullecourt, Fontaine, and all along the Hindenburg Line. Eleanor began to think she might be better off reading white crosses in France than staring at the *Globe*. But even there she'd be sadly out of luck. They weren't likely to list "artist" along with names and serial numbers.

She read through June – with the German aeroplanes savaging England – and into July, and was about to knock off for coffee when she opened the July 13 issue to:

TORONTO ARTIST MISSING IN NORTH

TOM THOMSON MISSING FROM CANOE LAKE SINCE SUNDAY – A TALENTED LANDSCAPIST

Toronto art circles were shocked yesterday at the news received from Algonquin Park that Tom Thomson, one of the most talented of the younger artists in the city, had been missing since Sunday and was thought to have been drowned or the victim of foul play. Mr. Thomson was last seen at Canoe Lake at noon on Sunday, and at 3.30 in the afternoon his canoe was found adrift in the lake, upside down. There was no storm, only a light wind prevailing, and the fact that both paddles were in place in the canoe as if for a portage, adds to the mystery. Mr. Thomson carried a light fishing rod and this and his dunnage bag were missing.

A Lover of Wilderness
Mr. Thomson who made his home in the city at the Studio Building in Severn Street, was especially fond of the woods,

and spent more than half of each year in the northern wilderness. He has risen rapidly in esteem as a landscape painter, his interpretation of north country having an indefinable charm and feeling that could only come from a deep love of nature. One of his paintings, "Northern River", attracted much attention a year or so ago, and was subsequently bought by the National Gallery at Ottawa.

Once Lived in Seattle

Mr. Thomson comes from Owen Sound, where his father still lives. Part of his 40 years of life were spent in Seattle. After coming to Toronto a few years ago, he was engaged for a time in commercial art. There is still a chance that Mr. Thomson may be alive, but this is considered doubtful as four days' search has failed to find a trace of him.

Eleanor raced through to the end without actually reading. She swallowed, ran her tongue around in her mouth to wet things down, then began again. Slower this time. "... was thought to have been drowned or the victim of *foul play*." *Killed* then. *Maybe*. "... There is still a chance that Mr. Thomson may be alive, but this is considered doubtful as four days' search has failed to find a trace of him."

Eleanor could not contain her excitement. She rose to her feet – loudly scraping the chair legs behind her, an act she once considered a heinous crime – and began rummaging quickly through the next day's issue, and the next. The paper was fragile and twice it tore along the fold – something that Eleanor could never forgive as a librarian herself – but this didn't slow her down.

Five days later the *Globe* had another report. Eleanor sat down to read it and this one she read very slowly, praying with every word:

TORONTO ARTIST DROWNS IN NORTH

Body of Tom Thomson Found In Canoe Lake,
Algonquin Park

Standing as Landscape Painter Was High –
To be Buried in Park

The mystery surrounding the disappearance of Mr. Tom Thomson, the Toronto artist, at Canoe Lake, Algonquin Park, on Sunday, July 8, was solved yesterday by the finding of his body. Word which reached the city last night indicated that he had been drowned. His canoe was found adrift a few hours after Mr. Thomson was last seen, and the fate of the artist was a mystery until yesterday's gruesome discovery. His brother, Mr. George Thomson of New Haven, Conn., also a painter, who had been visiting the family home at Owen Sound last week when the news first came, went to the scene and joined for a time in the search. The body, it was stated in last night's telegrams, will be buried in Algonquin Park, which had been the artist's happy sketching ground for years.

An Artist of Charm
Mr. Thomson, who was about forty years of age, was a landscape artist of rare charm and promise. His work steadily grew in esteem among art lovers for it represented one who not only saw, but felt and understood nature in her varied moods. His pictures were steadily sought for the collections of the Ontario and Dominion Governments.

A Critic's Tribute
"Critics," said Eric Brown in a recent article in The London Studio, "look to him to carry forward the Canadian landscape painting far beyond anything at present realized. Wandering alone the best part of the year in Algonquin Park, inured to hardship and reputed the best guide, fisherman and canoeman in the district, he lives with these wonderful seasons and they live by him. Here, again, is the decorative sense strongly developed and visible in every composition. There is no loss of character; the northland lies before you, whether it is a winding river fringed with

gaunt black pines, or whether the green blocks of melting ice float on blue liberated waters of the lake."

Eleanor sat back in the library chair and breathed deeply. *Drowned*. Odd, she hadn't ever considered drowned when she had tried to envision him dead. Stabbed, maybe. Or shot. But not drowned – people didn't drown in her thinking. *Lost at sea*, sure. Philadelphia had a huge harbour and shipyards. But drowned sounded like kittens to Eleanor; it spoke more of pity than tragedy.

When nothing more turned up in the paper that year she turned instead to the index files, and was quickly rewarded with *A Study of Tom Thomson*, written by a Blodwen Davies some twenty-five years earlier. When the librarian returned with it, the copy was dusty and grey, but Eleanor saw nothing but hope shining through, when she opened to Tom Thomson's photograph: tall, dark, long of nose, high cheekbones. Her fantasies were running away with her by the time she peeked into the first paragraph. Davies' book told of a romantic farm boy from Ontario's Georgian Bay, who never amounted to much until the last few years of his short life. And yet, in a flurry of painting between 1912 and 1917, most of it in Algonquin Park, Thomson had probably done more for the recognition of Canadian art than anyone before or since. His work was of the same stumps and rocks and water that had distinctly unimpressed Eleanor at the art gallery, but there was something different about Thomson's approach. Eleanor couldn't quite put her finger on that difference, but it was almost as if his paintings had electricity running through them – some life she could neither see nor understand. She laughed at the thought. Why did she always feel compelled to contrive sentences around art?

Thomson's life fascinated Eleanor. He'd gone from a farm to the city, but by the time he died at age thirty-nine he was, according to the author, a true bushman. Thomson was an acknowledged guide and canoeist, and meticulous in almost everything he did.

But Davies' book had been written more to illustrate the great mystery of Thomson's death than to describe his paintings or romanticize his life – and it was this that Eleanor grabbed onto. Thomson had drowned in Canoe Lake, Eleanor already knew that from the newspaper account. What she didn't know, and what Davies told her, was that Thomson's canoe had been found only a hundred yards from shore or so and that he'd set out to fish on a relatively calm day. The author strongly questioned the "accidental drowning" version of the makeshift inquest – held at a cottage on Canoe Lake by a coroner who didn't even view the body, let alone demand an autopsy – by pointing out that Thomson's body had a distinct wound on the temple and that blood was seeping from an ear. Only a living body could be bruised or bleed, so it couldn't have happened as the drowned body bumped along the lake bottom. Also, there was no water in his lungs; they were filled with air, which hardly seemed the way a drowned body would be.

Eleanor felt her palms dampen as she read this part. Then he *was* killed, just as Rita had said.

Everything in Davies' account fascinated her. The body had taken eight days to rise – not nine as the *Globe* had reported – and this had been in the warm waters of July when bodies generally rise to the surface in two or three days. There was fishing line wrapped around an ankle. Thomson's portaging paddle was fitted to the canoe, in an amateurish manner that he would never have allowed, and his working paddle, one easily recognized by everyone who knew him on the lake, was never found, though they searched the shoreline diligently for months, even years after, and paddles do float.

Blodwen Davies made it abundantly obvious she suspected foul play:

Who met Tom Thomson on that stretch of grey lake, screened from all eyes, that July noon?
Who was it struck him a blow across the right temple –

and was it done with the edge of a paddle blade – that sent the blood spurting from his ears?

Who watched him crumple and topple over the side of the canoe and sink slowly out of sight without a struggle? . . .

Did Thomson's body take eight days to rise in a shallow lake in the middle of July?

And it didn't stop there. Thomson's friends had buried him almost immediately upon finding the body, buried him wrapped in a shroud and placed in a pine box in the little graveyard on the knoll overlooking the north end of Canoe Lake. An undertaker, F.W. Churchill, had come to exhume the body, claiming the Thomson family wanted it returned to their family plot in Leith, Ontario. Churchill had arrived on the evening train, worked at night by lantern, and then left on the morning train with a coffin everyone who lifted it claimed was far too light to hold a body, let alone the bloated body of a man who'd been in a lake for over a week.

But it wasn't totally encouraging for Eleanor. Nowhere could she find any reference to a wife or girl friend. In fact, from what she read, it would appear Thomson had led a perfectly celibate life in the bush, usually camping and sketching alone or else guiding fishing parties of men. Her only hope seemed to be that perhaps there was someone back in Toronto, where he returned each winter from Algonquin to work on the larger canvases he made from the small sketches. Trouble was, that didn't fit with what Rita had said about Eleanor's mother coming from a small town in Ontario.

Eleanor kept the Davies book out past its due date. She had never done that before – when she was a librarian she considered such an act the ultimate in ignorance – but she couldn't return it to the library even to check it out again. It was as if if she dared let it out of her hands, even for a new stamping, she would lose any chance the book might hold. The librarian might ask her what it was she found so interesting . . . someone else might have put in for it (though she checked and saw the last time it had been checked out was four years ago). She kept it and she studied it, hoping she had missed a name, a hint, a small hope. But there was nothing.

After a month of praying the book might have rewritten itself to suit her, Eleanor decided to try out the idea on the one person she felt she could trust – Joyce, after all, was a member in good standing at the Art Gallery of Ontario and had lots of "artsy" friends. She was a guaranteed sympathetic ear.

They met at Old Angelo's for an early dinner. Joyce listened graciously to what Eleanor told her – which was only that Rita was having the family tree researched and there was a possibility that Thomson was a distant relative – and she agreed to ask around to see if there were any untold Thomson stories, particularly, as Eleanor had asked, about any possible marriages or engagements. The annual gallery meeting and ball were coming up at the end of the month, Joyce said, and she promised to try to find someone, who was up on their Thomson, and zero in.

Eleanor marked the date of the art gallery ball on her calendar and phoned Joyce again on that day to remind her of her promise. Eleanor wasn't particularly expecting anything, but was nonetheless extremely disappointed when Joyce didn't call the following morning. She was wondering if perhaps she should go back to the papers, back looking for a new artist, when Joyce phoned.

"Eleanor?"

"Joyce! What's up?"

"Sorry I didn't call earlier. Hung over, I'm afraid."

Eleanor laughed to hide her impatience.

"I think I might have something for you," Joyce said.

Eleanor caught her breath.

"Tell me."

"It's just a *maybe*, now, remember that."

"Sure."

Eleanor had the sudden sensation of delight. She was now

a character in a mystery novel, a central character, and she finally had something to occupy her bored mind with that was somewhat more stimulating than taking inventory at Eaton's.

"You've heard me talk about Lucy Baronskill?"

"Who?"

"Oh, never mind. Anyway, her husband might know something."

"About Tom Thomson?"

"Yes, of course."

"What about him?"

"Well, Lucy's husband works part time in the Walker Galleries over on Bloor Street – you know the place. He's very connected, if you know what I mean. And Lucy says that there's more than a dozen Thomsons in the basement of that gallery. She thinks they belong to some strange old woman, who won't let anybody buy them or even see them. Maybe she can tell you whether Thomson's a relative."

Old woman! Eleanor crossed her legs with excitement. It might be a sister, she cautioned herself, or the wife of an old friend. Then again, it might be...

"Who is she?" Eleanor asked.

Joyce giggled.

"How would I know? That's all Lucy said."

Joyce was eager to set up a meeting – too eager, it seemed to Eleanor, but she didn't dare ask Joyce if she suspected Tom Thomson meant anything other than "distant relative" to her. Joyce arranged for them to visit the Walker Galleries on a Friday night, after Eleanor was off work. George Baronskill would be expecting them.

He turned out to be a work of art himself, perfectly dressed in grey flannel slacks and navy-blue blazer, polite and charming, beautifully spoken. He first showed Joyce and Eleanor around, as though they were wealthy Rosedale matrons, not apartment dwellers. Patiently, he explained the current exhibition to them, detailing the intentions of the realist from New York and the mushrooming value of the landscapes by the recently deceased artist from New Brunswick. Eleanor felt if she could only remember all he told her, she would have all the party talk concerning art she'd ever need over the rest of her life.

When they neared the office space near the rear of the galleries, he dropped his voice discreetly.

"You were wondering about Tom Thomson, Mrs. Philpott?"

"Yes,' Eleanor said, her breath catching. "Where are they?"

He pointed to the cellar. "Down there."

Joyce spoke. "Couldn't we see them?"

Baronskill shook his head.

"No. They're locked in the safe."

"You've never seen them?" Eleanor asked.

Again he shook his head. "Only Mr. Walker and the owner, but there's twelve, thirteen, maybe fourteen in there. Small ones."

"The owner?" Eleanor asked, backtracking.

"She used to come sometimes and look at them. I've never seen her, though."

"Do you know her name?" Eleanor asked quickly. The small muscle in the fatty part of her left thumb twitched, and she moved the hand behind her back.

"No. I'm sorry."

"But she lives in Toronto?"

"No. She came on the bus, I think. From up north. But I'm not sure."

Eleanor decided to ask. "Could you find out her name for me?"

George Baronskill looked at her carefully, sizing her up. Eleanor felt uneasy.

"She's very old," he said, as if explaining why not.

Old? Eleanor hoped old enough.

"She won't sell," he added.

"I just wanted to talk to her," Eleanor said.

He didn't pursue the point.

"Could you try to find out her name?" Joyce pleaded. "Please, George."

Baronskill smiled. "I'll try."

Two days later Eleanor had her information in a beautifully scripted note from the Walker Galleries.

Mrs. Philpott,

The owner of the Tom Thomson paintings you are interested in is Miss Janet Turner of Vernon, Ontario.

Good luck. And if I can be of further assistance to you, please do not hesitate to call.

Yours,

George Baronskill

Miss Janet Turner! Eleanor read and re-read the note. *Miss!* Then it was not a sister. Nor was it the wife of an old cronie. It was someone who knew him as a friend, who had obviously been close to him. Why else would she have the pictures? And they must have meant something special to her, otherwise why not sell them? Why not, at least, let people view them?

Perhaps...

Eleanor felt she was close. She was in Vernon, anyway. All that dreaming and puzzling might be leading to something she could use.

She choked out her second cigarette and decided to get ready. She washed her face and put on her make-up, barely enough eye shadow for elegance and certainly not enough for suggestion. She chose a light lipstick, a delicate line between pink and soft orange, and checked twice to make sure there was no smudging. She brushed her hair until it shone in the rough light in the tiny bathroom, then back-combed and teased it into the proper lift and bounce. Eleanor chose her black-and-red-flecked wool suit for authority, softening the effect only slightly with a rose-coloured scarf.

70

First a little breakfast. Eleanor buttoned her grey gabardine coat with the imitation fox collar, grabbed her shiny black patent-leather purse – her work purse, she called it – and left.

Just as she brushed through the lobby of the Muskoka Hotel she heard the first peal of the morning school bell. The town was quiet, a few delivery trucks and salespeople double-stepping to work, and the bell tones hung over the town like a lingering smile.

7

Russell Pemberton walked back from Zendal's welding shop carrying the top section of a fishing rod. He was sucking on a caraway seed that he'd stuffed in over the single tooth he had left in the front of the top row. A legacy from his mother; the seed sweetened the breath. He was thinking of Abigail Pemberton now, thinking of another of those little rhymes she'd pounded into his head when he was a boy:

> Wilful waste makes woeful want,
> If I should live to say,
> How I wish I had that crust
> That once I threw away.

Mother was so right, Russell thought, as he walked away from Zendal's. You take the tip of that fly rod. Most people would have thrown it away, just as Russell had thought of doing when he'd snagged it casting for rainbow trout this past September at the Locks. It had snapped right near the top eye and the eye had slid down the line and into the water and probably out to the lure and whatever deadhead he was stuck to; he never knew for sure, for the whole thing gave that last pull and he was minus lure, swivel, line, and rod tip.

Fortunately, he'd remembered some of what Abigail Pemberton had taught her boy. "Bring the rod in," Zendal had said. "I can probably fix it up good as new for a dollar and a half." Better that than a new rod, Russell thought, one he'd have to get used to all over again at his age. No, he'd done the right thing and he was proud of himself. He wondered what was wrong with people today that they wouldn't think of something like that.

Hearing what Zendal had to say was the first good thing that had happened to Russell this morning. He'd awakened early with a headache, and though he'd rummaged around in his bottom drawer for the packet of dried and crushed rosemary to make up some tea, as his mother would have done, he hadn't been able to find it. Most likely it was gone, used up after all these years. He'd ended up bumming a couple of aspirins off Archie and they'd upset his stomach. So he hadn't eaten anything.

And he'd almost passed out when he went up to the fourth floor around nine and opened up the closet for his fresh rolls of paper towels and toilet paper for the washrooms on that floor. Somebody had vomited on the floor of the washroom and he'd had to go back to the closet and get out the mop and pail and clean it up. Days like this, Russell thought, it hardly seemed worth while to take care of the washrooms for a measly four-dollar-a-week reduction on his rent. He'd thought momentarily about giving up the job, but when he heard his mother's own voice rattling around the washroom—"You never miss the water till the well goes dry, Russell"—he'd regretted even thinking such a thought.

There was a good smell in the air now; sharp, crisp, brittle. Didn't matter what you called it, Russell knew that the autumn air was energized differently. He sucked it deep and thought about partridge hunting, the sound his shins made as they pushed through a tight growth of small spruce, the smell of the grease and gun oil, the sharp, exciting taste of a spent Number Six shot shell, the popping sound a partridge made when you slipped your open hands in around the rib cage between the skin and the breast meat and shucked the feathers and outer skin like an overcoat.

Russell fancied himself a man of feeling and he thanked his mother for that gift. Abigail Pemberton had been a coarse-looking woman, tight-lipped and low-browed, and with hair that was short and curly and snapped free of the bands she wore like wire wool shreds. But she'd been beautiful inside. A mystic, Russell thought. She believed all health and feelings were connected to what you ate. She told Russell once, just a few months before she died, that there were two ways of seeing the world. There was the way things appeared to be, and the way things were, and you could only see the way things were if you first understood, and were able to overcome the way things appeared. Most people, she said, only got as far as the way things seemed and settled for that. They weren't interested in the rest.

Russell also knew, thanks to his mother, that there were two sides to everything, and as often as not they balanced out. Tit for tat, she called it.

In his younger days, Russell had two distinct feelings about his town, the overriding one being that he loved it. And, because he thought himself a man of feeling, if poorly educated, he kept a whole file of Vernon in his mind, which he could thumb through without even opening his eyes. The reservoir hill in May, for example, and the Dutchman's breeches. The morning mail, with everyone gathered in the mailbox area, sorting keys and talking about things that never will matter. The skull on stone sound of a lacrosse ball against the tannery wall. The school bell. The tannery whistle at noon. (Damn shame it was now shut down.) Watching the ice break up and give in as it washed under the river. The sound of a back street in fall.

They were corny thoughts and he knew it. All comfortable and sure and full of confidence. Russell sometimes wished he'd been born simple and had passed a worthless life running errands around the town, his head full of sights and sounds and smells and not a damn thing else.

On the other hand, there had been times when Russell hated the town, though he'd been younger then and most of those memories were faded. They included the little things that hurt, the discovery that friends have lied to avoid your company or being too early drunk, and caught out with being so.

But there was none of that now. Russell's mind had worked the miracle of total rationalization and he had now become virtually evangelical about it: Vernon was the *only* place, not the best place. Its people – and by this he meant the real people, those who had roots here that usually ended in a tangle of common relatives, preferably those, like Janet Turner and himself, whose parents or grandparents had been original settlers, good, dependable pioneer stock – those people were the finest people the Lord had created. When God gave out a bonus he gave it to Vernon.

Russell had come to the opinion over the last ten years that city people were empty inside. Nothing at all there. And to make up for that pathetic deficiency they tried to pass it off by gussying up the outside; lots of loud talk and fancy clothes and silly airs. Sometimes in the summer, when he saw one of those Toronto tourists stopped in town with a fancy boat and motor and an Airstream silver trailer back of him, he felt like going up to the guy and asking him if he knew how to work a canthook, or if he knew what an adze was for, or if a cord of bird's eye maple would burn longer than a cord of hemlock. Russell had a million questions they'd never answer.

Why did Abigail Pemberton always call dill seeds "meeting house" seeds, for example, and why did she always push several of the foul-tasting things into Russell's mouth prior to a church meeting that was destined to have an especially long sermon? What month was the crayfish in berry? What was a devil's darning needle? But he'd never bother asking such tourists. What was the use? They'd only try to purchase the answer from him anyway, if they thought they couldn't live without knowing. That was city training. Want something, buy it. Slip the old codger a buck and a wink. Great old character, eh? *Horseshit!*

Russell, thank God, hadn't been raised that way. Nor had any of the other people he respected. Look at Jenny Turner, he told himself cockily, enough money but no hot water in her place. His mother, bless her, had once told him if people were going to live and die by money anyway then they may as well change the system. Give everybody a certain amount when they turn eighteen, she'd said to Russell, and when it's all gone, pop them off. Russell loved that one. That would mean the end of the Toronto tourist, sure enough. None of them would even last long enough to complete the drive north to Vernon.

Russell was working himself into a state and he knew it. Shut up and settle down, he told himself, or you'll start talking to yourself like you did last Friday in the post office. He'd gotten all worked up about the young people again, this time for the way they ran on the sidewalk and never bothered watching where they were going or what they were doing, knocking good people over or half scaring them to death anyway. He was running it over in his mind for about the sixth time when suddenly there was a tap on his shoulder and he turned around and saw Bill Deems, the postmaster, standing there asking him if he was all right. Certainly he was, Russell had said, as he kept on walking, and then he realized he had been talking to himself.

No more situations like that, Russell promised himself. He switched subjects. He thought of how fine the new paving up Hunter's Street looked. He thought how much his old bones needed this rare sun after an October that had been overflowing with cold rain. He thought of Rocket Richard and how there'd never be another like him.

And then he saw the city woman.

She was headed down toward the river and the bridge. The city was in the opposite direction. She was poking around like a tourist, but Russell knew that no one in their right mind – apart from hunters, and she was hardly after venison – would come to Vernon at this time of year. Russell had long ago decided there were two things Canada could do without, November and Manitoba. He'd been across the country by train and he had no trouble deciding that anything within a couple of hundred miles of Winnipeg wouldn't be missed, and he'd seen enough Novembers in his life to know there wasn't a good one in the lot. What she was doing here in November was beyond him.

And then he remembered what Archie had said, and the reference to Jenny Turner and the funny question the woman had asked.

This was going to take some figuring. He walked back up to the post office, said the proper things to the proper people, picked out his seat – the one that held the sun till early afternoon – opened up his big coat and sat back.

Russell decided to drift off. It was a perfectly conscious decision, a deliberate one, and it struck him odd that people looked on old people who tended to drift as if they'd lost, or were losing, control of themselves. Russell, on the contrary, never felt more in control than when he closed his eyes and shuffled through the past. No surprises there. No hurts without a laugh now. Even about Jenny. No passion without a result, one way or the other. Lord, that sun felt good... eyes closed... a final great spit... a roll of the shoulders against the bench back... warm... curl the toes... there... there... that's just about perfect...

He had turned sixteen on January 22, 1901, the very day Queen Victoria died, and Russell could still remember the loss he felt as he went charging about the town looking for people to slap his back and shake his hand, only to run into drawn window blinds and black arm bands. They even muffled the tannery whistle for the day.

No one seemed interested in Russell, not in his birthday or even in his new job. No more herb deliveries for Abigail Pemberton's boy. He had a paying job with Muskoka Wood Manufacturing Company. Odd jobs around the new mill mostly – turning the big birch logs in the hot pond to make sure the bark softened, working the big "Red Deer" stamp as they cut flooring, keeping the "nigger" well-oiled while it moved logs in for cutting—and it was all fascinating to Russell. He'd discovered he loved wood, loved to run his hands along the grain and smell the chips and watch the storms of wood dust around the huge saws as they screamed through log after log of good Muskoka hardwood.

And already he was something of a celebrity around the mill. During his first week of work—the tail end of a month of damp and cold weather from the north—his mother had given him a large sack of tiny little cheesecloth bags filled with asafoetida and sewn together with little catgut ties to hang around the neck. He'd argued that it would make a fool of him if he offered them around but his mother had told him to try it just to see what would happen, and to his surprise the old-timers had jumped at his offer, saying they hadn't seen things like that since their cambuse days when they were moving square cut pine down to the Ottawa River. Some of the younger men had laughed at first but later took them and tied them on. And when after the first month not a man who had a bag on had had a cold or even a sniffle, Russell was besieged by requests for more. At twenty-five cents a shot, a dime of which Russell got to keep, the Pembertons had made a killing.

He'd never been happier. For the first time in his life he had money and, better yet, his hair was starting to stay put when he watered it down flat to his head. His mother even kidded him that he was getting good-looking, and he'd run to the mirror to check. Jaw widening, freckles vanishing, nose longer, perhaps too long, and thinner, eyes blue and clear—Lordy, Russell thought, she just might be right.

In March, on Jenny Turner's sixteenth birthday, Russell came home from work on the run. He bathed in the steel tub in front of the kitchen fire while his mother poured steaming kettles of water at his feet, put on his church clothes, had his mother try the tie a second time, flattened his hair down till it looked as if his head had been painted black with a thin silver ruler line down the centre, cleaned up his

78

black Wellingtons, grabbed the ju-jubes he'd bought at Morley's the day before, and said goodbye to his mother.

"Just hold on one minute, Russell," she called as he reached for the front door latch.

Abigail Pemberton bustled over to her work counter, opened a tiny bottle and hurried back. She had a half-dozen caraway seeds pinched between her thumb and forefinger.

"Open up," she commanded.

Russell did as he was told. Abigail placed two inside his mouth and slipped the other four into his vest pocket. She then stood back and winked at him. Russell smiled and hurried out the door. From that moment on, the caraway seed sucking was a habit with him.

At Jenny's house the birthday was a quiet affair. Her father, Harvey Turner, was a camp foreman for the Vernon Lumber Company and was away in the bush getting the logs cut and skidded out for the spring drive.

But the rest of the family was making the best of it without him. Jenny had her hair tied up over her head and held with a carved wood clasp; some of the hair had been allowed to fall in evasive wisps down the sides and over her temples, and Russell found that enchanting. She was dressed in a white cotton dress with a yellow waist tie, and Russell thought her the most beautiful girl he had ever seen. And considering he had never been outside of Vernon in his sixteen years, she undoubtedly was.

All considered, it had been a most successful evening. Russell had wanted to be witty and he'd made them laugh several times. He'd wanted to be gracious and mature and there'd been no missed etiquette points and no spilled tea. He'd wanted to catch Jenny's glance and for the most part of the night, he'd seen nothing else but her eyes flashing back at him.

She was, as far as he was concerned, his girl. Some of the older fellows at the mill began kidding Russell a bit, and he denied it all categorically, puffed out his chest, and began swaggering a bit more while he worked. He was delighted to find out he was popular, that people could actually like him for things he said and did, almost as if he really mattered to them. He knew they'd only kid someone they genuinely liked, and he discovered he was feeling like the luckiest guy in the world from the moment his mother called him in the morning until he leaned over from his bed and blew down the chimney of the coal-oil lamp at night. He was Russell Pemberton, a *somebody*.

And it only got better. He got promoted in the early part of the summer to assist one of the inspectors. Russell suddenly found himself in training to become what amounted to a "professional" in that part of the world. His new mentor, a soft-hearted curmudgeon named Ainsley Lewis, kidded him relentlessly – good, Russell figured – and spent noon hours showing him how to calculate board feet on the metal-tipped inspector's rule that at first made less sense to Russell than a Chinese abacus. Lewis also pounded him daily with information on how to grade lumber, what it should weigh, what a strong knot was in comparison to a weak knot, what the better grains were. Soon he could tell just by looking at the lumber how long it had lain in the bush before it had been cut, how long it had been in water, sometimes even how big the original tree had been.

In late August, Lewis even let him work some birch piles down at the shed one afternoon. Russell had climbed up like a conqueror about to be knighted, had reached down with his special yardstick, hooked the metal edge under the first board, lifted, placed his boot under and kicked it entirely around, the twelve-foot length of board spinning in the air like a log in water, and he had called out the grade. To the side Lewis nodded his approval. Russell went on to a second and soon he'd gone through the entire pile, workmen hurrying at his whim to move the checked boards on to designated piles, and he'd worked out the gradings and board feet entirely on his own.

And when it was all finished and Ainsley Lewis got up from his crouched position on the next pile over and checked a couple of Russell's calculations, he'd reached into a cubby-hole along one side of the shed and pulled out a brand-new inspector's book with clean yellow sheets and a new, leather case. He'd handed Russell the book and Russell had slipped the straps over the thumb of his left hand and the first three fingers of that same hand so he could open and close it with one motion, and when he looked up Ainsley Lewis had walked away.

One day Russell would try the Ontario hardwood exams and one day he'd be a full inspector. Then he'd have it made. He could see his future unfolding ahead of him, perfect and predictable as lilac bushes in May. He decided that one day Janet Turner would form a part of that remarkable future.

On October 10, 1901, the future King and Queen of England, the Duke and Duchess of Cornwall and York, were to pass through town on their special train. It was the first–and, Russell came to realize, the last–time royalty would ever see Vernon, and he always considered them poorer for having looked but once.

It hadn't been a particularly nice day. The wind was burrowing down from the northwest, turning the bay to raspy whitecaps and the water for the first one hundred yards off shore was black as old coffee. Russell's mother had been up grinding herb leaves since before dawn, and when he came down and filled a big bowl from the bubbling porridge pot she never even bothered with a good morning.

"Black sky in the northwest, we're in for another bath," she said, as she always said when she saw black clouds over the bay.

Russell hoped it would hold off until at least noon. He knew she'd be right, but she generally allowed her weather predictions a four-hour leeway.

"No work till ten today, Mother," he said. "Everybody gets to see the train."

Russell finished his breakfast, wiped his mouth, rinsed it with salt water, rubbing his forefinger up and down over the

81

front teeth to shine them, and left. He was due to pick up Jenny at seven.

Jenny wore a fine black wool coat with a sheepskin collar and muff, both dyed black. Russell wished he'd dressed warmer, for their breath hung in quick balloons before them as they waited for the train. But he wanted to show off his new waistcoat and, particularly, the silver-coated watch chain that led arrogantly to his vest pocket. His rationale was that he'd look his best for the Prime Minister and the future King and Queen – Lordy, all anyone there was talking about was how ill King Edward was supposed to be from all that liquor and high living – but the real reason, of course, was to pull Jenny's eyes away from the tracks. He would race home and change to his work clothes after the train left.

The wind slashed in across the bay and cut through their clothes. Hardly anyone said anything; they were all too busy saving themselves for the train when it arrived. Russell looked into the sky and it seemed night was gathering for a comeback in the hills just across the bay. He prayed the train would beat the storm.

Twenty minutes later it did. Two huge black and glistening Canadian National steam engines came at the tip of a massive white smoke roostertail. They were pulling ten cars, the last being the Cornwall, and stopped and hissed and clunked to a second stop right in front of Russell's spot, just where he'd told her it would.

Jenny turned and nodded her approval at him. Russell fingered his watch chain.

"I'm impressed," she said. And laughed.

The crowd pressed in on them, and her laugh was lost.

Never before had Russell been so delighted to be pushed around; in a pure reflex action he put a protective arm out toward Jenny and she snuggled close as he carved out a space. Quickly, he dropped his arm from around her waist, but their shoulders continued to touch under the force of the crowd. Russell felt she was talking to him through her shoulder, and he found his entire concentration was centred there. It seemed to him they were both pushing harder than needed, and after a minute or so he could no longer distinguish between what would be a natural force against Jenny and what would be unnatural. He looked quickly at her and realized that her shoulder was up against the wooden car, and it suddenly occurred to him that he might be squashing her.

He eased up just as the Duke appeared.

The Duke came out onto the platform alone, wearing the finest black serge suit Russell had ever seen. He was very pink of face, particularly around the cheeks, and looked, Russell decided, like a jolly good soul.

When the rest of the crowd recognized him, a mighty cheer went up. P.D. Duncan, the skinny, tight-lipped, bespectacled principal of the school jumped from his view along the sidelines and made an odd hand signal that moved the teachers into motion. One of them raised a hand, did a quick conductor's three-count, and the children moved awkwardly into "God Save the King." Most of them were so awestruck by royalty that they could do nothing but stand there with their mouths open, and the song would have died on the spot had the rest of the older crowd, led by Russell and Jenny, not taken up the song.

The door to the royal coach opened again and the Duchess herself stepped out, severely wrapped in a great scarf and a huge coat with a fur collar. Her face was barely visible but what could be seen was beautiful. Apart from the girl pressing against his flabbergasted shoulder, Russell thought he had never seen such beauty.

In a moment he felt his fist lock and his arm rise pumping into the air.

"*The Duchess!*" Russell yelled.

"*The Duke!*" someone else called.

"*Hurrah for them both!*" Russell yelled. He wondered if this was really him.

"*Hurrah!*" the crowd called.

"*Hurrah!*"

With the last yell some of the men in the crowd tossed their hats. Russell turned and looked upon his creation: hats climbing and spinning back at odd angles as they skipped over and away from grabbing hands, hundreds of schoolchildren, mechanically waving their little flags, their faces shocked by the immensity of the moment, women, men – people Russell *knew* – cheering and laughing and pushing tighter and tighter toward the royal coach. Russell had never felt such power before, and he decided there and then that he could do perfectly well without it.

But it was no longer in his hands. The Duchess had noticed Russell as the one who had started it all. She was now pointing to him and calling for him when Russell turned back toward the car. He couldn't hear her but he could read her lips, *and she was calling him there*.

Russell turned and looked at Jenny, who was laughing up at him. *She's laughing at me. She thinks it's funny that I'm trapped.* He decided he wasn't going. He decided he'd simply run away. Under the circumstances, it seemed like the only sensible thing to do.

But when he turned he went straight into Tommy Lynch's arms, and he couldn't have picked a worse refuge. Tommy called for the other men nearby to help him and they pitched in eagerly. In a moment Russell found himself held by more than a dozen arms and hoisted completely above the crowd.

They were handing him along! Russell lay there – for what other word was there for it but that? – he *lay* there in absolute terror, thinking that it was all a nightmare and that it would soon end and he'd be glad for it. But it didn't end. He felt hand after hand poke up and into him. He felt the thrusting from around his head and shoulders and he felt the new hands accepting him around his knees and feet. He looked out and saw a flood of madness, eyes wide and mouths open with shouts he couldn't decipher. He turned – or rather, they turned him – and he thought he saw Jenny laughing and pointing at him, and he decided he regretted ever knowing her.

He turned again and he was facing the Duchess, who was leaning out over the platform railing. She was smiling, not a teasing smile like he'd seen in the crowd, but a gracious smile and one of great appreciation, or so Russell thought.

The crowd quietened.

The Duchess removed the corsage she was wearing. She held it up for the crowd to see, the crowd cheered its approval, and she reached up and pinned it onto the chest of a crimson Russell Pemberton.

Russell lost track after that. He was dizzy, almost sick. There was the roar of the crowd, the hands handing him back, the chugging, very slow and deliberate, of the train as it pulled out, the school kids singing "Maple Leaf," and the royal pair waving backwards to the townspeople, many of whom were gathered in a respectful circle around the Mayor and scrambling for position as they sought to slap a congratulatory message into his back.

Russell was vaguely aware that a lot of them were sending backslaps his way as well. And he heard his name called out a lot. Not in laughter, either – more as if he'd scored the winning goal or something.

When he came back to reality he was strolling up the walk toward Jenny Turner's house and she had her hand tucked into the bend of his elbow.

Russell checked his watch and it was only nine-thirty, which gave him a full half-hour to change and get over to the mill yard. Together they looked the Duchess's corsage over: orchids, Jenny said, and she seemed greatly surprised that someone had been able to get them in this area at this time of year. She decided several corsages must have been packed in ice back in Ottawa, and the Duchess simply took out a new one each day. There were little paper bells and green paper-coated wires in the fashion of leaves. Russell wondered what it would have cost.

"Russell, it's beautiful," Jenny said as she delicately touched it.

"I still can't believe she gave it to *me*," he said, and looked at the ground sheepishly.

"Who else?" Jenny said mischievously.

Russell smiled.

"If I," he began, "if I gave it to you, would you take it?"

Jenny looked up from the corsage and smiled.

"You don't sound overly confident about it, Russell," she said.

Russell blushed and checked with his left hand to make sure his hair was still plastered down.

"Would you, though?" he asked.

"Of course I would," she said and looked straight into his eyes.

Russell thought he was passing out. He wanted to say something but couldn't. He stammered, stopped, looked at her. She smiled back, and Russell thought it made the corsage pale in comparison. He fumbled with the pin. She moved deftly, removing the corsage from his breast with two quick motions.

"Thank you," she said. "You'd better get going, don't you think?"

"Yes!" he said, far too loudly. "Yes, I do. I've got to get going. Bye." He moved backwards down the boardwalk. "Bye, Jenny."

She just stood there smiling.

Rain was beginning to fall in thick drops now. Russell ran through the streets to his house, did a spin in the front yard, and opened his mouth to the rain as if he'd drink the sky dry. He spun and spun, and when he stopped he looked up toward the house and saw his mother at the window. And she was shaking her head.

8

Eleanor had driven to the local cemetery, having gotten directions at the gas station, on the off-chance that she could get more information – names, dates – about Janet Turner. She found herself at the Turner family plot, near the rear of the cemetery, covered in soggy, rust-coloured pine needles. She jotted down the names and dates of what she presumed were Janet Turner's parents. Next stop the local newspaper.

The door to the newspaper office was opened by the editor himself, a fat, bald man with a remarkable smile. Eleanor had no difficulty gaining his sympathy, having said she was researching her family tree for a book, and there was a hint – only a hint, she emphasized – that Tom Thomson had been a distant cousin. He invited her into his office and scrambled out for a couple of coffees for them, and she fashioned a clearing on the busy desk, found an ashtray, and was sitting quite contentedly smoking when he returned.

"My uncle knew Tom Thomson," he said as he grunted into his chair and took a desperate sip of his coffee. "And I've read every word they've ever written on him, too, and it's all a bunch of bumph as far as I'm concerned, for what that's worth."

"Tell me," said Eleanor. She offered him a cigarette. He accepted one, tapping it thoughtfully on the desk.

"You ever read that plaque they built for him up at Canoe Lake? Here. I got it here."

He got up and fumbled with the books in his bookcase. Eleanor noted not a single one had been stood up; rather, they were stacked, with no effort to bother making sure the spines faced out for easy reading. Yet he went directly to the book he wanted.

"Yah, here. *Algonquin Story*, by Audrey Saunders. You've read it?"

"Actually, I haven't," Eleanor confessed. "I've just begun looking into all this, I'm afraid. But I have read Blodwen Davies' book on him."

"Borrow this one, then. Here. Yah, here it is. Page one eighty-five. 'He lived humbly but passionately with the wild – it made him brother to all untamed things of nature.' And here, too. 'Artist – Woodsman – And Guide.'"

The editor shut the book with a loud smack. And then he laughed, a long, drawn-out, wheezy laugh.

"If you'll pardon the expression, Mrs. – uhhh – Philpott, but what a bunch of *crap*. '*Humble!*' If my Uncle Vince and the old-timers I've talked to are right, Thomson was one of the most arrogant sons of a female dog they ever knew."

"Where did your Uncle Vince know him from?" Eleanor asked, resisting the urge to get up and defend her unknown artist. She was already starting to think of him as her father.

"Here . . . there," the editor said, blowing on his coffee, which skipped over slightly onto his desk. He simply wiped the drops clear with the flat of his hand. "Mostly there, at Canoe Lake. Uncle Vince was a walking foreman for the lumber company there. He told me some of the old boys despised Thomson. Wouldn't talk with them, wouldn't eat with them. Half the time, that is. The other half he wanted to be their best friend – especially if somebody had a crock of good hooch.

"Jesus Christ. I'm telling you, a lot of that stuff about him is hogwash. Hogwash! Thomson drank with the best of them and cursed better than most of them. My uncle fished

Thomson more than once out of the lake after he tumbled in drunk."

Eleanor took a sip of her coffee.

"So he might have drowned," she said.

"Might have," the editor said. "Might have. Who's to say now? I heard all that talk about the big party at George Rowe's..."

"George Rowe?" Eleanor asked.

"Yah, you know. The guide," the editor said.

"Of course," Eleanor said, pretending to know.

"Anyways," the editor continued, "him and this Martin Bletcher were supposed to have been in some big argument about the war or something and Bletcher's supposed to have threatened him when the party broke up. 'Don't get in my way,' or something dumb like that, and when Thomson couldn't be found the next day a lot of people started saying Bletcher had done him in."

"You don't seem to think that," Eleanor said.

"I don't. No, I don't," the editor said, and he swirled his coffee thoughtfully and looked into the cup's bottom. "I met Bletcher a few times – he just died a few years back, and *there* too, at Canoe Lake, isn't *that* odd? – and he never struck me as the type who could murder. A lot of others don't think so either. Bletcher had a big mouth and drank too much, but he couldn't bop some poor guy on the head and then anchor him down with a rock and send him to the bottom. Not bloody likely, I don't think..."

"Any ideas, then?" Eleanor asked.

"Ahhh, you hear lots of talk. But it doesn't add up to much."

"Such as."

"Well, maybe it was an accident. Who's to say he didn't trip going over that portage and bang his head on a rock and drown?"

"Davies says there was no water in the lungs," Eleanor offered.

The editor smiled. He finished his coffee and crumpled the

cup and tossed it into the wastebasket, until that moment the cleanest space in the office.

"I read that book, too," he said. "Lot of Thomson buffs around here, Mrs. Philpott. You'll find yourself in good company."

"What about the other talk?" Eleanor asked.

"Well," the editor began. "You've heard the talk about suicide because of him knocking up—getting a girl pregnant?"

Eleanor almost choked on her coffee. *Pregnant?* She found herself nodding. She hoped the flush she felt wasn't going to give her away.

"Do you believe that?" she asked.

The editor shrugged. "Probably not."

Eleanor wet her lips. "Who was this girl?"

"I wouldn't know," he said. "I wasn't around, of course. Certainly, it wasn't Miss Janet Turner—no child!"

Eleanor shivered. *Her* name. A *child*.

"Janet Turner..." Eleanor said the name as if her mouth had never used the phrase before.

"*Miss* Janet Turner," the editor corrected her. "*Miss*, please. I think it's her first name."

Eleanor smiled. "But there was some connection between the two, Thomson and *Miss* Janet Turner..."

"I can't say for sure. Most old-timers take it for granted they were engaged but the death put the kibosh on that. She apparently says they were and that's enough for most people around here. She wouldn't lie."

Engaged!

Eleanor felt faint and was glad she was sitting. What enormous good fortune! So much—and she'd given so little. Maybe it was too easy... perhaps there was a hitch... a trick, a dead end.

The editor leaned forward earnestly. Eleanor felt it coming, anticipated the worst, and actually felt relief when he only asked, "You're not thinking of talking to her, are you?"

Of course I am, she thought. Whatever could he mean.

"I shouldn't?"

"Suit yourself," the editor said and pressed back in his swivel chair. He folded his hands behind his head and stretched. "I wouldn't want to be you, that's all."

"Meaning?"

"Meaning Miss Janet Turner is a very difficult subject, that's all. Don't forget, she's had forty-four years now of people pestering her, and the crazy thing about it is that it doesn't get any better, it gets worse. More people this year than last year. More people next year. All wanting to know about Tom Thomson or look at her paintings or ask her what really happened."

"What's she like?" Eleanor ventured.

"Well, there's lots of talk about her around here, I can tell you that. And the kids don't like her." The editor laughed. "Some of them call her a witch, my own two kids included. But she's not that bad, not by a half."

"You know her well?"

"Only a tad, really. She loves this old place 'cause she once worked here when she was a teenager. Long before my time. She kept books or something for a couple of years around the turn of the century. So she phones me up every now and then to tell me whether I'm right or wrong. She's eccentric, I'd say. Eccentric—yes, that's it."

"Doesn't she have any friends?" Eleanor asked.

The editor leaned forward and sprawled out over the paper-covered desk, resting his chin on his folded hands.

"A few," he said. "Can't say who they are at the moment but maybe I'll think of some. If I were you I wouldn't count on her helping you."

Who else can? Eleanor wanted to say.

"You'll find out more about your Tom Thomson sticking to other things, I suspect," the editor said.

"Yes, well, what about your files, then?" Eleanor said and drained her coffee. "You're sure you don't mind?"

"Not a bit," the editor said when he rose. Then he laughed. "Not if you don't, that is."

Eleanor soon understood what the editor's little joke had

been. He guided her down some narrow, winding steps into the basement, helped her around several large rolls of newsprint, fitted an old key into a steel door and, with a loud grunt, followed by the creak of the door, opened the files.

"No one has the time to keep them up," he said apologetically as he stepped back to let her see. "Too bad, too. Probably lots of valuable history in there."

"I'm sure," Eleanor said.

"Probably not much on Thomson, though. The odd social notice, perhaps. Maybe an obituary, but I think I looked myself once and couldn't find it. See what I mean about him? He becomes more important every year. Say he died yesterday. It'd be front-page news on every paper in the country."

The editor began his laugh again and ended it with several huge coughs into his fist. Eleanor noticed the fist was white as he coughed into it, as if the man were desperately trying to hold onto something.

"Please," said Eleanor. "I've already taken up so much of your valuable time. You just leave me here and I'll be fine."

The editor coughed once more and looked up and smiled.

"You just call me if you need any help, Mrs. Philpott. Some of those folders can be pretty heavy."

"Yes," she said. "Thank you for your help."

"Wait'll you see what's there before you thank me," he said. And then he was gone.

The papers had been filed by simply bundling together the year's issues between heavy cardboard and bolting the packages together. They were piled in no apparent order, and the only designation as to what was what came from a grease-pencil mark on the top or side binding which announced the year. The older the bundle the narrower it seemed; the older the more yellowed, as well, and once Eleanor had actually touched one of the very old bundles from 1896 she realized that it was dried and fragile to the point where a page could disintegrate in her hand. It felt like moth wings. She determined not to touch anything she didn't absolutely have to know about.

The only light came from a bare bulb that hung on a cord from the ceiling. Eleanor had to use both hands and much of her strength to pull the bundles free, step outside the fire door, and spread them over the newsprint rolls. She then opened her purse and pulled out the notebook with the information from the graveyard.

Harvey Turner had died on February 9, 1932. He had been seventy-five years old and, according to the obituary that appeared in the papers two weeks later, a man of comparative good health until just the year before. He died with his wife and daughter Janet at his side.

The funeral had been held at his home. Harvey Turner had been a native of New Brunswick, had come to Ontario at the age of seventeen, and married Melissa Burton in 1883. Two years later, with their newborn daughter, they had come to Vernon, where Harvey Turner took a job with the local lumber company.

He eventually rose to become a camp foreman, which Eleanor took to mean he was a resourceful and clever man, and he was, according to the write-up, considered an expert timber cruiser and evaluator. For twenty-three years he had been in charge of the mill's bush operations. Several years before 1932, he'd retired and moved to Hemlock—Eleanor made a note that she'd have to find out where *that* was—but had moved back home to Vernon just prior to falling ill. He'd been operated on in Vernon but he'd lasted only four days. He was, the paper declared, "a man of quiet, but jovial disposition, whose friendships were sincere, and who enjoyed the respect and confidence of all who knew him. Many beautiful floral tributes gave silent testimony to the high esteem in which he was held."

But even though Eleanor could find out nothing more of the man than what was offered up in the obituary, she could discover something of the times he lived in. The year he died, rolled oats were selling five pounds for fifteen cents and the talk of the world was the kidnapping of twenty-month-old Charles Augustus Lindbergh, Jr., "Lindy's baby."

There was a fifty-thousand-dollar ransom, and it was obvious that no one as yet knew the sad truth about the child. *The Silent Witness* was playing at the theatre in town, and Gregory Clark was due to arrive in Vernon for a speaking engagement. The big fad in Canada was fourteen-day dieting.

After a while, Eleanor began to feel as if she was driving. The more she tried to focus on the faded print of the old papers the more difficult it became to see properly. She looked at her hands and they were greying around the fingertips and down the side of the palm she was smoothing the sheets with. She took a deep breath and turned to 1935, the year of Mrs. Turner's death.

Again, the obituary appeared two weeks after the event. Again, it was merely a skeleton of the person it described.

Melissa Turner née Burton died on October 3, 1935, at the age of seventy-seven. She'd been active in the Women's Christian Temperance Union, and once again "There were many beautiful floral tributes, which gave silent testimony to the high esteem in which she was held."

And once again Eleanor found no help in the rest of the paper. Partridge season was about to open and made-to-measure suits were selling for $22.50. The big advertising push was on for Good Humour Frumenty, a granular wheat food, which was supposed to be the ultimate in breakfast treats, and sold for twenty-three cents a large package.

On the day of the obituary R.B. Bennett and the Conservatives were put out of power. Under Mackenzie King the Liberals won the largest majority in the history of the country, taking 168 seats. In Muskoka, the first Liberal was returned to Ottawa since 1878. People were obviously much dissatisfied with their fortunes.

Eleanor went back over the issue prior to the one in which the obituary appeared, and she was rewarded with a short item that she had missed, though it had appeared prominently on the front page. "Our readers will regret to learn that Mrs. Harvey Turner, one of our highly-respected citizens, passed away at her home Tuesday."

"Highly-respected." Eleanor liked that. She wondered for a moment what it would be like to grow old and die gracefully in a tiny town. Obviously, you did not die alone. Something went with you and something stayed behind, and Eleanor could think of nothing else but that it was a definition of who you were: no need here to worry about who you were to yourself, the town would take care of all that.

Eleanor felt envious. She remembered her father's death and how no one but family and a few of his colleagues had showed up in the little chapel, and how no one had even bothered to look at the little funeral cortège as it wound its way to the cemetery. No, that wasn't quite true, someone in a hurry had honked.

In the afternoon the door opened at the top of the cellar and the editor came down with a small brown bag containing two coffees and a double cream for Eleanor. It was a welcome relief. With the heat of the basement and the rough light and the agony of concentrating hour after hour on nine-point typeface, Eleanor was beginning to swim on her feet.

"Find anything?" the editor asked, as he fumbled with the bag top.

"No," she said. "Not really."

"I didn't expect you would," he said. "Here, this is yours. No, hold it. This one has double sugar marked on it. Here. And here's your cream."

Eleanor thanked him for the coffee and sat back on one of the newsprint rolls to drink it.

"You know about the Tom Thomson ghost, eh?"

Eleanor blinked to hide her astonishment. "Ghost?" she asked.

The editor giggled, coughed once. "Sure. Thomson slipping out of the mist on a cool August morning. Thomson calling from the shore—hell, that's the one I like best, this guy claiming Tom Thomson called to him from the shore to say his brother had just drowned up ahead and him racing back to find out sure in hell it was true. Happened damn near where Thomson himself drowned, too—and all that talk about Thomson skulking about at night looking to avenge his murder. *Great* stuff, that!"

"That's the first I've heard of it," said Eleanor.

"And there's all the stuff about his grave, too," the editor went on excitedly. "Where the hell's the body? What about that light casket they loaded up and took to his home? And that skeleton they dug up there a few years back and all the government whitewash about it being some Indian who was just passing by. Bull-oney, I say. *Bull*-oney. If they really dug him up and moved him back, then I want to know why Janet Turner always went up there and cleaned up his gravesite, that's what I want to know."

Eleanor grabbed at this. She looked at the tiny notebook she'd placed beside her work area and tried to will the information into it, and she burned with a sudden worry that she might lose what the editor was saying.

"So you got a lot of good stuff to look into, Mrs. Philpott," the editor said. "But I really don't think you'll find much there." He pointed at the files.

"Yes," Eleanor said. "Well, I want to look anyway. Where would you suggest I start after I've exhausted the files?"

"Where?" the editor said, checking the bottom of his cup, and seeing nothing, crumpling it with a quick fist. "People, I guess. People. Talk to people."

"And who would you recommend?"

"Yah, well, trouble is, not too many of them still kicking. Janet Turner'd be your best bet, of course, but you'll hit a stone wall there, sure as hell. You could, of course, go up to Canoe Lake. Still a lot of people there who talk about it. Watch it, though. There's lots of them willing to tell you the most incredible eye-witness accounts, which fall apart once you discover they weren't even born when Thomson drowned, or got killed, or whatever..."

"Any other ideas?"

"Not that I can think of now. But I'll work on it. You got about another hour before closing, then I'll call down, okay?"

"Okay," Eleanor said. "Thanks a lot."

96

The editor disappeared up the stairs and Eleanor went back to the newspapers.

She looked through a few pages of 1894, only to find out the pages were as fragile as the mantle of an old lantern. Before she quit, though, she discovered Janet Turner had been bright in spelling – scoring ninety-five in a third department test – and terrible in art – standing second from the bottom. She found other marks: an eighty-five in grammar and a fifty in history. Eleanor followed the school reports to 1897, when Janet would have been twelve, and suddenly discovered that her name was missing from the weekly reports.

For some reason it bothered her that her mother – *perhaps* her mother – may have had no further education. It was at this moment that Eleanor entered her great dilemma, a worry that would grow and grow in the time ahead. She was *judging* Janet Turner, trying to find out enough about this unsuspecting woman to decide whether she was worthy of being her mother.

Then she felt the depression. It seemed to wash from deep inside, a funny, creeping feeling that picked up strength as it ran toward her thoughts. She'd found from time to time before that she could stop the wash, or flutter, or whatever it was that bore into her, and she could do it by concentrating very hard on something totally unrelated. She'd found television helped. Or doing dishes. This time, though, she could not stop it. She looked around and *everything* was related: the newspapers, the notebook, even the fact that this office basement was in Vernon. She put her hands on the nearest roll of newsprint and closed her eyes while the feeling ran its course.

It was a terror, a dread, an emptiness – most of all an emptiness. Nothing mattered. Nothing. None of it ever would. She thought she'd cry. She thought she'd fall down on the floor and they'd have to come and take her away somewhere because she'd never stop crying about all the emptiness, and she'd never try to tell them about it or even look at them when they asked her what was wrong. They'd

97

have to find out for themselves. She wouldn't help them. She couldn't help them.

She thought of Doctor Klotz. She remembered what he had said. "You can fix it, Eleanor. *You* can fix it. You won't believe it possible while you're still under this cloud, but you can fix it. You have to remind yourself that it *will* pass."

It was gone!

As quickly, no, *quicker* than it had come, it was gone. Eleanor fumbled in her purse and pulled out the container of barbiturates. She took one, wincing as she swallowed without water. She cleared her throat. It was down and the dread was gone. The pill, the doctor had said, was just to make sure it stayed gone.

She went back to the files, stacked some of the years back that she'd been through, and pulled down others. In 1902, she was relieved to find that Janet Turner's education picked up again. She was seventeen and her parents enrolled her in a business academy in Kingston. It was an acceptable school that had three other local girls in it as well. It was a year-long course and Janet, who was always very good in mathematics, graduated as an office bookkeeper. And on October 1, 1903, she was hired at the local paper to take care of their books.

Eleanor felt a sudden chill.

What she was reading told her that this woman she didn't know had probably stood in this very spot fifty-eight years earlier. The great difference was that Janet Turner would have been only eighteen, with all the promise of her life ahead. Whereas, Eleanor reminded herself, she was forty-three, had blown her life, and was right now looking for the link that might allow her to go back and adjust her past. She thought about that a moment. The present, obviously, is the final measure of the past. If she then goes and alters her past, would it also change her present? She hoped so.

Eleanor rubbed her eyes. They felt like they'd been strung up all afternoon over a bonfire. And yet, she hadn't had a single smoke, which was most unusual for her. Fear of fire had been the main restraint, but she'd also been too preoccupied.

The rest would have to wait until tomorrow. Right now, she needed a drink. The pill must be making her feel tired. And a smoke. That too. And something to eat.

Eleanor looked at her wristwatch. Five. She put the files back in a better order than she'd found them and was just starting up the stairs when the door opened and the editor's smiling face loomed into view.

"Get what you wanted?"

"Not exactly. No. Would you mind if I went at it again tomorrow?"

"*Mind?*" The editor smiled, a large, jolly smile that revealed a set of strong white teeth – Eleanor was somewhat surprised that he'd have such a treasure in his mouth, for he hardly looked the type to take such good care of his teeth. "You can stay all month for all I care. I'm glad to have somebody new to talk to."

They walked together to the front door. The editor was carrying a folded piece of paper in his hand and he reached for the door handle with the other.

"I wrote down the name of someone who might help you, Mrs. Philpott," he said. He handed her the paper.

Eleanor didn't even look at the folded note. She was overwhelmed that he had even bothered – typical of her, in keeping with someone who wondered why anyone ever did anything for her.

She thought for a moment she would invite him for a drink, but her better judgement told her that would hardly be right. She felt her ring anxiously, as if its weight had startled her. She stepped out the door thinking she'd thank him in a gracious manner and then perhaps *he* would invite her, but when she turned to speak he was shutting the door on her. Of course, Eleanor told herself, he'd have a car parked out back.

Eleanor was furious with herself. She tried to call thank

you through the glass but it just steamed up when she spoke at it. The editor tapped lightly from the inside, waved, and then was gone. The light went out in the newspaper office.

Unlocking the door to her car, Eleanor realized how cool the air had become. Just as she was about to start the ignition, she remembered the note, still clutched in her left hand. She read the scrawled message. "Mr. Russell Pemberton, Muskoka Hotel. (P.S. Go easy with him. He's a bit funny.)"

In the upper apartment of the brown frame home opposite the Muskoka Hotel, an old hand moved to the handle of the out-of-date Kelvinator ice box, removed a fresh lemon from the keeper box, closed the door and set the lemon on the small kitchen table with the blue-and-white-checked oil-cloth. Beside the lemon were two fresh Kleenex, carefully smoothed and separated. The lemon was halved with a paring knife, then quartered, and three of the sections were returned to the Kelvinator. The fourth was set on the Kleenex nearest the only chair, the chair was moved back, and Miss Janet Turner sat down slowly and sighed.

She was glad last night's storm had passed. She didn't care for storms, apart from the one small blessing that they kept the tom cats away, but twice she'd seen from the porch of her dried-out little cottage at Canoe Lake a fire ball run along the water surface and slam into a big hemlock on one of the islands. Both times the trees burst apart and into flames as if they'd been wired with dynamite. Lightning had also struck houses before in Vernon, and on nights like that she was glad she didn't live higher up on the reservoir hill.

Storms also made her think of Tom. A lot of things did, actually, but especially storms: the way his eyes had widened and those crazy, electric bursts of energy. There'd been times when she'd held fast to the bannisters of the old cottage steps while he'd tried to pull her out into a downpour, and when she wouldn't follow he'd go himself, running up and down the shoreline, spinning like a small child to make himself dizzy, laughing like a madman, and making her giggle at his wild abandon.

Tom said he liked storms, that they told him the world was really alive and not just sitting around waiting for things that never came true. He especially liked the smell of the storm's aftermath, how, when you sucked deep, it seemed your lungs were made of fresh cedar boughs. She thought he was foolish, and said so, and he said maybe so, but then he was damn proud of being such a fool.

More than forty-five years ago Tom had sat with virtually the same view as she would have had had she lifted the blind. It was early April 1915, with winter hanging on by its claws and everybody talking about the Germans supposedly having a new weapon that you couldn't shoot back at – gas. Tom had gotten off the train in a melancholy mood, she remembered, and had come over the next morning from his room at the Olympia Hotel, now called the Muskoka.

Over coffee with her mother they'd talked about the war and Tom told her his good friend Alex Jackson was going to enlist and get over to Europe. And then he'd turned and looked out the lower kitchen window and over the bright, snow-covered lawn and sat silent, the index finger of his left hand rubbing down his long nose as if it were trying to smooth something out. He just shut up completely, and when she had looked at her mother she'd simply raised her eyebrows and then her coffee cup and said nothing. After several long moments Tom's thoughts came back in from the window and he turned to her mother.

"If I hurried and finished before lunch would you mind if I painted that?" he said, the war mood lifting like a momentary steam. "I'd clean up so you'd never notice, I promise."

And he'd flashed that childlike grin, the big teeth begging permission, and her mother nodded with a large smile and began cleaning up the breakfast dishes herself while Tom rushed back for his paints and a small canvas.

Jenny had a damp cloth and was running the toast crumbs into her cupped hand when she thought to look at just what

101

it was Tom planned to paint. There was nothing outside but the sun shining on the bare bushes, and across the road at Stevenson's Photographic Gallery the windows were partly covered with great, dripping icicles, which hung down from the eaves. Signs of the last storm of the winter. Nothing, she thought. Not a darned thing there.

But she'd seen it take shape while she stood with her mother back of Tom's right shoulder. It had been the icicles he'd wanted, actually, and after he'd worked a while on getting them to hang from Stevenson's, as if the sun were just beginning to soften the exposed parts, her mother shivered as if one of the icicles had just been slipped down her back.

Tom must have liked the way it had gone, for he talked the whole while. He started to show her what mixing cerulean blue and alizarin crimson would do and she laughed and said she would just leave the icicles bare because that's what they were to her: white. He shook his head and asked her how she ever got through art class at school and her mother mortified her by running off and coming back with a flurry of report cards and reading out her marks.

"Let me see," she began, with great drama. "Drawing, 55 – drawing, 60 – drawing, 50, 54 . . . Shall I go on?"

"Mother, *please!*" she had said.

Tom had just chuckled and continued to paint, and soon the small canvas was completed. His mood, so low when he'd first arrived, now soared, and he filled his pipe, lit it, and decided that the two of them should go for a walk around town and really enjoy the beauty of this early spring day. And they had paraded up and down Main Street as if the future was firmly held in their coat pockets.

Ha!

The hand took the lemon quarter off the Kleenex, pinched it slightly, and raised it toward the face. *So many changes.* Her skin had once been tight and clear and beautifully textured. In the picture that Tom had taken of her holding his fly-fishing pole, and the four tiny bass they'd caught in the rocks

102

of Joe Lake Dam, she'd looked, she thought, fresh. Thin and straight and dark. Beautiful even. Or so he'd said anyway.

She ran the lemon slice over her forehead and rubbed it tight along the lines, working away from her eyes, quickly using the second Kleenex to wipe away the juice that ran toward her eyelids. The skin, once so healthy brown in summer, was grey now, lined and worn. The lemon refreshed and perhaps tightened a bit, but it could never bring back that crinkly smile and smoothness of her younger face. Nor would her dark hair swing lightly and drop loosely against her face any more if she turned too quickly. Grey and dull now, it turned with her these days, slowly and deliberately as if afraid it might hurt itself, protected by a hair net and tinted a subtle tinge of blue.

How could she even compare?

This autumn of 1961 she was seventy-six years old. Once too tall and square-shouldered, and blessed with a full figure, which caused a great many proud blushes, she was now somewhat stooped and weighed 170 pounds. Her health, once a matter of personal pride, had become a burden. There were small prescription bottles on the shelf with odd names like Serpasil and Tuinal for her high blood pressure. But while that seemed to be under control, the diabetes was worsening. There was talk of injections. She hoped it remained talk.

They were almost all gone now. Mother. Father. *Tom.* Of all those once gathered here for Sunday meals only she was left. She was left... yes, *left. Abandoned.*

9

Russell Pemberton came along Main Street from the post office, headed toward the warmth of the hotel. He could see his breath, thinly. It was hard to believe he'd sat out most of the day drowsing in the sun. He looked up toward the reservoir hill and saw several fine, wispy fingers of purpling-over pink. Abigail Pemberton would have been pleased. *Red sky at night*, she'd have said, *sailor's delight*.

Russell felt good, full of the promise of tomorrow and pleased with the outcome of the day just passing.

He would have a drink, he decided. Maybe a couple. It had been a fine enough day that it deserved a proper evening, and with the new month's old age pension cheque just cashed, there was nothing to prevent him from enjoying life as it was meant to be. He'd go to the draft room.

First of all, he wanted to put the majority of his money under the mattress. So he went up to his room, hid the money, left his coat and toque, and went to the washroom. One of the toilets was running, and though he removed the china top and fiddled with the ball cock for several minutes, he couldn't get it to stop. The cut-off valve wouldn't sit properly.

Russell cursed several times, placed the top back on, and went back to his room to call Archie and have him call for a plumber.

It was Russell's opinion that plumbing was a profession for perverts. Bad enough that their main job was the traffic of the body's expulsions, he thought, but it was positively sick that everything had to have dirty names like nipple, cock, joint, coupling, ball, male and female adapters, with the male twisting into the female, usually with a lot of lubrication. Russell had been forever grateful that he'd always been something sensible, like a lumber grader or camp foreman. Something you could be proud of and talk about in any company.

So he was in a bad mood when he reached the fifth-floor elevator and pushed the down button. It didn't make him any happier when he had to wait for the damn thing to rise up from the basement, either. Nor did it please him when the doors broke open on a perfect display of Georgie Quill's ass.

Russell had no trouble recognizing Georgie, even though Georgie was lying on his side and facing the back wall. Russell had seen him in this position too many times before. Georgie would pass out after a full afternoon's drinking and, inevitably, some of the boys would carry him over to the elevator, unbuckle his pants, stack him in on his side with the bare ass winking back, and leave him there for the edification of whoever happened to be fortunate enough to call on the elevator. This was the second time Russell had won the pleasure. And for the second time Russell simply rode the elevator to the basement draft room and stepped off, leaving Georgie Quill's ass behind as a hand-me-down shock for some other unsuspecting soul.

He went straight to his chair halfway down the wall row on the men's side, and he barely had time to set his cane on the chair opposite when Chris, the head waiter, came over with the purple velvet pillow they kept for Russell behind the bar. It was a custom, now, and Russell accepted it with gratitude; otherwise, his piles wouldn't let him sit through even a single draft in the hard chrome and plastic chairs.

105

He loved this beer room as he loved the town. But unlike the town, it could never properly be called beautiful. The best part about it, Russell often thought, was that there were no women gabbing. It was men only. It was a murky, foggy, black-and-white room where the smoke hung in twisting drapes and where the wall hangings were old, faded shots of the tourist boats that once worked the Vernon River system, shots from Russell's heyday. When you walked in, the floor made sticky, tearing sounds from past beer spills. You sat with your back to the wall – a cardinal rule among regulars – at a formica and steel round table where you could run a hand over the rises of hardened glass-bottom rings and tiny black gullies dug by abandoned cigarette butts. Textures you could count on, Russell liked to think.

There were other men there, some of them regulars, but very few of them Russell bothered with. Some of them either talked too much – always about what they *might* have been had it not been for the war, the bad knees, the old man dying, the wife, the babies, the flood, any goddam number of things they could come up with – and the others spooked him. Some of those crossed their skinny legs so tight Russell thought it would make their eyes pop out, and they sat there smoking roll-your-owns and fingering their change on the table, as if they had an appointment coming up. Russell didn't like any of them.

What he did like was to salt down the first two drafts, down one of them in two big tips to the mouth and then sit back sipping on the other while he checked out of the present tense. Russell didn't need any of those others sitting with him anyway. He'd known for years that he'd never find a finer and more congenial drinking buddy than his own memory. Never an argument. Never a scene. Never any trouble. The sole complaint he had was that he couldn't always control the drift, couldn't always be sure where he was headed. No great pleasure to find himself back on the day Jenny left for the business academy in Kingston. But he couldn't always stop it.

———

106

The day she left on the train he'd smiled and waved. But it wasn't really him.

Then he'd hiked up the Rock Trail and sat on an overhanging rock, looking at Vernon and trying to understand. He traced the river all the way from Birch Lake through town and out past the narrows, and he bet he knew every bass spot along it and every shoal and spring feed in the bay and both lakes. He ran his finger along Main Street as far as he could see and then up Princess and Hunter's and Maple and East, and even out the Fourth Concession, and he figured out he knew who lived in every house he could see and what they did for a living and how old their kids were. He could see the reservoir hill and even see the clearing beside the best trillium patch around town. He could even see the tip of the railway station and the siding where the Duchess had given him her corsage.

He began throwing rocks off the Rock Hill bluff to see if he could reach the river. He heard one splash and he ran and found more rocks and came back with an arm-cradle full. He started throwing them as far as he could, pretending he was firing them at spots in the town. Morley's store. The Olympia Hotel. His own house. The Turner house.

He started yelling as he threw. He gathered up another armful of fist-sized stones, climbed to the crest of the hill, and began screaming with each stone he tossed, throwing so hard and with such anger that his arm soon had no feeling in it below the shoulder.

And then all the rocks were gone. Russell looked at his throwing hand and saw that the rocks had shredded the skin and several very small balls of blood were rising out of the torn tissue. There was no pain, but Russell Pemberton sagged to his knees and cried anyway.

But as hard as he cried that day, the pain dissolved the moment Jenny came home from school. The memory of that peculiar day sat as handy as the jack-knife in his pocket; a day seldom went by without Russell tapping both of them lightly just to make sure they were still there.

He'd been out in the garden staking his mother's tomato plants when Abigail Pemberton came out through the back door with a cup of steaming water—her bowel rinser, she called it—and the news that Jenny and her new diploma were coming home today. She'd heard it from Mr. Morley, who claimed to have it direct from Mrs. Turner herself.

Russell remembered he didn't move, just knelt and continued tapping the stake slowly with the flat side of the axe. He wondered why he hadn't noticed the strong earth smell before. He cleared his throat.

"Did Mr. Morley say when?" he asked and deliberately looked down at the black under his fingernails.

"Eight o'clock train," his mother said and took a slow sip of her hot water. She swallowed, smiled. "You've enough time, son."

Russell dropped his axe and raced up the steps past his mother, who held the door open for him. He went through without looking at her. Inside, a basin of hot water had already been laid out, and around the basin in their natural order were Russell's shaving mug, brush, soap, razor, pumice soap, towel, and some of the translucent pink lilac water his mother had made only the week before. A clean shirt was over the chair and his suit, also pressed, was hanging on the kitchen door. Obviously, his mother had been home some time, keeping the news from him.

At a quarter to eight a brand new straw skimmer with Russell Pemberton beneath it was by the station boardwalk. Russell was in a state, absolutely convinced the stationmaster could smell him, and was sending messages about him down the telegraph line. He kept looking up from his key and scowling Russell's way, and Russell kept pretending he wasn't even in the man's line of vision. Damn his mother and her enthusiasm, slapping that perfume behind his ears and all down his collar as he raced out the front door. She'd laughed—he could hear her for nearly two blocks as he ran down reservoir hill. Christ! This was hardly a laughing matter.

At five minutes to eight Mrs. Turner and her husband arrived by carriage. Russell recognized the black and red rig as their neighbour's, Western's, Democrat. Harvey Turner pulled up the team sharply, jumped down, and marched over to shake hands with a cringing Russell. In Russell's little world, which ran between the reservoir hill and the Rock, Harvey Turner was a god, a big, tough, highly-respected walking foreman with the Vernon Lumber Company – as good a camp man as there was in the district.

"Evening, Russell," Mr. Turner said. He was smiling, his big, yellow teeth barely visible under the large haystack of a moustache. Russell looked at the moustache, watching carefully to see if it shivered when the lilac struck.

"Good evening, sir," Russell replied. "And Mrs. Turner." He doffed his skimmer, wished he'd practised.

"No ball game tonight?" Mr. Turner asked, and winked obviously toward Russell.

"Certainly is," Mrs. Turner said quickly before Russell could answer. He looked at her, caught the sting of her stare, and was about to say yes but his team wasn't playing, when the train whistle rose faintly from somewhere out over the narrows. Out came the stationmaster and the baggagemen, the stationmaster nodding curtly at Russell and tipping his green visor generously toward the Turners.

The train hissed and screeched to a halt just in front of them and a wooden step dropped perfectly out of the first car, followed by a porter who stepped down, bounced assuredly on the boardwalk, and turned to offer his hand to the only passenger disembarking. Suddenly, Miss Janet Turner was back in Russell's Vernon.

She had on a summer dress Russell hadn't seen before, blue the colour of robins' eggs, and set off by a white lace bonnet. But what struck him more than the bright clothes, so emphasized by the sober tones of everyone else, was the intensity of Jenny's eyes. Dark, they seemed to glisten in the evening light, and when they fell over Russell the impact very nearly sent him to his knees. Jenny ran first to her father, hugged him, was lost in his hug, stood back at arm's length from him, laughed, and went directly to her mother, who gathered her up in her arms as if the movement of her hands could weave a cocoon. Russell waited patiently, and was more than rewarded when Jenny spun her mother around so she had her back to him and he and Jenny could look at each other. She winked. *Winked.* And Russell prayed silently.

When Jenny finally broke away from her mother she came over to Russell and shook his hand. A small gesture, perfectly in keeping with the occasion, but for the instant her skin tightened to Russell's time froze solid for him. There was the train sighing and steaming, the grate of luggage being pushed over wood, the babble of the porter and the stationmaster, and yet for Russell it was nothing but this moment forever. He told himself he could see it for what it was: a message. By the time he left his Jenny this evening she would have heard his question, that much he knew for sure.

And sure enough, even though that moment passed into others, they were not much different. Everything seemed to go as if Russell himself had outlined the scene. Jenny talked for several minutes with her parents, talked about more things than Russell could keep track of as he helped the grumpy stationmaster hoist Jenny's three large steamer trunks onto the Democrat. And when they were loaded Jenny suggested in perfectly reasonable tones that she walk back with Russell and tell him all about Kingston and the academy while her parents hauled the luggage home. A few happy shouts by Harvey Turner, a sharp slap of the reins, and the wagon and parents were gone, leaving Russell alone with his wish.

"So tell me," Jenny said, as she took his arm in both of hers and began up the hill toward town, "what's the latest? All the details, now. You can hear *my* stories later."

Russell distinctly felt her nails scrape across his wrist, three times back and forth. He could see the conversation stretching out before them as clearly as the way home. Some gossip, some talk for talk's sake, an admission of mutual missing and then *it*, the innocent little question that would set in motion the marriage of Russell Pemberton and Janet Turner. *Mr. and Mrs. Harvey Turner of Vernon request your presence...*

But right after the gossip, right after all the little talk about who was in jail and who was sure to end up there, Jenny's conversation took a detour into unfamiliar territory for Russell. They'd just crested reservoir hill and the town was rising out of the hollow to meet them. Jenny stopped and shook free of his arm, as if he'd been the one who'd taken hers. She stared at the town.

"What's wrong?" he asked.

She smiled, smiled as if she hadn't realized he'd noticed. Russell felt confused.

"Oh nothing, Russell," she said, not convincingly, and took his arm again. "It's nothing. I'm sorry."

This time Russell stopped and shook free. "No," he said. "What is it? Something's bothering you."

She looked up at his eyes then, as if to make sure he really was Russell Pemberton. Then she turned – Russell would always remember the sound her dress made as it continued turning after she stopped – and she did something he hadn't seen her do since they'd been in public school together: pull two blades of grass from the side of the path and hand him one. Russell recalled it was timothy, a sweet-tasting grass, and he never chewed on it again after that.

"It's exactly the same as when I left," she finally said.

Russell wanted to say the right thing. Did she mean the grass? Not likely. This was far more important than that.

"What is?" he asked.

"*This*," she said, waving the grass wand-like over the town below them.

"Of course it's the same," Russell answered. He'd try and make her laugh: "You were expecting maybe Montreal?"

But Jenny didn't laugh.

"Look at it, Russell," she said. "It may as well be the day after I left."

Of course, Russell thought. That is precisely what's fine and good about a town like this. You can count on a place like this. He would try another lightener: "Cuthbert's barn burnt down."

"Oh, Russell," Jenny said, her exasperation showing. "So what if it burned down or turned into a butterfly. That's not what I mean and you know it."

"No, I don't," Russell said. "What do you mean?"

Jenny threw her grass in a short, high arc toward the town and watched it land ahead of them. Russell stopped biting his, took it out of his mouth and spun it in the fingers of both hands behind his back for several moments before discreetly dropping the blade. He heard her sigh.

"Maybe it's me that's changed," she said. "All that time away and you can't expect to fit back in as if nothing happened, can you?"

Russell didn't know why not, but he realized he should say nothing.

She continued: "I'm not so sure there's much here for me anymore, you know, Russell."

Russell looked away from her and swallowed. *I'm not so sure there's much here for me anymore.* She said that. He went over it again. Where did that leave the big question? What about him? He couldn't look back at her but he could hear her breathing, thinking almost. He looked down toward the lumber piles by the bay and picked out a fresh cut and tried to decide what it was from the distance. White pine. He thought about the grade. Number two. He puzzled over the number of board feet he could see. He figured 1,400. Maybe 1,500. For a brief moment he felt soothed.

He felt Jenny's arm on his once again, the nails along the wrist again. And he heard her voice. "Thank God I've got you, Russell," she was saying. And then she kissed him on the cheek. But by some black magic this kiss had less meaning to Russell than the handshake. It felt like a kiss from his

112

mother, but it also had a message, one that could not be missed: shelve the question.

They talked on other levels the rest of the way back to the Turner house. Jenny spoke freely and animatedly about her classes, her bookkeeping certificate, which was going to guarantee her a job, her friends—"You'd like them, Russell," she said; *I'd hate them*, he thought—and the books she'd been reading, particularly Susanna Moodie's *Roughing It in the Bush*, which she'd just have to lend him. Russell asked her if it was about camping, which made Jenny laugh, and the laugh seemed to have a settling effect on the awkward air they'd felt between them since she'd stopped upon first seeing the town.

"I'm sorry about the way I acted back there," she said as they arrived at the path leading up to the Turners' stoop.

"There's nothing to feel sorry about," he said.

She laughed. "No," she said. "I was wrong. Besides, something *has* changed."

"Uh huh," Russell said. "And what's that?"

"*You*," she said. "You smell like old Mrs. Grimes."

Before he could even blush she was gone, the door snapping shut on the remnants of her laugh. Russell stood a while outside, hoping she might come out or at least look out, but she didn't. So he went home and washed. And refused to speak to his mother for a week.

It was a constant source of wonder to Russell Pemberton how so many moments in the past were arranged in different sizes. And he could never understand how something so seemingly disconnected—the feel of his jack-knife, for example, or the taste of chokecherries—could conjure up those larger memories. And yet, while the day Jenny Turner came home from Kingston stood as clear and familiar as yesterday, there was nothing that made the next few years anything more than what they were: a time Russell Pemberton passed through and seldom saw again.

Over those years the months moved like ants at a picnic: orderly, persistent, with each one much the same as the one ahead and the one behind. And quickly. Russell and Jenny took up much as they had left off before she went away: the passionless couple. Together they were invited to parties, together they went, together they sat and talked, walked and were silent, drank tea, and laughed. In the town it was not seen as a true romance, not the way so many others were. Russell saw other romances begin, turn into gossip, turn into acceptance, turn into marriage, turn into nothing – his, however, took no turns at all. Jenny and Russell caused no giggles or knowing glances; they were, simply, a natural local occurrence, causing no more speculation or wonder than fish being found with water.

It was hardly a case of being each other's last chance, either. Jenny was an acknowledged town beauty, after all. But it was also accepted – particularly by the local bachelors who tried courting her and failed – that she wasn't much interested in any male company apart from Russell Pemberton's. And opinions – the few times they were ventured – were divided over that, some believing Russell was actually the chosen one and some believing Russell was nothing more than convenient camouflage, someone Jenny could use to hide from the local dullards while she waited for something truly fancy to come along.

As for Russell, he was certainly popular and, at least according to his mother, "a devil of a handsome man." He knew that wasn't quite true; he was, if anything, pleasant looking. But he had a good job and was dependable, and that was probably better in the long run. He also knew he had a bit of a reputation as a wit and a deserved reputation as an athlete. He was one of only three men who'd ever completed the long swim across the bay, and that had even been written up in the paper. Little wonder then that Alva Thornberry made it well known she'd be nothing short of delighted to be seen with Russell, and Tommy Lynch's little sister, Mae, was obviously tongue-tied and crimson whenever she encountered Russell at a social or in the streets.

Still, Russell would have none of it. Not until he knew for sure the full extent of his chances with Jenny. He had no doubt he loved her and would make her a fine husband. But he had grave doubts that she felt the same for him.

Ironically, his life apart from Jenny saw great progress during those years. The mill was so impressed with his grading skills that the bosses began testing Russell for possible promotion. They put him first in charge of the board pilers and work immediately picked up; they made him an assistant yard foreman and saw morale surge. The largest mill problem, however, was not in the yards, where the owners could keep strict eyes on everything. It was in the bush where the cutting and hauling were done and where the men were very much on their own. Russell was offered a five-dollar-a-week raise to foreman over a bush crew cutting near Algonquin Park in the winter of 1910-11 and he lept at the opportunity. When spring breakup came, Russell's crew had produced more board feet of good lumber per man than any bush camp before in the company's history.

It was this instant reputation that got Russell an offer from the Vernon Lumber Company in the fall of 1911. He knew without being told that the offer had been inspired by Harvey Turner, as Mr. Turner's own bush camp the winter before had been barely fifteen miles from Russell's and he had been much impressed by Russell's command of his men. For Russell it was the job dream come true and he took it without even asking what his salary would be, only to find out it was a dollar a week less than what he'd been making the year before. But he never complained. This was what he'd been waiting for, the chance to work closely with Harvey Turner, and the fact that the company wanted the two of them to supervise the logging in the timber rights Vernon Lumber held inside Algonquin Park meant that Russell would practically be working side by side with Harvey Turner. They were assigned immediately to go to Canoe Lake.

That night at the Turner house there was, in honour of Russell's new job, a celebration dinner: a large roast, corn on the cob, peas and Yorkshire pudding presided over by an expansive and enthusiastic Harvey Turner. Mrs. Turner had even baked a special cake and Jenny had a present for him, a glistening new two-bladed Sheffield steel jack-knife. There was a note as well: *To my dear friend, Russell – in case you need some help in "cutting it."* When Russell laughed and looked up from the note he saw Jenny sitting with her chin resting on her fists, smiling back proudly. He thanked her and – in what seemed like a finer present yet – Jenny suggested the two of them go for a walk. Harvey Turner agreed that this was a splendid idea and offered to help with the dishes, a gesture that caused his wife to choke on her tea.

This is my endorsement, Russell thought. *I am now a fellow worker; why not family as well?* Jenny got her coat and Russell's, and his straw skimmer, and they were off, moving down Hunter's Street toward the river, their way shown by fugitive light from the kitchens they passed. Jenny took hold of Russell's arm, as he had hoped she would. They went down past the Anglican church, the rectory, and then along the pathway to the bridge. It had rained heavily for several days before and they could hear the water boiling around the piers as they approached.

"You're going to miss all this, Russell," Jenny said.

"I'll be back in April," he said. "Maybe even out for a few days at Christmas."

"You'll be back at Christmas," she said knowingly. "My father says some of them are so stark crazy by then they're dancing with brooms."

"You forget. I've been there. I've seen them dancing with each other."

"What do you think about when you're there?" she asked.

"Think about? Oh, I don't know. How the cut's going, I suppose. What I'm going to do if the ice doesn't freeze thick enough to let the cutters through. Stuff like that."

Jenny giggled. "No, silly. That's work thinking. I mean when you're lying there trying to get to sleep."

"I never have any trouble getting to sleep."

"All right, then. When you're walking. You know, other stuff. What goes through your mind?"

Dare I, Russell wondered. If only he'd rehearsed the question as carefully as he had that night years ago. He knew he had his opening. But it closed as quickly as he saw it.

"Do you ever wonder if this is all there is for us?" she asked. "Didn't you ever want to ride down some fancy street in Toronto, and nod or not nod to the people you passed, just depending on however way you felt?"

But Russell felt he had her this time. Beaten. "Gosh, no," he said. "That'd be putting on airs."

"Not airs, Russell," she said, disappointing him. "You're just not with me. All I wanted to know was if you are perfectly satisfied with things the way they are, that's all."

"Perfectly," Russell answered with great pride and efficiency.

"That's what I figured," she said icily.

They both went quiet then, the swirl of the river rising to fill the silence. Russell went back on the conversation, hoping to sort it out, but it was already too distant and cluttered with dead ends. All he really had was her last sentence and the feeling of sadness and dissatisfaction he thought he had detected. He knew it had grown out of her wondering whether or not he was satisfied with things the way they were, and then suddenly it hit him – the opening. So perfect. So obvious. He shut his eyes. *Handed to you on a silver platter, dummy, and you almost dropped it in the river.* He opened his eyes and loudly cleared his throat.

"Well," he said, "there is one thing."

Jenny looked back from the river abruptly, almost as if she'd been standing there alone and he'd crept up on her.

"One thing what?" she asked.

"One thing I'd change," Russell said, smiling widely at her. She smiled back. "What's that?"

Russell swallowed. "You," he said, his voice on a higher pitch. "I'd change you."

She laughed, looked down the length of his buttoned coat and back up.

117

"How?" she asked.

"Make you Mrs. Russell Pemberton."

There. It was out and on its own now. Russell was glad for the lack of light. Glad, too, a dog barked while she digested what it was he had said. *Barney*, Russell thought, *I'd know that bark anywhere.* He was aware of his own warmth, aware that it all—the question, the dog barking, the river—had a sense of total familiarity. Of control. The question was out, an answer would have to come back. If you fish hard enough, his mother often said, even when he came home empty-handed, you deserve to eat.

"You surprise me, Russell," Jenny finally said, and looked back down the buttons.

Surprise, he wondered. *After all these years it's a surprise?*

"Why not?" he forced his mouth to say. "We're always together anyway. People always put us together, don't they? So why not get married?"

She moved away to the bridge railing and looked away from him. He knew what was coming.

"Please, Russell," she said. "I care for you more than anyone. You know that. You're my dearest friend."

"Well, then?" he asked. He would force it.

"It's just that it's not like *that*. Not yet, anyway."

"When then?"

"I don't know when. Maybe never."

Russell felt his anger taking over. "Christ, Jenny. We're both twenty-six years old!"

She turned quickly back to face him. "Yes, we are," she said. "And that's not even halfway, is it?"

Russell stiffened. *Now what in hell does that mean? Marry me and it all ends?* He felt like he'd like to spit. The dog barked again, its hollowness surprisingly loud across the river.

"Barney," he said.

"Yes," she said. "I thought so, too."

What happened after that was forever blurred, perceptible only—and not accurately—when Russell Pemberton tortured himself in later years by looking back on it. He knew

Jenny had bussed his cheek, for only the first time in all their years together, when he walked her to her parents' front door that evening she returned from Kingston – he was beginning to think of those two kisses as pats on the head. After Jenny's rejection he went immediately into the nearby Olympia Hotel, where several of the boys from the millyard were gathered around a long pine table covered with draft beer. They were both surprised and delighted to see Russell and it struck several of them that his appearance at the Olympia watering hole was reason enough in itself for a celebration party, and Russell knew he couldn't talk them out of it without a detailed description of precisely why he was hardly in a party mood.

After the initial order of four trays of draft, there were only pockets of recollections for Russell. He wrist-wrestled and he won. He threatened Boyd, the bartender, when Boyd began moving about the room stacking chairs for closing. He vomited on his shoes in the alley back of the Olympia.

But the memory that stung so badly came out of Gully Cavanough's dowdy little cabin on the town line. There was an exchange of money – a great deal, judging from Russell's empty billfold the next day – and there was too much dandelion wine and far too much of Cavanough's common-law wife, Hazel.

Hazel would become and remain the island in that particular sea of painful memories. Always, Hazel surfaced as a vivid and perfect memory, actually growing clearer with the years. Sometimes before he slept he'd see again her mammoth breasts, the way they wobbled like tight cow's udders when she shifted her weight. He could even smell her breath, hear her cackle, hear also the hysterical squeals of the boys in the kitchen, as if they were watching. Unless he caught the recollection and stopped it, it would fly into Russell lying atop Hazel with his pants down around his ankles and his suitcoat and vest still on, and she grunting and moaning and heaving, tossing Russell helplessly in the air over her, his head spinning and focussing in and out on the filthy bed beneath them and the matted grey wool blankets that were itching against his legs.

If he got that far he would finish out the thought. He would remember vomiting again, this time in great drawn-out and searing heaves, and he would remember wishing he was not lying there with his pants trapped around his ankles, and that he could somehow reach the knife Jenny had given him earlier that same night.

Harvey Turner and Russell Pemberton set out on October 7, 1911, in a drizzle so faint it was impossible to say whether the drops were rising or falling. To the east, however, the haze was gilt-edged with sunlight, a message of a fine day coming. For the longest time after the train pulled away north from the Vernon station, Russell leaned out of the window watching the town shrink until eventually a knoll and a quick turn erased it completely. There was only the trip ahead.

They went first to the Hemlock junction, then changed over to another, slower train of four cars, only one of them passenger, which headed down the old Ottawa, Arnprior, and Parry Sound railway route to the Canoe Lake station. By the time the station came into view the day had fully arrived, late but all the more welcome because Russell had been given the privilege of seeing it coming.

Russell never forgot his first sight of Canoe Lake. His first thought was that it made a better calendar picture than a first day of work, and he wished he could just wander off and walk with it. Not a cloud in the sky, not a wrinkle in the water. He could look out over the lake and pick out the far shoreline simply by tracing the natural fold between two identical pictures, the far shore and its reflection.

Fall colours had always been a matter of personal pride to Russell, since Vernon people maintained nothing on earth equalled theirs. But this, he had to admit, was a full step beyond. Sugar maples the colour of blood, birch like fire, tamarack as soft and yellow as cat's fur, deep red sumac, tan poplar – and all of it crocheted neatly into thick evergreen stands that seemed to roll up and beyond the horizon. One of the far hills had been recently burned out, and there were signs of logging on two of the closer ones. But Russell was a logger, and to him the burnt and worked hills were no less beautiful than the others. He thought he had never before seen a natural setting so perfect. Had he not come from Vernon he would have thought this the most beautiful place on earth. But, of course, it wasn't.

The first week passed and Russell couldn't have been happier. He missed Vernon and his mother and his friends – particularly Jenny, though he wasn't sure he could ever look her in the eye again, not after what he'd done with that, with that *whore* – but he was discovering that the bush life was as good as anything town life had to offer, and often better.

That he was only twenty-six years old and in such a position of authority naturally led to early trouble when the men started arriving. He began meeting the morning train down at the Canoe Lake station when the men were due; they were scheduled in lots up to twenty over a four-day span. Some of the older fellows thought Russell was joking when he greeted them as their camp foreman, and a couple of times he felt he was damned lucky to have had Harvey Turner standing there beside him with his sleeves rolled up and his huge fists clenched when the men started kidding. But he figured his best stroke of good fortune came on the last day of train-meeting, when six stragglers rolled off the car stinking of whiskey and barely able to stand up. Russell didn't even speak to them. He had his axe in the wagon and he walked back to get it. When he returned carrying the axe the drunken men were trying to pull their baggage turkeys out with the help of a flustered conductor, and one of the bags slipped and fell with a great crash. The men, who'd been laughing and singing up to this point, stopped dead; there wasn't a sound as a small stain grew on the canvas turkey and then began trickling out over the station platform. Russell walked up, reached down and dipped

121

his finger in the spill, put his finger to his tongue and, still not saying a word, methodically drove the flat end of his axe into all six bags, until the entire platform was glistening with the tears of spilt whiskey.

That single incident made Russell's reputation. From then on he was not only assuredly the boss, but highly admired by his men, for two of the six stragglers were known hell-raisers. As it turned out, these two eventually numbered among Russell's strongest supporters. He'd had the good sense to supply them with his own extra clothes while they waited for their own luggage to dry out enough so they could knock out the broken glass.

The men cut until just after Christmas. Russell was disappointed that he missed getting home for the holiday, but he was far too busy to brood over it. Mostly they felled birch, though also a surprising amount of white pine, thanks to a small burst in the market. The skidding gangs worked as the rest of the men cut, and the skidding was completed by the end of January. From then until spring breakup they hauled by sleigh, and Russell found this by far the most difficult and dangerous part of his job. It was his responsibility that the huge bunks of logs, some weighing more than twenty tons, were moved easily and without mishap by a small group of men and work horses.

Those mornings Russell was up long before dawn, usually checking to see how quickly the simple warmth of his thumb and forefinger could pinch off the tip of an icicle. If Russell determined there was going to be a small thaw that could work to their advantage, he'd have the horses out on the trails by the time the sun rose in the white sky. Then, once the horses' hooves had flattened the trail down tight, he'd bring out the two tanker trucks and their teams to flood the sleigh runners' tracks all afternoon. Once that froze over, they'd haul by night, the land so cold they could hear a tree crack for half a mile and had to breathe through their mouths because their nostrils kept freezing shut.

Russell thought these lonely night hauls to be the most peaceful times he'd ever known. Sometimes he'd walk along the trails after the sleighs and look up and see the Northern Lights dancing like the flicker on the edge of charcoal; the sky purple and narrow orange, shimmering like a drying sheet in the summer wind. He used to look out at the stars and try to name the constellations and even try to guess at what was out there. One clear night, when the only sound around him was the growling of his own feet on the dry snow, he saw a star shoot off and drop behind the hills to the west, and he decided then that there was indeed an awful lot more to the universe than he or any other human would ever understand. Russell vowed then, and stuck to the vow, that he would never again laugh at his mother's mutterings about spirits and grand designs. At least Abigail Pemberton had the guts to think about such things, Russell thought, and that was a whole lot more than he could say for most people.

His life in the park fell into a happy pattern. He got on well with his men and, when he saw him, famously with Harvey Turner. They met every second Sunday for a game of whist – and on the infrequent Saturdays off – and though the age difference kept the relationship somewhat formal, Russell never felt comfortable calling him "Harvey." The similarity of jobs and mannerism made them appear more father and son than casual, on-the-job friends. Having never known his own father, Russell was eager to accept Harvey Turner as a ready replacement. One day, with a little luck, they'd truly be related.

Russell's bush work ended on April 7, 1912, with the first blast of dynamite that opened up the ice at the mouth of the first creek leading back toward Vernon. Russell went home by train, back to his mother's house, back to his friends, and back to his job inspecting the lumber under the watchful eye of belligerent old Ainsley Lewis. Periodically through the coming summer he'd be sent up to the park to check on things there, perhaps blaze a new skidding trail, and come the fall he'd be back up again for the winter.

As far as Russell was concerned, his life could revolve around Vernon and Canoe Lake forever. The two finest places on God's earth, and Russell had them both.

In the year 1912, Jenny Turner was working at Miller's General Store as a bookkeeper-accountant-clerk and Russell began meeting up with her at the end of the day and walking her the short two blocks home. He wished Jenny lived a mile or two out of town, anything to make the walk last longer, but it wasn't as bad as two blocks sounded. On a nice day they'd barely manage a snail's pace home, and even on the days that weren't so nice, Russell generally ended up leaning against the railing post on one side of the porch entrance while she leaned against the other post. It never seemed they talked about anything that mattered, but it also never seemed they were stuck for things to say. And Russell was always sad when Jenny's mother would come to the door and announce that supper was ready and say "Good evening, Russell," as if that was his signal to swing off the post and head down the walk with a happy smile and a wave – which is exactly what he always did, almost every day that summer.

By now Russell was fairly content with the way things were between them. He'd resolved himself to the fact that it was a one-sided love affair, at least as far as passion was concerned, and he even sometimes wondered if his own desperate love for Jenny was fading. Sometimes he even thought of her as a sister, and he thought then he must be getting very old indeed.

One muggy August day he met her outside of Miller's. Not a breeze off the river, not a cloud in the sky.

"You'll never guess what, Russell," she said.

"What?"

"Guess. It's got something to do with Canoe Lake."

"You're going fishing."

"No."

"You've quit Miller's and you're going to become a logger."

"No," she giggled. "Get serious."

124

"Only two things you can do there, fish or cut logs. I'm afraid that's my best shot."

"Father's bought a cottage there," she said.

Russell felt faint! *The heat. No, what she had said. Surely she was joking.*

"Go on with you," he said.

"No. I'm serious. He just bought it. We'll be going up next weekend."

Lordy, Russell told himself, what more could he ever ask for? Here she was being practically *delivered* to him. She'd spend her holidays at Canoe Lake and be coming up most good weekends. All Jenny Turner had to do was see Russell Pemberton in his *real* element – bossing men, having their respect and admiration, working hard, making important decisions – hell, he wouldn't even have to do a thing. *They* would tell her for him all those things he'd prayed she'd somehow ask him about but could never figure out how to tell her himself. What a massive stroke of good fortune!

"Whose cottage?" he asked.

"Well," she said. "Nobody's really. Father says it used to be a ranger's station."

Russell started to laugh. He knew the building. Cottage be damned – it was little more than a lot of baked boards in need of oil and paint and with an attic full of squirrels' nests and bats. Christ, the floors weren't even straight.

"What's so funny?" Jenny asked, the smile on her face anxious to join in on Russell's joke.

"You'll see. You'll see."

But in the end it was Russell who had seen. When he arrived at Canoe Lake in October to begin cutting, Harvey Turner invited him down for a Sunday dinner. Mr. Turner had been working at the cottage all that month, and the rest of the family – Jenny and her mother – had come up the weekend before to help. The four of them sat down to a huge ham cooked up with brown sugar basting, cauliflower, baked potatoes, string beans, home-made relish and

125

chutney, thick, hot fresh bread, and pumpkin pie and tea for dessert. Russell had to reach under the table and loosen his belt while the women cleared off the dishes, and after dinner he'd been given the grand tour.

The first thing he noticed was that the floor was level. Mr. Turner had jacked up the front and put in new footings. There was also the smell of linseed oil in the air and he could see how the dry wood had darkened with the oil. Inside there was wallpaper, new linoleum, cleaned and replaced windows and a newly-set door and step down into a brand-new kitchen shed. From his seat in the big wicker chair in the living room he could look out past the newly oiled porch railings, past the yellowed leaves of the single poplar in front and count the deadheads bobbing up in front of Little Wapomeo Island. It was a cottage indeed.

A squirrel scratched quickly up one side of the roof and down the other.

"The squirrels?" Russell asked. "What did you do about them?"

"Smoked 'em out," Mr. Turner said.

"And the bats?"

"The *what*?" Mrs. Turner called from the kitchen.

"Come on, Russell," Jenny said quickly, removing her apron and folding it over the back of the chair nearest the box stove. "Let's take that walk now."

Russell wanted to say "What walk?" but knew better than to blow this good fortune. He jumped up, waited while Jenny pulled a light sweater over her head and burst through the other end with her hair running wildly over her face, and then opened the door for what he would come to think of as the finest single walk of his life.

They walked back up the knoll to the little hillside behind the new cottage. Russell heard all about Mrs. Turner's fear of bats and Jenny heard all about the difficulties of moving logs over the short rapids on the Little Madawaska River.

It was a rare, warm October day, with a small breeze out of the east and the air full of floating milkweed fluff. Jenny ran ahead trying to catch one, but every time she grabbed for it the gush of wind from her hand shot it further away. Russell stayed back with his hands on his hips and laughed the way he'd heard Ainsley Lewis laugh in the summer when Russell lost his balance and fell ten feet from a pile of Number One grade cherry.

He breathed deeply: a crisp mouthful, dazzling in its variety—decaying leaves, pine needles, the distant, faint smell of cut lumber, earth, mushrooms... Jenny saw the mushrooms first. She checked underneath the hat, decided something must be right about them, and picked several dozen large ones which she laid on the path and announced she would pick up on the way back.

"You seem to know your way up here, Russell," Jenny said as they came up onto the hill. Behind them Canoe Lake spread out and down past the first several points to the south. The lake, cradled by six or seven hills that this time of year looked like the fresh coals of a fire, was simply breathtaking.

"I've seen just about everything around here," Russell said. He worried that it sounded too conceited. He added: "There's something up here worth seeing." He felt better.

"What?"

"You'll see."

They came to what once had been a clearing. Now there was a single birch, not too large, a stand of white pine and a lot of new growth: tiny princess pine, seedlings, dried and yellow broken ferns, where a deer had recently lain, cedar sprigs, and several dozen foot-high hemlock.

"Over here," Russell said.

They hurried over. Jenny stopped suddenly and went wide-eyed with surprise. There, not ten paces in front of her, was a grave marking. It was solid granite, a rock rough-cut in the shape of a more formal marking, and someone had obviously spent days working on the inscription.

"In memory of Ja's Watson," it read along the top. "The first white person buried at Canoe Lake. Died May 25,

1897, being one of about 500 employed at this camp by the Gilmour Lumbering Co. Age 21 yrs."

Below that there was a cartoonish-styled hand pointing toward some verse that had been chiselled in at an awkward slant and embossed with a holly vine.

In a quiet voice, Jenny read it aloud:

Remember comrades (when passing by)
As you are now so once was I
As I am now so you shall be
Prepare thyself to follow me

When she'd finished they both stood there staring at the grave for a while. Russell thought about Watson's age. Just a kid, he told himself, probably killed in some damned fool accident that could have been prevented. Jenny thought about the loneliness of being buried in such a place. Probably, she thought, no one from his family had ever even been here. She turned and looked out over the lake with its tiny whitecaps smiling periodically. Off toward the east there were high clouds, bare wisps, soft and gently curved as gull feathers.

She turned back to Russell.

"Can you think of a finer place than this to be buried?" she asked, her voice a church whisper.

Russell thought as he'd been asked to. He thought about the Rock Hill, about the trillium patch in the reservoir, thought even about the soft grass back of the kindling pile in his mother's back yard. But he knew what answer was expected—and in actual fact wouldn't have minded this spot himself, except that he had no plans of ever dying and certainly no thoughts of actually being dead.

"No," he said softly. "I honestly can't."

Returning to pick up the mushrooms, Jenny seemed in a wistful, melancholy mood. They walked slowly, Russell with his hands behind his back, holding some leaves he'd picked for her, and Jenny with a milkweed frond in her hand, picking the tiny parachutes off one by one and releasing them from the palm of her upheld hand. And she talked. She talked about how the time had flown since they were kids together and about how poor Ja's Watson had lived an entire life in less years than they had behind them.

They arrived back at the cottage with their hands and Russell's jacket pockets bulging with mushrooms. Jenny hurried ahead inside and returned with a six-quart basket and Russell emptied his hands and pockets out.

"Why don't you come in for some tea," she said.

"That's okay," Russell said. "I've got to be getting back to the camp."

When he dumped the last mushroom out of his pocket she took it, leaned up and brushed against his lips.

"What was that for?" he asked.

"Just for being you," she said.

And then she was gone.

That first blast of dynamite the following spring, 1913, was like an alarm clock for Russell. Winter was over. Jenny would soon be up to the cottage. Again in *his* element.

Tiny freckles of earth began forming where the sun stayed longest. Russell began seeking them out, standing over them and sucking in the smell of dead leaves and pine needles as if he could gain strength from it. The larger the openings grew, the closer it was to May and the arrival of the Turners for a weekend. He began walking in the bush looking for signs of spring: an old stump ripped apart by a hungry bear, Dutchman's breeches, early Mayflowers, ants, a fresh beaver chew. At the end of April he saw a robin picking through the garbage the cook had set behind the camp. It was gone in an instant, startled by Russell's sudden arrival, but Russell had seen enough.

Spring was here.

On the third weekend of May the bull cook came back on the supply wagon and told Russell that the Turners had come up to Canoe Lake and were staying to the end of the month, opening up the cottage. Russell worked as hard as he could that Saturday to make sure he'd have the entire day free on Sunday. And on Sunday afternoon he took a bath in the big cast iron tub the cook kept to wash clothes and dish towels in, scrubbed himself head to toe with yellow Comfort soap, forced the cursing cook to pour hot pails of water over his head to rinse his hair, dressed to the nines in a borrowed white shirt and his own best pants, slapped some extra soap behind his ears and began the long walk down to the cottage, turning onto the footpath that led to Turners' and looked out over the lake.

And then he heard Jenny's laugh coming from beyond the turn ahead. He felt his heart sputter. He thought he'd lost his breath. One more corner and the winter's wait would be over!

Then he heard another laugh, this one deeper and rumbling. A man! And not Harvey Turner – that laugh he knew.

They came around the corner. Jenny was dressed completely in yellow with a matching tie in her hair. Whoever she was with was quite tall and, Russell had to admit, quite good looking with all that dark hair and those elegant features. Probably a cousin, he told himself.

"Russell!" Jenny called when she saw him. "Russell Pemberton!"

"Hi, Jenny," Russell called back, and instantly wished his voice were deeper. He thought he'd squeaked.

Jenny ran ahead to greet him. She grabbed his hands and spun about him. Russell thought she had never looked better.

"Oh, Russell," she said. "Is it ever good to see you again."

That made him feel better. He looked awkwardly at the fellow coming toward them with his pipe in his mouth and a large smile that Russell thought was composed of far too many teeth. He was all dressed up in a fancy suit with one of those short collars Russell had seen in the last newspapers he'd had around. A dandy! Russell told himself. A real dandy.

Jenny turned to the stranger. She nodded back at Russell

130

in a most serious manner, as if Russell were a great piece of horse flesh.

"Tom, I want you to meet my very dear friend Russell Pemberton," Jenny said to the man.

Russell's chest swelled. *Very dear friend!*

"Russell," she said, "meet Tom Thomson."

10

Eleanor ate an early supper in a back booth of Charlie's Restaurant, halfway up Main Street between the newspaper office and the hotel. She sat in a corner seat, a huge and hideous illustration of a moose crossing a mountain stream behind her, a massive mirror to her immediate left. Through the mirror she could watch a tiny, flat-faced man sitting on the end counter seat, who was ripping a paper into tiny pieces, licking them and placing them in his vest pocket. The restaurant owner and the counter waitress went about their work as if the peculiar little man wasn't there, even though he periodically laughed hysterically at one of his miniature scraps.

Eleanor was fascinated with the treatment of the man at the counter. The owner put a cup of coffee down without a word and the little man took it, also without a word, and when he had finished he hopped down from the stool and left, still without saying anything or appearing to pay for it. In Philadelphia he would probably be dead by now, the owner standing over the bloody little man with a smouldering handgun, calling him a thief and kicking at him. It was a difference in attitude that was difficult to measure; in North America the time zones change from east to west. Eleanor thought that wasn't quite right. Having come from Philadelphia, she knew first-hand that it was the north that awoke so much later than the south.

Eleanor ordered a coffee and a small bowl of vanilla ice cream, and while she worked through the ice cream she wondered if anyone from Vernon would ever shame themselves with psychiatry. For someone from Philadelphia it had been a relatively easy step; she had, after all, known any number of people who had turned to therapy in their darker moments. Some of them, she thought, considered their treatment to be virtually recreational. They turned to it as their friends turned to tennis or jazz, and its value was probably more social than medicinal.

She wondered what it was Dr. Klotz gave her. Certainly he wasn't the only one she could talk to, for there was Joyce, even though she seemed to shy away from the topic and shift the talk on to other things as soon as she could. What it probably gave her was, well... a hobby, an exercise, a project. Some people took night courses to better themselves; Eleanor took up her personal history. At the moment, anyway, there wasn't a great deal of sentiment involved in her search for her real mother. It was, rather, more like an assignment from Dr. Klotz. Both of them wished to one day uncover the real Eleanor Philpott – she'd delay her sentiments for that moment, if it ever came – and until then they were simply dividing up the work.

She had learned years ago not to wish too hard. Her father had made sure that was the one lesson he passed on to her. An unadventurous man himself, he was not about to let his daughter suffer the wounds of an unrestricted imagination. Once Eleanor had arranged an audience with him simply to ask if he would put up ten dollars so she could join her friend, Liz, and sign up for ballet lessons at the "Y". He called her to his den. She tiptoed in, shoulders hunched, and sat tensely on the edge of the stuffed chair opposite his desk. She tried to put her elbows up onto the chair's high arms, but the action made her feel like a little kid trying to fly and so she'd quit, tucked her hands in between her legs and asked him.

"Speak *up*, Eleanor! For heaven's sake, child, pronounce your words properly."

Eleanor had rallied and spoken again, slightly louder.

"*Dancing?*" Her father had said and rummaged his pipe around in his leather pouch, all the while staring at her until she looked back down at her knobby knees and began wishing they looked like Liz's knees, as true as bannisters.

"I think not, Eleanor," he finally said, lighting up.

"But Liz is," she said, convinced she was going to cry.

"If Liz were sick would you want to be sick as well, Eleanor?"

"No sir, but –"

"No buts. Just because Liz is doing something is no reason for you to want the same, is it?"

"No."

"Well, then. The answer is no. Ten dollars for something like that is ten dollars wasted, as far as I'm concerned. Your trouble, child, is that you're just not practical about things. And that's something you should remember: *be practical*, Eleanor. Think about it – what possible good would ballet do you twenty years from now when you'll have a husband and a family to take care of?"

Eleanor said nothing, just looked at her knees.

"Well?" her father said, his impatience edging the practiced calm of his voice.

"Nothing," Eleanor finally said, her voice barely audible above the sizzle of the pipe bowl.

Her father smiled and removed his pipe.

"Exactly. It's settled then."

Eleanor pushed herself out of the chair. She would *not* cry, she told herself. She wished him dead. She wished him worse. She walked toward the door glad only that she would at least deny him the pleasure of her tears.

"Eleanor," he said when she was at the door.

She turned. He was smiling at her in the poor light of the room.

"Any time you want to talk something over like this, you just come ahead in, okay?"

134

But that had been, as far as Eleanor could remember, the last time she had ever asked him for anything.

Not surprisingly, that was one of the very first stories she'd told Doctor Klotz. It seemed to fit into her idea of the type of thing a psychiatrist would find of some value. But he hadn't reacted with any obvious interest. She'd even looked up and back at him, as if to say "It all lies there, doesn't it?" but he wasn't even looking at her. Doctor Klotz was clipping his nails. And the rest of the interview had been tied together with a lot of Eleanor's ramblings and the steady click of the clipper.

Eleanor had been furious. She'd attempted to gather herself for an assault, wondering if she'd dare or what the penalty was for it, when suddenly Klotz began talking. A lot of it made little sense to Eleanor, as it seemed too filled with talk about repression and functional personality, but one thing stuck with her firmly. A phrase, really, just a phrase.

. . . the Eleanor that never was. . .

How bloody goddam true, Eleanor told herself when she got back to the apartment that evening and poured herself a relaxing sherry. How true, how true, how true. She was in mourning for herself, keening for the Marilyn Monroe inside that never stepped outside. No, not the Marilyn Monroe – the Eleanor Philpott.

Eleanor drove slowly back to the hotel. Past a few houses, their lower windows flashing with the blue hint of television and the light washing warm and secure out across the lawns. She still couldn't fathom what it was these people did or thought, but there was something about the town that she found remarkably seductive.

That soured slightly when she came in through the empty hotel lobby and pushed the elevator button. She looked at the indicator and saw it coming from the basement. In a moment the doors opened, and Eleanor was staring straight at a naked rear end.

She must have screamed, though she hadn't realized it or ever decided upon such action. But she must have, for in a moment the man called Archie was there, sticking his big elbow of a nose in through the doors and cursing at the bare buttocks that lay sideways, smiling up at him.

"That's it, Georgie! *That is it!*" Archie shouted. "Come on, now. Up with the pants. Up. Up. Up!"

Eleanor cringed back out of eyeview while Archie moved in and grabbed Georgie Quill around his shoulders and turned him upright. With a great grunt, he then lifted Georgie to his feet and leaned him precariously against the wall while bending down and pulling up the man's pants.

"Waaaz goin' on?" Georgie asked.

"Your pants, pal. Your pants," Archie said.

"This won't happen again, Mrs. Philpott," Archie said as he stumbled past, carrying Georgie.

"Thank you," Eleanor said, and immediately thought it was rather an odd comment for her to make.

She was about to step onto the elevator when Archie called her name anxiously. She stepped back. He hurried up to her, rubbing his hands together as if washing them, which, Eleanor supposed, he probably intended to do immediately.

"Gosh, Mrs. Philpott," he said. "We can't tell you how sorry we are about that incident."

"It's all right," she said.

"No. It's not. It won't happen again," he insisted.

She smiled at him, nodded and again took a step toward the elevator.

"Look, Mrs. Philpott," he said, still not sure she was on his side. "If there's anything I can do for you while you're here . . ."

"Well," she said. "Perhaps there is."

Archie nodded anxiously.

"Do you know a Russell Pemberton?"

"*Know* him!"

Russell had to grab the bannister at the top of the basement stairs. He looked about him at the sparks. Tiny lights, quick, close, and bright. Inside more than out. And he had no breath. None to push out, none to bring in. There was nothing but the sparking and a heavy, heavy pounding in his neck and temples.

He would wait it out. He would sit this one out as he had sat them all out in the last couple of years. Damn time-wasters, he called them, and often thought about the days when he could run straight up Rock Hill, around the top and back down in under ten minutes and with the sweat barely budding on his forehead.

The hardest part was not the wait, never the wait. The damn pounding would stop soon enough. But until that time Russell had to look like he was doing something, not just standing there in a fog like some old geezer about to kick the bucket. It unfortunately seemed to happen most when going up stairs, and Russell had noted over those times that stairways were mercilessly boring. No pictures, nothing to read, no windows, not even any interesting furniture he could pretend he was checking out the wood grain in. So he stood there helpless, unable to move or breathe, or stop the pounding.

"Russell! You got a minute?"

Russell realized that it was Archie calling. He saw him wave. A woman standing beside him. The spots were fading finally and, when he deliberately moved his chest, air flowed in. One day soon, he promised himself, he'd go see a doctor.

"Russell?" Archie repeated.

Russell moved away from the bannister.

"Yes, Archie. What is it?" he said in a loud voice that carried agitation with it. As if he'd been interrupted from something important.

Archie looked hurt. "Could you come here a minute, please?"

Russell went over to the elevator slowly, his cane echoing as it tapped on the slate flooring. He arrived and stared at the woman smiling at him – the city woman.

137

"Mrs. Philpott, this here's Russell Pemberton," Archie said. "Russell, Mrs. Philpott."

"How do you do, Mr. Pemberton. I've heard an awful lot about you."

Well, thought Russell, at least she's started on the right foot.

"Mrs. Philpott," Russell said, and bowed slightly as he always did when meeting a lady.

"Eleanor. Please," she said.

Russell decided he would deal with that later, once he'd checked her out. At least she looked all right, all clean and not too gussied up, and with the right kind of smile: loose, that was the way Russell liked it, loose, never tight, pinched, forced – Lordy, he'd known women who turned their upper lip white when they smiled.

"Could I buy you a drink by any chance, Mr. Pemberton?"

A *drink*! Russell was less than three months away from turning seventy-seven. And not once in all those years had a woman bought him a drink.

"No," he said. He concentrated on keeping his face expressionless. Then smiled: "I'll buy you one."

They sat in the lounge, in a far corner where the distant television barely whispered. Russell sat with his cane resting tight to his thigh and was glad his chair was a couple of inches higher than the wall bench she sat on, so he looked down on her. The other way around and he wouldn't have been able to talk at all. She had a gin gimlet – Russell had never heard of it, and she'd explained it in a way that didn't make him feel stupid, and he'd liked that – and Russell had a rye and Coke. A gentleman's drink, Russell commended himself, the kind of thing you drink around ladies.

"It's about Tom Thomson, Mr. Pemberton," Eleanor said eventually. "I understand you knew him quite well."

"And who told you that, pray?"

Eleanor smiled knowingly and looked at Russell as if he were kidding her.

"Oh, I have friends," she said. "Actually, your name comes up no matter who I talk to." *Well, at least that's not a lie.*

"I see," Russell said. He liked that. He wondered who.

"I'm doing some research on him," she said. Still true. "Particularly on what he did around here and in the park. I understand you knew him here."

"And there," Russell added proudly.

"Yes, of course," Eleanor said, suddenly hopeful. "Would you mind, then, if I asked you a few questions about him?"

"Tom was a man like myself or a hundred others around here in those days," Russell said. "Nothing special. 'Cept he could paint and we couldn't."

"Was he a good man? A good person, I mean."

"The very best."

They both sipped their drinks and looked at each other. Russell thought about all he could tell if he was of the mind to; Eleanor thought she was getting nowhere.

"A good outdoorsman?" Eleanor asked.

"Not so good as they'd have you believe," Russell said. It was out before he could check himself. He hadn't meant to go even this far.

"Tell me, please," she asked.

Russell sighed heavily. All right, he thought. I will, goddam it. About time this malarky came to an end anyway. He moved his cane out from between his legs and placed it on the chair beside him, a sure sign that he would be staying.

"First time I saw Tom Thomson in a canoe he was sitting in the wrong end and paddling side to side like he was slapping water bugs. He pulled out from the dock, goes in a big circle of the bay–didn't even know how to draw his canoe straight–and comes back in and tips arse-over-tea kettle, reaching with his paddle for the mooring."

Eleanor laughed appropriately. Russell licked his dry lips with three nervous flicks of his tongue. *Imagine that, me swearing in front of a lady.*

Eleanor tried flattery, hoping to urge him on. "You remember things as if they just happened yesterday," she said. "But that must have been forty years ago or more."

"Forty-eight years ago, to be precise, Mrs. Fullpot," Russell said, and he nodded proudly.

Philpott. Eleanor wanted to correct him.

Russell seemed to be drifting:

"Did he ever give you any of his paintings?" she asked.

"Yes, he did . . . gave me two or three. I always gave them back."

Russell laughed, then looked away.

"What's so funny?" Eleanor said, showing an interested smile.

"Oh, nothing, nothing," Russell said, and laughed again.

"No. Tell me. Please."

Well, Russell thought, if she must.

"I was just thinking . . . You know, one thing you must remember is that no one thought too much of his painting. Some of the guys thought he was, well, kind of 'odd', if you get what I mean. I remember we had one guy on the gang who saw him painting down by the dam one day and came back and yapped about it over supper and I told him Thomson was an artist and the lad said, 'What's that?' Can you believe that? He didn't even know what an *artist* was, so you can see the kind of place it was back then.

"Anyways, I remember this one time we were all over at his cabin and somebody had some hooch there – pardon me, some liquor – and Thomson was pretty well gone, if you know what I mean, and he had all his paintings spread around, just the little ones, and these guys got into an argument over who was going to go out and grab some kindling for the fire. Big argument. Lordy, I thought there was going to be fisticuffs over it. But Thomson he just jumps up and yells – if you'll excuse the expression – 'To hell with you all then, *here*!' – and he tosses two small paintings into the stove. You should've seen them burn, I'm telling you. Pretty as a fire as they'd been as pictures too, if you ask me."

"Did you know anybody who kept any of the pictures he gave away?" Eleanor asked.

So that was it, Russell thought. An art dealer, that's what she was. Up here trying to pull the wool over the dumb bumpkin's eyes. He'd already said far too much.

"No," he said.

"No?"

"No."

Eleanor decided to change tactics. "Are there many left from those days?"

"Pictures?" Russell asked. Hadn't she heard him?

"No, people. It was a long time ago."

"Not too many," he said, and smiled that he was the one out of that Canoe Lake group who was able to say that. "Not too many."

"But you're not the only one," Eleanor suggested.

The only one that's talking to you, Russell wanted to say. Good thing she's a woman.

"No," he said. "Not the only one, no. There're a few. Only two of us still in town, though. Miss Janet Turner and me." Russell wanted to bite his tongue off. A stupid slip, that.

Eleanor took too quick a drink and choked. Stupid, she told herself. A sure sign of nerves. She cursed the gin. She cursed her inability to come to any lasting truce with those emotions that kept betraying her. He *had* to know she already knew about *Miss* Janet Turner – Vernon was too small a town for secrets.

"Are you close to her?" she asked, desperate to get back into Russell's good books.

"She lives just up the way," Russell said, gesturing with a toss of his head.

"Still good friends?" she asked.

"The very best."

"And you were both friends with Tom Thomson?"

"Yes, both of us."

How good a friend? Eleanor wanted to ask. But if she'd read Russell Pemberton right, she didn't dare.

141

"Would you suggest I talk to her?" she asked, and was pleased with the phrasing. Perhaps the editor was wrong.

"No," Russell said, and was pleased with his phrasing. That would put an end to it right there. But when he looked at Eleanor and saw her looking back, hurt, he couldn't leave it where he should have. "It's nothing personal," he added. "It's just that she's had so many people pestering her over the years that she just says no to them all."

But none of them had my question! Eleanor wanted to shout. "I can understand that," she said instead.

Eleanor again felt a sense of loss, as if the talk were finished. Russell Pemberton made a move, but it was not to get up and excuse himself, much to Eleanor's surprise. It was instead to order another round for them.

I shouldn't have been so brusque, perhaps, Russell thought. She's a nice enough girl. Not pushy like some of those city scholars and all their high-faluting words. He'd buy her another drink and that would be the end of it.

"What's she like?" Eleanor said, when the waitress put the second drink down before her.

"As fine a woman as you'd want to meet," Russell said.

"She never married?"

"No. Never."

"She lives alone, or...?" Eleanor asked.

"All alone. Just like me."

So sad, Eleanor thought. So very, very sad. *What a difference I would have made!* Then she caught herself: perhaps she was really no one at all to this woman. No more than she was to this old man.

"No family?" Eleanor asked.

"Not here. No." Russell said. He warned himself: *put a stop to this.*

"A brother? Sister?"

"Nothing."

"Any other relatives?"

"A cousin she was close to."

"Where is this cousin?"

"Dead," Russell said. "Dead like most of all of them. She died not too long ago."

"Did she die here?" Eleanor asked.

"No," Russell said, growing increasingly uncomfortable that he could not end this. "In the States."

The States! Eleanor wondered if this was the key she was looking for.

"How did she end up there?" she asked.

Russell took a long sip from his drink. End it quickly but courteously, he ordered himself.

"Well, not that it's of any importance, but she married a doctor from there. Or from here that lived there, I should say."

"Remember his name?"

"Of course I remember his name. Doctor Ray McAllister. I knew his brother, Don. Used to be a ranger in Algonquin Park."

"So he was from here?"

"Over closer toward Ottawa. Don lived in Whitney when I knew him."

"Any idea how they ended up in the United States?" Eleanor realized she was pressing her luck here. He might wonder why all the interest in this side of the story that had nothing, absolutely nothing to do with the artist or his work.

Russell thought a long, long time. He took a sip from his drink.

"I think perhaps they met there. Yes, I do believe they did. I remember Sally was nursing in New York, and she was still there when it happened, you know in the summer of seventeen. He was an intern down there somewhere."

Eleanor reached for her drink. She tipped it over. *Maybe Philadelphia!* The drink ran over the edge and down onto the seat where Russell's cane was.

"Oh, my God! I'm sorry. I'm so sorry!" Eleanor said and scrambled after the cane.

"Don't worry," Russell said. "No harm done."

"Oh, God, I feel so stupid. Please forgive me. Please," Eleanor said as she reached for the small napkin that had sat under her glass and began dabbing uselessly at the wetness. In a moment the waitress was there with a proper cloth and the spill was forgotten. Eleanor's first reaction was to feel foolish for having done it. Her second was to resent having blurted out how sorry she was, as if she'd run over him with her car—so absolutely, irrefutably, typically Eleanor.

But all she could think about was maybe he'd interned in Philadelphia. Maybe he had connections! And while she was running it around in her mind, another drink was delivered. Eleanor took a quick drink—she needed it—and thought she'd change the subject.

"You were there that summer?" she said, swallowing hard.

"I was," Russell said. "I helped look for him." He'd trapped himself by ordering her a third drink, and he knew it. But at least she'd moved away from Janet Turner. If he had to endure more talk, at least he could relax his guard a little.

"What's your interpretation of what happened?"

"An accident," Russell said. A little too quickly he thought. His guard went back up. Still, no doubt that's the simplest answer. No one can question much on that one. It's also the one Jenny uses most often, so if it's good enough for her it would be good enough for him, too.

"What about this fight there was supposed to be in that guide's cabin?" Eleanor asked, anxious to keep the conversation going.

"I wouldn't know about that," he said, lying.

"What about the line around Thomson's ankle?"

"Simple. He fell out of his canoe, the line fell with him, and they tangled together on the way down."

"The bruise?"

Russell smiled. "He obviously smacked his head on the stern when he fell."

"But there was no water in the lungs."

"I've read that, too. But what they forget to point out is

that was never proven by any autopsy because there wasn't any done. Just the hearsay of those who found him, that's all."

"Okay then, fine, but why then did they go and bury him without the coroner being there?"

Now Russell knew he had her and could nail shut this disturbing conversation. He smiled and took a long slug of his drink, chuckling to himself as he washed the rye and Coke around his throat.

"Mrs. Philpott," he began. "This is not the city. A body that comes up after eight days in warm water is not a very pretty sight, wouldn't you say? I saw Thomson when they found him. I know only too well why they buried him so fast."

"I see," said Eleanor. "Was Miss Turner at the funeral? At the one at Canoe Lake?"

"She was, yes. I was, too. And her father and mother."

"What happened to her after..." Eleanor couldn't help herself. Too much liquor. She was going too fast and knew it.

"After?" Russell asked, his brow knitting. "She went home. Same as the rest of us."

Eleanor felt incapable of stopping her questions. They were rising to her mouth and flying out.

"But after that?" she asked, and knew she shouldn't.

"I'm afraid I don't understand you."

"Did she go away, or anything like that?"

"She went home, Mrs. Philpott. Back to Vernon, and later on to Hemlock, all three of them. It's just up the road, north."

She would have to check out Hemlock. Perhaps tomorrow, after the next round with the newspaper files. Eleanor felt she should close off her talk with Russell as gracefully as possible. She'd run out too much of her line for the moment.

She finished off the third drink. Russell, fortunately, was also finishing his second. Quitting seemed the natural thing to do. Eleanor looked at her watch as if she'd forgotten something.

"My goodness," she said. "I shouldn't be keeping you so long."

145

Russell said nothing. Agreement by silence.

"Well," she said nervously. "I'm completely worn out from my day. Do you mind if I call it a night?"

"Not at all," he said coolly.

Eleanor felt it, reacted properly by sending him an apologetic smile. "I'd like you to know how delighted I am to have found you," she added.

Russell tried to calm it, but a smile tugged at the corners of his mouth. He still didn't like all that questioning. But at least the girl had the good sense to recognize that he knew his stuff.

What she didn't realize was that he planned to take it with him, too.

11

Another evening without supper. Russell Pemberton reached down into the bottom left-hand drawer of his dresser and removed four sugar cubes, a box of digestive biscuits, and a small jar of instant coffee. He moved to the tiny sink in his room and turned on the hot water until the steam clouded the mirror above, then took the chipped mug from the soap holder, rinsed it, and filled it with the water. He sat down on the velvet pillow of the desk chair, circled a heaped spoonful of the coffee into the water, dropped in the sugar cubes, still stirring, then removed two biscuits from the package, breaking one of them.

When Russell drank coffee his hand shook, and he invariably ended up hoisting the mug only a few inches, steadying it, and then diving his mouth down into the liquid to suck huge slurps of the drink in, frequently burning the roof of his mouth. This shaking was getting worse, he told himself. It had to be the city woman.

Maybe he'd been a bit testy with her but she could never say he hadn't been polite. Still, he hadn't told her much. Not that there weren't things to be told, mind, but they were probably better off between himself and whoever or whatever it was dreamed up this loony world.

Russell settled back in his chair, stretching out his bad leg. He broke off a piece of one of the biscuits and popped it into his mouth. In a few moments it would be soft as porridge;

he'd swallow it then, without a single chew involved. He looked up at his wall, up at the only picture of Abigail Pemberton he had left, all dressed in black and staring out with clear, grey eyes that Russell had never seen duplicated on any other person. Even the camera only hinted at them.

There were other pictures as well. Russell in front of a team of horses. Russell all gussied up in Charlie Hazel's zoot suit in 1943. Russell with the group at the Canoe Lake camp. And a picture of Jenny, slightly out of focus, standing near the Joe Lake Dam with a long black skirt on, a white frilly blouse, and a huge straw hat, which she's clamping tight to her head with one hand while the wind tugs at it. She is laughing, her eyes nearly closed and her teeth seeming to fill the space on her face the eyes have abdicated. She is darkly tanned in the face and hands. She is slim, perfectly straight, proud, so very much alive... obviously taken before July 8, 1917.

Russell never really came to terms with how quickly the love affair must have happened. If his eyes had been opened to such things he would have known immediately that they were in love, right when he met Jenny and Tom coming along that path in the spring of 1913. Jenny was as courteous as could be, but she made it rather plain to Russell that she had no intention of breaking off with Tom that afternoon and going off somewhere with Russell.

"Up for a visit?" Russell had asked the man shaking his hand, desperately hoping this Thomson was either a relative or else a weekend visitor to one of the lodges. As Russell found out later Jenny had met her new friend only three days before.

"Up forever, I hope," Thomson had said. He had such a smooth voice, not loud but carrying, and along a single plane. Russell instantly envied Thomson this, for Russell's voice was unpredictable, slipping from one octave to the next and absolutely unreliable when starting out. Russell had therefore developed a habit of clearing his throat before speaking, and his mother's threats could do little to dissuade him. He cleared it now.

"Well, there's not much work around here," Russell said. This man didn't look like a logger. Or a ranger. Just a tourist.

Jenny laughed. "Tom's an artist," she said.

Russell looked confusedly at her. He'd never met an artist before. In fact, the only ones he'd even heard of had been in school: that Italian who did Mona Lisa and wrote all his notes backwards in a mirror, a few others, all Italians, all dead. This guy didn't look Italian. But certainly Russell wished him dead.

"A painter?" he asked.

Thomson nodded.

Russell looked around with a deliberately puzzled look.

"Not many people around here to paint, Mr. Thomson," he said.

"Tom," said the artist. "Tom. Just Tom. I don't paint people."

"Wildlife?" Russell said. "Animals?"

"Maybe," Thomson said, and smiled. "Mostly scenery though. Landscapes."

That gave Russell new hope. To do that he'd at least be leaving on the train. Nothing worth painting around here.

"Tom just sold a painting in Toronto, to the provincial government," Jenny said.

"Is that right?" Russell said, feeling somewhat more comfortable and reassured that there was little to worry about here. "What of?"

"A lake," Thomson said. "Not unlike this." And he gestured expansively past the poplars.

"*Sold* it?" Russell asked. *Lordy, who would want it unless they owned a cottage there?* "What for?"

"Enough," Thomson said smugly.

"Tell him, Tom," Jenny begged.

"Two hundred and fifty," Thomson said.

"What?" Russell said. Perhaps they hadn't understood his question.

149

"Two hundred and fifty *dollars*, Russell," Jenny said. "Isn't that wonderful?"

Wonderful? Russell barely made that much in the whole of last year. And for a goddam *painting?* A painting of a dumb lake? What would anybody want with that when they could have the lake itself just by looking out their window?

"I understand you know where all the big trout are in this lake, Russell," Tom said, gracefully changing the subject.

Russell looked at Jenny. She was beaming, her bright eyes jumping back and forth between the two as if she couldn't decide of whom she was proudest.

"Oh, I don't know about that," he said and looked down at his polished boots. *Polished for what?* he asked himself.

"Come on, Russell," Jenny said. "I told Tom you probably catch more trout than anyone around here. Isn't that so?"

Russell couldn't catch his grin in time.

"Well, your Dad's pretty good," he said. "But I guess I catch a few."

"I'll swap you a painting lesson for an afternoon's fishing," Tom said.

Russell was flattered. Maybe he, too, could make two hundred and fifty bucks.

"Ah," he said, "I couldn't paint. But I'll take you fishing, if you like."

"Fine," said Tom.

"Next Sunday," said Russell.

"You're on," said Tom.

They walked together, back along the trail to the Turner cottage to see how it had fared the winter – some slight heaving only, easily remedied by Harvey Turner's insertion of a carefully-measured cedar post under the kitchen floor – and then over to another cottage where they all had tea with Annie Fraser, whose husband Shannon was the proprietor of a brand new lodge called Mowat.

By afternoon's end Thomson seemed a fine enough fellow to Russell. He told them he was a farm boy and a city slicker, that he knew next to nothing about bush life, and Russell had to admire such honesty. He was somewhat surprised when the man, who seemed so strong and healthy, admitted to being a sickly child and a sufferer of weak lungs, and Jenny added, much to Russell's horror, that spending time at Canoe Lake was probably just what Tom needed to set him right. Thomson thought that a splendid idea. He went on to tell them about working in Toronto and of his great friends at Grip, the commercial art business he worked for, and how he'd have to bring his Toronto friends up to Canoe Lake so they could see it for themselves.

Russell was amazed at how much he came to know of the man so quickly. It was all Jenny's doing. In a casual, harmless way as they walked, and even as they had tea with Annie Fraser, sitting out on the verandah, Jenny kept extracting information from Thomson and it kept flowing out with no apparent bragging nor, for that matter, reluctance. And for every point Thomson told about himself, Jenny seemed to trade one about herself, or about Russell, and Russell flushed with pride when she made him the gallant hero of the Duchess story once again.

Tom and Jenny seemed, Russell later reflected, in a tremendous hurry to know everything there was to know about each other.

It took less than two weeks, thanks to Russell and the ranger Mark Robinson, for Thomson to get his canoe stroke down perfect. Soon it became a pleasure to see Tom coming across the lake on a crystal clear day, the canoe tilted dangerously into his stroking area and the bow weaving no more than a palm's width off course as he stroked deep and then quickly turned it true with his out stroke.

As for fishing, Tom was a remarkable student. He already knew quite a bit about bass habits – caught some lovely ones just off the rocks by Jenny's cottage – and had what Russell considered a fair motion with a fly rod, working the light line through his fingers well and casting in a relaxed and very high figure eight. They even had a contest one calm day

151

off the Turner dock. Russell brought a bag of wood chips from the cook's kindling box and he paddled out around the dock in the canoe and set out a dozen in a wide arc at various lengths from the dock. When he came back they tried hitting them, and Tom tapped three out of the dozen with his casts, one more than Russell. Thomson even began making his own flies, at first using gull feathers he found and painting them, later bringing up the proper feathers and ties and hooks and clamps from Toronto, enough for Russell as well, which was a generous gesture.

But it was Russell who taught Tom how to troll. He first made Tom abandon his string line and turn to wire line, something that could drop down where the big lunkers were. He showed Tom how to make his own lures out of shiny metal, how to hook up the lead, how to harness a minnow, how to set up a rhythm, a motion that would be consistent and attract the trout, and he showed him how to work a line with your knees while paddling.

One thing Russell could not teach him, but Tom had the gift anyway, and that was to be able to *sense* what the line is doing two hundred and fifty feet away from you. Russell had fished with a dozen fellows who came with good intentions and tried their best, but who could never come to understand the fine click a good lure makes as you move it slowly ahead and let it fall back. Nor could they tell the difference between silt bottom and trout nibbles, nor, sometimes, between rocks and actual bites. These were not things you could teach. Tom quite simply had a knack.

And Tom could also play a fish. Nothing panicky about him. When he felt a strike he did nothing, and Russell rarely saw that in anyone but the very best. Tom watched his brake and his line and knew instinctively when he should set his hook in the fish's mouth, and he seldom missed. Russell always believed you could tell a good fisherman even if you never saw him let his line out or work the rod; all you really needed was to see the way the fish had been hooked and how much ripping of the flesh had occurred. Tom's fish invariably were set cleanly in that fleshy little recess just inside the lower mouth, the spot Russell liked to think God made especially for fine fishermen.

With Russell working five and a half days of every week, Tom soon began leaving on solo fishing trips. But he took more than fishing gear with him. He'd pack a supply of what he called "boards," which were neatly measured and cut eight-by-ten-inch panels, and he'd return with each one painted up. He'd show them to Russell and to Jenny and they'd invariably approve, and after a while Russell had to admit that Tom had something there. They were pretty—well, not exactly pretty, but when Russell looked at them he kind of felt the way he would when he was back in Vernon and longing to be back cutting in the park: you wouldn't be able to see it exactly the way it was, but you sure could feel it the way it felt.

Jenny came up to Canoe Lake every weekend and she was obviously completely taken with Tom Thomson. And no wonder. Russell knew he was a fine-looking man, and he was certainly polite enough, but he also had an uncanny way of talking. He'd sit there and tell Jenny about their fishing trips and it would sound like no trip Russell had ever been on in his life. Tom would have animals in it, as if he were telling a children's story; he'd have the names of the plants down pat, which was something Russell could never do, but which his mother surely would have admired; and Tom would also talk about the clouds, or the way the wind whipped up the lake, or the colour of a group of ferns he found on a hill. All things Russell himself liked but he had never before thought interesting to anyone but the actual observer. Lordy, he'd always been so careful not to bore anyone with dull tales of the bush, and yet here was a guy holding everyone, Russell included, completely entranced with a subject Russell himself wouldn't dare broach.

As for the romance, it was soon evident to more than just Russell. He was over at Mowat Lodge one afternoon having a nip of whiskey with Shannon Fraser in the back shed and

Fraser said it probably wouldn't be long before Jenny snared herself a man. Russell never let on that he was hurt at all by it – what was Fraser to know? – and simply covered up by having an especially long pull at the bottle.

Russell found himself on the fringes of the romance, aware but not involved, present but not invited. It was impossible not to notice, harder though to admit to. He would be still fishing over by Wapomeo Island and hear her coy laughter float across the water the way sound will on a quiet night. He would hear Tom talking – though not be able to make it out – and Jenny's laughter would follow practically everything he said. One evening, overcome by curiosity, Russell paddled close to the shore but could see only the lantern turned low on the Turner porch. He knew they were sitting out enjoying the evening, their silence more disturbing than talk he couldn't make out. Enjoying it more than him, that was for sure, for Russell went back to the camp that night empty-handed and depressed.

For Russell, proof of the seriousness of this romance came the following winter, when Jenny was separated from Tom by 150 miles of snowbound road. But he knew she was receiving weekly letters from Tom and returned letters twice a week. By spring Russell had given up hope and, like so many others, was ready to concede an engagement announcement was due before summer.

But for some reason – almost as if he were shying away – Thomson seemed to go cool on the relationship. When he arrived, as promised, in the spring of 1914, he came with a friend, Arthur Lismer, and for three solid weeks he and Lismer camped down on Molly's Island on Smoke Lake, fishing and painting.

One thing that astonished Russell was that Tom had had his fondest wish come true. He had a backer, a Doctor James MacCallum, who he said was as fine a fellow as you'd want to meet. Tom quit his job at the printing company – an action Russell could not comprehend no matter how hard he tried – and he was setting out to make it or break it as an artist.

Jenny's reaction to this bit of news was puzzling to Russell. He'd been delighted for his friend, even if he didn't quite comprehend what it all meant. All this talk about patrons and support for the arts and complete freedom to paint – Lordy, obviously nobody was telling Tom what to paint, or else he'd have never ended up at Canoe Lake painting dead stumps and swamps. But Jenny. Well, Jenny had seemed downright put off by it all, as if MacCallum had either done something that was none of his business, or else she'd lost Tom.

Which turned out to be partially true.

For the three weeks Tom and Lismer camped down on Molly's Island they didn't come up once, despite the fact that a three-hour paddle would have brought them to the far shore of Canoe Lake, and despite the fact that Jenny and her mother went up on the train for two of the weekends to their cottage.

She was fit to be tied. Russell stopped over on the last weekend and they played some whist and Jenny ended up throwing her hand and running out of the room just because her mother trumped a trick Jenny had needed. The other two didn't say a word. They sat there while Mrs. Turner poured more tea and Russell absent-mindedly shuffled the deck, and several minutes later Jenny came back from the porch wringing her hands, and with her eyes red from rubbing, telling some ridiculous story about how she'd seen a loon dive just off the point and come up with a large perch. Russell figured she hadn't been looking at anything but her own palms.

Next thing he knew Tom was off to his new patron's cottage at Go Home Bay over on Georgian Bay. Jenny got a letter, maybe two, during this time and Tom talked of nothing but how hard he was working at Dr. MacCallum's and how one of his paintings had been sold at the Ontario Society of Artists exhibition in Toronto and he'd be happy to get the money because he was flat broke. She read the letter out loud to Russell, presumably skipping over some parts, but when she came to that section about Tom having no money he remembered her adding a rather sarcastic aside: "Broke. What a *real* pity. Most people who aren't broke have jobs, Russell, did you ever think of that?"

Tom did return to Canoe Lake in mid-August, acting as if he was just taking up where he'd left off, and certainly Jenny did the same.

From what a discouraged-again Russell could see, Jenny and Tom's courtship was back in full swing. They spent a few Sundays together in the park, particularly when the fall colours were at their height, and Tom continued to write Jenny throughout the winter.

In April 1915, Russell received a short note rather formally asking him to supper at the Turner cottage the coming Sunday. He at first took it to be a special invite aimed at himself – thinking for the moment that Tom, who Russell had noticed had a rather wandering eye, had staked out new territory – but by the time he was walking up the path to the little cottage he'd come full circle and was thinking he was walking into an official engagement announcement. So be it, he'd told himself. They'll get nothing but best wishes from me.

But it was nothing of the kind. Tom was there, all right, though not Mr. Turner, and he quite honestly could never remember seeing Jenny so excited or happy, but the big deal was a silly letter Tom had from one of his Toronto pals telling him he'd just sold *Northern River* for five hundred dollars.

"Isn't it wonderful, Russell?" Jenny asked as she knelt on a chair and leaned across the table delicately holding the letter between her thumb and forefinger.

Russell couldn't quite understand the excitement. He was making five hundred a year now, with bonuses, and no one ever gave a party for him for doing that.

"Yes," he said. "Great. Uh, what's this northern river? Some property you own?"

Jenny positively shrieked. Russell could feel himself blushing and he felt like he wanted to hit something. Tom, thank God, showed no amusement.

"The name of a painting, Russell. I did it over the winter from one of those sketches I showed you."

Five hundred dollars for something like that! Russell was impressed. He'd seen Thomson do a sketch any number of times, once right from the canoe while Russell trolled, and often it didn't seem to take him much more than ten minutes or a half-hour. Five hundred dollars for a half-hour's work! Not at all bad, thought Russell.

"Well," he said. "Congratulations."

"Thank you," said Tom. "Let's hope it isn't the last of it, eh?"

"Come," said Jenny. "Let's sit down and eat before the food gets cold."

It was a meal Russell remembered more for the conversation than for the food – which was rare for Russell, particularly rare when he ate at the Turners', where the table was usually set like a late-morning daydream – and the notable thing was that the talk of Tom's success very quickly bowed out in deference to the real subject of the day: the war.

Russell hadn't been keeping up very well. Since he'd been in the bush the Princess Pats had gone over to fight in France and Canada's own first division had also crossed the channel. More disturbing, there'd been another battle for Ypres and the week before the Germans had launched the first gas attack. The Canadian casualties had been heavy.

"Gas?" Russell asked. "How can they fight with that?"

"It doesn't rise," said Thomson. "It sinks. The Krauts just blow it over toward the trenches and it settles on the soldiers. Chokes them to death or burns them."

"God spare us," said Jenny.

"Papers say maybe as many as fifty thousand are dead," said Thomson.

"Canadians?" asked Russell.

"Canadians."

A new mood seemed to be settling over Tom. Russell had come in the door and Tom had been all smiles and teeth and flashing eyes and full of the delight of the letter. Now,

157

almost as if it had been something he'd eaten, he seemed downcast, and his eyes looked deeper and full of sorrow. Russell thought for a moment he must have lost somebody.

"Did you have anyone – know anyone over there?" he asked.

Tom looked up as if he were replaying the question.

"Me? Oh, no. It just seems so futile to me, that's all."

"Futile?" said Jenny. "What would you have us do? Sit here and do nothing, let the Krauts overrun Europe, maybe even take England?"

"No, no, no. That's not exactly what I meant," he said. "It's just that, well, those are everyday people over there fighting. Most of us know someone there. Probably none of them realizes that it isn't even in their hands."

"And what do you mean by that, pray?" Mrs. Turner asked.

"Well, it's just that what can one man do with a rifle when it's governments and industry at war."

"I don't follow you," Jenny said. "If people don't fight how else can we win the war?"

"Win? Well, it's not really a matter of winning or losing – oh, never mind. Don't get the idea I'm not for Canada or Britain, because I am. It's just that I'm not entirely sure I'm for war, if you know what I mean."

"No, Tom, I'm not sure that I do," said Jenny.

"Anybody for more tea?" asked Mrs. Turner.

Tom seemed changed from that point on. He seldom spoke of war. Actually, he hardly talked about anything. Most times Russell saw him he was sullen, sometimes downright nasty. A lot of the others around Canoe Lake quite simply didn't like him anymore, considering him sulky, arrogant, sarcastic, and moody beyond their comprehension. Russell always stood up for him, but the defence became at times harder and harder to present.

The following spring, 1916, Tom returned to Canoe Lake just before leaving for a fire ranger's job he'd applied for and been given in the north of the park. One of the local guides,

George Rowe, had a cabin on the other side of the trail away from the shoreline down by the Turners' cottage. It was late April and still snowing, and the men had retired to Rowe's cabin for some liquid warmth.

Tom was drinking quite heavily. Russell put it down to nothing important; so was everyone else drinking too much. But when the talk got around to Mark Robinson and the war – about how volunteer enlistments were falling off and how Borden might end up bringing in conscription – Tom gathered himself and Russell and a bottle of whiskey in a quiet corner and told him all about his friend Lawren Harris, who'd gone overseas as a gunnery instructor. Harris's brother had been killed in combat, and Harris had suffered a nervous breakdown. Russell had asked what a nervous breakdown was, exactly – his mind instantly jumping back to how his mother always prescribed sage for a shaking hand – and Tom had looked up from his drink and said in a very surly voice, "It's worse than death."

It struck Russell at that moment that this man barely resembled the man who'd been his friend. But Jenny, as far as he could see, never changed a bit, always seeming optimistic and gay even when Tom would float off into one of his moods. Thank God she was the one person who seemed capable of breaking him out of them, for the only times for the next many months that Russell saw the old Tom was when Jenny was around. Almost as if she had some spell over him.

There was a remarkable happening that fall when Tom came back to Canoe Lake. The Turners were up for Thanksgiving weekend, staying over two nights, and Russell was, as he fully expected, invited to supper. It was an ugly day, with a sharp wind out of the northeast and the ground still sour from the rains of the week before. But Jenny insisted on going out with Tom as soon as Russell arrived at noon on Sunday and they didn't come back until a somewhat perturbed Mrs. Turner was starting to light a coal oil lamp and set out the plates.

159

Nobody said a thing. Russell sat through the quietest meal he'd ever attended at the Turners. The turkey was excellent and he even had a second helping of dark meat and cranberries, but he had to reach before it was offered and felt uncomfortable doing so. He'd look up and Mrs. Turner would be looking at her plate and Mr. Turner out the window toward the lake.

Jenny – well, that was the strangest part of it, she was looking straight at Tom and poking her fork down into her food without even deciding where it should go. As for Tom, he was doing about the same, looking at her and sneaking smiles – something Russell would never dare do, on the chance that food might be caught in his teeth.

Russell didn't find out what it was all about until he showed up at the station to see the Turners – all in noticeably better humour – off on Monday. The rain had cleared up and the sun was doing its best to cheer up through the wind, and Russell was thinking there might be some hope yet for a break in the weather. He was trying to tell Jenny this when she practically dragged him off the platform and down toward the path.

"But the train?" he said.

"We'll hear the whistle. Never mind," she'd said. "Come on. Let's walk up toward Coulson's store."

Once they got into the shelter of the path it seemed much warmer, with what leaves as were left cutting the wind somewhat. Jenny slowed her pace and walked a while looking at her boots, as they jumped out from her dress and stepped. Russell tried to think of something to say. All this was far too strange for him. He was still confused from the previous evening's supper.

"If I tell you something will you promise to keep it absolutely to yourself?" she asked in a little girl's voice.

"Why tell me then, if you don't want people to know?" he asked mischievously.

"Because I want *you* to know, silly. Because you're perhaps my dearest friend and I've got to tell somebody."

Russell laughed.

"What is it?" he asked. "You're getting married?"

Jenny stopped, turned and looked at him incredulously. *"Who told you?"*

Russell now stopped.

"Nobody. You mean... you and Tom?"

"No, silly—George Rowe and me. For God's sake, Russell, *of course* to Tom. Who else?"

Russell fought the urge to blurt his own name out.

Instead he asked: "And when did all this come about?"

"If you'd had your eyes open you'd have seen it coming for months. We decided for sure today."

Russell hoped the sadness was not apparent. So that was what spoiled the supper: a showdown. He deliberately forced himself to smile and extend his hand, as if Jenny were a stranger and they were meeting for the first time.

"My congratulations," he said.

"Oh, don't be so formal," she said, and laughed.

Before Russell could react both of Jenny's hands had a hold on his and he was pulled forward for a quick buss on the cheek.

"You approve then?" she asked.

He looked at her, aware of how easy it would be to hurt her at this moment, to really hurt. He wondered if he wanted to.

"I approve," he said, and insisted on the handshake he had initiated.

Jenny's hands tightened around his and they looked at each other. He felt the handshake had more farewell in it than greeting.

It was a rough winter, the snow waist deep and blowing into well-disguised drifts and hidden traps. Because of the war effort manpower was down and timber demand up. Russell had never worked so hard in all his life. But for a short rest at his mother's home at Christmas, during which time he didn't even get to see Jenny, he worked in the bush straight through the winter.

161

By the end of March, with a new storm howling down the stovepipes and bouncing the lids as if the firebox were boiling not burning, and with choking smoke backing up all through the camphouse, Russell decided he had had enough. He'd grown a thick moustache and shaved it off because he'd gone two straight months with a cold – the price he paid for not taking along *everything* his mother advised – and not only couldn't he plug up the sniffling but his proud growth would freeze up in the outside cold and pinch him mercilessly. So he'd taken the moustache off. There were fights in the camp and the cook had packed it in on the first of March with a loud kicking of the unscrubbed pots. Russell himself had cooked until the replacement cook arrived and the men had snarled through every meal for nearly two weeks.

He was exhausted.

He thought he was getting bushed, as well, though he'd never actually seen anyone go out of their mind in a logging camp. But he felt it coming on.

The wolves were coming in so close to the camp area after garbage that Russell had become concerned enough to get some poison from Mark Robinson and throw it out mixed in a potful of boiled pig liver. Next morning, they found five wolves, all of them twisted up with their tongues hanging out, all caught in a hideous, frozen pose of death. One of the men had a new box camera and Russell told him to bring it out and wait around while Russell and the bull cook assembled the frozen wolves in an attack position, propping some of them up with snow chunks and branches, leaving others lying dead in the snow with beef broth spread in the snow about their heads to give the appearance of having died from crushed skulls and broken necks. Then Russell had taken his big axe and stood in the centre of the macabre assembly with the axe held threateningly over his shoulder.

While he was waiting for the cameraman to position himself properly in regard to the light, Russell looked around at what he'd just created, and even before the camera was aimed, he'd decided he'd leave camp and spend a week in town, even if it cost him his job.

Russell called on Jenny the next day and found her knitting in the living room, more Kitchener socks for the Red Cross. They talked lightly of the weather until she finished stitching in the toe, and then she went to the kitchen to brew up some tea, shoving a book in Russell's hand to keep him occupied until she returned. Russell had never seen it before. It was called *With The First Canadian Contingent* and had been published by the Canadian Field Comforts Commission in order to raise money. Russell had only a quick glance through it and wondered if this represented her view of the war. In the dozens of tiny brown photographs – not printed, really, but pasted to the pages – not a soldier had a speck of dirt on him, not one needed a shave, not a single man was injured. Even the few photographs of men in the trenches showed happy, smiling soldiers, warm and dry and full of fine meals.

The most impressive photograph of them all showed General Sir Sam Hughes, he of the misfiring rifle Russell had heard about, in full military dress – sabre, braids, medals – standing over his title, Minister of Militia and Defence, and facing his immortal address to the First Contingent of the Canadian army: ". . . the principles for which you fought are eternal."

"A fine book, isn't it, Russell?" Jenny said as she came back in with the tea pot, two cups, and the shortbread Russell loved so dearly.

"Interesting," he said.

"You should read the section on letters from the front," she said. "Incredibly moving."

Russell decided he would rather not. He'd envied the departing soldiers for the anguish they'd been able to arouse in their own families as they left, but he still knew enough to realize such melancholy pleasure would be short-lived. He remembered Tom's story about his friend Harris, and he always wondered if just being related to a war trag-

163

edy could do that to a man. And if so, then what would it do to those actually there: all that rain, mud, the noise, the nights, the terror, the gas...

"Have you heard from Tom?" he asked to change the subject.

"Of course," she said rather quickly. "He's coming up the end of this week or next, said he'd spend a day or two here and then head up to Canoe Lake, so you'll see him."

"Have you told him I know?"

Jenny handed the cup to Russell, who took it and two shortbreads, setting them along the side of his saucer. He wanted to dunk them, but his mother kept telling him to at least not do it when visiting, so he didn't.

"No, I haven't," she said. "He'd be furious."

Russell looked puzzled.

"But why? If you're going to get married you can't keep it a secret forever, you know."

Jenny shrugged and picked a shortbread for herself.

"He'd rather we just did it, it seems. He'd rather nobody knew until it was done with."

"Well, men are like that sometimes," Russell said, aware he had no idea what he was talking about. "They'd as soon not admit to something until it's over, I guess."

"He's probably just afraid of the ribbing he'd get from all his painter pals," she said, nibbling on the cake. "All that 'free spirit' talk and 'freedom to paint' and all that. Far as I'm concerned they're just running away from reality. His pal MacDonald's married and it doesn't seem to restrict him much."

Russell knew Jenny well enough to tell when she was getting down in spirits. He decided he'd rescue her by talking of cheerier subjects.

"When's the date?"

"Date?" she said absent-mindedly.

"You know – when're you going to actually tie the knot?"

Again Jenny shrugged.

"Tom keeps saying he can't be pinned down yet. He wants

to see how his sales go this year first, to see if we can afford it."

"*You've* got a job," Russell pointed out.

Jenny smiled.

"Tom says *he'll* pay the way."

"Sounds like he needs a good push to me," Russell said.

"We shall see," she said.

Russell was back at Canoe Lake three days when Tom arrived on the train. Winter was going to persist through April, it seemed, and Russell took out his axe when he got back to camp, hiked out fifty yards onto the ice, and spent thirty-five minutes hacking through eighteen inches of tightly-crystallized ice. He hardly saw a squirrel around and only the odd early crow. For the most part the month had consisted of a foggy reel of heavy cloud rolling over from the northeast, every so often shaking out a few inches of new snow.

But Tom hardly seemed to mind. He moved into Mowat Lodge, took over the upstairs bedroom on the cold east end, and proceeded to paint at a driven pace. Russell had never seen such a flurry of activity, and he took it to mean Tom was out to make money for the wedding. But though he gave his friend several openings that month, not once did Tom even hint that there was anything more between him and Jenny than good friendship.

Russell had known Tom for close to four years now, but only lately had he become fully aware of the vast personality shifts Tom was capable of going through – momentarily laughing like a child, instantly dour and nasty like a forgotten old man. But at least the dark clouds came with a stiff wind behind them and were soon gone. Tom had this grandiose plan that he was going to paint a long series on spring, maybe try to do the same scene sixty days in a row so he could demonstrate the drama of the snow running off and the buds emerging to their June fullness.

The idea fell apart after several attempts, but it was not really Tom's fault. Some days it was impossible to paint.

Cold, pin-tipped rain replaced the howling snow; mud took over pestering the feet where the ice had left off. Both Russell and Tom agreed that neither had seen the black flies so dense or the mosquitoes so organized in the years since the two of them had been coming to Canoe Lake. Nowhere was there any escape.

For a while Tom set aside his paintings to put in gardens at Mowat Lodge for the Frasers. Russell came over to help him on the day he put in the turnips and string beans, bringing a bottle of whiskey with him. The rest of the men were on the log drive, and Russell had little else to do but spend his time closing up, checking over a few new cutting areas and getting ready for his train ride back to town.

By supper time they were both pretty tight. Tom started asking Russell what his plans were for the summer and whether or not they'd get out fishing much. Russell saw it as good a chance as any to find out about the secret wedding. He wanted to hear it from Tom himself.

"So what about yourself?" he asked. "What big schemes have you got up your sleeve this year?"

At first Tom looked at him sideways, and Russell noted the tightness of his brow, almost as if Russell were some total stranger in a bar, picking a fight with him because he didn't like his looks.

"Me?" Tom said. "Well, I'd like to get out and see the Rockies, you know. Maybe do a bit of painting there for a while. I'm also going to take out a proper guide's licence this year. Maybe it'll pick up some."

Not even a hint. And the Rockies! Did he mean as a honeymoon? Russell didn't believe so. Apart from Jenny coming up one weekend and Tom going down, he hardly seemed like a man with marriage on his mind.

Another thing that worried him was that Tom seemed to be getting awfully friendly with a pretty young woman who'd come up to Mowat with her ailing husband, a Major Tom Cassidy. The Major had a spot on his lung – tuberculosis – and his doctor had prescribed a treatment that demanded the poor fellow be wrapped up in a huge officer's blanket filled with goose feathers and placed in a hammock outside in the cold all day long. His wife Daisy would stay out beside him as long as she could bear the cold, and read to him. But she had to spend at least half of her time inside getting warm, and she usually sat in the summer dining area where Tom had his paints set up.

Russell got over his worry when he happened to eavesdrop on them. It was as simple as it looked: Mrs. Cassidy asked Tom questions about painting and he answered them. She seemed intelligent, was certainly very pretty, and Tom was merely enjoying the chance to talk to someone whose only interest wasn't fishing lures or whiskey.

He even painted her up a rather exquisite vase to hold the wildflowers she was able to find. He took an old jam jar, cleaned it, and painted pussy willows all around it. It was really quite beautiful, and the young woman made sure it was full of fresh spring wildflowers each day.

But then Annie Fraser, the proprietor's wife, broke the vase. She said it was an accident, that she'd done it while cleaning, and certainly Russell had no reason not to believe her, for Annie was about as soft-hearted a person as you could wish for. But the incident threw Tom into a terrible mood. He refused to eat with them that evening. Later, he came downstairs with his Izaak Walton book and turned a chair toward the far corner of the sitting room. Russell swore there wasn't even enough light to read there.

And Tom got into one quarrel that Russell was witness to. Martin Bletcher, the sour-dispositioned German from the cottage closest to Turners' had been ranting for three years about the lunacy of going to war against Germany. Each summer since 1914 Bletcher had loudly praised America for having the wits to stay out of a fight that wasn't any of its business, and although no one ever agreed with him no one ever bothered much getting him to shut up. He was an American, after all, from Buffalo, and at the time the Americans weren't involved in the war.

167

But now they were.

Bletcher came over to Mowat Lodge one afternoon in early June just after the papers had arrived on the train telling the story of Vimy Ridge: the Canadians had done the impossible, they'd taken it, but it had cost them dearly – eleven thousand casualties. Bletcher had his pet groundhog, Digger, on a foolish little dog leash with chain leading out the first several inches from his collar so the poor thing couldn't chew through it. Bletcher put the pet up on his knee and began to tell everyone that the whole thing was a tremendous waste of time and lives, that Vimy Ridge wouldn't matter a good damn to the Germans, and wouldn't mean a thing in the end. Funny, Russell thought much later, Bletcher ended up being right about that.

It was certainly the wrong thing to say there. Major Cassidy, sitting out to the side in the hammock, all wrapped up in the blanket, had been a veteran, had actually picked up his lung spot while serving in France, and when Thomson heard Bletcher going on about the futility of fighting the Germans, something snapped. He came out through the door, grabbed Bletcher by the scruff of his neck and threw him down the steps so Bletcher skidded in the mud and fell flat on the seat of his pants. There was a hollowed-out stump at the bottom of the steps where Mrs. Fraser planted pink petunias, and Martin wrapped his arms around the stump as if everything else were sinking around him.

Russell figured that was the end of it all, but then Tom bent down and picked up the terrified groundhog by the scruff of its neck and carried it squealing and kicking past Martin and the others, past the woodpile and up the path to the main outhouse where, in full view of everyone, he opened the door, raised the seat, and dropped the helpless animal down the hole.

Martin started to whimper, but he didn't dare say anything. Instead, he shook and watched as Tom came back, wrenching the axe clean of the chopping block as he passed by the woodpile again. When Martin saw this he closed his eyes and began to sob in choking sputters. Russell didn't know what to do. He didn't think Tom would kill anyone, but then again he didn't even think Tom could ever drop an animal into an outhouse hole.

Martin wasn't about to die, however. Tom walked up, stood a moment over Bletcher to prolong the agony, and then slammed the axe into the stump just over Bletcher's head.

"All right, Martin," Tom said in a supper-table voice. "Let's see now what *you* think of the trenches."

Martin looked up, one eye open.

"What do you mean?" he asked, the terror tugging his voice back in.

But Tom was in no mood to answer him. He simply walked off down the path to the dock, hoisted his canoe into the water, steadied it, and pushed off. And after a few quick licks of his paddle Tom was gone. The only sound remaining was the muffled squealing of poor Digger.

Russell got up and walked off himself, not at all sure what to do. Like everyone else, he was speechless: this was so completely unlike Tom. He set out along the path to try and forget what had happened, but though he walked all the way up to Coulson's store by the dam he couldn't forget it: the scene stitched slowly into his mind forever with each blow of the axe. Only when the chopping stopped did Russell know Martin had worked his way through the outhouse floor to Digger's prison.

A few days later, with Tom away on a week-long fishing trip – alone, which probably meant he was painting as well – Annie Fraser started a rumour around Mowat Lodge that Russell swore neither Tom nor Jenny Turner would ever hear, at least not from him. Annie claimed she'd gone in to clean Tom's room – saying his absence gave her the chance for a proper cleaning and airing – and she had come across a letter with a Vernon postmark. Annie blushingly told Russell that she couldn't avoid the letter as it had been spread out page by page on Tom's bed. Russell had somehow managed to keep a blank face through all of this.

The letter was apparently from Jenny and in it she was insisting that Tom get back the money he'd loaned to Shannon Fraser because they'd need it for the wedding. Russell thought nothing of this, though the select few Annie also told were astonished. Some of them claimed they simply had no idea, but Russell decided they must have been blind then, not to have seen it coming. It didn't surprise him: what did surprise him was that Tom had lent Shannon Fraser money, an accusation that Shannon was having a troublesome time denying to his wife. Where, Russell had wondered, did Tom get the money in the first place?

That was an easy subject to approach with Tom. All Russell had to do was ask him how the sales were going. Tom said very well indeed, judging from what his friend Doctor MacCallum had reported, when he stopped overnight at Mowat, on his way to holiday at Highland Inn, a few miles further into the park. Then Russell came right out and asked him about Shannon and the money and Tom, miffed at first that Shannon had mentioned it, admitted it was true, that when he had ordered his own new canoe Fraser had asked him to get him a couple as well, and Fraser had promised to pay him back later. The amount Shannon Fraser owed him, he said, was about two hundred dollars, which caused Russell to whistle.

"And so far, the son of a bitch hasn't come up with it," Tom concluded.

"How badly do you need it?" Russell asked.

"Badly," Tom said, but he didn't expand on why.

Russell recognized the end of the conversation.

Russell returned to Vernon late this year, in mid-June 1917, and took up his duties grading lumber with Ainsley Lewis, who was by now so old and infirm from his drinking that it only seemed a matter of time before he would take over from him entirely. But that would mean giving up forever his split life between the lumber yard in the town and the timber cuts in the park. When he thought about that Russell made mental lists: more money, prestige, security in town; no more park, no more Canoe Lake, no more clear winter nights in the bush. And he decided that he hoped Ainsley Lewis lasted at least a few more years. He wouldn't change his life as it was right now if he could avoid it. Unless, of course, he could add a certain somebody to it. But he couldn't, and he knew it.

Amidst a great furor, Prime Minister Borden introduced his conscription bill, but still Russell had no inclination to volunteer, as many of the millhands were doing. If they want me bad enough, he decided, they'll have to come and get me. He'd at least wait until conscription became law.

Yet Russell's attitude was best kept silent, as the town was still falling head over heels over Corporal Rodney Furness. Furness had come home earlier in the spring without his right arm. Not a person didn't know the story: shelled in France, his arm ripped clean off, and the buddy beside him knocked cold by a blow in the head. Furness had carried his unconscious pal two miles using his one good arm and his teeth, his bloody right stump hideously tracing their retreat in blood. He was Vernon's first great war hero: a handsome, friendly lad who spoke politely to everyone and was worshipped by the younger men and kids around town. But all Russell could think of was that Corporal Furness was nineteen years old and had no arm.

He saw little of Jenny in those days. With the mill short of help he was working long hours. When he had any time off, he found he was too exhausted to use it any way but wisely.

Russell did see her, however, toward the end of June, just before she was about to take off for her holiday at the lake. She was helping her mother pack when he came over, and Mrs. Turner seemed delighted with the chance to escape the hot town for a while. Jenny had other reasons to be excited.

"Tom's reserved a cabin at Billy Bear for us in the fall, Russell," she whispered, when her mother went upstairs for some last minute packing. "Isn't that swell? You know Billy Bear, out past Limberlost..."

"Yes, yes, I know it. Great place. For your honeymoon, eh?"

"Of course, silly. We'll probably get married here. We'll want you for best man, I'm sure."

Russell swallowed. He looked out the window and over the deep grass toward Stevenson's photograph studio. Why hadn't Tom mentioned anything to him? Why was Tom being so silent about it all?

"When do you figure on announcing it officially?" Russell asked.

"Mother has this bee in her bonnet about doing it Saturday night, at the party at Mowat Lodge. Sounds dreadfully formal to me."

Russell smiled. "How's it sound to Tom?"

"He doesn't know yet. I'll tell him when I get there, I suppose."

On Saturday morning of the long weekend Russell caught the early train out of Vernon and arrived at Canoe Lake around nine o'clock. He took his old shortcut to the Turner cottage, wading through the high grass and raspberry bushes of his neglected trail, and arriving at the back door with his pants soaked from the knees down with heavy dew. Rather than knock and be seen in such an undignified state, he decided instead to spend a half-hour drying on Hayhurst's dock, just off the point, where the morning sun fell earlier than it did on the heavily-shaded Turner dock. It was here that he first realized he had forgotten completely about the Canoe Lake Regatta.

Sunday was July 1, 1917, Canada's fiftieth birthday, and since no one would dare suggest a competition on a holiday, the anniversary regatta had been set for Saturday, the last day in June. Russell could see craft already in the water: the two row boats from Mowat anchoring buoys for the canoe races and a half-dozen or more canoes setting cedar bough and wildflower floats for the parade to follow. Russell realized he couldn't have picked a worse place for his pants to dry off in privacy.

"Russell!"

He heard the call but couldn't place it. He looked down toward the narrows but the glint of the sun on the water made it impossible to make out anything other than the trace of morning.

"Hey, Russell!"

It came from there all right. Something flashed like a mirror: a wet paddle, raised. Tom's signal.

Russell waved back and squinted, saw the canoe move out of the sun line and swing in a slow, graceful arc toward the Hayhurst dock where he stood. He recognized the stroke before the face, the deep pull, and the shoulder shift into a J-stroke. Between the gunnel on the paddle side and the water there couldn't have been more than three inches. Tom's impress-the-tourists stroke. Russell shook his head and spit.

"About time you got here," Tom called as he approached the dock. He was smiling widely and was already brown as a berry. He looked like the Tom of 1913 and 1914, the same orchard-raiding glint, the same astonishment with everyday life. Perhaps his depression had lifted for good.

"I'm not like you," Russell called back. "I got a job."

Tom slapped his paddle down hard on the water, sending a wide wing of water up and across Russell's already wet pants. This time, though, the soaking was somewhat higher.

The two of them looked where the spray had struck and Tom roared. "That train have no washroom facilities?"

Russell didn't know what to do: laugh or cover himself. There was an oar on the dock. He grabbed it and reached out and into the docking canoe so the blade of the oar set firmly between the front thwart and the gunnel. He gave the oar a gentle prod and by the time the vibration hit Tom in the stern it nearly dumped him overboard.

"Hey!" Tom shouted, genuinely worried. "Not with all my clothes on!"

173

"Tit for tat," Russell said and gave another push.

Tom reached out for the dock frantically, catching the end of the diving board.

"For Christ's sake, Russell. We'll both be in soon enough anyway."

Russell pulled back.

"And what does that mean, pray?"

Tom looked up, his confidence rising with the sureness of his grip on the board.

"The Cedar Point swim," Tom said, looking puzzled at Russell. "Looks like it's going to be between you 'n' me."

"What's between you 'n' me?"

"The race, for Christ's sake."

"I never entered any race," Russell protested.

Tom looked up at Russell as if he were seeing him for the first time.

"Well, somebody put you down for it."

"Are you set, gentlemen?" Shannon Fraser's voice barked through the makeshift megaphone.

Russell looked down at his knees. Odd the way they folded in a smile when he leaned over this way. He could see the frayed edge of the leggings, grey on black, and could feel also the way the huge bathing suit—Shannon's—sagged out from his chest and stomach. Russell felt he was in a shell, which was at least a change from a trap, which is where he knew Jenny had put him earlier in the afternoon as she stood over the pots of soaking beans and tried to slough a grin off into the wooden ladle she was carrying. She'd signed him up for this foolish event; he knew that without asking.

He looked down the length of the dock from his crouching position at the diving-board end. Tom was at the far end, head down and arms pointed out as if he were afraid to get close to his praying. Martin Bletcher was beside Tom. Perhaps, Russell thought, Tom will get so distracted by his opportunity to drown Martin that he'll forget about me. Surely, there were no other serious challengers to him.

174

Martin was barely past the dog-paddle stage. Taylor Statten was too gangly. The big tourist from the lodge was obviously more floater than swimmer, and the two kids from down the east shore were short of breath already, judging by the way their rib cages shook as they waited. No, sir – this was definitely going to be between Russell Pemberton and Tom Thomson. And Russell had no doubt as to the winner.

"Ready!" Fraser shouted.

"*Go!*"

Russell pushed out with his legs, then his toes, and felt another measure of time receive him. There were the shouts, fading; the long and graceful slip through air; and the inevitable opening up and shock of the water itself. And the silence – no, the forgotten sounds of being underwater; low, thick sounds that began within and stayed within, sounds with no direction. He kicked hard and opened his eyes. Below were the aimless wanderings of clams, a glint of a can, then the dropoff into black silt and hell-bound branches. This was the only way to enter the water – straight in, without rehearsal. Russell knew why river baptisms worked. People mistook the utter shock and sudden water for the Lord Himself. It was a feeling so instantly alien that they automatically had to know from where it came, and looked up, where they were told to, rather than upstream, where they should.

He surfaced to shouts. He could hear his name, Tom's, even Martin's. He listened for Jenny but either couldn't hear her or didn't want to hear her. He shifted over into a side-stroke and surveyed the competition: Martin in a panic to keep up, the kids already falling behind, Taylor Statten with an early advantage, thanks to his long dive, and Tom up ahead of Shannon sending up a great, challenging foam. Tom was doing the crawl, though, and couldn't see Russell. Foolish, Russell thought; the secret is in the pacing.

It was warm water for the end of June and after a while Russell rolled over onto his back, let his hands drift along his sides, and moved by footpower alone while he watched the

175

clouds. With both ears under the water now he could hear his own breathing, deep, gritty snores that were coming from everywhere else but within himself. He thought of weeds and how they could startle him if he slid across one as he swam; he thought of leeches and how they frightened him sometimes; and of snapping turtles and how they terrified him. And he had no sooner laughed at how foolish such imaginations were than he had scared himself with the thinking, and so rolled back over and went into a thrashing crawl.

He left Martin, who was beginning to tire and grunt for breath. He passed Statten who was making great churning motions and getting nowhere. He went into a breast-stroke and looked for Tom. For a long while he couldn't locate him.

And then, far ahead and already through his turn at the point, there was Tom. *Swimming back at Russell*. Tom was still in the same long, powerful crawl-stroke that Russell had seen him using at the start. Russell floundered for a moment, sputtered, then went into his own high, deep overhand-stroke and tripled his kicking pace. Every third stroke he looked up, astonished at how fast the two of them were closing the gap between them. He could hear Tom coming: on every held breath of Russell's he could hear Tom gulping for more air.

Then, in an instant, they passed, and Russell distinctly heard Tom's laugh.

Not in front of Jenny, you don't. Russell steeled himself to the thought. He dug in deeper, faster, gauged the distance to the deadhead at the turning point, dived, somersaulted and kicked off it, surfacing a good ten yards closer to the dock finish line. He heard the tail end of George Rowe's call to shore that Russell had actually touched the deadhead. And he heard the cheer that followed.

The cheer was like a burst of oxygen. Russell began breathing only every fourth stroke and upped his kick even faster. Each time he came up he measured Tom's distance. Fifty yards... four strokes... forty-five... four strokes... forty... thirty... twenty. He could hear the cheering grow, could hear his name rising with Tom's as if the two words were waging a separate battle above.

He looked at the dock, now completely loaded with people. He could make out faces: Harvey Turner's, Shannon Fraser's, and he knew that to be this close meant Tom was all the closer and would soon be touching. He knew what his mother would say – no one ever failed by trying – and decided to give a final burst. For himself, if nothing else.

Suddenly he was even with Tom, then past him. Impossible, Russell thought. He actually leaned back to see and only then realized. *Tom was in trouble*.

There were still shouts in the air. But with a different edge: fear. Russell turned back.

"*I've got a cramp!*" Tom screamed.

"Keep still!" Russell shouted at him and reached out.

Tom knocked his hand away.

Russell reached again. Tom hit him away again, then smashed Russell's face, one of his fingers landing square in Russell's eye. It felt like a match bursting.

"*Let me help you!*" Russell shouted.

He reached and coiled an arm around Tom's neck, turning him so Russell had the advantage of seeing what was happening. Tom's legs seemed to be knotted up: he had them crossed baby-fashion and drawn up tight to his stomach. Russell got a firm grip on the neck and turned Tom onto his back so his arms flailed out behind them, and Russell dragged him the few feet to the drop off where he got his footing and there were others wading in to help. He passed Tom to them, then sagged face first into the water.

From water to hands to the dock – it all meant nothing. There was only the pain in his eye. Someone placed a handkerchief onto it, Russell grabbed it, pressed it even tighter and stood up.

"For God's sake, Russell!" Shannon Fraser's voice burst into his ear. He could feel Fraser's breath against his cheek. "Stay lying down, will you?"

"I've got to see Tom," Russell said.

"He's all right."

"I've got to see."

Russell found himself pushing through the crowd on the dock, heading instinctively to the circle formed around the shore. He pushed through. Tom was lying there resting on one elbow, his head down, and his breath coming in chokes. He looked up, then hustled to his feet despite the hands that were trying to tell him to stay there.

Russell reached out and grabbed his shoulder. Tom shook it off. He looked at Russell. Russell looked back, confused and unable to read the mood.

"Sorry about your eye," Tom said coolly.

Russell started to say that it was all right, that he was just happy he was still alive, when Tom pushed past him and wedged through the still-startled crowd. No one said a word: they turned and they watched as Thomson walked up the path and over toward Mowat Lodge.

Russell could hear the water dripping between his legs onto the ground and could feel it trickle down his leg. And he suddenly felt very, very tired.

He could sense Shannon Fraser was beside him again. "It's a good thing that lad's full of himself," Fraser said in disgust. "God knows there's nothing else there."

Russell could feel Fraser's hand on his shoulder. He moved away intentionally, so the hand fell. Right now, he didn't want anything to touch him.

That wasn't quite true, of course. Had it been Jenny Turner's hand he would not have shaken it off. But he'd looked for Jenny and hadn't seen her. Her mother was there, though, and was quick to tell Russell to get some iodine on the scrape below his eye. A simple look of concern from Jenny would have been far more medicinal than any iodine, he felt, but in the end had to settle for the iodine. Mrs. Turner took him over to her kitchen for the annointing and he expected to find Jenny there, but she wasn't. She must have followed Tom to the lodge. For a few moments, while Mrs. Turner was rummaging through her medicine cabinet,

Russell allowed himself a single, wicked thought – what if he'd been unable to save Tom? – but the thought vanished with the first burn of the iodine. Just as it deserved to.

He didn't see Jenny until that night. Russell arrived at Mowat Lodge with a swollen, blue shiner. She was in the kitchen putting cookies out on the platters and making the tea, and wouldn't even look up when Russell peeked in and tapped on the door frame to get her attention. He thought she hadn't heard him and was about to call her name out when he felt a sharp tug at his sleeve. He turned around quickly, noting the cautionary finger of Harvey Turner as it pressed to his mouth. Mr. Turner signalled Russell to follow him and they walked out onto the front porch and stood in the moonlight.

"Tom hasn't shown," Mr. Turner said simply.

"Maybe he's not recovered yet," Russell ventured.

"He was well enough to be seen paddling up toward Little Joe Lake around supper."

Russell shrugged, unsure what to say. "He'll be back."

"Not tonight," Mr. Turner said. "He had all his gear with him."

"Who saw him?"

"George. He was fishing up there."

"Oh." It was settled then.

"There'll be no announcement," Mr. Turner said, looking out toward the lake and the moon. "You haven't mentioned it to anyone, have you?"

"No, of course not."

"Good."

For a while they both stood looking out over the lake, almost as if they were unaware the other was there. Russell watched a blue cloud skid over the moon and vanish in the black to the east.

"No announcement ever?" Russell finally asked.

Harvey Turner coughed. "Not tonight anyway. I'm sorry about what happened today, son. It's been rough on you."

Russell said nothing.

"Sometimes I wish it was you, not him, you know."

Again Russell said nothing. What was there to say? He simply nodded, afraid he was going to cry if he stayed around talking. He took a step down off the porch, then another and soon he found himself walking away from the sounds of the dance, the laughing and the violin tuning and the ringing of spoons on saucers. The further he moved away from it the further he wanted to be away from it.

There was someone on the path up ahead. Whoever it was stood motionless, tucked into the tree break, where the lake had eaten in under the roots. Hoping he hadn't been heard, Russell stopped and stared at the shadow, wondering who it was and what they were up to. He smelled something. Perfume. Jenny's perfume. She had just passed by this way. He stopped breathing, unsure what to do now. Turn and leave? Call?

It was much too dark for him to see her well, but he could hear, and there was no difficulty distinguishing sobs from the chatter of the lake playing around the roots. Jenny seemed to be muffling the sound, trapping it, and knowing she was struggling only made the thought all the more painful to Russell. He knew why she was crying – the engagement, so certain this afternoon, had vanished with Tom. Where had he gone? *Why?* Russell felt a sudden urge to hurt Tom. Then he wondered if it all wasn't partly his fault, as well. He hadn't had to press him so hard; Russell had caused him to cramp up by trying too hard. And what did the race mean to Russell? Nothing. He should have let Tom win and then everything would have been all right. What was he out to prove by making a fool of Tom? It wasn't Russell's day. It was Tom and Jenny's. And he had ruined it.

His eyes burned now with something apart from Tom's bruise. He tried to swallow but that hurt too. He waited until she was completely finished, afraid even to pull out his handkerchief for fear it might cause her to notice him. He didn't want her to know he was weak, that he, Russell Pemberton, was crying as well.

180

12

For breakfast Eleanor had only a cold Danish and black coffee. She ate quickly, thinking less of the food than what she might find this morning at the newspaper office. It was a bitterly cold day, the clouds high and without threat, though she passed a score or more drifting, lonely snowflakes as she hurried down Main Street. Inside the newspaper office it was warm and busy, deadline day, and the editor was tied up with the layout of the front page. A note had been left at the front desk: Eleanor was to go ahead on her own.

She knew what she wanted. The local coverage from May 1917 to early 1918 wasn't likely to make any references to out-of-wedlock births, but right now she needed only to recreate the death of Thomson and Janet Turner's movements in the following months. Eleanor was building a case; the first evidence would be circumstantial – if there was to be any at all.

The binders weren't in order. She found 1917 between 1941 and 1953. But there was little to encourage her. The first mention worth noting came under the Hemlock section – *that name, Hemlock, yet again* – and was tucked in with all the visits and sicknesses and the skunk under the Catholic church steps. ". . . met his death in some unknown manner about 10 days ago, and his body was found on Sunday. An inquest will be held."

The next mention came on July 26: "Strange to say, prior to his arrival the body had been buried, and it was his unpleasant task to exhume it"–the story far more concerned with the undertaker, Churchill, than with Thomson, about whom the paper said only that he was "about forty-two years of age" and that the "deceased was well-known by several in Vernon." No mention of any engagement; nothing at all about Janet Turner.

Eleanor placed the so-called pregnancy in its proper context. From what Eleanor could recall, clothes were loosely worn during the First World War years, but with fairly tight waists. Say she was pregnant in May or June, then it would be expected to show up by four months, which meant that by October and November it would have been a difficult thing to disguise. An impossible thing to disguise. Rumour would have had to be fact by then.

Eleanor was beginning to lose hope, drifting through the remainder of 1917 as if she were sleeping. Then, in October, Janet Turner's name came up.

She was off for a prolonged train journey, up into northern Ontario. And a few weeks later Eleanor discovered in the personals column that she had visited a Mrs. John Barkley in New Liskeard, a Mrs. Boone in Haileybury, and a Miss Wilma Burford in North Bay, who was reportedly seriously ill. Still, Eleanor took very little from this information: it was perfectly natural for Janet Turner to go off somewhere, after what she'd been through. It wouldn't necessarily have been to disguise a pregnancy.

She turned to the November 14 issue of the paper.

"On November 8, 1917, a Thursday, Mrs. Harvey Turner and daughter Janet left on a prolonged holiday to the United States!"

Eleanor sat down. She took out of her purse, first a barbiturate, which she gulped down without water, then a cigarette, which she lit and dragged on with shaking hands, blowing the smoke in long trailers into the ceiling lights and trying to gather herself.

Hope again!

She must now concentrate on finding out where they went and how long they stayed.

She finished out the year. With each new week she held her breath as she ran a blackening finger down the personals column.

Nothing!

Not a mention. In all likelihood they had not returned home, as the town personal items seemed to mention even trivial happenings: a cold, a cut finger, a visitor from a town just down the highway. Surely it would have said whether Mrs. Harvey Turner and daughter Janet were back. And where they had been.

Philadelphia?

She put 1917 back on the shelf and looked for 1918. Not on the left-hand shelf. Not on the right. She rechecked the left, then the right.

It was not there.

She shoved her note pad back into her purse, picked it and her coat up, and raced upstairs. The editor met her just on the other side of the door.

"Mrs. Philpott! Just on my way down to see you."

Eleanor smiled, her anxiety hidden. "And I to see you," she said.

"Something wrong?" the editor asked. He had seen through her smile.

"Well — I'm afraid I can't find 1918 in the files."

The editor showed no surprise at all. "I'm afraid the files aren't in very good shape," he apologized.

"It wouldn't be anywhere else?" Eleanor asked.

The editor shrugged. "I'll look. Perhaps... but he was dead by then, you realize."

Eleanor nodded.

"But you want to look through 1918."

"Yes."

"What's it all about?" he asked. If he was suspicious, Eleanor thought he hid it well.

"Well," she said. "I'm interested in Janet Turner as well."

The editor smiled knowingly. "I guessed as much," he said. "Try Russell Pemberton yet?"

"As a matter of fact, yes."

"Funny old duck, eh?"

Eleanor knew she didn't need to say anything.

"Russell knows if anybody knows," the editor said. "I mentioned the suicide theory to you the other day, didn't I? About Thomson getting a girl pregnant?"

"Yes."

"I don't buy it myself. You have to expect that a small town like this would have a few stories like that, especially with him being so famous. But don't make the mistake of believing any of it. A fancy theory, but one big problem."

"What's that?" Eleanor said, responding to the cue.

The editor smiled, slapped his palms against his huge chest. "No baby."

"Of course."

The editor looked at his watch. "Deadlines, deadlines, deadlines. Look, I promise you we'll scout around for that year. Might turn up, might not. You've got some other leads to follow?"

Eleanor said she did indeed and the editor excused himself by wishing her luck. She would need that, and more, for it was becoming more and more apparent that the truth, if it lay anywhere, was neither in books nor newspapers. Only two people might confirm it – Russell Pemberton or Janet Turner – and she knew better than to count on the old man. As for Miss Turner herself, Eleanor knew it would not be a case of going to her and asking her. It would, rather, be going and *telling* her. Then waiting for the reaction.

The best idea, given that 1918 was nowhere to be found, would be to go investigate this place called Hemlock. There was always the chance that someone there might be able to help. If Eleanor could establish that Janet Turner had arrived in Hemlock to live prior to February 26, 1918, the day of

Eleanor's birth in Philadelphia, then she would know that Janet Turner was not her mother.

Charming, this road into Hemlock. Eleanor was unused to highways that required concentration. It slowed her down considerably, forced her to observe. Tiny little houses squeezed onto lots someone had taken the time to wrestle out of the bush; the hanging laundries stretching out toward the bushline; the women out splitting wood; everyone turning to watch her pass by. The engine knock, she told herself, they can hear me coming for a mile. Her car looked little better than the ones she saw abandoned in the clearings back of the false-brick houses, weeds partying under the propped-up hood where the engines had once been. May you soon join them, she said aloud to the old Chevrolet.

Eleanor couldn't be sure what to look for in Hemlock. It was a pretty enough town, to be sure. Make that a village; Vernon was barely a town and probably had close to ten people for every one Hemlock could produce. Eleanor thought Hemlock looked like something out of Rudy's Ottawa Valley memories, something that couldn't, or shouldn't, exist now. But it did. And it was beautiful, cradled into a river bend, as if the river were charged with keeping time from crossing over.

It had only taken her forty minutes to drive up from Vernon, and she hadn't driven fast. She found herself in Hemlock too quickly, unprepared, but knew there was nothing for her to do but ask. She had no names, no hope of even guessing.

She struck gold on her first try, selecting, for some reason, the older looking of the two stores, a white clapboard building, with workshirts and shotgun shells in the window, and a massive Pepsi door push. She walked in and a bell rang, startling her. She looked up and realized that the bell was attached to the door. A friendly-looking woman – too young, was Eleanor's first thought – came bustling through, her bulk squeezing through the narrowness between the wall and the desk shelves near the front. She was carrying knitting, purling as she walked. Heavy, but with a remarkable air of good health to her.

"Hello," she said, and Eleanor instantly knew from the cautious tone that the woman had hardly expected to find a stranger calling, on a Friday, in November.

"Hello," Eleanor said, and was surprised that her own voice sounded so sure.

"Can I help you, ma'am?" the woman asked. She hustled the yarn and needles into the pull-out drawer by the register.

"Well," said Eleanor, looking about the store. "I certainly hope so."

"We haven't got much in, I'm afraid," the woman said, following Eleanor's glance. "No use carrying too much this time of year, you know, with the tourists all gone, and all that."

"Well, actually, I don't really want to buy anything," Eleanor said. *Am I doing it right?* she wondered. *Should I maybe buy something first and ask later as an afterthought?* She smiled: "I'm really looking for some information."

The woman relaxed, rather than becoming suspicious, and this puzzled Eleanor.

"Yes?" the woman said. Eleanor felt she was being encouraged.

"It goes back a long way," Eleanor cautioned.

"So do I," said the woman. "And after that there's always my mother."

"Between 1918 and, oh, 1931? . . ."

The woman smiled. "I cover part of that," she said. "I won't tell you how much."

Eleanor felt a warmth from the woman. *Why aren't they ever this way in the city?*

"Ever hear of a woman called Janet Turner?" Eleanor asked, figuring there was no reason to sneak up on it with a woman like this.

186

"Tom Thomson's girlfriend?" the woman asked.

Eleanor nodded, aware that her excitement was racing up from her heart. She would fight it off.

"Oh," said the woman. "I only knew her to see her – still know her, I should say, 'cause she still comes up once in a while, though she didn't look none too good last time, last summer . . . or the summer before. Anyways, I only know her as a person who used to be around here. Probably haven't spoken two dozen words to her in my life."

"Your mother?" Eleanor asked.

"My mother knows her well," the woman said. "Very well. I was just thinking there that mother was saying she should write her, you know, get in touch to see if she's all right, eh? She *is* all right, isn't she?"

Eleanor smiled.

"She's fine."

"You know her then?" the woman asked.

"No. Not well anyway."

The strange smile returned to the woman.

"Would you like it if I called my mother and asked her to come over?"

"Very much," Eleanor said. "Thank you very much."

"Oh, Miss Turner was very, *very* respected around here," the old woman said, as she and Eleanor marched down the main road toward the west. "Marched" was the only word for it; Eleanor had never seen a person so old move so deliberately; long, fluid strides, with the arms swinging out and away with clenched fists. Eleanor was puffing, double-stepping to keep up, trying not to let it show. She knew she must have appeared an awkward contrast to the old lady, so obviously city compared to her companion's men's woollen pants, heavy boots, and ski jacket dappled with cigarette burns. The old lady smoked as she walked, never taking the cigarette from her mouth, and she made curious clicking sounds with her false plate as she sucked on it.

187

"Here's where she lived," the old lady said, swinging off the main road and onto a dead-end street leading down to the river edge.

"Nice house," said Eleanor, looking at the white frame house with its neat hedge and tiny holders set in along the porch railing for summer potted plants.

"Not there," the old lady said. "This here is a new house. Miss Turner lived here when it was a string of wooden frame houses; they had one floor of a half house, rickety old place, I know, because my husband and I lived in the other half for over a year. Drafts, you wouldn't believe the drafts, Mrs. uhh..."

"Philpott."

"Philpott. This here was where they used to pile slabs and down there a bit is where Sheffield's had their mill. That's where she worked, of course."

"...As?" Eleanor asked.

The old lady laughed, a long, modulated cackle.

"As everything. People used to say Janet Turner ran things here. Did everything but fell the trees. She paid the wages, kept the time, kept the books, you know, ran the office end of it pretty well."

"How did the workers treat her?"

"Oh, just fine, fine. You could count on Miss Turner, you know. Her word was good as gold. And she didn't mince words, either. You always knew where you stood with Miss Turner."

How unlike myself, Eleanor thought.

"Was she well-liked in Hemlock?" Eleanor asked.

"Popular you mean?" said the old lady. "No, not really popular. She was very proper, if you know what I mean. Not one to skip about, so to speak. She went to church and played some euchre and she belonged to the women's institute. But she was respected more than popular. Very respected. My goodness, her own boss came in to work one day three sheets to the wind–"

"Pardon?"

188

"Tight, you know. And she jumped up and sent him packing straight home and said if he ever came in like that again she'd quit on him."

"And?"

"Well, he never did, of course."

"Why did she go back to Vernon, then?"

Again the old lady laughed.

"Mill closed down, that's why. That's always why. Look out over there, eh? Will you?"

Eleanor's eyes followed the old lady's bent finger to a point where the river widened and looked more like a lake. She could see bullrushes, beige and grey now, and leafless poplars, and what looked like old foundations and an ancient dock.

"Hard to believe that used to be a fine, big mill with steam pouring out of it, isn't it? Before that there was a chair factory there, dang fine chairs, too, with hickory ribs and good maple seats. Gone, though, just like the mill."

Eleanor wanted to haul her back.

"What about the houses? What happened there?"

"Burned down," said the old lady. "Burned down in... 1921, same year my first baby was born. Janet and her parents were lucky to get out you know. The Wheelers were living in the part we had then and they lost four. Terrible fire. Lots of fires in this town."

"They lost everything?" Eleanor asked.

"Lost enough," the old lady said. "They got some things out. Valuables and that."

The paintings! Were they there? Were any lost? What about letters from Tom?

"You knew her well?" Eleanor asked.

"Well enough. As I say, she wasn't really popular, mostly because she had a very sharp tongue and if she took a mind to use it on you, watch out. But if she liked you you'd hardly find a better friend. Certainly not a truer one."

"Was she, uh, strange, back then?"

Again the laugh.

"Strange? Hah, unmarried women are always said to be strange, isn't that so? Well they aren't. And Janet Turner certainly was not. She was very proper, outspoken, dependable. She had her moods, all right, and you stayed out of her way if she was in a bad one, but she was not in the least strange, my dear."

"Did she ever talk to you about Tom Thomson?"

"Only to say if only his paintings had been selling when they were engaged and if only he hadn't drowned—and it's obvious what she meant by that."

"So she didn't talk much about him then?"

"No, of course not," the old lady said. "He was dead and that's that. You can't worry about the past all your life now, can you?"

Eleanor didn't know. Lately, she certainly seemed to be.

"Do you remember when she came here?" Eleanor asked, preparing herself. "How soon after, I mean?"

"After his death? I don't know. When did he die? During the war, wasn't it?"

"July 1917."

"Well, then, it must have been 1917 or 1918. Not long after."

Eleanor's heart sank.

"Can you be more exact?" she asked, desperately.

"What's it matter?" the old woman asked. She looked at Eleanor; it was obvious that she could see no reason for knowing.

"It matters to me," said Eleanor. "A great deal."

The old lady graciously did not ask why. She thought a minute, pulled out another cigarette, lit it, and let it hang as if pasted to her upper lip.

"Well, maybe I can find out. They weren't in the house when we moved out, I'm sure of that. But not long after. We moved out in 1918, yes, it was 1918."

"When in 1918? Do you remember?"

Again the look from the old lady. She puffed on the cigarette and let the smoke race off without inhaling.

190

"I guess it'd be on our deed," the old lady said presently. "We're still in the same place."

A brisk walk to her house, during which Eleanor learned all about the 1932 gold rush in Hemlock, which fizzled as quickly as it began. Soon, Eleanor found herself waiting in the kitchen over a cup of disturbingly strong coffee while the old woman buried herself in papers she was pulling out of a piano seat. Eleanor could see no piano in the living room.

After several minutes she came out into the kitchen, her glasses tilted by one hand as she looked closely at an old document held in the other hand.

"June 12, 1918," the woman said. Eleanor's coffee cup shook. "I'd place their moving to Hemlock somewhere around the fall of that year."

Plenty of time, Eleanor calculated later, after she'd thanked the woman, turned down a second cup of coffee and excused herself. *Time to have me, recover, and get on back to Vernon and then move to Hemlock.*

All the way back to Vernon she pored over the speculations. Why had Janet Turner gone to Hemlock? Was it simply that Hemlock was where the work was? Or was there too much shame to carry around in the home town? Perhaps no one else even knew; it was simply a move insisted upon by shocked parents? If so, was it then considered all right to move back in the early 1930s? Fourteen, fifteen years wasn't long enough for people to forget—not *that* type of thing. If there was something wrong then it was unlikely anybody outside of the immediate family would have known what had happened.

Except, perhaps, Russell Pemberton, who isn't telling all he knows.

13

Earlier that day, Russell had taken some food in and kept it down, poached egg over toast, a buttermilk, and a dish of ice cream. He'd become dizzy on the hotel stairs because, he decided, he hadn't been eating properly. In fact, he hadn't been eating properly for months; too many of those cursed digestive biscuits and chopped egg sandwiches with the crusts cut off – eating like a silly little baby. Time was, back at the winter cutting camps, Russell Pemberton would put away three boiled chickens in a sitting and half an apple pie.

Well, he'd decided, that was the last of them, that one last night. From now on he was going to get some proper nutrients into him and have a nap so he wouldn't tire so easily. He'd been for the mail, kidded poor Odon Fuller about his flying saucer – "Find any little green fellers to pilot her, eh?" – and he'd come back to his room, just as he'd decided he would, to lie down for a spell.

The phone rang.

It rang again. And again.

Russell twisted out of bed, grunted, fumbled for the phone, and finally picked up the receiver.

"Yes," he said, his anger hidden.

"Uh . . . Mr. Pemberton?" said a woman's voice, strangely distant, shy.

"Yes," he said, a slight irritation evident.

"I'm sorry," said the timid voice. "Are you sleeping?"

Lordy – Russell paused – *am I sleeping?*

"If I am," he said, deliberately and slowly, "then this is a nightmare, right?"

"Oh, God," the voice said. "I'm sorry. I didn't think I'd be bothering you. I'm so sorry..."

That voice. He knew it. Mrs. – oh, Mrs. – that woman from the city.

"No, no, it's all right," he said. "How're you making out, anyway?"

"How do you know who this is?" the voice said, still timid, though now surprised.

Russell laughed. He liked that. He'd show them.

"I know. I know," he said. "What can I do you for?"

Do you for? Eleanor had never heard that before.

"Well," she said. "I was wondering if maybe we could talk some more, that's all. But I don't want to disturb you. Maybe some other time..."

"May as well talk to you as to myself," Russell said, and chuckled at his humour. "Where are you now?"

"My room."

No way for that, Russell thought. I may be nearly seventy-seven years old, but nobody's going to get any chance to spread anything about Russell Pemberton. Not now or ever. Abigail Pemberton had taught him well: "All you really own is your self-respect," she once said. And he planned to take his with him.

"I could meet you downstairs, I guess," he said.

"Fine," Eleanor said. "*I'll* buy the drinks this time."

Russell said nothing. His pension wouldn't permit another squandering like last night.

"The lounge."

"When?"

"In an hour. I want to get a bite to eat first. Have you eaten?"

He lied. "Yes."

"I'll call you when I get there, then," she said.

"Fine," Russell said. "I'll be here."

193

"Okay, *ciao*."

Chow? Russell had never heard that word before except at the camp, meaning food. He didn't know what to say. So he hung up.

An hour. He checked the table clock – five-thirty – time enough for a quick snooze. He would need his energy. He settled back on the bed and automatically began to drift.

Russell had never spent a week as confused as the one immediately following the botched engagement party of June 30, 1917. His eye still throbbed where Tom had scratched him, but that he could deal with. It would go away. What wouldn't was his wonder over what was happening. He couldn't see where he stood with Jenny, where Tom stood with Jenny, where, for that matter, he stood with Tom. When he thought about it, and he did very little else, he saw only a complicated maze that made his sore eye throb all the harder as he tried to work his way clear in it. Distracted, when it lingered on the fringes of his thinking, he would become convinced he could finally understand just what was what; but as soon as he pulled the thought closer to the front of his head it seemed to tangle. So he gave up.

And the maze took another unpredictable turn on the next Saturday evening when Tom Thomson, all smiles and laughter, came to the Joe Lake cookhouse and burst in on Russell as he was putting beans in a pot to soak. George Rowe was right behind Tom, and they'd been drinking.

"There you are," Tom shouted as he came through the door. "We've been hunting all over hell for you."

"You were in the wrong neighbourhood, then," Russell said, proud of his joke. Tom rolled his eyes.

"We're going fishing," Tom announced.

"It'll be dark in half an hour," Russell said. They certainly had been drinking.

"That's the way we want 'er," George added.

"Come out here a minute," Tom said and threw an arm around Russell's shoulder. He followed, reluctantly.

194

Tom flicked a finger at Russell's shiner as they went outside, which made Russell wince in pain.

"Mosquito bite?" Tom asked, as if it had all been in good fun, then jabbed a fist hard into Russell's shoulder. Tom laughed loudly, and Russell lost his grip on the smile he was holding back.

"Wait'll you see what we got in mind," Tom said.

On the path to the left of the cabin were three one-gallon paint cans, each with a half-dozen or so bullrushes sticking out upside down. Russell smelled gasoline.

"Oh, no you don't!" he said and took a step backwards toward the cabin.

"Ah, Russell. Come on," pleaded George Rowe.

But Russell stood his ground and shook his head. "No, no, no," he said. "Mark Robinson sees us with that and we'll all be strapped to the caboose first thing in the morning."

"He won't see us," Tom said with confidence. "We'll stay up here on Little Joe. Here – take one of these buggers."

Russell knew when he was beaten. He took the tin of soaking bullrushes and simply fell into line with the other two, who were already stumbling down the long path to the slip where Russell kept his square-stern canoe. Tom's canoe was tied there as well, loaded with fishing gear and packs, and he slowly stepped out onto the planks Russell had dropped along the shore, splashing a portion of the gasoline into the lake, where it spread out in dark purple and waving rings.

They loaded up the canoe – Russell transferring his own pole and kit over to Tom's craft – and, with Russell and George Rowe firmly positioned, Tom pushed out off the planks. The canoe shook worrisomely as Tom got down on his knees, settled, and then they were off. Russell paddled bow, Tom stern, and Rowe sat flat on the canoe floor and rolled a cigarette.

"Don't light that!" Tom shouted when he realized what George was up to. "You'll have us all killed!"

Russell turned, saw what was happening, turned back, and cringed. He wished he'd just followed his first inclination and told them both to go to hell – even if that became the literal result of their crazed expedition.

A few minutes of hard paddling brought them to the high rocks opposite the island. Russell let up and Tom drew the canoe to a stop. Rowe let out the anchor, a netted stone that he handed out slowly until the line went slack, then he tied the rope to the thwart.

Tom reached and pulled out the first of the soaking cat-tails.

"Give us that light now," he said to Rowe. "And be care-ful."

Rowe stroked a match outside the canoe, under the gun-nel, and held the flame out over the water as far as he could reach. Tom held out the bullrush into the match; it caught and lept, a roll of flame sliding off the tip and up into the night sky, where it dissolved. He let the flame settle, turning the bullrush as if he were candy-coating an apple, and then held the blue fire far out over the stern.

"George," he said in a royal tone, as if Rowe were a ser-vant. "Open us a can of the holy water, would you?"

"By all means," Rowe said and then played around in his creel until he came up with a Mason jar. He screwed off the top, tossed it and the rubber ring overboard, and then passed the open jar to Russell who, knowing better than to smell it, took a quick drink, and a quicker swallow, to ensure his taste buds spent as little time as possible with whatever liquid was dropping into his stomach. It felt as if he'd swallowed the flaming cattail Thomson was holding.

"Present your flies, gentlemen," Tom said, in his mock aristocrat's voice. "I do believe it is time. And George, do light us up another torch like a good chap now, what?"

A half-hour later, with all but two of the bullrushes spent, they had twenty-three lake trout, twenty-one of them an identical one and a half pounds, one barely a pound (but so badly hooked it was already dead) and one, caught by a delighted Russell, weighing a very impressive four pounds.

They were in understandably fine moods when they set

196

out for Rowe's cabin on Canoe Lake. Thomson sang "A Bicycle Built for Two," his clear tenor moving above the canoe as smoothly as the first bottle, a second and then a third had worked from bow to stern and back again to bow.

Down the narrows, over the dam, and across the bay, they came, singing and rubbing their paddles heavily along the gunnel—a sound that a sober Tom Thomson would never permit. They hit the makeshift dock in front of Rowe's cabin before they saw it and the canoe slid part way up the water-logged boards and tipped over onto its side, spilling Russell and George onto the dock and throwing Tom halfway into the water where he barely saved himself from a complete bath by submerging paddle, arm, and shoulder and catching a hold on the bottom just in time.

"Save my fish!" Russell called, as he scrambled to his knees.

"Piss on your fish!" Tom yelled. "Save *me*!"

"The booze!" George called out.

"Jesus! Grab it quick!" Tom yelled.

"What about you?" Russell called back, laughing.

"Get it first! I'll hold."

Rowe was already scrambling into the canoe. He came out, clutching the creel to his chest, and let Russell take it from him. Russell also grabbed the burlap sack with the fish in it, then helped George up to his feet, steadied him, and guided Rowe over the walkway to the shore.

"Hey!" Tom called.

"What?" Russell yelled back without turning.

"Get me up!"

"You said you'd hold," Russell said matter-of-factly. "So hold."

All the way up the long path toward the cabin they could hear Tom shouting. Just as George put his hand out toward the door, they heard a final curse and a splash.

George pushed open the door. He and Russell were still laughing when the light and heat hit them. Both men winced,

197

then focussed slowly on the one-room cabin and its smiling residents.

"What the hell's going on here?" Rowe asked.

"Nothing. What's going on out there?"

Russell recognized the voice before the face cleared sufficiently. Lowrie Dickson—Rowe's buddy. And Martin Bletcher was there, too. And Shannon Fraser. All with their shirts open, gathered around the blazing fireplace and a single coal oil light. On the makeshift table by the wicker chair stood four of the same Mason jars the three fishermen had been working their way through. Two of the jars were empty. Each man inside had a glass in his hand.

"Leave that damn door open," Shannon Fraser said. "I'm starting to sweat alcohol."

"Where's Tom?" Bletcher asked. Russell thought he detected a quiver in the voice.

"Washing up," Russell said.

Rowe snorted but no one caught on.

"Catch anything?" Dickson asked.

Russell answered by simply turning the bag upside down and letting the catch slide out onto the floor and spread in a slimy, glistening mass.

"Holy Lord Almighty!" Fraser said.

"And that's not 'em all," Russell said.

"Sure it's them," Rowe argued.

"Nope," Russell said. "Still one to come. There—that'll be it."

When Russell turned they all turned with him. A heavy sloshing up the last few strides of the path announced Tom. He stopped at the doorway, the water pouring from him, his thick, black hair flat from the crown down across his ears and down his neck. He was grinning.

"So, Pemberton," he said. "We're even, are we?"

"Even," Russell answered.

Tom came over, smiling, with his hand outstretched and Russell, pleased, reached for it. Tom took Russell's hand, pulled down quickly, and Russell went head first into the pile of fish. He could hear the laughter. He'd been suckered and knew it, knew also that there was nothing he could do but make the most of a bad moment.

Slowly he moved into a sitting position. With Tom leaning over and howling into his face, Russell grandly ran a forefinger along his face and slowly shook off the fish slime. Then, just as slowly and dramatically, he reached for a fish, held it in both hands between his legs, while Tom pointed and laughed, and then squeezed until the fish shot out from his hold and hit Tom square in the mouth. When Tom turned, sputtering, Russell grabbed another fish, jumped up, and forced it down the back of Tom's pants.

In a moment fish were flying about the cabin. Bletcher ran out the door to safety and Dickson wrestled with Fraser, as he tried to shove the four-pounder down the front of Fraser's pants. Fraser, however, was much too strong. With one swat of his hand he sent Dickson into the fish pile with Russell, where Russell put a trout down Dickson's collar. Rowe jumped into the bunk and pulled the covers over his head, but Tom countered by slipping a fish into the pillow and covering Rowe's head with it.

Tom then grabbed one of the full jars of liquor and threw it so it smashed into the fireplace, exploding the logs and sending a high kick of flame out into the room and against the wall.

"For Christ's sake!" Rowe screamed from under the covers. His head poked out just as the flames were drawing back into the fireplace.

For several moments no one said anything. Tom laughed self-consciously, then covered his mouth and sat down heavily. Russell turned in disgust and stomped outside, where the fresh night air was as welcome as his mother had been after a bad dream. Down toward the landing a bullfrog grumped and Russell saw Martin Bletcher standing on the walkway, slowly swaying back and forth and, Russell was sure, humming to himself.

It appalled Russell that he was sometimes capable of acting this way. Good old Russell Pemberton, the essence of dependability, who couldn't keep his own devils within. Those times when the rot spilled out of him he wished he could rip it off like a shirt and bury it. Then he'd be done with it forever. But he couldn't fool himself anymore; those times when he thought it was finally done with, it invariably returned, and there were times, like tonight, when he could hold only himself responsible for inviting it back.

Tom. So often it involved Tom. The few times he'd seen Tom act this way – like a cat suddenly turning on the hand that retrieves its ball of yarn – he'd felt responsible for righting things, even though he knew there was little use in trying. It was part of the penance, part of what Russell paid for his own cleansing.

"Martin," he called quietly. "You all right?"

Bletcher jumped, unaware that anyone had come up on him, and very nearly slipped off the boardwalk into the water. He turned, and even in the distance and the bad light Russell could see Martin had been sick on himself.

"Let me alone," he called back.

But Russell couldn't. He came down and stood on the shore where the boardwalk began. He put one foot on it and felt it shake with the added weight.

"Stay off!" Martin said.

Russell laughed. "Why? You look like you need a bath."

"Go back to the cabin," Martin said.

"Not without you."

"I don't want to go back."

"You should get something into your stomach, don't you think? There's bread back there. We can toast some."

Martin shook his head.

"I'm better off here," he said.

Russell knew what it was that was eating at Bletcher.

"Tom?" he asked.

From behind, and in the light off the water, Russell could make out Bletcher nodding.

"I'll be there," Russell said.

Bletcher then shook his head violently from side to side. "He scares me," he said.

Russell laughed, hoping his own apparent lack of concern might rub off onto Martin. "Look," he said. "Tom couldn't hurt a fish in the condition he's in, now could he?"

Bletcher didn't react.

"Now could he?" Russell repeated.

"I guess not."

"Well, come on then."

Martin Bletcher came, unsteadily, across the rotting board-walk and jumped onto the higher, dryer shore where Russell caught him by the arm and began leading him back with a gentle push of the elbow. They walked back toward the closed door and the muffled voices, and Russell didn't allow Bletcher to slow his reluctant stride until they came to the door and Russell had pushed it open.

Tom was down on his hands and knees, unsuccessfully pushing the fish back into their bag as Shannon Fraser and Lowrie Dickson kicked them toward him. George Rowe sat on his bunk with his hands over his face; he looked on the verge of throwing up.

Tom looked up from his chore and grinned.

"Martin!" he shouted with unexpected delight. "Just the lad we need. Shannon here needs a Kraut low enough to crawl in under poor George's bed and throw the fish out. How'd you like to do us a favour, eh?"

Russell scowled at Tom but he couldn't stop the insult. He looked at Martin who was pure white, but whether that was from the comment or vomiting, Russell could not say.

"Get them yourself," Martin said. "You threw them there."

Tom looked astonished. It wasn't like Bletcher to talk back so forcefully.

"Are you telling *me* what to do?" he asked.

"No," Martin said calmly. "And you're not telling me what to do, either."

Tom's smile vanished. "Is that a declaration of war?" he asked.

Bletcher sagged and closed his eyes as if he could see what was coming. "No," he said.

"Then get the fish."

"Tom..." Russell began.

"No! Damn it!" Tom said, standing up. "Get down and get the fish, Martin!"

"Go to hell!"

"What?" Tom said, obviously startled at this development.

"Leave me alone, Thomson," Martin said. "I'm warning you."

Tom laughed, the laugh uncomfortable, loud and phoney.

"Leave him alone, Tom," Shannon said. "I can get them out with the broom."

"No!" Tom said. "Martin'll get 'em." He grabbed Martin by the back of the neck, his fingers whitening as they dug in and forced Martin's head down. He swung feebly at Tom. Russell stepped between them and pulled Tom's hand free.

"Forget it, Tom," Russell said.

Shannon Fraser's big hand settled on Tom's shoulder. Thomson angrily hit it away. Fraser grabbed him around the wrist, hard.

"Get some sleep, Tom," he said gently. "We're all tired, okay? I'll finish cleaning up."

"Sure," Tom said with sarcasm. "And maybe rifle my pockets while you're at it, too."

"Now what the hell's that supposed to mean?" Fraser asked, the thick vein in his neck rising with his voice.

"You know goddam well what that's supposed to mean," Tom said.

Russell knew he should move. He gently placed a hand on Tom's shoulder, a move Tom seemed to take as a sign of encouragement, and he turned back to Russell.

"Shannon Fraser's a thief, you know, Russell," he said.

Russell wasn't sure what to do. He smiled slightly and tried to push Tom back toward the bunk.

"I'll give you one chance to take that back, Thomson," Fraser said.

"I can't take back the truth, Shannon, and you know it."

It's time to stop this, Russell thought. Just then Fraser's big right hand slammed into Tom's jaw, sending him reeling straight back and over into the fireplace. Russell moved, late, but in time to pull Thomson out onto the floor before anything caught fire. He rolled Tom over. The eyes were flickering, white as far up as Russell could see.

And then he saw Tom's temple: blood oozing out and down into his ear and hair. The wound was only a half-inch long, but deep. Russell quickly pressed the flat of his palm against it to stop the bleeding.

"Lord Jesus!" Russell called. "Get a towel! *Quick!*"

Dickson scrambled toward the washstand but George Rowe was already there. He threw the towel; Fraser caught it and handed it down to Russell, who quickly pressed it against Thomson's bleeding temple.

"I only hit him on the jaw," Fraser said.

"I know," Russell said. "He hit his head when he fell."

"Oh, God," Fraser whined.

Russell bent low over his friend. Tom was breathing well. The eyes were settling, too, and Russell could make out part of Tom's pupils, dilated and not seeing, but at least now visible. The pupils dropped lower and began quickly expanding, then shrinking to the size of a pin. Russell knew Tom could not see him. But finally the pupils also settled, and Russell knew that Tom was looking at him and wanting Russell to say something comforting.

"You're okay, Tom," he said. "A little cut on the temple, that's all."

"Tom!" Fraser shouted into his face. Russell saw Fraser's spit land along Tom's right cheek. He brushed it off. "Tom! Speak to us!"

Tom's mouth moved, then tightened as he ran his tongue over his lips. Then he tried again.

"Go to hell, Shannon," he said.

Fraser whooped and buried his face into Tom's chest.

Thomson pushed him off, then reached for the towel Russell was still pressing tight to his head.

"How bad?" he asked.

Russell shrugged. He didn't know. With Tom staring anxiously at him, Russell moved the towel back very slowly from the wound. It caught on the towel where the blood had already hardened. The bleeding was stopping; Russell placed the towel back in place and moved Tom's hand to hold it tight.

"You'll be all right," he said. "Just hold this tight until we can get something better on it."

"I'll take him over to the lodge," Fraser said eagerly. "Annie'll fix him up and we'll get him into his bed."

"I'll give a hand," said Dickson.

"Pick him up easy," Russell said.

They did, very gently. Shannon Fraser's big arms folded under Tom's arms and around his chest while Dickson took the feet. With Tom holding the towel tight they stumbled out the front door, which was held open by George Rowe.

"You better stay here and clean things up," Russell said as he passed Rowe. He was beginning to grow pleased with the way he was taking charge. "There's nothing you can do, anyway. I'll go along with them to make sure they get there all right."

"Okay," Rowe said. There was defeat in his voice. Russell thought of the job Rowe had to look forward to and decided he, too, would prefer anything to cleaning up the mess of the cabin.

As soon as Russell got outside, however, he realized Martin Bletcher was kneeling just to the side of the outhouse path, retching and vomiting. He left the others and hurried over.

"Martin," he called. "You okay?"

Bletcher turned, crying, and slumped over onto his side. Russell knelt down and propped him up again and held him. Bletcher was soaked and shaking.

"Can you walk?" he asked.

"I... don't think so..."

"If I help you?"

"Yes... maybe."

Russell got Martin up onto his feet, steadied him, and threw his arm around Martin's waist for balance. With his other hand he reached and took Martin's right arm and hoisted it up around Russell's neck, where he held it fast. He looked down the path: Fraser and Dickson were already off down the path with their injured load. He knew it was only a short walk to Mowat Lodge, so they wouldn't need his help as well. He'd be better off going in the opposite direction with Martin Bletcher, who looked as if he had far less chance of surviving the night than Tom.

Russell decided he'd cart Martin back to his sister, Bessie, and then borrow Martin's centre-prop to get himself back up to the Joe Lake camp in time for a bit of sleep before Art Galer arrived on the morning train from Hemlock. Galer had written from the Vernon office saying he wanted to go north of Joe Lake to check into setting up a third winter camp—an idea both Russell and Harvey Turner frowned upon—but first they'd have to see if the rivers in that area would be able to handle the logs.

He knew he'd be back down first thing Monday morning to put a disappointed Galer on the train. He'd return Martin's boat then and also check up on Tom, just to make sure Shannon's blow had knocked some sense into his head.

On Monday, however, a very serious Mark Robinson met Russell and Art Galer at the train. He shook Russell's hand—a strangely formal act—before pulling him away from Galer to tell him the news.

Tom Thomson was missing.

Mark told Russell that Shannon Fraser had seen Tom Sunday around noon, when the artist had paddled away from the Mowat Lodge dock. And now they were already moving to set up search parties. Personally, he said, he wasn't too worried; he'd even figured Tom would show on the morning train after having sneaked off to town to pick up some paint supplies or something. But the conductor said he hadn't seen him in weeks.

"Off on one of his crazy fishing trips, probably," Mark said.

"Sure," Russell said.

"Me and him were supposed to go off together this morning, though," Mark said. "It's not like Tom to break a promise."

Russell didn't like the tone of Mark's comments. But he still couldn't take seriously any suggestion that something might be wrong with Tom.

"Some of the men are going to scout around," Mark said. "Can you give a hand?"

When Mark and Russell arrived at Mowat Lodge, Shannon Fraser was leaning down toward them from the verandah railing, his pink face quivering.

"We found Tom's canoe," he said. His voice was cracking.

"Where?" Mark asked.

"Down past the island."

"On shore?"

Fraser shook his head. "No. Drifting empty," he said.

"Who found it?" Russell asked.

"Martin Bletcher."

"Where is it now?" Mark asked.

"On the dock," Fraser said and pointed down toward the canoe which was raised out of the water and turned on its side. It was Tom's all right: grey-green, with a metal strip.

Russell and Mark ran down onto the large dock and examined the canoe closely. Shannon followed, and stood behind them, wringing his hands as they turned the canoe over and back on its side again, with Mark talking all the time how it made such little sense to him.

"When did he find it?"

"This morning," Shannon said. "But he says he and Bessie saw it yesterday."

"Yesterday?"

"Yah, yesterday."

"Why didn't they report it then?"

206

"Martin says he didn't know it was Tom's."

Robinson turned and stared at Fraser.

"Shannon," he said. "There's only one canoe like this around here."

"I know," said Fraser. "He says it was too far away to see clearly."

Robinson took off his cap and wiped away the sweat. "They went over to investigate, surely."

Fraser shook his head to say no.

"Where'd they see it?" Russell asked.

"Just between the islands," Shannon answered and pointed to the large channel between Little and Big Wapomeo.

"How far off shore?" Mark asked.

Fraser shrugged. "Look for yourself. Couldn't have been more than a hundred yards no matter where, could it?"

"I don't understand," Mark said. "A canoe drifting between the islands and they don't go over and investigate..."

"Martin says he thought it had blown free of a dock and they'd pick it up later if it was still there when they came back."

"Back from where?" Russell asked.

"A picnic."

"Picnic?"

"Picnic."

"Wind doesn't blow that way," Mark said.

"What way?" Russell asked.

"Toward the island. Whose dock could it blow off of to end up there?"

The three men stared out toward the islands. Mark was right. To the southwest there were no cottages.

"Besides," Mark said. "It was calm yesterday."

They thought about that a moment, then Mark walked to the end of the dock and leaned out. "Say it drifted," he said. "Could have come from the Gill Lake portage, couldn't it? Tom might be hiking her back right now."

"Maybe the Tea Lake portage, if not that," said Russell.

It was decided Mark would check out Gill Lake and Russell would go down to Tea. Shannon said he'd wait around the lodge and tell some of the people, particularly the Turners, what was up.

"Don't go worrying anyone for nothing," Mark warned.

Russell, in one of the lodge canoes, headed down the western shore of Canoe Lake toward the Tea Lake dam. How Tom's canoe might have blown so far up-lake he couldn't say, but that was hardly the only thing without explanation as far as the disappearance of Tom Thomson went. With a little luck, he'd find Tom camped by the first portage point frying up a feed of freshly-caught speckles, waving his knife and threatening Russell in his usual way that he'd have his balls for taking so long getting there...

...But there was no Tom at the Tea Lake portage.

Russell docked at the lodge, tired and puzzled. There was something wrong with the way this whole thing was going. He decided he would go and see Jenny.

Russell thought of his mother, Abigail, as he walked down the wide path to Turners'. She would have looked for signs. She would have heard something, a cricket maybe, or simply the way the short waves were licking along the shore on the way over, and she would have claimed to know something about it. Once, when her own mother died, she claimed to have seen her mother walk into her bedroom and place her hand on Abigail's forehead and smile, and this on the night before they found her dead, wasted away with whatever had been eating her insides up.

But all Russell could do was listen. If there were signs, he couldn't identify them. He supposed deep down he simply didn't believe anyway.

He went up to the Turners' back door, lightly tapping and having his knock instantly answered by Mrs. Turner who looked tired and didn't say a word. She signalled Russell inside and pointed with a jabbing finger out toward the front porch.

Russell could feel the rim of his straw hat as he squeezed it, but nothing else. He looked around the little cottage and everything seemed to shine with polishing and cleaning, even the wall plates which he'd always felt needed a good dusting. Not that he cared.

He opened the front door and felt the breeze off the lake push in on his face. At least he could feel that. He poked the screen door out past the catch, heard it click, and peeked around the corner with one eye.

Jenny was sitting there, alone. She was staring at the water.

Russell looked at her but she did not move; whether she knew he was there was impossible to tell. She simply looked straight ahead. She looked fresh, but only in dress, the yellow one with the ribbon sash, and her hair seemed lately combed and tied, for there wasn't a loose wisp, which was hardly in keeping with Jenny.

Russell came the rest of the way out onto the porch and let the screen trip the catch when he closed it.

Jenny started. She turned like someone just waking to a sudden noise. At first, Russell had the feeling she didn't even recognize him. But how could that be?

"Hello, Jenny," he said, and nervously fingered his hat. "How are you?" *Damn*, he immediately thought, *what a fool thing to say!*

Jenny got up. She looked at Russell while Russell nervously picked at his hat.

He was trying to find some way of fixing what he'd said. He was looking for another question. Something more proper. He stared helplessly at her, hoping it would either come to him or else she would speak up and help him.

She started to shake. Russell had only seen a person shake like that once before, and then after he'd fallen through the ice. Jenny shook as if the ground around her was shivering, not her, and she was only trying to keep her balance. She had a handkerchief in her far hand and held it to her mouth, chewing on the fingers that wrapped around it.

Russell knew he must do something. He threw his hat onto the other chair and moved toward her. And then he did something he'd never done before. He held her.

Jenny buried her face in his shoulder. Russell stood there totally flummoxed. The arm closest to her he naturally put around her and onto her back. But the other arm he worried about, and he left it dangling, the fingers running back and forth furiously over the thumb, the entire arm desperate for something to do.

He had to hold her tighter and tighter to stop the shaking, and before he knew it both his arms were tight around her back and he was crushing her into his chest and shoulder, as if he could somehow absorb the shakes and remove them from her.

He thought he could detect her sobbing. It was hard to tell. Her face was completely buried in his coat. But after what must have been several minutes he knew for sure: he felt the wetness seeping through to his skin.

Russell was beginning to feel desperate. No one had ever used him for this before. He felt off-balance. He felt he was holding her too tightly, too loosely, incorrectly...

Jenny backed away and moved to the railing. She dabbed at her eyes. Russell noticed the hankie was clinging to her fingers, soaked.

"Russell?" she said, not looking at him. "What am I going to do?"

She looked out over the lake again. Russell moved to stand beside her, focussing his eyes on nothing. Not looking at her made it less real, more manageable. He patted her back with the flat of his hand, the way his mother had always done when he'd been upset or sick or frightened by a dream. He had no idea what else he could do.

Over the next two days, Russell walked most of the portages leading from Canoe and Tea Lakes without luck. Around four on Wednesday, he came back to Mowat, his boots slurping and his pants soaked to the knees. The others were already back, also without success.

210

At dawn Thursday morning, with still no sign of Tom, or word from him, Russell set out to paddle the Canoe Lake shoreline, completely convinced that a floating paddle might be the key to finding Tom. The canoe, after all, had been found floating. Paddles don't sink. And Tom wouldn't carry his paddle off into the bush with him.

But nothing.

When Russell came back to the lodge that afternoon, late, he passed by the Turner cottage. He was about two hundred yards off shore, with a light mist beginning to settle. But he knew he was still very much in sight. And he saw Jenny clearly enough, sitting out on the porch, staring right at him.

But when he waved, nothing.

At the lodge people were beginning to show their discouragement. Lots of talk about dragging. Martin Bletcher was insisting Mark Robinson send to headquarters for some dynamite that they could drop down off Wapomeo, about where the canoe had been found. "That'll bring him up if anything will," Bletcher maintained.

Russell figured Bletcher was eager to see Tom actually drowned just so he'd have some proof that he hadn't anything to do with it. With everyone sitting around trying to figure out what had happened to Tom there were more than a few hints that Bletcher had his hand in it. The story about the picnic and the day's delay in reporting the drifting canoe didn't sit well with anyone, particularly with those who had seen Tom's cruelty toward Bletcher and his groundhog weeks earlier.

But Mark, who'd taken charge of things, would hear of no dragging or dynamiting. He firmly believed Tom was still alive, and that they would soon find him.

Friday it rained all morning, big, lazy drops that tingled in the water and dripped off Russell's hat as he paddled down and rechecked the portage over to Smoke Lake; it was obvious by the prints that they had looked everywhere. The others searched mostly in the bush, and as Russell paddled he could hear Robinson's eerie whistle floating across the lake like a hoarse loon's call. Twice he heard Robinson firing shots, as well, and he took that to mean the ranger was beginning to feel a bit desperate.

The best thing about Saturday was the weather, clear, bright and hot. With the water still as glass, Russell went out early, before breakfast, and paddled gently around both Little and Big Wapomeo Islands, believing he might see some sign of Tom's tackle in the fifteen or so feet he could see down to. But there was nothing, and the shoals quickly dropped off into deeper water.

Mark Robinson was so exhausted from tramping through wet bush the past several days that he stayed at home while the others searched.

If Shannon had been right about the time he had last seen Tom, it would have been some thirteen hours after Russell himself had seen him. Shannon had been there then, too, helping to cart Tom and his ugly wound back down the path toward Mowat Lodge. Shannon had told Russell that Tom seemed to have recovered well. He said they'd roused Annie and with a bit of grumbling she'd come down to the kitchen and cleaned and dressed the cut, and next morning Tom complained only of a "hell of a headache."

Russell wondered if perhaps Tom had become dizzy out fishing and fallen overboard. Perhaps that was it. At least it was an explanation. Everyone knew about the party, but no one had yet mentioned the fight.

By Sunday it was obvious the searchers were simply repeating each other's steps. Russell went over the portage to Gill Lake and found only signs that others had walked this same area: three gun shells told of Mark Robinson himself.

It was now a full week with no sign. Even Mark Robinson seemed discouraged.

On Monday the two guides, Lowrie Dickson and George Rowe, headed down the lake to continue the disappointing search. When they got abreast of Little Wapomeo Island, Doctor G.W. Howland, who was staying there in the cabin belonging to Taylor Statten, called out to them and asked them to check on an object he could see floating ahead of them and to the right. They quickly paddled over.

It was Tom.

They lashed the bow line to the body, towed it over to the low campsite on Big Wapomeo Island, and there tied the body to some spruce roots in the shallows by the shore. The body would be sheltered there, and Lowrie Dickson took up a watch while Rowe paddled over and told Doctor Howland and then left to round up Mark and the others. Russell heard the news as he was stashing his lunch up under the bow of the canoe he'd been using. It came as no shock to him.

Russell went down to the island with some of the other men. Doctor Howland had already come over by boat and had placed a blanket over the body. Mark Robinson jumped in with his boots and pants on, waded over to the blanket with the water up over his knees and gently folded the blanket in half and removed it.

"That's Tom Thomson, all right," he said.

Russell knew he was right, but it was hardly the Tom he had known. This thing was bloated, sickly pale, and beginning to decompose around the face. There was a thick bruise over his temple – Russell recognized it immediately – and blood coming out of the ear beside it. The flesh hanging from the wound was clear and drifting in the water. Russell had seen frogs and crayfish go that way when they were dead and left in the water, but he'd never seen it happen to a human.

The sun was hot on Russell's neck. He thought he could smell something rancid. He closed his eyes.

"What'll we do with him?" Charlie Scrim, another of the guides, asked.

Russell kept his eyes closed waiting for an answer. There was a long silence. He could feel the heat. He could hear the body rubbing against the roots. He felt sleepy. He heard Mark Robinson sigh.

213

"I don't know," he said. "There'll have to be a coroner here, I suppose, and he'll want to see him. Cover him up, I guess, and leave him for the time being."

They paddled up again to the lodge dock. Russell had never heard it so quiet, not a paddle ran against a gunnel, not a paddle even broke water. When they neared the dock Russell looked up to see who was there. Most of the guests were assembled, Shannon and Annie Fraser, and – at the front of the dock with her hands on her hips and her yellow dress on – Jenny Turner.

Mark's canoe pulled up and docked first. He didn't even look at her, though she was staring at him. He got out in a crouch, stayed in the crouch, and slipped his tie through the bent spike and pulled it tight. Then he stood, wiped his forehead clear of sweat, and looked at her.

"Well?" she said.

Russell was amazed at how forceful her voice was. Not cracking. Not weak. Not afraid.

"It's Tom," Mark said. "I'm sorry."

Everyone was looking at her to see the reaction. She didn't even blink.

"Will you paddle me there?" she said. "I'd like to see him."

"Now, Janet," Mark said. "You wouldn't want to see a thing like that. It's Tom and he's drowned."

"Wet maybe, but hardly drowned."

Mark looked at her with astonishment. The onlookers pressed closer. Not a word was said.

"I want to see him," she said, evenly, as if there was no question about her right to it.

"No," Mark said. "No, Janet. I'm sorry."

She looked at Mark for a long moment, then at Russell. No expression, but he could tell from her eyes she was pleading. He did nothing. He looked away, down at the slip knot Mark had tied. When he looked up she was walking briskly off the boardwalk and away up the hill. Russell wanted to call to her but he didn't dare. He knew he had failed her.

The coroner had been sent for, Doctor A.E. Ranney of North Bay, but he did not arrive, as expected, on the eight-o'clock train. Robinson had been down to the station to meet the train and he came back furious. What was obviously bothering him was the fact that Tom was going to have to sit out in the water all night, in the hope that Ranney could come tomorrow and there could be an inquest.

That night Russell was unable to sleep. He was put up in one of the lodge's front rooms and kept the window open with a screen to keep out the mosquitoes, and as he lay there he could hear the water gently cuffing the underside of the dock. He could think of nothing other than the body out there tied to the roots. He thought of the fish he and Tom had often tied in much the same manner, to keep them fresh, and he thought of the time last summer when a snapping turtle had ripped the entrails out of their catch. He shivered.

He got up and went to the window, kneeling so he could look out the screen and down the lake. He pushed the screen open on one side and shoved his head entirely out and looked down toward Big Wapomeo Island. Through the growth he could make out the faint glow of a campfire flickering.

There was really no decision involved. Russell simply ended up dressed and in his canoe, paddling toward the light. It seemed the proper thing to do. He went out around the far end of the island, rested his paddle along the gunnels and simply drifted. A trout rolled not a dozen feet from him and in the starlight he saw the white belly flash and vanish. A bat flew madly across his bow and swept twice across the paddle blade, but stayed clear of Russell himself. From the far end of the lake he heard a loon cry, long and haunting and echoed, and when the call ended the silence seemed oppressive.

He drifted and he named constellations. He drifted and he remembered: the first time he'd met Tom Thomson; the shudder of realization when he saw Jenny looking at him... the reel Tom gave him... the fishing trips... the long paddles down rivers, where they could go from breakfast to lunch without a word and not seem awkward. He remembered Tom's eyes the snappy winter night when Russell called him outside to see the Northern Lights, and how he had insisted on painting them, and how his brush hand had frozen and Russell had to bring back the circulation by rubbing snow on it, and how Tom had laughed and howled simultaneously over the sharp pins that were closing in around his fingers.

As Russell came around the island he heard voices, low and slurred by the distance so he couldn't make anything out. The sound came from the campfire.

The men started when Russell's canoe grounded, but when they saw it was him they sat right back down with a wave for him to join them. Russell pulled his canoe up and walked over. He could see them now: Lowrie Dickson and George Rowe, the guides who'd found Tom.

"Couldn't sleep, eh?" Rowe said.

Russell said nothing. There was no need to.

"Can you understand it?" Dickson asked.

"No," said Russell.

"You saw him?" Rowe asked.

"I did," said Russell.

"You saw the line wrapped around his ankle?"

Russell looked up and his expression said he hadn't.

"More than a dozen times," said Dickson. "Neat as you'd care to see, too."

"Whatever for?" Russell said.

"You tell us," Rowe said.

Russell looked at them both. The way the light from the fire rose below them made their eyes jump with shadows. Russell thought they all must look half mad out here. He just looked at them, shrugged, and looked back down into the coals of the fire.

They went over and over the death. Nothing made sense. Not the line, not the fact that he'd taken eight days to come up, not the way the portaging paddle had been lashed to the thwarts, not the fact that the working paddle could not be found. Nothing. They remained silent, looking at the fire and listening to the way the body rubbed against the roots of the spruce tree. A few laps of bouncing water, then the groan of the rubbing.

It was better to talk. Even if there was no purpose to it. At least then they didn't have to hear Tom.

"Lowrie," Russell said. "You helped Shannon carry him back from George's. How'd he seem?"

Dickson shrugged and threw a small branch into the fire. "Okay, I guess. Walked up the steps himself."

"What about the cut—it okay?"

"I don't know. I left soon as Annie came down. She was fit to be tied."

"You can see the mark," Rowe said and pointed toward the body though there was no light.

They looked but of course couldn't see. And no one spoke for a long time, as if they were actually studying something other than their own confusion.

By dawn there wasn't a star to be seen. Cloud had moved in, black and thick as steel wool, and the first drops of rain were ringing off turned-down coffee mugs. The guides had blankets with them and a spare for Russell, and they all huddled under cover trying to catch a couple of hours' sleep. But Russell still could not sleep. He closed his eyes and saw his mother, Abigail Pemberton, leaning over him and pinching his chin so he had to look straight into her eyes. *Mind your own business*, she was saying, *and let others worry about theirs*.

Mark Robinson's eyes were red and sore-looking when he came over in the morning.

"It's going to be a close one," he said when he stepped out of his boat. He looked up at the clouds to make sure the others knew he was talking about the weather.

"Hotter today than yesterday," said Rowe.

"Glad for the rain," said Dickson.

Robinson went and stood by the bank overlooking the

217

body. Tom was shifting in the water, bobbing up and down, and a root was bared where his arm had been rubbing up against it. Robinson stared a long, long time, and none of the others spoke. They still wore the blankets, huddled in under them and looking exhausted, which they were.

"Undertakers are here," Robinson said, as if speaking to the body. "But not the coroner."

"What does that mean?" asked Dickson.

"It means we can't bury him," said Robinson. "But we shouldn't leave him like *this*, for heaven's sake."

"Well," said Rowe. "What can we do? I sure don't want to spend another night here."

"Christ, no," said Dickson.

"We'll have to see," Robinson said.

He left then, paddled back to the ranger's station and returned. The park superintendent, Bartlett, had given his permission for a burial.

First thing they did was take the body out of the water and lay it out on some planks set first over the rocks. They stripped Tom while Doctor Howland did a medical examination – but no autopsy – and Robinson cut off the fishing line from Thomson's ankle with his pocket knife. They placed him in a shroud then, and transferred him by Mark's boat over to Mowat Lodge and then into a rough pine casket.

They loaded the casket onto Shannon Fraser's black wagon – an act Russell thought appropriate, as it had been a hearse before Fraser bought it – and everyone, barely a dozen people, fell in behind the wagon as the team pulled it up past the Turner cottage and on toward the hill. The Turners – Harvey, his wife, and Jenny – joined in the procession at the closest point to their cottage. Russell noted that Jenny's face seemed completely white, ghost-like, and that her father had to steady her for the climb up the hill. She never took her eyes off the ground immediately in front of her.

The rig stopped and the men unloaded the casket and carried it over to a freshly-dug grave. Russell figured Fraser and Charlie Scrim had come up and hurriedly dug it. It was far too shallow for a real grave, and the sides were already caving in for lack of support.

Much to Russell's surprise, Martin Bletcher's father was the one who carried the Bible and said a few words over the casket.

But Russell didn't hear what he said. He was too busy watching Jenny. She had sagged against the arm of her father when they first stopped but now was standing entirely on her own feet at the foot of the grave, staring directly at the casket. The rain was steady now. Russell could hear it on the birch and poplar leaves. He had his hat off—he felt that was the proper thing to do—and the water was running out of his hair and down his forehead, hanging on his eyebrows like a small itch. He kept running a finger along, knocking the water free.

Jenny turned during the ceremony and looked through the overgrowth to the Ja's Watson marker they had puzzled over nearly five years before:

Remember comrades (when passing by)
As you are now so once was I
As I am now so you shall be
Prepare thyself to follow me

Russell followed her movement, guessing at what she was thinking, but there was no hint in her face. That blank look was there, the same as that first day he'd seen her after Tom had gone missing. She'd asked him then what she would do, and he still didn't know. Neither for her nor himself. And what of her strange behaviour when they found Tom? Did she feel there was more to the story?

"I don't know, Jenny," Russell said under his breath as he looked at her. "I just don't know. I'm sorry."

There was the sound of dirt striking wood. He turned and realized the ceremony was over, that they were tossing wet sand back into the grave and some of the people were already beginning to move back down the hill. He put his hat back on, took one last look at the casket and turned and left himself.

Janet Turner was never the same after that day.

Never.

She and her mother went out on the evening train. Russell stayed and went back the next day. But he was not invited to the inquest they held that night after Doctor Ranney finally arrived from North Bay. The coroner was met by Martin Bletcher's father, who seemed eager to assume some measure of authority over the incident, and Doctor Ranney was treated to a fine meal at Bletcher's where, immediately after, they held an informal inquest in the evening. Ranney completely accepted Doctor Howland's verdict of death by drowning, and he saw no need for exhumation and autopsy.

Ranney left on the first train next morning without ever even seeing where Thomson had been buried.

In the evening another undertaker arrived, H.W. Churchill of Vernon, claiming the Thomson family had authorized him to dig up the body, put it in a proper casket, and ship it back to Leith for burial in the Thomson family plot. Shannon Fraser met him at the train and took him and the new casket up to the graveyard where Churchill insisted on doing the job, immediately and alone, by lantern light.

Fraser returned a few hours later, following the light of Churchill's lantern through the pitch-black trail. The undertaker was sitting waiting, looking rather refreshed. Fraser looked at the grave and saw that it had been disturbed somewhat: at least some dirt had been shuffled about. He helped Churchill load up the casket, and it struck him that the casket was exceedingly light for having a man's body in it.

Stationmen at the Hemlock junction, who would transfer the body to another train for the ride to Leith the next day, would say exactly the same thing.

14

Eleanor wondered what it was that was different about Russell Pemberton this time around. He looked the same, but that was all. She felt he was treating her differently this time, as if she'd somehow been stamped "Approved." And he was ordering beer this time, no longer rye and Coke; she found herself smiling within as she realized rye and Coke was Russell's *formal* drink. But what led to the beer, whatever it was that had caused him to decide he could let down his hair around her, she couldn't understand. All she knew for sure was she wasn't about to waste this opportunity trying to find out.

The Muskoka lounge was quiet and she was easily able to catch all he said. He was much more animated this meeting, his voice rising loudly then fading to a discreet whisper. She got the distinct impression he was enjoying himself.

As for Russell, he thought Jenny would have wanted him to be more open, so he told Eleanor about the missing paddle they never found, about the way Tom's portaging paddle had been so poorly tied across the thwarts, all about the search itself, and even a bit about the gossip. He left out the letter Annie claimed to have found and also failed to mention the fight the night before Tom disappeared. He didn't mention them because he had never formed appropriate words about the two incidents, and Russell Pemberton never spoke of things he hadn't practised alone first. He noticed her perk up when he mentioned the local talk about Tom having been killed.

"But you yourself said it was an accident," Eleanor interrupted.

"I did, yes, and do. But people cause accidents as well as have them, don't they?"

What? Eleanor thought. She said, "Yes."

Russell was pleased with himself. A nice touch. He wasn't sure what it meant, but he did know it sounded good.

"All I do know for sure is Tom did not kill himself, that I promise you."

Why would he? Possibly because of the pregnancy? Eleanor did not know how to pursue this. She wished she were better at leading people, but they always seemed to set their own routes and she was simply invited to follow.

"Tom Thomson would not kill himself," Russell went on. "He was just starting to make it as a painter and things were smelling pretty rosy for him." He knew he'd have to be careful here. "Besides, he was likely going to be getting married in the near future – things were looking up."

"To Miss Turner?" Eleanor tried to ask casually.

"I'm not mentioning names," Russell said, deliberately trying to be cute about it.

There was an uneasy pause.

"You might ask *her*," Russell finally said.

Eleanor blinked several times. *But hadn't he told me the last time we spoke that I shouldn't bother her?*

"Could I?" she finally said.

"You could try," Russell said.

"You've been talking to her?"

"I've been talking to her."

"You told her about me?"

Russell nodded and lifted his glass, peering at her from both sides of the misty circle the glass bottom made over his nose. He had seen Jenny, all right, this morning when she surprised him by walking up to Western's stable and catching Russell and Western at one of their bull sessions. Hadn't looked good, he thought, pale as tracing paper. But she'd been in fine shape. "I just checked the obituaries, boys," she'd said, "and you'll be glad to know we all missed it this week again." He smiled at the thought. He'd told her about the Toronto woman, all he knew about her, and just when he figured she'd be thanking him for driving the snoop off, Jenny had asked, "Did you like her?" Kind of caught Russell off guard. He hadn't put his words together exactly the way he'd liked to have in retrospect, and it kind of came out that, yes, he did like her. "What did she look like?" she next asked. "Did she say she was going to call on me?" Russell was pleased. "I told her not to," he said. Jenny had frowned. "I'm not an old bat, you know, Russell Pemberton. You tell her I'll talk to her – maybe."

"Mr. Pemberton?"

What? Oh – Russell came back. He tilted his head to invite the question.

"When should I try to see her?" Eleanor asked.

Russell shook his head as if to clear it. "Tomorrow maybe. Try around noon. Not before that, mind."

"I won't," she said. Eleanor was still puzzled at the change in the old man.

Russell moved to get up, his bad leg cracking loudly. It startled Eleanor and she moved to help.

"No. Don't," he said. "I can manage, thank you. And thank you also for the drink, Mrs. Philpott."

"You're welcome," Eleanor said, but it wasn't heard. Russell was already off toward the elevator doors.

Up in his room Russell rummaged around in his bottom drawer until he found what he needed: a small green-tinted medicine bottle with tape on the outside and his mother's cramped writing in fountain pen over the tape. *Ground curly mint. October, 1926. Prepare a tea with hot water, let sit, drink, improves digestion.* If it'd been my decision, he thought, Jenny would never see that woman. But it's up to her. He went over to the sink, ran the water steaming hot, filled his old mug, and dumped in about three shakes of the medicine bottle. Then he sat back in his pillowed chair with his bad leg up to await the drink...

... Easter, 1918. Lordy, Russell would never forget it: the rector's timing could not have been worse. Russell himself was feeling bad enough, Ainsley Lewis down at the mill having finally drunk so much his heart burst wide open at work one day and he died gurgling like a newborn baby in Russell's arms at the side of the drying shed. Russell had been appointed head lumber grader on this thirty-third birthday

But Ainsley Lewis meant far, far less to Russell than Tom Thomson had meant to Jenny Turner. She came back with her mother from their long winter in the States and she looked as pale as she had on that miserably rainy day when they'd lowered poor Tom down. She was also putting on weight. And hardly ever smiling.

No doubt about it—from Tom's death on, Jenny Turner changed. Russell had thought it would only last a few months, then maybe a year, then two, but after that he just accepted it, and she was never again the Jenny Turner of the days before July of 1917.

She came back to Vernon near the end of March 1918, not long after her own thirty-third birthday. She was home for Easter, and she made sure she called on her old friend Russell and got him out to church.

What an unfortunate service. It was pleasant enough when they arrived: checking all the new bonnets, approving the white brocade hangings back of the altar and the Easter lilies, pink roses, and carnations spread throughout the church. But it soon became practically unbearable. Russell began fidgeting first when the choir came out singing Simper's "Awake Thou That Sleepest," and found himself actually sweating when the choir later launched into "O Death! Where Is Thy Sting?" But the worst part was the sermon: Rector Deanny rose to the pulpit, set out his notes, and announced, in his rumbling and earnest voice, that he would speak on the fear of death. Russell cowered as if he were praying, and when he looked over at Jenny he found himself looking at that same vacant expression he had first noticed on the evening he visited her after Tom had vanished.

But she only stayed in Vernon a couple of days. She returned to Toronto and stayed with relatives until mid-fall and she quickly passed through Vernon on her way to join her parents at their new home in Hemlock. After that, Russell seldom saw her. Once a year, if lucky, he'd be up to Sheffield's, the mill where Jenny was working as office manager and bookkeeper, to discuss some timber purchases, and he'd drop in and see her at the offices. Her health had returned, but not so much her fun. She seemed, well, straight-laced, older, much older. He knew enough of the boys around Hemlock to soon find out she was very highly thought of and respected throughout the town, but he noticed they spoke of her as if she were, oh, a schoolteacher, some untouchable who you might like and get along wonderfully with, but never fully know. Possibly her few close friends did, the doctor and his wife and the schoolteacher, but for the most part Jenny seemed to be living quietly and very much to herself with her parents. Harvey Turner, his legs unable to take another winter of hauling timber, got on with the railways, working in the small Hemlock switching yard. Jenny, however, soon took on the personality of the family breadwinner, particularly during her father's frequent bouts of illness. She became preoccupied with her work. And Russell knew enough Sheffield's men to know she was damned good at her job. The only thing he'd have changed for her was to have her doing it back in Vernon.

He toyed with the idea of offering himself to her as second best but better than nothing at all, yet that seemed an impossible concept to phrase in a marriage proposal. Whenever he saw her, there seemed to be others around, whether her parents or Hemlock friends, and he came to think she had engineered matters that way. Jenny acted more like an old widow than a fairly young woman who had had her engagement spoiled. A second chance was there for the taking. Russell felt Jenny would know that without him ever having to say it. But she just didn't seem interested.

He decided not to press, not ever. He would wait and be there if she needed him. And even if she never took up the opportunity, Jenny Turner would know there was one person who could always be counted on. And that was Russell Pemberton. Unlike Tom, he would be there, forever.

As for Tom Thomson, Russell was able to forget all about him for the most part. Every once in a while he'd come across a reference to the artist in a newspaper or a magazine, but no one in town talked about him. And Russell very seldom got up around Canoe Lake anymore: the company wasn't cutting around there any longer, and Russell's additional yard duties with grading and handling the men kept him tied to town almost permanently.

At times it seemed as if the Thomson memory was diminishing with time, as it should have. Had anyone told Russell in 1930 that in another thirty years the Thomson years would be in even clearer focus and the man himself a nationally-known legend, Russell would have laughed. By the spring of 1930, Tom Thomson was virtually forgotten, remembered only by those who preferred their artists dead or by those who had been there when it happened and could not forget, ever.

In the summer of 1930, however, all that quickly changed. Russell was drinking at the Olympia Hotel when he heard it and at first he thought it was a joke. But then a couple of rangers came in and they, too, had heard about it: a woman was claiming she had seen the ghost of Tom Thomson.

Russell went to great pains to sort the story out. The woman and her guide – Russell didn't recognize the name – claimed to have been coming across Smoke Lake after an afternoon's fishing when Tom Thomson pulled out of the mist in his canoe and hailed at them to follow him to the landing. He said he had something to show them. Both swore it was Thomson, right down to properly describing the very shirt he had on the day he drowned, but when they pulled up on the sand after him he simply vanished. Nor could they find the mark in the sand that the canoe should have left.

The story hit Vernon with unfortunate timing. The Turners were in town making arrangements to take over their house once again. They were coming back from Hemlock. Sheffield's was closing up and pulling out. Jenny was out of work. And her father was seriously ill.

Russell went immediately up to the Turner home, hoping to soften the blow of the story. He didn't think he could stop her from hearing it, but she should at least hear it from him. He knew how best to temper things. Especially where it concerned Tom.

Mrs. Turner met him at the door. She looked distraught.

"She's already heard, Russell."

"Where is she?"

"The garden."

Russell could hear the swing creaking as he hurried around to the back. The grass had been scythed that day and smelled strongly and hummed with disturbed insects, but even that sound, coupled with the rusty chain of the swing, could not disguise the fact that she was crying. He came and stood behind the swing.

"Jenny . . . I'm sorry."

She turned quickly, her eyes black, her cheeks flushed and streaked, then simply shifted over and made room for him. He came around and sat with her, and for several long minutes they swung, Russell worried over whether he was pushing too fast or slow. He wanted to be perfect with Jenny.

"How could they be so cruel?" she finally said.

Russell shrugged. "It's just a story."

"Story. Sure, just a story. Why can't they leave him alone, Russell?"

"I'm sorry you had to hear."

She looked at him. "Russell, even if I didn't hear on my own, I'd expect you to tell me, wouldn't I?"

227

"I suppose so." Russell knew he wouldn't.

"You haven't kept things from me before, have you, Russell?" she asked, suddenly calm.

Russell was startled. "No," he said.

"You're sure."

Did she know about the fight? Did she know he'd failed her before? Couldn't have.

"I'm sure. Why?"

"I'm sorry," she said. "I just don't know myself sometimes."

"About what?"

"About Tom."

"What do you mean?"

"You know. About the grave and all that."

Russell looked at her, scarcely believing what he was hearing. "That still wouldn't make a ghost, Jenny."

"No... no... of course it wouldn't. But I still don't understand it, Russell. You can appreciate that, can't you?"

"Yes," he said. "I don't either."

For a long moment they said nothing. She stared out at the shed, where some swallows were shouting about the invasion.

"It's unfair," she said, very quietly and seemingly to herself.

Russell said nothing. They continued swinging until Mrs. Turner came out with tea and biscuits.

They were not good years for Janet Turner. She was forty-five when Sheffield's closed operations in Hemlock, forty-five and single and unemployed, with both parents to care for. She had their house to get into shape and a job to find during lean times. She'd put on weight in Hemlock and now dressed almost solely in black clothes – like a widow, Russell thought – and apart from going to church every Sunday morning at nine, she seldom left the house and the side of her father's bed. When he died she retreated further into the house.

Russell's mother was also very ill. Abigail Pemberton was eighty-two years old then and spent most of her evenings sitting in the rocking chair in front of the stove, heating up water in the kettle and pouring it into a basin of ground up boneset leaves. All it did was make her sweat, and Russell told her so, but she argued that that was precisely what she wanted, to push out the bad chemicals. She'd start up immediately after supper and by sundown the kitchen would be like a steambath, the vapour clinging to the windows and forming dripping beads along the upper beams. Fortunately, Abigail Pemberton hummed when she took these footbaths, so Russell never tripped over her as he hurried through the kitchen in a blind search for his coat.

Abigail Pemberton died on August 27, 1933. She had lost her voice toward the end, which was a bit of a blessing: in the last few months she'd taken to talking out loud and constantly to the ghost of her grandmother, a gentlewoman from England, who had come out to settle in the Ottawa area with her dissatisfied husband, and who had so despised the pioneer life and Canada that she'd died strapped to a bed in an insane asylum. Abigail Pemberton, who once vehemently denied this family story, had later decided that she was most proud of this relation, that the poor woman had simply seen the world for what it was and had died for it.

But when Abigail Pemberton's voice went, so too did her interest in her grandmother. She turned again to her potions, convinced that constant drinking of rose hip tea and maple syrup would regenerate her throat. It didn't, of course, and later that summer she had died in her sleep, barely three days after taking herself to bed and lying back with her hands folded over her breast.

Russell was hauling pulpwood – trying to make a few extra dollars to make up for cutbacks in time at the mill – when Jenny's mother died. When he heard about it, the funeral was already past and there was little he could do but feel guilty. He should have been there when she needed him and he knew it. He decided to write her, though he knew he usually appeared even more awkward in print than in person.

In the letter he tried to perk Jenny up. He attempted, in a wandering, roundabout way, to have her take a good look at herself and to appreciate some of her good fortune. She had a house, a fine house, all paid for. She had an education and loved reading. She had her memories and she had her admiring friends, and Russell counted himself first among this group.

But it hadn't worked. She didn't write back. As soon as he could, he'd come into Vernon for a Sunday and together they walked up and down both sides of Main Street, looking at the Christmas displays. It was a cool day with great scoops of white cloud sliding across the sky in a manner that brought great shadows over Main Street in an endless parade of cold draughts. Russell told Jenny some camp jokes and she laughed and kidded him mercilessly about the potions he was mixing up and selling. "You'll turn into your mother, yet," she warned. And he had laughed and agreed with her as if he'd always known it was inevitable.

"How will you make out?" he asked as they walked up past the bowling alley and examined the town hall decorations.

"Oh, all right, I suppose."

"There's a worry?" he asked.

"I don't know yet," she said.

"Money?"

"Yes, perhaps."

"Tell me."

"Well," she began. "I can live upstairs, I think, off the rent from below. And there were some savings. The house is all paid for. And the cottage. And my friends would always help me out. I'd just hate to run into an emergency, that's all."

"What about selling some of the paintings? They're worth something these days, surely?"

"They're worth a lot."

"Well?"

Jenny turned and looked directly at him. She was no longer smiling. Stern, rather, and Russell instantly regretted ever bringing up the paintings.

"I have no intention of selling them," she said. "Not ever."

Russell left it at that. It didn't matter much. She was all right for the time being and he couldn't see any emergency arising short of the house burning down. Her needs were few and hardly likely to grow at her age.

They walked a while longer until the sky was completely clouded over and the sunless street too cold for comfort. He escorted her back, planning to catch a ride back to the camp with a couple of the men who had families in town and drove the supply truck back and forth.

She asked him to come in a moment and he did, standing near the hall rack fidgeting his hat about in his hands. The house seemed so empty to Russell now, no dishes banging in the kitchen, no bark from the big radio in the living room. It was also dusty, something Mrs. Turner would never have allowed. It had obviously been a very sad time for his friend.

She came into the hallway clutching a cardboard box with glue on one side giving way and caught with tape. She held it in her hand, looked at Russell, and smiled.

"Any idea what's in here?" she asked.

Russell laughed.

"None," he said.

She opened it. Inside was what looked like dried out and yellowed tissue paper, held together with a number of wires coated in green-black paper. There were also a number of tiny bells. Russell looked, looked again and finally saw.

It was the Duchess's corsage!

"For God's sake," Russell said. "Wherever did you come up with that?"

Jenny giggled.

"I kept it," she said. "First in the ice box and then in the refrigerator. But obviously it didn't fare as well as I'd hoped it would."

Russell touched the yellowed tissue with his finger and

realized this was once an orchid. He had never been more flattered in his life: *she'd kept something he had given to her*. When? Lordy, it must have been more than thirty years!

"But why?" he asked. He had to.

"Why what?"

"Why keep a silly thing like that?"

"Because I always knew I'd find a use for it one day."

He looked up at her. She was smiling, the warmth of the house and the cold from outside bringing a lovely flush to her cheeks.

"And have you?" he asked.

"I have," she said. "I want to give it back."

"Back? But why?"

"Just because it's important to me, that's why."

Russell took it, though he couldn't be quite sure what she meant. He puzzled over it all the way back to his house, which was now rented out—though he never bothered to collect—to a family driven off one of the nearby farms. He thought about it still when he went to meet the men in the supply truck for the long ride out to where they were cutting pulp.

It snowed then. The flakes came in through the no-draughts and through the holes in the canvas roof and up through the floorboards. Russell and the men wrapped themselves up in the two bearskins the truck always carried and shared a bottle of home-made sherry one of the men had picked up down in Vernon's little poor section out by the tannery. Russell snuggled into the fur, felt the liquor drop like fresh coals into his cold stomach, and wondered some more.

What was to become of him? What of Jenny? What, for that matter, of them both?

In October of 1956, on the drizzly day when four men went up to the tiny Canoe Lake graveyard carrying picks and shovels, Janet Turner and Russell Pemberton were both seventy-one years old. In truth, not much had become of them in the two decades since Russell had worried so about them. Jenny had finally given up her demeaning job washing sheets at a lodge on nearby Birch Lake, and Russell had retired from the mill on a small pension and had moved into the Muskoka Hotel. They remained friends, neither closer nor farther apart than they had been at the turn of the century. Both were firmly established as town eccentrics; neither could care less.

But that October they were ready to fight back. Kids trying to trip Russell as he hobbled along on his bad leg, or playing nikky-nikky-nine-doors on Jenny, failed to upset them, but four grown men disturbing a friend's grave – even if there was no one in it – certainly could.

What was most disturbing, at least to Russell, was that the four men actually found a skeleton. The skull had a hole in one temple and had at one time been covered with a shroud – just the way Russell remembered Tom on the day they buried him.

Naturally, everyone – Russell included – figured it for Thomson. The shroud, the naked body (except for one sock they must have forgot), the hole in the temple. Jenny was in a snit: she was so furious at anyone going up and deliberately desecrating a grave, whether a body had been there or not, she wouldn't even speak. Except to Russell Pemberton.

A week later Russell had been over at Jenny's for tea when some people were over pestering her about the digging. He sat watching her fidget, wondering if perhaps he should take the matter into his own hands and shoo them out.

"It's not him," she finally said. "It's an Indian."

"An Indian?" one of the men had asked incredulously. "There's no Indians around there."

"They were passing by," she said, "and one of them died."

"And how did they come to bury him there?" the man asked.

Russell had wished he was forty years younger; he'd have shut that mouth up permanently.

Jenny's lip had trembled and she'd looked down.

"They asked me," she said. "And I gave them permission."

"Permission to do what?" the loudmouth asked.

"To bury him in Tom's old grave," she said.

Russell had closed his eyes and looked down. He could not bear this humiliation.

There was a long pause, then Russell stood up and his bad knee broke the silence before he spoke.

"All right, gentlemen," he said. "That's just about enough, isn't it. Miss Turner has had a busy day and she's pretty tired."

They went without argument. Russell saw them down the stairs to the front door, made sure all were gone, then came back up to collect his hat and coat and leave himself. When he came into the living room she was crying, her face buried in her hands and her body turned toward the window, as if Russell might not then notice.

He went over and stood by her, himself looking out the window, and saw the men who had just been there crossing Maple Street and heading down toward the Muskoka Hotel.

They were laughing.

Russell closed his own eyes and touched Jenny's shoulder. He tried to read the touch, hoping to find some message there telling him what to do. But the shoulder neither moved away nor pushed closer, and after a moment he felt ill at ease standing with his hand stretched out as if she were a railing and he resting. He thought about hugging her but couldn't gather the courage to draw closer. He thought about saying something but couldn't decide on what.

Eventually he turned, gathered up his coat and hat, and let himself out, carefully closing the storm door so it wouldn't startle her.

A month later a report from the Ontario Provincial Crime Laboratory in Toronto confirmed precisely what Janet Turner had told the men that day. Dr. Noble Sharpe, who headed the investigation, concluded that the skeleton was approximately five-foot-eight, whereas Tom was six feet or more. Sharpe

234

said the man was between twenty and thirty, whereas Thomson was nearly forty, and he said the skeleton was that of a Mongolian (either Indian or half-Indian), and Thomson was certainly not that, though he may have looked like one. As for the hole in the skull, rather than being the work of Martin Bletcher or Shannon Fraser, this Doctor Sharpe speculated that the Indian "at some time... likely had an operation on his head for haemorrhage following a blow."

Russell simply couldn't buy it. What was an Indian doing there? There wasn't even a lake to be portaging to. What Indians bury their dead naked? What band of Indians would be likely to have performed intricate surgery?

Balderdash, to put it bluntly.

Russell knew there was only one way the whole crazy thing could ever be settled, and that was to take a shovel and crowbar to that grave down in Leith. If Tom was there, which Russell severely doubted, then it would all be settled. If Tom wasn't there... well, then, Jenny keeping that grave clean all these years would make a whole lot of sense, though how she knew anything, or if she indeed did, was beyond Russell.

Just as Russell knew it would, the official government version of the Canoe Lake skeleton only served to stir up the murder controversy again. Everybody had a theory, and when they couldn't try it out on poor Jenny they ended up coming to Russell. But he took his cue from her: say nothing further. She'd already tried to explain it and only made matters worse. It was surely best to say nothing. With Thomson's possible murder being talked about so much there was a lot of renewed interest in Martin Bletcher, but he was already dead by 1956 and couldn't answer the charges. Lots of others were eager to talk about Thomson but they hadn't been there that night. Unlike Shannon Fraser and Russell. But Fraser had never mentioned the fist fight and injury to Tom, nor would Russell. If it hadn't been for those headline-seekers the grave might never have been disturbed and it all would eventually have been forgotten. They obviously hadn't learned the lessons Russell Pemberton had from his mother. *What's done is done. Let sleeping dogs lie.*

... Lordy, the tea! Russell leaned over and dipped his thumb into the mug. Room temperature! He looked at his watch and jumped quickly to turn on the radio. He took a sip: amazing how good the mint tasted, so fresh and full of summer though it had been fully thirty-five years since Abigail Pemberton had ground it up.

The radio faded in, out, then in again, and stuck with a static rasp. Irritating, but not loud enough to drown out the hockey scores.

15

Indian summer skipped town some time during the night. Saturday noon, and Eleanor found herself sitting in the old Chevrolet with the heater blasting and the wipers groaning back and forth through heavy slush. She had parked directly across from the house belonging to Miss Janet Turner. As Russell Pemberton had suggested, she would try and see the old woman now. It would be her last chance. The $100 she'd arrived in Vernon with had dwindled until it barely covered the hotel bill when she checked out around eleven. There wasn't any time left either, so she wouldn't have stayed even if the money had been there. Monday was the first day of the Fall Home Furnishing sale and she was pencilled in for a full forty hours next week. Beek had warned her once about taking time off for minor things like the appointments with Dr. Klotz and she knew he had the power to drop her to twenty-four hours from her regular thirty-two, or even to dismiss her altogether. At thirty-two hours a week she was barely surviving. Beek had her and he knew it, and she knew it, too. The distance made no difference: she hated him even thinking of him, as much as if he was at that very moment picking at the buttons of her blouse.

It was sleeting now and Eleanor was unable to see through the slush packs that built up where the wipers stopped. Through the pie-shaped clearing of the wipers, Vernon seemed nothing less than wretched now, cars with their headlights on, people running and slipping on the sidewalks, their hands held up in front of their faces, eyes closed, cheeks glistening red with the sting of the wet snow. Eleanor wondered how a town could change so drastically in a single day. Weather just didn't seem to have the same status in the city as it did here.

After leaving the hotel, she had dropped down to the newspaper office to leave her address for the editor. He wasn't in, so she left it in the mail slot along with a short note begging any news, thoughts or, better still, discovery of the year 1918.

Eleanor turned off the wipers, then the ignition. The silence was overwhelming. A leaf splatted soggily on the roof, then another on the windshield. By the end of this miserable day, Eleanor figured, there would not be a leaf left: Vernon would be naked and as inspiring as a black and white photograph.

She did up her fur collar tightly, picked up her purse, and reached for her gloves. For some reason she checked herself in the mirror and found herself stabbing about her purse for her powder. A delay tactic, that's all. Anything to avoid the truth. She snapped the compact shut and pulled her gloves on quickly. She opened the door, wincing as the wind cuffed large drops of slush in on her.

She hurried to the shelter of the porch, pulled the storm door and it gave reluctantly, snapping back from the bottom and digging into her foot just above the ankle. The door inside was oak, with ornate designs, very baroque, around the window. No knocker. She changed her purse over into her other hand and hammered hard with her right knuckles.

She waited.

Nothing.

Eleanor knocked again. Much harder and longer. She pressed her ear to the misted glass and listened. Nothing still. Odd, no one had mentioned her being hard of hearing. And certainly no one would be out on a day like this, most of all an old, stiff-jointed woman.

238

She knocked again, a loud, extended hammering that made her hand sore.

She waited.

A light came on in the stairway.

Eleanor caught her breath and held it. She wet her lips, though they were wet enough already from the weather.

She could hear someone on the stairs. A dragging sound, a slight knock, a pause – step, place the cane down, rest. Eleanor closed her eyes, took another breath. The sound continued, growing as it came closer. Eleanor felt guilty that she'd made the old lady move. She wished she could just burst through the door and tell her not to bother, that she would come up and make them both a fine lunch and take good care of her.

The flat side of a palm came against the pane. Eleanor could see the wrinkles, the whiteness around the bones. The hand began moving in a circular motion, clearing the mist away: a hole grew in the window.

The hand moved and was replaced by an eye. From what Eleanor could see the eye was clear enough, intelligent, but it was nesting in a dark tangle of lines and sagging skin.

Eleanor smiled. Last time she'd used that smile was during her job interview at Eaton's. It felt phoney, little-girlish.

The eye moved away.

Eleanor heard the latch jangle, then there was a lift and the doorknob turned, slowly, then quickly with a burst of effort. The door opened inward.

Miss Janet Turner looked older than seventy-six. Large and heavy. Sad. Her face was white, the hair blue, grey, and white, and somewhat dishevelled, and there were several light black hairs on her upper lip, so stark against the whiteness of the old skin that they seemed to have been inked onto paper.

The mouth, with so many lines running away from it that it seemed stitched to the face, moved, spoke.

"I'm sorry I made you wait so long," the old lady said. The voice had a strength the skin did not. It did not sound old; in fact, to Eleanor, it sounded much purer than her own, which lately seemed to be getting more and more throaty from her smoking.

Eleanor cleared her throat. Twice.

"Miss Turner," she said. "My name is Eleanor Philpott, from Toronto. I...uh...Mr. Pemberton said perhaps I should call on you, if you felt up to it."

"I know who you are," the old woman said.

Eleanor felt her lip tremble. She cleared her throat again, but the old lady spoke before she had a chance to say anything.

"Come in, dear. I'll make tea."

"Thank you," Eleanor said. She eased in through the door. There was hardly room for the two of them on the small landing. The old lady turned awkwardly.

"I'm afraid you'll have to help me up."

"Of course. Here..."

Eleanor felt it was like hauling up a trunk. She stepped first, then pulled. Miss Janet Turner followed, breathing heavily; her cane rattled along the step edges as she held it loosely in her right hand. The left knee seemed stiff, and she did all the stepping with the right foot, dragging the left after it and resting after each completed step. Eleanor realized it must have taken just as much effort to get downstairs—no wonder she had waited so long.

The stairway smelled musty. *Old*. At the top of the stairs a bare bulb glared down. On both sides of the steps there was dust piled high, and several of the rubber treads were broken.

By the time they reached the top the old lady was wheezing loudly, but she wouldn't rest. She let go of Eleanor and moved across the short upper hallway to the doorway leading into the living room. Eleanor was obviously supposed to follow. She passed another door leading off the hallway into a side room, and the door had two large bolts and two heavy padlocks on it. *The Thomson paintings?* No, they were supposedly with the Walker Galleries in Toronto. What, then? Letters? A diary? A lock of baby's hair? Eleanor's imagination was running away with her.

240

The living room was a mess. Newspapers and magazines were piled everywhere and there was a large blue oil stain on the red linoleum around the space heater. It was cool inside, the heater obviously not on, and Eleanor noticed the old woman was wearing heavy boots, which dragged across the floor. Her hose had fallen and hung sloppily over the top of the boots.

With Eleanor's help, Miss Turner stepped down the two narrow steps leading from the living room to the dining room. Here, more newspapers and stacks of mail were strewn across a round oak table. She pulled out one chair with a worn red cushion on it, sat down heavily, and then rattled another chair with her cane, an indication that Eleanor was also to sit.

"I-I could get the tea if you like," Eleanor said.

"Sit."

Eleanor sat.

"There's plenty of time for tea, my dear," the old woman said. "Where have you come from?"

"Toronto."

"You have an accent."

"Yes, well, I'm American. At least *was* American."

"Oh, indeed. Where? I had relations in the States."

"Philadelphia," Eleanor said. She looked hard for any hint. But there was none.

"I see."

Eleanor wanted to ask if she had ever been to Philadelphia but she didn't know how to do it to make it appear casual, particularly if she was right in her guess. It would seem obvious.

"I'll get the tea now," the old woman said, and got up slowly. Eleanor moved to help but she was too late.

She sat and looked around while Miss Turner moved about in the kitchen. The house was desperately in need of a cleaning. She looked at some of the magazines stacked on the chair closest to her. None could have been newer than five years old. There was a china cabinet but the glass was dusty and the cups were stacked rather than hung. And a box of newspaper clippings. She leaned forward to see – *Thomson?* – but they were all obituaries, neatly cut out by scissors, and all of the names meaningless to Eleanor.

Miss Turner came back from the kitchen with the tea and a tray of cookies. The tea wasn't steaming and was very black. It had probably been steeping since morning. Eleanor said nothing, took one of the shortbreads and a quick sip of the sour-tasting tea.

"Now, what is it you wanted to see me about?" Miss Turner asked. Her hand trembled as she raised the cup to her mouth.

"I'm curious about Tom Thomson."

"Isn't everyone," the old woman said sarcastically.

Not in the same way! Eleanor wanted to say.

"I understand he gave you several paintings," Eleanor said.

"Are you an art dealer?" the old woman asked.

"No."

"What are you, then?"

Eleanor coughed for time, knew it gave her away. She hadn't prepared for that kind of a question. *She* was supposed to be asking the questions.

"I'm... doing a study on Mr. Thomson."

"What kind of study?"

"On his life."

"His death. Posh," said Miss Turner, "no one does his life. They do his death. That's where they all begin."

Eleanor felt a sharp pain in her temples, which left as quickly as it had come. She groped for something to say.

"... and where it ended for me," the old woman went on matter-of-factly. "So I'm not much use to you, am I?"

"But I'm interested in *you*, as well..." Eleanor said, anxious for the conversation to return to its casual beginnings.

"My paintings?" the old woman said defensively.

"No. In you."

"Why?"

"Well. . . because you were close, for one thing."

Miss Turner took a quick sip of her tea.

"I was there when he died, if that's what you mean."

"No," Eleanor said, also pausing for a taste of the tea. "I meant you were close friends."

"We were?"

"Mr. Pemberton. . . he suggests you may have been engaged to marry."

Miss Turner fixed Eleanor straight on; the eyes seemed too clear for their age. They were the eyes of a child. Eleanor felt they were focussing just behind her, looking through her.

"Russell Pemberton does not know everything, my dear, despite what he may think to the contrary."

Eleanor's mind was racing. The hard edge, sheathed momentarily, was emerging again in Miss Janet Turner. Eleanor looked to her teacup for comfort. Her mind was concentrating as hard as it could on the conversation, looking for hidden meanings, breaks, shifts, slammed doors, anything that might tell her something the words were not. The pain shot again, then cleared.

Eleanor looked up, smiling. She gambled: "But you *were* engaged."

Miss Turner nodded, then sipped her tea, her eyes staying with Eleanor. Or just behind her.

Is she looking for my reaction? Eleanor wondered. *Who is interviewing whom?*

"I've read the papers from that time," Eleanor said. "There was never an announcement."

"Not officially, no," Miss Turner said.

"When would it have been?" Eleanor asked. "The marriage, I mean."

"September 1917."

Eleanor's mind did a rapid calculation. *Yes. September at the latest.*

The old woman put down her cup and saucer with a loud

243

rattle. Eleanor wanted to read something into that, but the woman was seventy-six, after all. She would have to watch to see if the hand steadied.

"You've been through the town paper, have you?" Miss Turner asked.

"Um hum," Eleanor said, swallowed. "Yes."

Miss Turner smiled. "That must be something, to read it all again. But there wasn't much on it, was there?"

Eleanor shook her head. "No."

Again the smile, quizzical. "You see, it didn't matter then. Just to me. And a few others. It's bigger now than it was then, if that makes sense."

"Well, he's very famous," Eleanor said.

"He's dead." Miss Turner looked through her again, and again the mysterious smile.

"Yes, of course," Eleanor found herself on the defensive. "But people are interested –"

"Why are *you* interested?"

Eleanor was again caught off guard. "Because of my study, of course."

"What will the study tell anyone that they don't already know, though?"

Eleanor could feel herself scrambling. "Well... perhaps something about what influenced him."

Miss Turner smiled condescendingly. "You don't seem like much of an art scholar, my dear."

"Yes, well, as I said, I'm interested in your life, as well."

Miss Turner looked about her. "In this?"

Eleanor's pain returned, lingered this time.

"But *you* influenced him –"

"So some might claim."

"No. I didn't mean that."

"You think he killed himself?"

"No. I didn't say that."

"But others have."

Eleanor felt she had no choice but to follow along. The conversation was no longer within her control. She was chasing now; she'd imagined herself leading. Perhaps everything else was to turn out differently as well.

"He didn't," Miss Turner said.

"He didn't," Eleanor repeated.

"Of course not. Why would he?"

Eleanor could only shrug. *How would I know?*

"You're interested in me because you think I pushed him," Miss Turner said.

"I–"

"Well, I did not push him. You don't wait for four years just to have it all burst by squeezing."

Unless, Eleanor thought.

Miss Turner leaned forward.

"You think I was pregnant, don't you?"

Eleanor felt dizzy. She cleared her throat, could feel the heat rise in her face.

"It's all right," Miss Turner said. "Get it out in the open if that's what you're thinking."

"Well, it is a rumour," Eleanor began.

She was cut off.

"Precisely that – rumour. A lie." Miss Turner said firmly.

Eleanor fled to her tea. It was now very cool, bitter.

Miss Turner's odd smile returned; it attacked her face like a plastic surgeon, tightening up, smoothing, cutting decades from the truth.

"Besides," she said, "you only have to look around you."

Eleanor was again caught off guard. The conversation had moved so far out in front of her that she found herself doing its bidding, gawking around as if she'd suddenly awakened in this strange room. With this strange woman.

"You see?" Miss Turner asked, delight surfacing.

Eleanor could only stare back, totally confused.

The old woman shut her eyes a moment, then opened them with the focus behind Eleanor.

"If I was pregnant," she said slowly, "where is the child?"

The headache settled to stay. Eleanor winced, felt faint.

What is going on here?

"So you see," Miss Turner went on. "We really haven't anything to discuss now, have we?"

Eleanor felt she had to move quickly to salvage the moment. Her head was throbbing; she felt woozy.

"Couldn't we go back to when you first met him?" she began, but she knew it was futile.

Miss Turner shook her head. "There'd be nothing in it for you. And I'm really quite tired, my dear." She closed her eyes, as if she slept sitting.

Eleanor gave up immediately, hated herself for it, but she felt nauseated. She *had* to leave.

"Perhaps we could meet again," she said in desperation.

Miss Turner shook her head again. Her eyes were still shut. "It would be a waste of time," she said.

Eleanor stood, reached for her purse.

"How old are you, my dear?" Miss Turner asked.

How old am I? Eleanor's stomach was turning.

"Forty-three."

The old woman clucked her tongue several times. "Forty-three," she repeated. "So young to waste your time on idle gossip. There was *no* baby, I assure you. Save yourself the trouble, my dear. Direct your attentions to something that's there, and matters. Not some malicious slander."

Eleanor found herself nodding, thanking Miss Turner. Yes, she could see her way down by herself. The time was appreciated. She hoped they could meet again. Goodbye and thank you, thank you.

Three miles out of town Eleanor turned in at a White Rose gas station. She parked and hurried into the washroom, slamming the cubicle door behind her. The seat was filthy, streaked, and the bowl hadn't been flushed. Eleanor flushed it carefully, twice, then cleaned the seat with the hard, waxen sheets from the dispenser. Then she was sick, twice, and the incredible heat in her temples shifted to a cool band across her forehead. She sat down on the lowered toilet seat and buried her face in her hands.

What had happened? She'd lost control of the interview. All her questions were lost. *What had happened? What did it mean?*

"*Look around you . . . Where is the child?*"

I'm here!

Here!

"*How old are you?*"

But you know how old I am!

"*Save yourself the trouble, my dear. There was no baby.*"

But there was a baby!

Me.

She heard her own moan, distant, frightening, and only then realized she was crying. She looked up at the cubicle door, flecked paint, lipstick drawings of breasts and penises, and she saw her own breath, noticing for the first time that the washroom wasn't heated.

She felt the cold sink in then, and started to shake. She shook with the cold and with her own sobs. Her stomach tightened and bent her forward and she vomited again, over the floor. She sat there still, ripping the unruly sheets from the dispenser and cleaning up the slimy mess between her shoes.

When the heaving finally stopped, the calm returned. She stood up and rubbed her eyes, then saw in the mirror how smudged and red they were, how startling against the paleness of her face.

Instinctively, Eleanor reached for her make-up. She pulled the lipstick free first and automatically opened it. She only stopped when she had the lipstick to her mouth.

Eleanor then did something she had never done before. She reached out toward the mirror and scribbled two words.

ELEANOR THOMSON.

The lipstick broke on the final letter and she threw it on the floor and kicked at it, smudging the red grease hideously along the battleship-grey floor.

She started to laugh at what she'd done *You, Eleanor?*

16

Russell Pemberton made a porthole in the window by blowing on the frost and then rubbing with his palm. When it gave way he could see the sun cresting Rock Hill, its light firing on the single open spot left on the frozen river. It was a bitterly cold day; the smoke from the wood fires squeezed into the sky like thick toothpaste, the air so cold and still and brittle it tightened Russell's nostrils just to think about it. He'd never seen the dawn from this side of the river before. Hell, he'd never been in a hospital before.

Between his window and the river stood a thick oak tree, and not a half-dozen feet away an ash. Both uncommon trees in town. Russell knew why they were there. He'd seen his own mother plant ash and oak side by side in their yard further up on the hill close to seventy years ago, and he remembered still the rhyme she taught him on how to read spring.

Oak before ash, summer of splash,
Ash before oak, summer of smoke.

Dry summer, wet summer – who gave a damn? All Russell hoped was that he wouldn't be there when the leaves came out. It was already the end of January. If he had to stay here until May he was dead for sure.

The humiliation of it all! Here he was, standing at a window wearing a silly little starched shirt with no back in it, his bare ass presented to anyone who happened to pass by the doorway. He had a crib to sleep in – a bed with *sides*, for God's sake – and a bunch of surly nurses shoving bed pans at him every time he grunted. He'd told them he wouldn't move his bowels until they let him go home and they'd answered that as if it were a challenge, sending in this twinkle-toed male orderly with a great tube of soapy water to insult Russell's rear end and cause him to spill his private business all over the bed. Wasn't his fault. But try and tell them that.

Tests, the doctor said. Tests. Have you been having the dizzy spells long? How's your appetite? Do you always feel bloated? Can you pass some water into this cup? Just one more tube of blood... one more... one more...

I will get out of here. And I will never, ever, come back in.

Russell went back toward the bed, elbowing the glucose drip stand out of his way as he moved. At least they hadn't used that since they brought him in. Damn that it ever happened – should have taken those steps slower, blacking out just when they were loading up the Timmins bus, in front of all those poor people. He sat and put his feet up.

Not long till supper now, not that it matters. Can't swallow anyway. He looked at his night table. Two cards, the gaudy one from Jenny, the plain one from Archie. And the envelope. He reached for it and took out the letter again.

Jan. 23, 1962

Mr. Russell Pemberton,
c/o The Muskoka Hotel,
Vernon, Ont.

Dear Mr. Pemberton,

I don't know whether you'll remember me or not, but I was the woman who spoke to you several times last fall about Tom Thomson.

I've nearly finished my research but I've hit one hitch. I

had hoped to finish out what happened to those who were close to him that summer (1917) and, in particular, I was interested in Miss Janet Turner. She was good enough to see me (as you suggested) and though she was most helpful regarding Mr. Thomson, I foolishly neglected to ask her about her own whereabouts in the months after. You told me, you'll recall, that she went to live in Hemlock in the fall of 1918. So I need to place her between the tragic drowning and that time, the space of about one year. I believe you mentioned in passing that she took a long trip to the States, but I forget the details, I'm afraid.

Any help you could give me would, of course, be much appreciated.

I trust this finds you in fine health. I look forward to hearing back from you.

Yours sincerely,

Eleanor Philpott

Russell crumpled the letter and tossed it into the wastebasket. *What a crock of shit! I told that woman nothing about Hemlock in June of 1918. I said not one goddam thing about any trip to the United States of America.*

He'd hoped he'd seen the last of her when she pulled out that sleety day back – *when?* Fall, yes fall. He'd gone straight up to see Jenny after she'd left and she had been in a funny state. She shouldn't have agreed to see her. But she wanted to. Whatever she said it must have upset Jenny. And no one had a right to do that.

"What happened?" Russell had asked.

"Nothing," Jenny said.

"You've been crying."

"I was thinking about Tom and me, and the life we might have had."

"What did she want to know?"

"The usual – no, not the usual – she wanted to know about the engagement."

"Did you tell her?"

"Did *you*?"

They'd looked at each other then and laughed. Russell had pursued the point no further. But he knew that the conversation between the city woman and Jenny had disturbed his dearest friend.

And Russell Pemberton should never have allowed that to happen.

It was a bad winter all around. Montreal still hadn't recovered from the loss of the Rocket. It was enough to make a purist puke—one year after the great Maurice Richard retires some young whippersnapper named Hull scored fifty goals in a single season. Geoffrion he could take, but *Hull*? And this, how do you say it, Ma-hov-lich? Him scoring forty-eight goals. And him a goddam Maple Leaf? Russell couldn't even pronounce the new star's name, but he sure could hate him.

Maybe he was seventy-seven years old. Maybe he was in a crib. But he'd teach that young whippersnapper Mahovlich to respect the Rocket if he ever got hold of him.

Ma-ha-volich. Toronto. Figures. Toronto makes me puke. Him. That goddam woman. They all deserve each other. Goddam that city to hell!

Eleanor Philpott checked the mailbox as soon as she arrived home from Eaton's. Nothing. Nothing again. It had been more than two weeks since she'd written. It was near time to give up hope, surely. Perhaps he was dead. Should she phone the Muskoka? Would it matter if she found out he was?

Tom Thomson and Janet Turner had become an obsession. She thought Dr. Klotz was worried for her. Sometimes she thought he was encouraging her, though. Sometimes she thought she'd soon have him making house calls. Three times in January she hadn't been able to come into work. Not sick or anything, just couldn't come in. The third time she'd even dressed and come downtown, then circled the

College Street store for the better part of an hour before she decided she couldn't enter. And she was smoking more. Chain-smoking, if they'd only let her. Perhaps Eaton's wasn't so bad; at least it forced her to cut down.

How many times had she been back over that meeting with Janet Turner? How many times in the months since had she lain in bed late and tossed ashamedly as she remembered that immature "Eleanor Thomson" she'd scribbled in the gas station washroom? She could roll to her left side and break down the talk with the old woman until it became a clear, premeditated message—*she was trying to tell me*. Shivering at this thought she could shift to her right side and suddenly see the old woman's words crystal clear: "There was no baby, I assure you." Who could mistake that? There was no relationship between one Eleanor Philpott, late of Philadelphia, and one Janet Turner, of Vernon.

She is not my mother.

(Roll to the other side, sigh.)

She is, too.

It all related to words, and they could take on any form she wished. Back in her days as a librarian, Eleanor had taken great pride in maintaining an attitude only slightly above contempt for dictionaries. She never made mistakes in spelling. And using such an obvious cheater for the *New York Times* crossword was, well, immoral. Now she realized there was a third facet to her dislike. And that was distrust. Words couldn't be broken down like some chemical equation. Together they didn't mean the total of what they meant separately. Alone, they meant anything she chose for them to mean, in any context. Words were sneaky.

Perhaps the search for Jenny and Tom was diversion. Anything to avoid the realities of this mad situation. *Perhaps I am crazy*. Too many thoughts with barbed-wire edges. Jenny was a comfort, offered. It had only to come true and she would gladly take it.

The phone rang at eight-fifteen. She let it ring for some time, then answered.

"Hello?"

"Mrs. Philpott?" a crisp, clipped voice asked.

"Yes..."

"George Baronskill here, Mrs. Philpott. You do remember me?"

"Yes, of course." *But how does he remember me? What does he want?*

"I got your number from Joyce Maynard. She says you're still keen on Tom Thomson. That right?"

"Yes... right, I am."

"We're bidding on a new Thomson—sorry, an *unknown* Thomson—that's just come on the market. I went out to authenticate it yesterday. Real thing, for sure. Owned by a Mrs. Cassidy here in Toronto who's very old and says she was at Canoe Lake the summer Thomson drowned. You interested?"

Eleanor was stunned. It wasn't like her to have luck.

"Yes. Very..."

"Here's her number then." George Baronskill was all business.

Eleanor scrambled for a pen. "Yes, go ahead."

She wrote down the number. "I don't know how to thank you, Mr. Baronskill."

He chuckled. The first time she had heard him laugh. "Just put in a good word for Walker Galleries, okay?"

"Yes, I will... thank you, thank you."

She was incredibly proud of herself. First the phone call, the invitation to tea, the lie about a doctor's appointment, the rush for Bus 33 up Avenue Road, knock at the door, enter, admire the antiques and the war pictures of the late husband, and soon it was all sitting in her notebook. If she could pick the information up and hug it, she would have.

Mrs. Cassidy, a frail eighty or more—she wouldn't say when Eleanor asked—had been completely open.

"You were staying at Mowat Lodge in 1917?"

"Yes, my husband had tuberculosis. That's what they did for you then. Send you up for fresh air and sit you outside wrapped in army blankets."

"It worked, I hope."

"It worked," the old woman smiled.

Eleanor liked her very much.

"You knew Thomson well?"

She giggled. "Well enough. He thought I was, shall I say 'available.'"

Eleanor arched her eyebrows. "'Available?'"

"Come, come, dearie. You know what I mean. My husband was ill, after all. I was a young woman."

Eleanor glanced quickly at the faded picture on the mantel. And pretty, too.

"But didn't Thomson have a girl?"

Another giggle. "He most certainly did."

"Do you recall anything about her?"

"Janet Turner? Oh, I should say so, yes. She was very pretty. I think I might even admit in my old age to a little envy. And she had Tom wrapped around her little finger whenever she was around."

"She wasn't around all the time?"

"No, of course not. She had a job in – what's that name? – Vernon, yes Vernon. Darling little town. Do you know it?"

"Yes."

"She came up only the odd weekend. That's why I had troubles with Tom. He fancied himself quite a ladies' man. But when she was there she pretty well ran him, I can tell you that. They were going to be married, you know. Janet had written a letter."

"A letter?"

"Annie Fraser – the woman who ran the lodge – was yapping about it all over the lake. She read it when she was cleaning Tom's room. Janet told Tom to make sure he got back the money Annie's husband owed him, and to make

254

sure he got it back fast. They had to get on with the wedding as soon as possible. Had to."

"*Had* to?" Eleanor felt lightheaded.

"Well, yes. According to Annie Fraser anyway, the letter was quite definite."

"There was a baby coming?"

"Apparently."

Eleanor swallowed carefully. "But what happened then?"

"Did he commit suicide? I don't know, my dear. I don't know."

"No, not that. Do you know if there was in fact a baby?"

"There wasn't next summer when I went back, that's all I know."

But what happened over the winter?

Eleanor was shaking when she left Mrs. Cassidy's apartment. She had something new: a letter. *Miss Janet Turner was pregnant. It was down in black and white, in Mrs. Cassidy's words, in Annie Fraser's words. Didn't matter. She said it was written down. Well, you don't know that for sure. You haven't seen the letter. . . . It happened, I know it happened.*

She was the closest she'd yet been to the truth. It only required confirmation from one person, but that one person had already shown herself reluctant to talk openly to Eleanor.

But standing on Avenue Road, waiting for the Number 33 bus, Eleanor knew that she would once again have to meet with Miss Janet Turner.

Two weeks later, on her forty-fourth birthday, Eleanor raced up Yonge Street, toward Bloor. It was six o'clock, the street blue with streetlights and new snow. Cars growled as they moved away from intersections, whined as they accelerated. But Eleanor wasn't thinking of the weather, nor of her dinner date with Joyce. She was considering her luck. It had never occurred to her that it would ever require her coming

255

to terms with. Like royalty, or being a man – it was so far out of her daily thought that it came upon her like a foreign language. She felt lost with it. But luck was what it was. Forget the years behind her. Forget the depressions. She was lucky now. First the woman. Now the editor's letter. She was going to show it to Joyce, her sounding-board since Vernon.

It would be nice to show it to Joyce, all right, but how wonderful if she could only share her discoveries with Marilyn Monroe. She'd read in *National Geographic* about Eskimo women singing into each other's mouths to produce an eerie, wild, musical sound that could be traced to neither woman, that seemed to exist apart from the women and beyond the capacity of mere vocal cords. What sounds would she and Marilyn make together? The same sound, different sources. Somewhere, outside of their flesh, they would be exactly the same.

"Shall we have liqueurs with our coffee?" Eleanor said when the appropriate time came for the unveiling.

Joyce laughed. "The wine wasn't enough?"

"Not for what else I have to tell you."

Joyce laughed. "Bring it on, then. But this better be good."

Eleanor caught the waiter's attention first try – something she'd never been able to do before – put it down to more good luck (*Christ, it breeds!*), and ordered Grand Marnier for both.

She pulled the envelope out of her purse. "This came yesterday."

She spun it in Joyce's direction. Joyce picked it up and read.

February 20, 1962

Dear Mrs. Philpott,

Knowing my reputation for losing things, you should count your lucky stars that the scrap of paper with your name and address on it was still on my desk. And considering it's now been almost four months since it was put there, it should give you some idea of how clean my office is these days.

Which also explains how we lost 1918. One of the guys had the file out cribbing little "flashback" items for the paper. I finally found it by the paste-up table, covered by a half-ton of waste paper.

You're more than welcome to go through it yourself if you come back up to Vernon – and I, for one, hope you do. But you're undoubtedly immediately wondering what's in it concerning Miss Janet Turner and Tom Thomson. Not much, I'm afraid, but I'll fill you in on what I found.

At Easter there's a personal item about Miss Turner, saying she was home for the weekend and would be returning to Toronto – she was staying with relatives, I believe. Her mother was back staying in town and there was a mention that they'd enjoyed their winter stay in Philadelphia.

Next mention is for June 15, a short farewell to the Turners, who were moving up to Hemlock, and then, in July, that her mother was going to summer at the Canoe Lake cottage. No mention of Janet Turner – but of course we can understand her not wanting to be there, so close to where he drowned and all.

That's it. Deadline's upon us yet again.

Do come and see us, though.

Sincerely,

It was signed by someone whose name meant nothing to Joyce. Underneath he had written "Editor" and she knew it was the man who'd helped Eleanor.

Joyce read for emphasis: "... *enjoyed their winter stay in Philadelphia.*"

"Yes."

"Then you're right."

"I think I am."

"No. You *are* right. It's right here. Philadelphia."

"Della Street might point out to Perry Mason that it's all circumstantial evidence," Eleanor said.

"It convinces me."

"I'm going back up, just to make sure."

"When?"

"As soon as I can arrange it after the snow's gone."

"Why wait?"

"I haven't got snow tires."

"Oh."

"Besides, I want to see Canoe Lake."

"Why?"

"Just to see."

Joyce nodded. She understood. "It's starting to look like that's what happened," she said.

Eleanor lifted her glass. "Hold the congratulations until I'm sure. There's a very old woman has to have a say in this yet, you know."

Joyce toasted Eleanor. They finished. Joyce called for seconds. They came and she toasted again. "I hope it works out the way you want it."

"So do I."

Joyce paused. "What will it mean – if it's true."

Eleanor tilted her head. "I've been wondering the same thing."

"You'll be Eleanor Thomson. I mean you'd have *been* Eleanor Thomson."

"Perhaps I've been someone else all along and haven't known it."

Eleanor's mind couldn't stay on the session with Dr. Klotz. He was asking about her father and she was trying to tell him about his big study and the unused books, and how they used to read the comics together on Sunday afternoon.

"It's funny," Eleanor said, talking at random. "He smoked the same tobacco as you in his pipe."

258

Doctor Klotz cleared his throat, then spoke almost apologetically.

"I don't smoke a pipe."

Eleanor sat up abruptly, turned, flushing.

"Of course you do."

"No. I don't."

"But I *smell* it!"

"No, Eleanor, you *think* you smell it. There's a big difference."

Eleanor felt a total fool.

"My God!" she said. "You must think I'm crazy."

Instantly she realized what she had said. She closed her eyes. When she opened them she was relieved, not unlike a child who expects to be bitten by a dog which has run up close to it, but sees then it's friendly, as she saw that Doctor Klotz was smiling back at her reassuringly.

"Don't take it so seriously," he said. "It happens sometimes. You remember what he looked like; there's no reason you can't remember what he smelled like. The nose is often better at remembering than your eyes are."

But she still felt terrible. *There's a big difference*, he had said. And she could only think he intended that to apply to her obsession with Janet Turner. What exactly was the difference between *thinking* she was the woman's daughter and actually *being* the daughter.

She couldn't wait to see Dr. Klotz to tell him about the new developments. She wondered whether he was even interested in her pursuit of the old lady, though he had never changed the subject on her when she'd brought it up before. And this time was no different.

This time, he asked her to describe Miss Janet Turner as if he had never heard of her before. He asked her to use as few words as possible. She did it quickly, and was proud of it, using all the words she'd come to fit to this old woman she didn't know: self-assured, misunderstood, tough, outspoken, proper, respected...

259

"Are you sure," Doctor Klotz had asked in his usual measured tones, "you aren't really describing the Eleanor who never was? The part of you you're not willing to acknowledge."

Eleanor thought about that a while, toward the end concentrating more on the silence than on the question.

"Perhaps," she said. She wasn't sure just what to say.

There was a long pause. Eleanor could hear him sucking on his pipe—*no, he didn't smoke a pipe!* He must have been making the sound on his pencil. She didn't dare look.

"We've talked a lot before about menopause, Eleanor," he finally said.

"Yes."

"Have we talked about 'lost time?'"

"No."

"But you yourself feel as if you've missed out on things, don't you?"

"Well . . . perhaps."

"Clinically it sounds like this: the menopause brings on a terror, an awesome fear of having missed something or of not mattering now, and that terror manifests itself in depression. Sound familiar?"

Eleanor pretended to think about that for a while. She didn't need to.

"I guess so," she said. She was beginning to feel sulky. She didn't care for Klotz when he slipped into Klotz the lecturer.

"Would you rather look back on the life of Eleanor, uh . . ."—she knew he was checking his notes—"Thomson rather than Eleanor Philpott?"

Eleanor refused to answer.

He waited her out.

She felt herself getting defensive. "Well, it would have been different, wouldn't it?"

"In what way?"

Eleanor felt he was playing with her. "In every way," she said, instantly aware she was being needlessly sharp. "You

260

don't have to be a trained psychologist to know what different environments mean."

She turned further away from his eyes, afraid not for what he might see, but for what she might see him doing. Smiling.

"You don't have to be a trained psychologist, either, Eleanor, to tell someone to take a second look before they wrap up their former life and toss it away."

"I've *taken* a second look," Eleanor said. "And a ninety-fifth look, for that matter."

"And you'd throw it all away."

"I didn't say that."

"No. You didn't."

Again, a long pause. Eleanor would wait him out this time.

"You're forty-four years old, Eleanor, am I right?"

"Yes."

"And what have those forty-four years got to show for themselves?"

Eleanor was getting angry. She hated being led. She knew what he wanted. She also knew what she wanted to give him. *Nothing!* But...

"I don't know," she said. She knew that was what he was waiting for. It would soon be over now. She had opened the door. She would hold it for him, let him go first.

"Those years produced you, didn't they?"

Big deal!

"Yes," Eleanor said. She was tired of the grip he had taken on the conversation.

"And that's not so bad now, is it?"

How would you possibly know? she felt like saying. When did he ever see her except at a disadvantage, lying on some sweaty, sticky couch while he loomed over like some vulture waiting for her to drop some final proof that he did indeed have a role to play.

Eleanor nodded. She knew it was the easiest answer. She knew, too, it would end the conversation.

Following her session with Klotz she walked around the

261

Grange Park, thinking about the old woman in Vernon and herself in Toronto. She didn't need Klotz. Why hadn't she seen how shallow he was before? A fortune cookie could tell her as much. She thought of him noting the visit in her file: *getting through today*. She'd like to tell him to strike the first word. *Through today* – that was more like it.

"Lost time." Yes, but lost time implies there is something to be found. And once the good weather came, Eleanor knew just where to look.

17

Eleanor smelled sulphur as she turned off Highway 11 onto the business section exit into Vernon. Of course, firecrackers. It was Friday of Victoria Day weekend, with weather fit for a holiday. Earlier as she drove there had been a slight down-pour but now the rain had rinsed the clouds away as it left. The day seemed brighter than necessary. She passed a youngster on a bicycle and the sunlight flashed on the spokes and the wet chrome of his wheel rim. There was steam rising from the road. A day full of promise.

Despite his word, Beek had put pressure on her to stay and work that Saturday but she refused to give in to him. He had been far easier to deal with since she'd slapped his face for fluttering his hands over her left breast. She should have realized all along he was more frightened of losing his job than she was hers. Things were changing for the better for Eleanor.

Her spirits had picked up when she passed the sign about the North Pole, announcing to drivers that they were now halfway there. She'd worked out on paper the argu-ment for her relationship to Tom Thomson and had been satisfied with it, and she was off now to visit his grave – as any proper daughter should – and get final confirmation from her mother. She hoped.

She felt herself being absorbed into the business section of the town as the residential part of Main Street began appearing in her rear-view mirror. With the sun bouncing off the lake and the leaves still unfolding in light greens, Eleanor felt there might not be as pretty a town in the entire country, and she allowed herself the indulgence of thinking herself a part of it. How good it would be to walk along this street and know the face and name and business of everyone behind every door. How much finer, obviously, than riding an elevator with everyone staring at the floor-indicator as if the floors might have shuffled around overnight.

She slowed down and pulled into the hotel parking lot. From here she had a view of the big Turner house, though none of its windows looked directly out on her. She rolled down the window and put her arm out, feeling the warmth of the late afternoon sun on the car. She could smell lilac.

Nothing seemed changed but the weather. The house had no new coat of paint, though it certainly could have done with one. The grass, however, was neatly cut and raked, and the garden out to the east was as neat and structured as an illustration.

Perhaps we'll just sit in it this summer. Not even talk. Just sharing. Family.

The editor drained a second cup of coffee. In the hour they had been together, he had done little but listen and nod, whether in agreement or out of simple politeness, Eleanor could not tell. Now he leaned forward onto his chaotic desktop.

"Now I understand why you wanted 1918, I guess," he said. "It certainly appears as if something might have happened, that's for sure."

"*Might* have happened?" Eleanor said. She finished her cup of coffee.

"Well," the editor said, and grinned deprecatingly, "speaking as a journalist, I'd have to say you don't quite have the goods yet. You've got an old woman claiming that she heard another woman tell her over forty years ago that this other woman had seen a letter that mentioned a baby coming.

That's what – second – no third-hand information? Hearsay, in other words. You have yourself, born in 1918 in Philadelphia, you say in a home for unwed mothers, to an Ontario woman who'd become pregnant through some liaison with an artist who died."

The editor paused.

"You have Janet Turner leaving town for an extended train trip early in the fall and then, on November 8, we have her leaving with her mother to spend the winter in Philadelphia and not coming back until Easter, giving you time to be born and her plenty of time to recuperate. And the dates work out roughly from the date of the letter referring to the pregnancy to your own birth date."

"And," Eleanor interjected, "we have her leaving town almost as soon as she returned and taking up in another town, and changing drastically."

The editor shrugged and smiled sheepishly.

"But no proof," he said. "As I see it you've either got to have her confirm it to you or else you're never going to know. Maybe there never was a letter about a baby. Just gossip – malicious gossip at that. Maybe no baby. Maybe she just went to Philadelphia to rest. Maybe, too, she went to Hemlock because that was the only job open to her. Lots of soldiers coming back from overseas, you know. Jobs were tight.

"So, if she doesn't tell you, you better not tell anyone, particularly not anyone from around here, because you wouldn't find anybody – and I mean *anybody*, Mrs. Philpott – with a more respectable reputation than her. For most people to even imagine Janet Turner holding hands with someone would be impossible. You see what I mean?"

But Eleanor did not, not quite. She had no intention of telling anyone. It wasn't as if this thing was any kind of news story or anything. If Janet Turner confirmed it, it would simply be between the two of them, and perhaps a few select people in Toronto whom Eleanor might choose to tell. She certainly wouldn't broadcast it. After all, if Janet Turner was her mother – and she was convinced she *was* – then wouldn't Eleanor herself have a vested interest in her mother's reputation? Of course she would. The editor was just too caught up in having "the goods."

"Well, yes," Eleanor said. "I plan on seeing her, of course. First, though, I've got to go up and see Russell Pemberton."

The editor groaned. "Good luck with them both. Especially Russell."

"What do you mean?"

"I doubt Russell's of much use," he said. "Poor bugger's failed so much lately. He's getting wackier and wackier. Did he have his coat on when you saw him?"

"No," Eleanor said. "I didn't see him. Why?"

"Why? Because he wears the ugliest old rotten corsage you ever saw. Flowers all withered up and the bells broken. Looks like he made it out of some used pipe cleaners, for God's sake. He came down to the office last week and insisted we take a picture of it and run it in the paper. Claimed the Duchess of Cornwall had given it to him. The old sot's gone bonkers."

"I see," said Eleanor. "I guess I'll have to watch him when I'm talking to him then. What about Miss Turner?"

The editor turned to the middle of the week's edition, took one of the several pens out of his shirt pocket, circled something, and then turned the paper so Eleanor could read.

A GOOD RECOVERY IS WISHED ONE OF OUR ORIGINAL PIONEERS, MISS JANET TURNER, OF HUNTER'S STREET, WHO HAS BEEN ILL IN HOSPITAL SINCE THE FIRST OF THE MONTH.

Eleanor looked up, stunned. "What's wrong?"

The editor shrugged. "I don't know. But it must be important. The hospital administrator himself phoned this in. He does that about once a year, usually when it's hopeless and there's no family to do it."

Eleanor phoned from the pay booth in front of Charlie's Restaurant. She steadied the phone book on her lap and

266

dialled, her hand shaking. She hadn't a clue what she might say if they just put her through.

But her worry was wasted. "I'm sorry," a very pleasant voice told her. "Miss Turner is allowed no calls."

Eleanor felt strangely relieved. "When are your visiting hours?" she asked.

"She's listed 'family only', ma'am. Are you family?"

Eleanor couldn't answer. She stared at the receiver a moment and then quickly set it back in its cradle. She left quickly, slouching, as if by some madness the call were being traced.

Russell Pemberton, who was six weeks out of hospital and strong enough to sit most of the day in his usual place in the lobby of the Muskoka, unrolled a fresh supply of Tums. He popped six in his mouth and chewed. He hated the taste but at least they stopped a bit of the gas. He sometimes wondered what exactly was going on down there. It was as if his gut had been turned into a compost heap. Maybe there were worms there, or slugs? Whatever was there, the doctor said he wouldn't go in to see. Russell was just as glad. Anything, so long as they let him out of that goddam hospital.

And now Jenny was in. Diabetes. High blood pressure. *Tests*. He'd been over twice this week already, pretending to be her brother, just to sit and talk. She certainly took it much better than he had. He couldn't even stand visiting the place. She knew all about his cancer – how, he didn't know.

And Russell couldn't eat. He'd die of the cancer or starve to death. May as well just give up.

There wasn't much he wanted to do anyway. The smelts were running out near the Locks, but for the first spring in his life he had no urge to get out and net a bushel basket or more of the tiny fish. One thing he had wanted to do was see Odon Fuller become the first man in outer space, but the flying saucer had suffered a severe setback last month when Fuller's recycled Harley-Davidson engine had blown a piston through the cylinder head. A replacement was two or three pension cheques down the line, and Russell wasn't sure he'd be there next time to watch.

He thought he'd get some more Tums. Maybe go up and lie down for a while as well. He stood up, the knee cracking, and grabbed onto the arm of the chair until the spots cleared and the floor levelled out.

He shuffled over to the front desk to see if Archie was finished with the sports page. Russell cleared his throat and Archie looked up from the paper and smiled.

"So your friend's back in town, eh, Russell?"

"What friend?"

"Mrs. Philpott," said Archie and spun the register toward Russell. "See for yourself. You should remember her. It's only been about six months, surely."

Russell nodded, and checked the room number: 308. "I remember her, all right," he said curtly.

So she'd had the nerve to come back, had she?

"Where is she now?" Russell said.

"I don't know, but she left her key and went out some time ago."

"I'll see her later then," Russell said, trying to hide his rising anger.

He'd gather his energy first, then act.

Russell walked along the third-floor corridor shaking, fearing he might pass out. He had the key to the storage room out. He knew it worked on his own room; he'd tried it there often enough. He thought it was really a pass key. He hoped it was.

He felt lightheaded, his throat dry. He checked the corridor. No one. He checked the door: 308.

His hand shook as he moved the storage room key toward the lock. He missed, then connected.

The door opened.

Russell expelled his breath finally and clicked shut the attaché case. He had trouble with the right-hand catch: his hand was shaking so badly he finally had to work it with his left. He wanted to burn the case. He wanted to burn the city woman with it. He felt sick from what he'd seen.

Lies! All lies!

What he had seen was a neatly-measured and printed sheet of foolscap. It was divided in half, with "February 26, 1918, Philadelphia" written on the bottom of the right-hand side. From that notation an arrow rose toward the top of the page, and every two inches or less was printed: "(eighth month)... (seventh month)... (sixth month)... (fifth month)... (fourth month)... (third month)... (second month)... (first month)." Directly across from the notation "(first month)" was written "Tom Thomson receives letter: baby coming."

Below that, other notes appeared. "Tom Thomson drowns, July 8, 1917.

"Janet Turner leaves on train journey.

"Returns to Vernon.

"Leaves with mother for Philadelphia."

Across from February 1918, Russell's finger traced out the following:

"Eleanor born, Philadelphia."

Lordy, Lordy, Lordy, Lordy! What absolute horseshit!

Russell shoved the attaché case back where it had sat on the bed, turned, and moved slowly toward the door. He opened it a crack, peeked out, then moved out quickly, shutting the door behind him quietly. He started down the hall and stepped onto the waiting elevator. No one had seen him come and go.

When he got to the lobby he settled into his regular chair and tapped his cane on the slate floor. So now he knew. She was every bit as evil as he'd first suspected. The problem now was how to tell this woman it wasn't so without involving poor Jenny. Lordy, she'd never stand it. It would kill her. Russell would rather he was dead.

Russell knew a call to action when he felt one. When you boss men, he thought, it's in your blood no matter how

269

Christly old you get. He would fix things up, fix them proper. He would make everything all right again for Jenny.

Russell knew he had failed Jenny before, failed her when she needed him, needed someone. But he wasn't there. Tom was dead. And nobody else bothered. His fault, entirely.

He would never fail her again.

The Toronto woman was mad, loony – completely out of her mind – and she was about to upset poor Jenny with a pack of sick lies.

Not if Russell Pemberton could prevent it, anyway. And he could.

18

Eleanor came back from the restaurant hoping Russell Pemberton might have some news from the hospital. She expected him to be in the lobby – the deskman had nodded when she asked after Russell – but she hadn't seen him when she checked in. She looked about the lobby again, was about to turn to the desk when she heard a familiar sound, the cane tapping. *Russell Pemberton. What had happened?* He looked like a cadaver. Waxen, with his mouth hanging open. *He's staring at me!*

She went over, leaned down, and smiled.

"Hello there, Mr. Pemberton. Remember me?"

He rolled his eyes up. "Mrs. Philpott," he said casually.

Eleanor sighed in relief. He's not as bad as the editor said, she thought. And there's no corsage. Perhaps the editor has a bit too much imagination for his own good.

"How have you been?" she asked.

"Poorly, to tell you the truth."

"Oh, I'm sorry to hear that. Nothing serious, I hope."

"No. I'll be all right. What brings you back here?"

"You didn't get my letter?"

"No," he lied. "I was away part of the winter."

"I'd hoped to see Miss Turner again."

"She's not home."

"Yes, I realize that. She's ill."

"She's in the hospital," he said.

"Why is she in the hospital, Mr. Pemberton?"

"Because she's damned sick, that's why," Russell said impatiently. He hated her and was having difficulty disguising his feeling.

"Do you know what it is?"

"Diabetes, high blood pressure, she's got them all."

Eleanor worried about alienating him. After the phone call to the hospital, Russell was all she had to go on.

"Have you been to see her?"

"No. They wouldn't let me in," he lied.

Eleanor followed up. "Family only?"

"Yes, family only."

"They should make an exception for you," Eleanor said.

Russell looked up, agreement sparkling in his eyes. "Goddam right they should," he said.

He sat a moment, grumbling low so Eleanor couldn't make out what he was saying. When he looked up he was smiling.

"So you've come all this way for nothing," he said.

Eleanor nodded.

"You're going back then?" Russell asked eagerly.

Eleanor almost said she would, then she remembered Canoe Lake.

"I thought I'd like to go up to the park," she said. "I want to see where Tom Thomson was buried."

"Leith."

"No. Where they buried him first. At Canoe Lake."

"You'll never find it."

Eleanor hadn't thought of that. Forty-five years. It would be all grown over. She closed her eyes, thought she was going to cry. *Where is my new luck?*

"I know where the grave was," Russell said.

Eleanor didn't hear him.

"I say I know where it is," he shouted.

"You do?"

"Of course I do."

"But, can you . . . I mean, are you able to –"

272

"There's nothing wrong with *me*, Mrs. Philpott."

"But would you?"

"Certainly I would."

"When?"

"Tomorrow."

Eleanor looked at Russell. He was staring at her, daring her to take him up. *If he can't, who else is there? I must see it for myself.*

"Okay," she said. "Tomorrow."

They drove most of the way to Canoe Lake in silence. All the small talk was soon used up. Russell sat scrunched in the far corner, the drone of the engine and the wheels and the wind causing him to drift again. Not just that, but the road. It must have been ten years since he'd come out the park road. New lodges, another gas station, some much-needed work around the Oxtongue Lake turns.

"Do you mind," he said in an irritated voice.

"What?"

"Your ring. You're tapping it on the wheel."

"Oh, I'm sorry. I wasn't thinking."

Eleanor dropped her ring hand into her lap, realized she couldn't drive properly with one hand and self-consciously moved it back so just the fingers rested on the lower part of the wheel.

Up ahead she could see the west gate of the park with a red stop sign flashing on and off. She cleared her throat.

"How much do I have to pay?" she asked.

"Nothing."

"It's free?"

"Nothing's free. Tell them you're going on through. They only make you pay if you stop."

"But we're stopping, aren't we?"

Russell said nothing. Eleanor tapped the ring twice on the steering wheel, realized what she was doing, and flexed her fingers as if they were trilling on a piano chord. She was at the gate. A ranger in a handsome green uniform was stepping down from the steps, smiling. She rolled down the window.

"Good afternoon," the ranger said.

"Hello."

"Going to be stopping at all?"

Eleanor swallowed. "No," she said. "Going right through."

The ranger saluted. "Fine. Have a nice day."

Eleanor rolled up the window and pulled away. She could hear Russell chuckling in the far corner. She refused to look at him.

"You did just fine," he said.

She relaxed.

A few miles down the road Eleanor dared a question. "Why are you doing this, Mr. Pemberton?"

"Doing what?"

"This. Coming up here with me."

"So you can find his grave."

"No. I mean really."

"Turn up here, on your left."

Eleanor braked and turned off onto a gravel road leading around a gradual corner to a parking lot. She could see canoes piled.

"Canoe Lake?" she asked.

"Yes," Russell said.

"What do we do now?"

"Rent a boat," he said.

"A boat? We're going to row?"

"Of course not."

The years peeled off Russell Pemberton as the Evinrude outboard caught, coughed, and moved them away from the dock and the cloud of blue smoke that grew out of the engine. Eleanor was awed by Russell's obvious comfort. He seemed to fit the boat like an oarlock, sitting with his old legs crossed at the ankles and open wide at the knees; he guided the outboard by laying his forearm across the handle. From where she sat looking back at him she got the clear impression that he was looking everywhere but where they were going, as if the memory of the lake lay in his forearm, not his eyes, and he was free to do as he wished until the arm and the boat got him there.

Russell sat listening to the engine and remembering the tickle of the boat's vibration. He watched the shoreline because he wasn't sure what to do with his eyes. He imagined heavy copper line being let out, the William's Wobbler flashing in the sun back of the boat and then disappearing with the minnow tail, down toward the big trout. He saw the point where he and Tom had still-fished bass, the river leading off toward Tea Lake, where he and Tom and Jenny had gone on so many picnics in other years. He looked ahead toward the north shoreline, the roll of the hills in the distance clearer in his memory than in his sight...

... *Seventy-seven years old. You're seventy-seven, Russell, and full of cancer and not worth a damn to anyone. I once paddled down here in forty-two minutes, Joe Lake dam to the far point, and when nobody believed me when I told them, I did it again, on the same day. I've been drunk here. I've been boss here. Laughed here, cried here, eaten the best meals of my life here, made my best friends here, Lordy, been head over heels in love here...*

Where did that time go? How can it have been here once and now gone? Look at the shoreline – even it's changed. Water higher, fewer deadheads, more cottages, faster boats. What's to say for all we were back then? Who even remembers anymore? First Tom's dead, then Harvey Turner, Jenny's good mother not long after, Mark Robinson, Martin Bletcher – every goddam one of them, dead, dead, dead...

... Me and Jenny. That's all who's left. Me and Jenny. And pretty soon both of us dead, too. Me for damn sure soon. And then what's left? Nothing... not one goddam thing. Like we were never here...

... Maybe that's the way it's supposed to be. Who's to remember Abigail Pemberton after I'm gone? Nobody. And me after I'm gone? Just Jenny. All the rest of them think I'm some silly old fart who'd be better off dead anyway... Old Russell Pemberton, that's what they call me. I know. Well, they'll be old too one day. And

then we'll all be dead and there won't be anybody to remember them either. That'll fix them. Even this Mrs. Philpott. She'll be dead and gone and it won't have mattered a hoot in hell in the end. Just some flesh on a short visit. . .

. . . This woman. What am I going to do about her? She's getting so close to something that stinks to high heaven it damn near makes me sick to my stomach to think about it. If I had a stomach to be sick to. One thing's for sure: there's only one thing between what she wants and where she is so far. . .

. . . And that's me. . .

Up ahead Russell could see part of the Turner cottage, its bleached boards glinting in the early afternoon sunlight. Russell had been after Jenny to get some linseed oil on it last time he'd been there to see her, but she obviously hadn't. That must have been fifteen years ago. He'd kidded her about "preserving" the old place exactly as it had been in the days when they were all around Canoe Lake and she said that was exactly what she intended to do, that she never wanted to forget. He told her she should forget, but his heart obviously wasn't in it and the conversation trailed off into safer territory.

Russell didn't bother pointing out the Turner cottage or the spot where Mowat Lodge had stood or any of the other landmarks. Funny how he could look at them and see them plain as day or look and not see them. He knew the lodge wasn't really there, but to him it was. It had to be. He landed at the spot where George Rowe's cabin had been, but now there was nothing. A few rotten boards and not even the outline of the path up to the cabin, the very path he and Tom had stumbled up drunk on the last night of Tom's life.

"Graveyard's straight up from here," he said after cutting the motor. The boat rasped into the sand and he bent to pull the motor up and away from the rocks. It seemed heavy; he didn't think he'd be able to do it again.

"You're sure you can find it?" Eleanor asked.

Russell didn't bother to answer. He steadied the boat and motioned her out, and when she had stepped free of the boat

276

he wobbled over the seats and gingerly stepped out himself, grabbing the painter as he stepped and quickly tying it to a small cedar on the bank. With their weight out the boat floated free again, and though the drift was into the shore Russell didn't want to take any chances. Too often he'd seen the wind change its mind on this lake, and he wasn't sure either he or the woman could take the long walk back. A distance he once covered in under two hours, without even working up a sweat.

Eleanor's mind was racing erratically. She thought of graveyards and passed from that to names on tombstones, from that to names of people. Odd, the way some people seemed to become their names – Russell Pemberton *was* Russell Pemberton – and some other people seemed to wear their names like tight shoes or shirts with the buttons done up wrong. Her own name, for example. How absurd that Eleanor meant "light" and none was ever shed until now. She thought of Eleanor of Aquitaine and Nell Gwynne, people she found listed under a simple book of names when she had worked as a librarian: Eleanors, too. Ha!

She wondered what Tom Thomson and Janet Turner would have called her.

Russell went by her quickly, moving more easily over the rough terrain than he seemed to move over the Muskoka lobby. The cane seemed lighter, the steps more confident. His bad leg seemed suddenly inspired. She fell in behind him.

Eleanor breathed deeply, surprised the clean forest should smell damp and musty as a cellar. She stepped on a branch and it snapped, and she realized Russell was moving up ahead in complete silence. The forest felt close, protective. She felt good. Perhaps it was the way they had felt back then – before, that is.

"Just up here," Russell said.

Eleanor hurried on, breaking through to a flat clearing dominated by a huge birch tree that seemed too fat for its height. There was nothing to say anything had ever been here before. The birch, a few spruce, some bushes, rocks...

277

Russell saw none of that. When he came through the alders into the clearing he walked in on Jenny standing in her yellow dress staring at the stone and crying. He heard the buzz of Martin Bletcher, Sr.'s voice, and saw the men standing around with the light rain working down their foreheads in crooked lines. And he saw Tom's casket, sinking into the ground. Gone forever.

"Over here," he called.

Eleanor hurried and stood beside Russell, who was looking at a spot to the side of the large birch. He seemed deep in thought. Eleanor stared at him, at the spot he looked at, then back at him.

"Where?" she asked.

He nodded at the point in front of him. She stared back at nothing.

"Here?"

"Here."

"But there's no marker."

Russell looked up. "Mrs. Philpott," he said carefully. "There's no body."

"I thought from what you said you thought there was."

Russell looked back, shook his head.

"There's some that say he is. Lots that say he isn't. It's just another part of that whole story we'll never know."

Russell looked up at her to catch her reaction. She had none. She simply stared ahead at the ground.

But Eleanor hadn't missed it. *You're standing beside part of that story*, she wanted to say. But then, well, so was she.

"Miss Turner was here?" she asked.

Russell nodded.

"How... how did she take it? Badly?"

Russell looked up abruptly. "Of *course* she took it badly."

"Yes, of course, but..."

"They were engaged, you know."

"Yes, of course."

"It was a very difficult time for her."

"Yes."

278

For God's sake, she thought. Take the opening. Ask point blank.

"Mr. Pemberton," she began. Her voice failed her. She swallowed. "Do you think she was pregnant?"

Russell said nothing for a long time. He stared at the spot, thinking. You led her on, he said to himself. Do I now let her go on and trip her up? Stop her now? It can't get back to Jenny.

"No."

"Well, what do you think about Annie Fraser's rumour that she was pregnant?"

"Who told you that?" Russell asked sharply.

"Someone who was there," Eleanor said.

"Who?"

"You wouldn't know her. A Mrs. Cassidy. She lives in Toronto."

"Who the hell is she?"

"She says she was there."

"When?"

"Then, when it happened."

"Bullshit."

"Well, around then, anyway."

"'*Around* then' – I was there *all* the time, woman, and I am here to tell you what is true as the Lord Himself knows. *She was not pregnant.*"

Eleanor didn't know whether she was expected to respond. She wasn't.

"And don't you go spreading any such filthy lies, either," Russell finished.

"But Annie Fraser apparently saw a letter..."

"There was no letter, Mrs. Philpott. Annie Fraser talked a lot about nothing. She saw no letter because there was no letter."

"But apparently there was."

"Where is it, then?"

Eleanor didn't know what to do. He was clearly angry. He also must know, though. A little push in the right direction and it might be done with, the answer that would end the questioning. Why couldn't it be simpler?

"But nobody would keep something like that."

"Then you don't know for sure it existed, do you?" Russell said. He was beginning to worry. Word games – he hated them; he was trying to keep a clear grip on the drift of the questioning but it was beginning to get too big for his head to hold. He knew he was close to throwing the whole thing out and walking away from it, but he also knew he was close to shutting her down. If he could do this for Jenny, then he would have done all right. Why couldn't she take No and be satisfied with it? Russell clutched at a way, any way, of ending it all here and now. He concentrated until he thought he'd lost it. Something came, teased, lept away and then slowly returned. *Of course!* Her argument lay in that horseshit in the briefcase. Russell tried to picture the chart on the paper. He saw one word: *Philadelphia!* If that was the key to her madness, he could jam it right now. If there was one thing he knew it was that Janet Turner had never been pregnant and had never had a child. Not at Canoe Lake. Not Vernon. And most certainly not in Philadelphia. Good Lord – hadn't she gone there with her own mother?

Russell bubbled happily within. He had her, he had her, he *had* her!

"I swear to you," he said, looking directly at her. "There was no baby born in Philadelphia, so you may as well forget about it right here and now."

Eleanor felt faint. *That's it!* He's just given it to me on a plate. Poor stupid old Russell Pemberton. He doesn't even realize what he's done! *We* never talked about Philadelphia! For heaven's sake – he even argued that she never went anywhere that winter. He knows! *I know!*

World! Meet Eleanor Thomson!

Why has she stopped? Russell wanted to know. Have I won? It seems so. All I've done is said the truth. She must have bought it.

"There was no baby," he repeated.

"Yes," she said. "Of course."

Well, Russell, you've done it. He thought it over but the conversation rolled and rose in vanishing circles toward the inescapable fact that she had agreed with him. The trick now would be to move away from that talk, into safer areas.

"Come over here," he said, and moved off toward the left. She followed. He stopped, leaned over, and brushed back a large blueberry bush from in front of a rock. Standing with one foot holding the bush down he shuffled back so Eleanor could read.

Remember comrades (when passing by)
As you are now so once was I
As I am now so you shall be
Prepare thyself to follow me

She looked at the name and the date. J'as Watson. Twenty-one years old. Dead in May of 1897. She wondered if her mother and father had ever seen this stone before. She wondered if her mother had noticed it when they'd buried her father. She wished she'd been there to see.

In a way, she thought, I guess I *was* here.

Russell let the bush spring back, covering the writing.

"Lot of truth to that," he said. He tapped the rock with his cane.

"Yes," she said. "There certainly is." She suddenly felt sorry for Russell. He was obviously thinking of his own death.

"Can you show me where he drowned?" she asked.

"Nobody knows that," he said.

"I mean where they found him."

"Sure, I can show you that, all right. Nothing to see there but water, though."

No, she thought. But I want to see anyway.

In the past Russell had always found he did his best thinking on the fringes. Give him a job to do, something to concentrate on fully, and the little things that were bothering him would work out at the same time. The secret was to

281

avoid full concentration. Back in the logging days he used to figure out his quota deadlines while organizing a skid. It was as if his brain could work on its own: all he had to do was set things in motion and sooner or later the answer would come to him. And it never felt as if the thinking was getting too thick for his head.

Running the outboard and concentrating on getting over to the islands was a perfect main purpose for Russell. Something was wrong with what he'd said up on the graveyard hill–the woman had shut up too quickly–but try as he would, he just couldn't see what had gone wrong. All the way down the hill he'd gone over it again and again but every time he approached the answer, it spun away from him. Now, however, he could worry about the boat and getting where he was going. And it would come to him.

There was no baby born in Philadelphia! When it came he jumped, his forearm slamming the handle to the left and jolting the boat to the right. The engine roared out of the water, terrifying Eleanor, who grabbed frantically onto the oarlocks, but the boat settled again, rocked slightly, and then purred on.

"Deadhead!" Russell shouted.

"What?"

"Piece of wood floating!" he shouted, louder.

They were leaning close enough that their foreheads practically touched. "Oh!" Eleanor shouted.

She went back to staring ahead. Russell went back, terrified, to his thought. *I only know about Philadelphia from her notes!* He closed his eyes. *She knows I've been in her room! She knows I'm a thief!* Russell could feel his heart pounding. His chest ached.

For a moment he went back to the main thought: the channel in between the islands, that's where they found Tom. Better bear left.

But the fear flooded back. *She doesn't know! She thinks I knew about the baby and was lying to her. She thinks she is Jenny's baby! Oh Lordy, Lordy–now you've done it.*

282

*It's my fault now. I've screwed the whole thing up on Jenny.
Goddam my hide anyway!*

You did it, Russell. You better undo it.

He cut the engine. He turned off the gas and air valve, and
turned the engine so the boat cut sideways, slowed, and
began drifting. His chest felt tighter yet.

"They found him floating just about here," he said. He
pointed toward the flat corner of the larger island, where he
and Dickson and Rowe had passed that miserable night in
1917. "Over there's where they tied him up."

Eleanor looked over. She didn't like to think of her father
tied there all night like some raft that had broken loose. She
leaned over and looked into the water below, now perfectly
calm thanks to the sideways drift of the boat. She could see
down several feet and then the light seemed to powder off
into dark shadows. She thought of her father struggling
down there, trying to kick free of the line around his ankle.
She thought of the blow to his head and hoped he was dead
before he had even hit the water. She prayed for an easy
death – even if it was murder.

Here! He died right here!

She leaned over a bit further, her eyes not far from the dim-
pling water. Carefully, she slipped off her wedding ring and
let it drop into the water, watching the small circles spread
out from the ring and fall against the larger swells of the lake.

She watched the ring sink, swinging back and forth slowly
as if on a string, the gold flashing helplessly in the sun.

And then it was gone.

Russell's heart was pounding. He saw the way she was
leaning out over the boat and staring into the water. He
knew all it would take to make the world right again and he
did it. A quick shift of his weight and the boat turned
instantly, spilling them both into the water. He kicked out as
he fell, sending the wobbling boat upright and away, drifting quickly.

Russell wished Jenny could see him now. And then the
water closed over, congratulating him.

283

"You want to thank your lucky stars, ma'am," the ranger was saying as he wrapped a dry blanket around Eleanor's shoulders.

Thank them for what? She wasn't even sure what had happened. It all had the aura of a dream; she felt she should shake the blanket free, stand up, and say she'd had enough – time to wake up in her warm bed and puzzle over the crazy nightmare she'd been having.

But there wasn't any use in even trying. It might not seem real, but it was: the boat had tipped, Russell had drowned, and she probably would have herself had it not been for those hands grabbing her shoulders. That part she could barely remember: something about shaking the grip off, screaming for certain, and shaking, still shaking. She had a clear memory of how it had been at first, the boat dipping quickly and her own weight throwing her slowly, leisurely into the water, the water so cold, then warm, then very cold. Then freezing. And that was when she lost it. There were two moments she couldn't be sure of. The first when she reached the boat and grabbed the gunnels, screaming for help, the second when she felt the old man's hands go around her neck so she couldn't breathe. He was trying to pull her off the boat. He'd obviously panicked. Poor old man.

And now he was gone. She'd seen him slip away, quietly, and not down and up three times but straight down, vanishing in the shadows even more quickly than her ring had. She had thought she was slipping herself, and screamed again, louder, more terrified. And that was what had saved her.

She looked up at the ranger who was rubbing the blanket into her shoulder and smiling. "Who pulled me out?"

"The guy over there by the dock. The one with the white hair."

Eleanor looked. A slight man lighting a cigarette, then tossing the match into the water. Smiling. Now coming toward her.

"Feeling a little better?" he asked, smiling behind the sloppy cigarette.

"Yes... thank you."

The man grinned and nodded.

"This here's Johnny Winger," the ranger said. "Lives year-round on the lake. And you want to be grateful he does, Mrs...."

"... El... Eleanor," she said. "Eleanor Philpott."

She looked up at her rescuer, still smiling. "I don't know how to thank you, Mr. Winger."

"I'm sorry we lost your friend," he said.

Poor Russell! To go that way. Was it my fault? Leaning out too far? The ranger's hand came around from behind her holding a cigarette package with a cigarette raised out toward her mouth. She took it, surprised at how she was shaking. He lighted it for her, chasing the vibrating cigarette with the flame until it caught. She drew deep, her lungs cheering the warmth.

She blew out the smoke in the direction of her rescuer. "You're sure?" she asked.

Winger nodded. "I came around the channel turn just as he went down, ma'am. By the time I got there he was gone completely. It's a good forty feet deep there."

Eleanor drew again on the cigarette. She closed her eyes, thinking of Russell Pemberton and the terror he must have felt. She remembered him pulling at her, desperate to live. Could she have tried a little harder to save him? It didn't matter now.

"Here comes some dry clothes for you," the ranger said.

Eleanor looked back toward the parking lot, saw a middle-aged, plump lady get out with a worried look and a bundle of cloth. She came quickly.

"My wife, Mrs. Philpott," the ranger said.

Eleanor smiled. She didn't even know the ranger's name. The woman nodded and held Eleanor by the shoulders, urging her to move toward the boathouse. Eleanor stopped, and looked at the ranger.

"What will you do now?" she asked.

"The police should be here soon," he said. "They'll probably get a statement from you and then we'll get you back home."

"No. I mean about—"

"Oh. Well, we'll probably begin dragging for him in the morning. What did you say his name was?"

"Pemberton," Eleanor said. "Russell Pemberton. You must have known him. He worked around here."

The ranger shook his head. "No. No, I don't know that name. Johnny—you know it?"

"Know what?" Winger asked. He hadn't been listening.

"Russell Pemberton. He's the poor fellow that, you know..."

Winger thought a moment. "No," he said. "Can't say the name rings a bell with me. You say he was from around here, ma'am?"

"He used to work here."

"Must have been before my time, Mrs. Philpott. Not much about these parts I wouldn't know about."

The editor shook his hand cool of the steaming coffee that washed over the cup and doughnut he placed before Eleanor. She'd called him from the hotel after an uneasy night's sleep—the drowning had unsettled her only slightly more than the police escort back to town—and he'd said he'd be delighted to see her, both as a professional and as a friend. Eleanor was, after all, a story now. Grateful to have found him in so early, she quickly paid her bill and drove directly from the Muskoka, not even stopping for breakfast.

"There's nothing then," he said, "that you might have forgotten to tell the police."

Eleanor looked up at him surprised.

"No. Like what?"

"I don't know—" the editor began slowly.

Eleanor cut him off. "I went over it twice with them. What do you mean?"

The editor took a quick sip of his coffee, and looked at her carefully.

286

"I'm not sure what. Maybe the way Russell was acting or something..."

"Acting? Whatever are you getting at?"

The editor sighed. "Russell Pemberton spent his whole life in the bush and on lakes, fishing, river drives, you name it. He was a big name years ago in the regattas, you know. Unless he took a dizzy spell it doesn't seem possible a man like him would fall overboard. Was he standing up?"

Eleanor shook her head impatiently. "No. At least I don't think so. I couldn't see. I was looking over the side when it happened."

"At what?"

Eleanor felt her face warming. "At nothing. Just over the side."

"And he wasn't standing?"

"I don't know, I think not. Maybe he shifted his weight or something, how should I know."

"He wouldn't," the editor said.

"What do you mean he wouldn't."

"He wouldn't shift his weight. He knew boats. He knew what you can and what you can't do."

Eleanor was beginning to feel exasperated. "He was old and sick. Who's to say what he'd do now?"

"I suppose." The editor didn't seem convinced. He took a long drink of the coffee this time, draining it completely, though the steam hung a moment in the cup even as he finished.

Eleanor sought to leave gracefully. "You'll let me know," she said.

"The moment they find anything," the editor said, smiling and beginning to rise toward the door.

"About her, too," Eleanor said.

"About her, too," the editor agreed. "But don't get your hopes up too high, promise?"

"I promise," Eleanor said without conviction.

The editor opened the door. "We'll see you around here again?" he asked, the encouragement obvious.

"For the funeral?"

"You can't do him any good," the editor said. "I meant if Miss Turner takes a turn for the better."

"Perhaps. I don't know."

The editor winked. A strange action for him, Eleanor thought. Not in keeping.

"You're not through with her yet, are you?" he said happily.

Eleanor spoke without thinking. "I don't know."

She realized she really did not know.

Eleanor sat parked in the hospital parking lot, wishing she knew her trees better. The thick one by the river was an oak, she knew that from highschool botany, but the dark tree beside it she couldn't name. Ash perhaps? She lit a cigarette. Odd how the ash leaves were completely out and the oak leaves considerably behind. She looked back up toward the hospital and recognized the irony: the first half of her story came from an old woman dying in a hospital; the second half lay with another old woman, in another hospital, in another country, in another town. Perhaps they had one thing in common.

She butted her cigarette in the hope that action would naturally follow. She would at least walk in, that would be innocent enough. Perhaps no one would notice her. Perhaps she would be able to walk in and down the corridor – the hospital looked small enough to have only one, perhaps two, halls – and perhaps she would by pure chance come across Miss Janet Turner sitting by a window or reading a magazine and their eyes would meet and it would be all right. Smiles would say it all. No words. No words to ruin it. Two smiles, maybe a held hand, and the truth would be out.

But she was barely through the door when a blue-haired woman in a blue smock called to her from behind a candy counter. "May I help you?"

Eleanor smiled self-consciously. She had no game plan to fall back on. She would play it by ear, hoping.

"No thanks," she said. "I'm all right. I know where she is."

"Of course," said the old woman. "But I'll have to mark you down." She looked up and smiled brightly. "Two visitors to a room, you know."

Eleanor desperately sought another name to fall back on. There was none.

"I'm here to see Miss Turner," she said.

"Miss Turner, yes."

The woman held a pencil and went rapidly down the ledger, then down the other side. "I have no Miss Turner here, ma'am."

Eleanor was surprised. "But she's here."

The blue-haired woman flipped to another sheet, pink.

"Ah, yes. Miss Janet Turner. Room 113. Um, hum. Family only, I'm afraid. I'll have to have your name, please."

Eleanor simply followed through. "Eleanor Philpott."

The woman wrote it down without asking the spelling, which was unusual, then she hurried to the nursing booth with Eleanor's name and gave it to a heavy-set nurse, who looked at it and then smiled pleasantly at Eleanor.

"She's much better today, you'll be glad to know," the heavy nurse said.

"Oh, good," Eleanor said. She thought she was through. But the nurse took the slip of paper and moved down the hall with it. "I'll be right back," she said happily. "Just a formal check."

Eleanor felt dizzy. Would she be invited in? There was no reason to think Miss Turner would know she was restricted to "family-only visiting." Perhaps she'd be glad of any visit.

The nurse came back in a moment. Eleanor could hear her nylons whispering together down the hall, then the soothing squawk of her nurse's shoes. Eleanor looked up to give an air of confidence, but the nurse was flushed and Eleanor knew before she spoke that it was hopeless.

"I'm sorry," the nurse said. "She says she doesn't know you."

"I see," Eleanor said.

"They get this way sometimes," the nurse said, as if to help.

Eleanor smiled knowingly though she knew nothing. The old woman didn't know her, really. At least not as she was now. Eleanor hardly looked the same as she had back in February 1918, after all.

She went out to her car and found herself praying, reciting the Lord's Prayer from highschool though she now knew only snatches. She didn't know how to end it. Instead, she quickly looked up toward the sky and clenched her teeth. *Help her, please!*

Eleanor drove back to Toronto slowly, unsure about leaving, unsure about arriving. She drove with the windows down. The warm air, rushing in loudly, made thought difficult but not impossible. As soon as she could pick up CFRB, she turned the radio up full-volume, the distraction complete. This was no time for reflection. Behind her a man rolled lifeless in a lake bottom, dead there because she had taken him there. An old woman lay near death in a hospital, unwilling to acknowledge what Eleanor felt certain of. She felt awkward, guilty about leaving Vernon, but something told her it was better left behind. The best chance now lay ahead.

For three days they unsuccessfully dragged the lake, the second day alone being lost to high winds. On the fourth day, Johnny Winger and a provincial policeman from the Whitney detachment found Russell washing up against Little Wapomeo Island, straight out from the Turner cottage. Standing in the chilly waist-deep water they worked the body into a rubber body bag, dumped it over into the boat, climbed in, and hurried back to the main docks, where word went out to halt the search. The Whitney provincials drove him as far as the west gate of Algonquin Park, where they transferred the body into the trunk of a police car from the Vernon detachment, and from there into town and the funeral home. There Archie identified the old man.

Two days later they buried him. Eight people, mostly hotel staff, and Zendal, from the blacksmith shop, attended the brief ceremony in the funeral home's small chapel. The minister apologized for not having something special to say about Russell Pemberton, but the truth was he hadn't known the old man. Archie told the minister not to worry, that no family were present anyway, and the minister seemed to feel better after that. He stood back of the only bouquet of flowers in the chapel and raced through the ceremony, much to the relief of everyone present. When it was over Archie delayed the other pall-bearers just long enough to check the bouquet but there was no card saying who it was from. A card wasn't necessary.

Next day Archie cleaned out the old man's room. He took two large boxes up, one for throwaways and one for keepables, and he cleaned out the closet and drawers, and piled everything on the bed for sorting. Most of the clothes were too old or too torn and the ones that weren't would go to the Salvation Army. There were a number of old photographs in a black album with white pencilling underneath, but Archie couldn't make much of the writing out. Lots of lumber shots, dozens of pictures of fish catches, several of them showing Russell and a friend of his holding up large speckles on strings, and several shots of people doing silly things like diving and clowning in old-fashioned boats. There were also a few larger pictures pasted to the wall, and one of them was of a particularly beautiful young woman by a dam. He turned it over, looking for a name or a date but found nothing, and wondered for a moment whether it might be a relative, perhaps a cousin, he should be trying to contact.

But Archie knew there was no family. No one, anyway, who'd come to visit Russell in all the years he'd lived at the hotel. And in the end there was really no dividing to do: nothing was worth keeping. He used both boxes to pile the old clothes and pictures in, the second cane, and the dozens of very old, tiny bottles with blurred writing on adhesive tape. He even found a shrivelled old corsage in the drawer, the very thing Russell had been wearing of late. He threw that in as well.

Next morning, when the garbage truck made its round of town, the boxes were stacked back of the Muskoka Hotel with the other garbage. And by evening they were mere ashes in the town dump.

On the Wednesday following, Archie rented the room out on a weekly basis to an old woman. Someone else took over the washroom chores.

On Thursday morning, nearly two weeks after the drowning, Eleanor received a short note from the editor. She carried it with her all through the day, and read it again in the anteroom of Dr. Klotz's office, wondering why she was there and if she should show it to him, wondering if there was anything more for her to chase after.

Dear Mrs. Philpott,

They found poor Russell last Wednesday and he's buried now. I'm afraid I didn't make it to the funeral, but I'm not much for those kinds of things. I'd rather remember them the way they were.

Miss Turner didn't make it to the old man's funeral either, and, as far as I know, hasn't been told. She's critical, sad to say. I'll let you know soon as there is word.

Busy now that the tourists are here, but still hoping you'll be back up to visit.

As ever,

Eleanor knew she wouldn't see Vernon again. Unless Miss Turner miraculously recovered and then, perhaps more miraculously, embraced her as her own. She knew she could only lose by going there again.

Eleanor was grateful to the editor, not only for the note, though that was certainly appreciated. She had finally come to realize what he had been getting at, when he questioned her after the accident. *Russell Pemberton tried to kill me!* He knew I knew the truth. He knew it the minute he told me about Philadelphia. And he tried to kill me to stop me from telling. That was no boating accident. And he didn't grab onto my neck to be saved. He wanted to kill me because I *knew*.

But it still hadn't been confirmed by Janet Turner and never would be. Eleanor had given up going over the previous fall's conversation with the old woman: it was a cat's cradle, with straight lines leading to and away from every point Eleanor cared to raise. A conversation to suit the occasion. Miss Turner had categorically denied it, but Eleanor was convinced she had seen the truth behind the deceptive words. She knew. They both knew. And Eleanor wouldn't tell.

For that matter she wouldn't be telling Klotz, either. Let him think about it. Let him wonder about whatever became of Eleanor Philpott.

She got up from the waiting room and walked out. The receptionist didn't even notice.

That Saturday she told Wilson Beek that he could take his job and the whole notions department, for that matter, and shove it up his ass. She'd wished Joyce had been there to hear her say it, but she knew there would be other times to come when Joyce could see the new Eleanor. Oddly enough, Beek seemed almost grateful to see her go, as if his fingerprints were somehow all over the front of her dress.

She had enough to last a month, even two. With luck, she might find a library job, but she'd probably have to settle for another clerking job. It didn't matter. Giving up on Klotz was a bit like getting a raise; she could get by on less. It grated Eleanor a bit that Klotz never bothered calling, as if his concern fell off with her payments, but she gradually decided that he knew better than to call: she needed no reminder of the skin she'd discarded. Let him keep it in his notebooks.

She imagined her file: Philpott, Eleanor: Spongy personality. Weak. No resistance. No substance. No matter.

She had a new file now. And she could put anything she wished into it, take anything out for that matter. *She* was in charge of it. Not Rudy. Not Aunt Rita. Not even Eleanor Philpott.

But Eleanor *Thomson*.

The editor's next note arrived in mid-August and Eleanor welcomed it. She'd been expecting it, counting on it.

August 16, 1962

My dear Mrs. Philpott,

I'm sorry to inform you that Miss Janet Turner passed away on the tenth. She died in the hospital and I guess she died alone. There just wasn't anyone to be there, not since Russell went, anyway.

I asked and you may get some comfort in knowing she died in her sleep. They buried her from the Anglican Church and put her beside her parents out in St. John's cemetery. It was a sunny day. I can't explain why to you, let alone myself, but I went. So did a lot of others. Funny how they flock to you when you have no more need of them – but perhaps she knew they were there and it would make her happy. I just don't know, myself.

I'll send you a copy of the obit when it's printed. It falls to me to write it, me being a Tom Thomson buff and all, but you know, I can't even mention his name in it, can I? Not *officially engaged*. Crazy thought: her whole life formed by him and what happened to him, and I can't even acknowledge him in her death notice.

Oh, well, those of us who know, know. And that's what matters in the end. If anything does.

Sorry the letter's so depressing. Write when you get a chance and let me know what's happening. Better yet, come on up.

Eleanor knew that she wouldn't be writing back. "Those of us who know, know." That said it as well as anything she could think of. "And that's what matters in the end." It was all over. And though she at first denied it, by day's end she admitted she felt immensely relieved. Death was best in this case, best for all concerned.

They were all of them dead now, even Marilyn Monroe.

Six days before Miss Janet Turner's death poor Marilyn had been discovered naked in bed with an open bottle of sleeping pills beside her. Eleanor had kept all the clippings – one inconsiderate bastard had even claimed that Marilyn had once written her own epitaph, "Here lies Marilyn Monroe, 38, 23, 36" – as a reminder that when you cut away all the absorbent pores of a sponge there's nothing left. Marilyn hadn't been strong enough to fight it. They'd missed the real Marilyn by imagining something that was never there, and that, Eleanor swore, would never happen to her. Not now that she knew what was there.

She went out for a walk, knowing there were tears to come and proud enough of them not to bother hiding them. She could think about Tom Thomson and about Janet Turner and she could cry for them and for all their lost time. She would cry, too, for Russell Pemberton.

But not for herself. Not for Eleanor Thomson.

By the end of the walk she would have only herself left. And there the tears would stop. Then, finally, she would have reached the beginning.

Author's Note

There is no Eleanor Philpott, nor was there ever a Russell Pemberton or a Miss Janet Turner. All three are fictional creations, as is the town of Vernon, Ontario. The person of Tom Thomson has been fictionally recreated, and certain events are taken from known facts connected with the artist in the last years of his life. Many other incidents in the book are also modelled on what is actually known to have occurred, but this is a novel – a work of fiction.

Tom Thomson was engaged in the summer of 1917, and had, in fact, reserved a honeymoon cabin near Huntsville, Ontario, for the fall of that year. It has long been rumoured that he did receive a letter from his fiancée that summer, pressuring him into actually following through with the wedding, but it must be noted that such a letter has never been found and may, indeed, never have existed. Unfortunately, nearly all of those who were at Canoe Lake in 1917 are now dead, so the truth will always be beyond our grasp.

There are many theories concerning Thomson's death – whether it was accidental drowning, murder, or suicide – but all we know with absolute certainty is that an autopsy was never performed, and that no one is sure where Thomson was buried. Precisely what happened on July 7-8, 1917, or who, if anyone, deserved the blame, will not likely ever be known. And perhaps this is for the best. There are two treasures left us by Tom Thomson, one artistic and one romantic.

As for the possibility of a child, it will remain a speculation. After Thomson's tragic death his fiancée did leave the area in the early fall of 1917, first on a long journey to northern Ontario and then, in early November, to Philadelphia with her mother, where they remained until Easter of 1918. Whatever gossip there has been is overshadowed by the fact that no child has ever materialized and also by the personal physician of Thomson's late fiancée, who is still alive and who strongly argues that he would have known had there ever been a pregnancy. Certainly to some who knew her, the thought would be incomprehensible.

Six years ago the research began in earnest for this book, and the author has considerable debts to acknowledge. Much gratitude is due the Ontario Provincial Archives in Toronto and the extensive library and files of the *Toronto Star*. The generosity of Publisher Peter Rice, in opening up the fragile archives of the Huntsville *Forester* must be mentioned, as well as the kind help of Ron Tozer, Interpretive Services Supervisor for the Algonquin Park District of the Ontario Ministry of Natural Resources, who put the park files at my disposal. I interviewed a great many people who would prefer not to be mentioned, for a variety of reasons, but they will know what they gave and that their contribution was appreciated. Two who helped are now dead: Miss Addie Sylvester of Huntsville, Ontario, who knew Tom Thomson when she was a child; and Mr. Jimmy Stringer, of Algonquin Park, who tragically drowned in Canoe Lake only days after kindly giving me many hours of his time. For the sense and description of Algonquin Park in the early years, I owe my own family and relatives as well as Ralph Bice, of Kearney, Ontario, and Dr. Wilfred Pocock, of Huntsville. For invaluable suggestions, I am indebted to Dr. Paul Hurst, a Toronto psychologist. Two friends – Ralph Cox and Ann MacGregor – helped me with encouraging readings of early drafts. Of all the many names due credit there is only one left to take the blame: the author.

Roy MacGregor
Ottawa, December 1979

Also by Roy MacGregor...

THE LAST SEASON

What happens to has-been hockey stars?

Felix Batterinski enjoyed brief fame as a hockey "enforcer" with the Philadelphia Flyers. When he's cut from the team he tries for a second career as a playing coach with a Finnish club, but a controversial play spells the end of his come-back bid. Faced with his own obsolescence, Felix begins his personal descent into disillusion, despair and ultimately a bizarre death.

"A classic Canadian novel."

Calgary Herald

"[The Last Season] is so rich in meaning that to call it simply a hockey novel is misleading. . . In giving Canadians Felix Batterinski, Roy MacGregor has shown them a vital part of themselves."

Maclean's

"This is a novel that ought to stick around in readers' minds and in Canadian fiction for a long time."

Sunday Star

"MacGregor's description of this rural Ontario family is reminiscent of William Faulkner's descriptions of rural Mississippi families — the sense of foreboding, the family members bound together by dark secrets, the mentally retarded relative, the clash of organized religion and the occult. . . . Clearly then, *The Last Season* is much more than a sports book."

The Globe & Mail